THE WARDEN is the first in Trollope's sequence of novels known as the Chronicles of Barsetshire. The fictional Barsetshire is the setting for much of the action in the six novels, often centred around the county town of Barchester. The stories involve the clergy and the rivalry between different factions of the Church of England, as well as the uneasy relations between old and new wealth, town and country, and the aristocracy and the gentry. They have produced some of English literature's most memorable and best-loved characters, including Septimus Harding, Archdeacon Grantly, Bishop and Mrs Proudie, and Josiah Crawley. The novels are:

*The Warden* (1855)
*Barchester Towers* (1857)
*Doctor Thorne* (1858)
*Framley Parsonage* (1861)
*The Small House at Allington* (1864)
*The Last Chronicle of Barset* (1867)

NICHOLAS SHRIMPTON is Emeritus Fellow at Lady Margaret Hall, Oxford. His publications include *The Whole Music of Passion: New Essays on Swinburne* (1993) and *Matthew Arnold: Selected Poems* (1998). He is the editor of Trollope's *The Prime Minister* for Oxford World's Classics.

# OXFORD WORLD'S CLASSICS

*For over 100 years Oxford World's Classics have brought*
*readers closer to the world's great literature. Now with over 700*
*titles—from the 4,000-year-old myths of Mesopotamia to the*
*twentieth century's greatest novels—the series makes available*
*lesser-known as well as celebrated writing.*

*The pocket-sized hardbacks of the early years contained*
*introductions by Virginia Woolf, T. S. Eliot, Graham Greene,*
*and other literary figures which enriched the experience of reading.*
*Today the series is recognized for its fine scholarship and*
*reliability in texts that span world literature, drama and poetry,*
*religion, philosophy, and politics. Each edition includes perceptive*
*commentary and essential background information to meet the*
*changing needs of readers.*

OXFORD WORLD'S CLASSICS

ANTHONY TROLLOPE

# *The Warden*

and

# *The Two Heroines of Plumplington*

*Edited with an Introduction and Notes by*
NICHOLAS SHRIMPTON

OXFORD
UNIVERSITY PRESS

# OXFORD
## UNIVERSITY PRESS

Great Clarendon Street, Oxford, OX2 6DP
United Kingdom

Oxford University Press is a department of the University of Oxford.
It furthers the University's objective of excellence in research, scholarship,
and education by publishing worldwide. Oxford is a registered trade mark of
Oxford University Press in the UK and in certain other countries

Introduction, Select Bibliography, Appendix 2, Explanatory Notes
© Nicholas Shrimpton 2014
Biographical Preface, Chronology © Katherine Mullin and Francis O'Gorman 2011

The moral rights of the author have been asserted

This selection first published as an Oxford World's Classics paperback 2014

*The Warden* first published as a World's Classics paperback 1980
New edition 2014

Impression: 10

Published in the United States of America by Oxford University Press
198 Madison Avenue, New York, NY 10016, United States of America

British Library Cataloguing in Publication Data

Data available

Library of Congress Control Number: 2013956089

ISBN 978-0-19-966544-0

Printed and bound in Great Britain by Clays Ltd, Elcograf S.p.A.

# CONTENTS

# BIOGRAPHICAL PREFACE

ANTHONY TROLLOPE was born on 24 April 1815 in London. He was the fourth surviving child of a failing barrister and gentleman farmer, Thomas Anthony Trollope, and his wife Frances (née Milton), who became a successful novelist and travel writer. Trollope's childhood was dominated by uncongenial schooling. He was sent to Harrow, the boys' public school in north London, as a day boy, then to Sunbury, Surrey, while awaiting a place at his father's former school, Winchester College. Trollope was admitted to Winchester in 1827, but his father's embarrassing inability to pay the fees became known to fellow pupils. He was moved back from Winchester to Harrow in 1830 for two further years, which he later described as 'the worst period of my life'.[1] Unsurprisingly, he did not shine academically, and when, in 1834, the whole family fled to Bruges in Belgium to avoid imprisonment for debt, he obtained a clerkship in the London headquarters of the newly-created Post Office through his mother's connections.

The beginning of Trollope's long Post Office career was not encouraging. He soon became known for unpunctuality, and was, by his own account, 'always on the eve of being dismissed'.[2] His scanty salary led him into debt, and travails with money-lenders would later inform the scrapes of many fictional characters. Trollope was sustained by a habit of imagination that was first acquired during his unhappy adolescence. Daydreaming not only allowed him 'to live in a world altogether outside the world of my own material life':[3] it served as an apprenticeship for fiction. Yet it took a change of scene from London to rural Ireland to persuade Trollope to express his imagination in writing.

In July 1841, aged 26, Trollope was appointed deputy postal surveyor's clerk, based in Banagher, King's County (now Co. Offaly). His new-found professional success helped him to grow in social confidence. Ireland prompted his lifelong enthusiasm for hunting with hounds, too. That enthusiasm was never far from his writing, and sometimes it made life difficult for him at work, not least because hounds and horses were an expensive pastime. Within a year, he became engaged to Rose Heseltine, the daughter of a Rotherham banker who was holidaying in what is now Dun Laoghaire. Trollope proposed after barely a fortnight's acquaintance. The wedding was, for

---

[1] Anthony Trollope, *An Autobiography* (Oxford: OUP, 2014), ch. 1.
[2] Ibid. ch. 3.    [3] Ibid. ch. 3.

financial reasons, postponed for two years until 11 June 1844. Marriage
and the birth of two sons, Henry Merivale in 1846 and Frederick James
Anthony in 1847, helped Trollope to find what he called the 'vigour
necessary to prosecute two professions at the same time'.[4] His first
novel, *The Macdermots of Ballycloran* (1847), sold far fewer than the
400 copies printed. But it was favourably reviewed and was followed
by a second Irish tale, *The Kellys and the O'Kellys* (1848). Both kept an
uneasy silence on the Famine, to which Trollope was a horrified witness, but his recollections of the famine years would inform the later
*Castle Richmond* (1860). The failure of *La Vendée* (1850), on the French
Revolution, together with the increasing demands of his Post Office
career, conspired to deflect Trollope from fiction for some years.

In 1851, he was sent to the south-west of England to investigate
ways of expanding the rural postal system. His successful development
of the pillar box, which he first tried out in St Helier in the Channel
Islands in 1852, led to the spread of post boxes throughout the UK.
The project won Trollope promotion to the surveyorship of the north
of Ireland in 1854, and his family settled in Donnybrook. During these
years, he composed the first novel to bring him real recognition, *The
Warden* (1855). The first of six 'Chronicles of Barsetshire', *The Warden*
was set, like its successors, in a fictional county, based on the south-
west England Trollope knew. Although they dramatized changes in the
ecclesiastical world, the 'Chronicles' were also secular in their interests.
While *The Warden* brought him less than £10, Trollope 'soon felt it
had not failed as the others had failed',[5] and began work on *Barchester
Towers* (1857). It was warmly reviewed. But it was not until the publication of *Dr Thorne* (1858) that he met with unmixed success. The novels
following—*Framley Parsonage* (1861), *The Small House at Allington*
(1864), and *The Last Chronicle of Barset* (1867)—established his reputation, his popularity, and his fortune.

During the twelve years between *The Warden* and *The Last Chronicle*,
Trollope published seventeen novels, numerous short stories, and several collections of travel writing. This extraordinary scale of production was sustained by his habit of rising at five each morning to allow
three hours of writing—250 words each quarter of an hour, he boasted
in *An Autobiography*—before leaving for the office at nine. Other celebrated writers have written to a similar schedule, but Trollope's pride
in his achievement has never been entirely admired by critics. His
schedule made him an invaluable contributor to the *Cornhill Magazine*,
founded in 1859 by the novelist, William Makepeace Thackeray. The

---

[4] Trollope, *An Autobiography*, ch. 4.       [5] Ibid. ch. 5.

serialization of *Framley Parsonage* in the *Cornhill*'s first issues did much to secure the magazine's and Trollope's reputation. Through the *Cornhill*, he made lasting friendships with major literary and artistic figures. By 1859, he was living in the north London suburb of Waltham Cross, after a promotion to Post Office surveyor of the eastern district. He was soon elected to the Garrick and Athenaeum Clubs, and became a stalwart of the Royal Literary Fund. These were marks of serious literary success. He also, in 1860, met a young American woman, Kate Field, with whom he fell in love. The nature of *that* relationship is known almost as little as Trollope's relationship with Rose. But Kate mattered to him—and would do till the end of his life.

Trollope concluded the Barsetshire Chronicles on a high note, considering *The Last Chronicle of Barset* to be his best novel. Following the model of Honoré de Balzac's *Comédie humaine*, Trollope saw realist fiction as capable of depicting a complex culture through a multi-volume series. The Palliser volumes, beginning with *Can You Forgive Her?* (1865) and ending with *The Duke's Children* (1880), were his other major sequence. These novels, like the Barsetshire Chronicles, could be read separately and in different orders without irrecoverable loss—but they formed a continuous whole all the same. In the story of the Pallisers, Trollope developed one of his strongest themes—the difficult marriage and its negotiations. He also explored great political issues, including the 1867 Reform Bill and the disestablishment of the Irish Church, while inviting readers to map the Conservative leader Daubeny onto Disraeli, and the Liberal Gresham onto Gladstone. His portrayal of democratic politics has remained consequential for generations. The novels' political appeal, nonetheless, was carefully balanced against other enticements: 'If I wrote politics for my own sake, I must put in love and intrigue, social incidents, a dash of sport, for the sake of my readers',[6] he said, with characteristic pragmatism.

Trollope resigned from the Post Office in 1867. His earnings from writing had long outstripped his salary. The following year, feeling that 'to sit in the British Parliament should be the highest object of ambition to every educated Englishman',[7] he stood as the Liberal candidate for Beverley in the 1868 General Election. He was unsuccessful. That failure haunted his fiction as it must have haunted his private life. Trollope interspersed the Palliser series with other novels and studies. He was by this stage a professional writer whose commitment was broken significantly only by field sports and travel. Trollope's international voyages included Australia, where Frederick, his younger son, was a sheep

[6] Ibid. ch. 17.    [7] Ibid. ch. 16.

farmer: *Australia and New Zealand* (1873) was a result. Trollope and
Rose left London in 1880 for South Harting in Sussex, hoping country
air would ease his persistent asthma. This was no retirement: the last
two years of his life saw a further six books, including *Mr Scarborough's
Family* (1883), a study of parental domination, and the unfinished *The
Landleaguers*, a return to Irish matters (published posthumously, 1883).

In early November 1882, Trollope suffered a stroke, and, on
6 December, he died in London at the age of 67. He had written forty-
seven novels, five volumes of short stories, four travel books, three
biographies, an autobiography, and two translations from the classics,
together with uncollected pieces of journalism. His prodigious output
included a biography of Thackeray, and a study of Cicero whose political judiciousness was often a silent model behind his admirable fictional
politicians. Few who knew Trollope could avoid commenting on his
loud and bluff persona in public: at 5 ft 10 in., and around 16 stones, he
struck those who met him as burly—a man of bodily appetites. It was
difficult for many to imagine him dissecting the emotional complexities
of his characters with such delicacy and sympathy.

Trollope's posthumous *An Autobiography* (1883) startled a large
number of readers. Its dry discussion of how much money his fiction
made denied any Romantic model of authorship. Here was no account
of the creative flash of inspiration. Writing fiction was more like a trade,
the result of well-applied skill and labour. But, knowing at first hand the
cost of his father's failure, it was important to Trollope to demonstrate
to his family, if to no one else, that he had made such a success of his
life. He had no university degree, and was without the much-coveted
honour of a seat in Parliament. He wished to demonstrate too, in a culture less familiar with the notion of a professional writer than ours, that
writing could indeed be a life. His estate was valued at the huge sum of
£25,892 19s. 3d.

Biographies of Trollope are always to some degree doomed to follow the sparse facts laid out in *An Autobiography*. The nature of his
marriage, his feelings for Kate Field, his relationship with his sons,
let alone the secrets of his inner life, are among the topics on which it
is impossible to write with certainty. Trollope had no commitment to
privacy—but private he remains. Declining to reveal himself in correspondence, he is, perhaps, only glimpsed in the astonishingly fertile
novels about human lives, desires, and choices, which were his enduring bequest to English literature.

*Katherine Mullin*
*Francis O'Gorman*

# INTRODUCTION

*[Readers who are unfamiliar with the plots may prefer to treat the Introduction as an Afterword.]*

*The Warden* is a risky, experimental novel, which has come to be seen as cosy and charming. At first sight, this is a touching romantic comedy in the Jane Austen tradition. Set in the picturesque surroundings of a Victorian cathedral close, it invites us to eavesdrop on the personal and moral dilemmas of a group of sharply observed but fundamentally sympathetic characters. John Bold, an earnest young Radical, launches a campaign against the way in which the endowments of a local almshouse, Hiram's Hospital, are being used. But Bold is in love with the daughter of the warden of that almshouse, Septimus Harding. How can this tangle be resolved? For Henry James, writing in 1883, *The Warden* was 'delicate' and 'delightful', a novel which is essentially 'the history of an old man's conscience'.[1] As such, it lays the foundations for Trollope's best-loved *roman fleuve*, the Chronicles of Barsetshire.

At the time of its composition, *The Warden* was something rather different. Far from working to a formula, Trollope was anxiously searching for an appropriate model for successful prose fiction. By 1851 he had written three failed novels and an unproduced play. How could he catch the attention of contemporary readers and establish a place for himself in a competitive literary market? The answer, it seemed, lay in the enthusiasm for novels-with-a-purpose: the social-problem or 'Condition-of-England' fiction which flourished in the decade after 1845. Disraeli's *Sybil* (1845), Elizabeth Gaskell's *Mary Barton* (1848), Charles Kingsley's *Yeast* (1848) and *Alton Locke* (1850), and Dickens's *Bleak House* (1852–3) and *Hard Times* (1854) showed that there was an appetite for novels which engaged with controversial contemporary issues. Thackeray, in his 'Plan for a Prize Novel' in 1851, suggested that, 'Unless he writes with a purpose . . . a novelist

---

[1] Henry James, 'Anthony Trollope', *Century Magazine* (New York, July 1883); repr. in *Partial Portraits* (London: Macmillan, 1888), here quoted from Donald Smalley (ed.), *Trollope: The Critical Heritage* (London: Routledge, 1969), 534.

in our days is good for nothing.'[2] After two Irish novels and an equally unsuccessful historical narrative, Trollope decided that he might do better with a more up-to-date and fashionable kind of fiction.

Since there is no evidence in Trollope's letters or autobiography to support this claim, it might seem an unjustified supposition. *The Warden*'s setting, in the 'Elysium' of the cathedral close of Barchester, is far removed from the slums, mills, and sweatshops customary in social-problem fiction, and the language of the novel suggests comic exaggeration rather than serious engagement. 'Eager pushing politicians', we are told, 'have asserted in the House of Commons, with very telling indignation, that the grasping priests of the Church of England are gorged with the wealth which the charity of former times has left for the solace of the aged' (p. 10). John Bold's wish to achieve some modest reforms in an English country town is incongruously presented in the terminology of the French Revolution: 'Bold has all the ardour, and all the self-assurance of a Danton, and hurls his anathemas against time-honoured practices with the violence of a French Jacobin' (p. 14). This looks more like mockery of Condition-of-England fiction than a deliberate use of its procedures.

But if one turns to the autobiographical novel *The Three Clerks*, which Trollope wrote two years later and published in 1858, one finds an account of a young writer's adoption of precisely this formula for a successful novel. Charley Tudor, the character who most closely resembles his author, is trying to publish fiction in order to supplement his salary as a civil service clerk. The editor of the *Daily Delight* encourages him but gives clear instructions about what is required. These include a direct engagement with contemporary abuses:

The editor says that we must always have a slap at some of the iniquities of the times. He gave me three or four to choose from; there was the adulteration of food, and the want of education for the poor, and street music, and the miscellaneous sale of poisons. (Chapter 19)

Eager to oblige, Charley chooses both 'the miscellaneous sale of poisons' and 'adulteration', with the convenient consequence that the hero of *Sir Anthony Allan-a-dale and the Baron of Ballyporeen* is able to spring back to life after being poisoned with prussic acid because the quality of the chemicals used in its preparation had been so poor.

---

[2] 'A Plan for a Prize Novel', *Punch*, 20 (22 February 1851), 75.

After the successful publication of his first two novels, the editor asks Charley for another serial and again insists that it must involve topical social issues:

'We have polished off poison and petticoats pretty well,' said the editor; 'what do you say to something political?'

Charley had no objection in life.

'This divorce bill, now—we could have half a dozen married couples all separating, getting rid of their ribs and buckling again, helter-skelter, every man to somebody else's wife; and the parish parson refusing to do the work; just to show the immorality of the thing.'

Charley said he'd think about it.

'Or the Danubian Principalities and the French Alliance—could you manage now to lay your scene in Constantinople?'

Charley doubted whether he could.

'Or perhaps India is the thing. The Cawnpore massacre would work up into any lengths you pleased. You could get a file of *The Times*, you know, for your facts.' (Chapter 47)

Although the scene is comic, the recipe for commercially successful fiction is clearly identified as one which involves the treatment of social and political problems.

How much bearing does this have on the composition of *The Warden*, a novel first published in 1855? *The Three Clerks*, after all, is based on Trollope's life between 1834 and 1841, when he, like Charley, was a clerk in London. Such early experiences might not seem relevant to a literary decision made more than a decade later. But *The Three Clerks*, despite its use of some personal circumstances from the 1830s, is actually set between 1853 and 1857 (certainly after December 1852, since Napoleon III is on his imperial throne in Paris), and Charley Tudor is an amalgam of Trollope the struggling civil servant of the later 1830s and Trollope the struggling would-be novelist of the early 1850s. *The Warden* is the real equivalent of Charley Tudor's imaginary Condition-of-England novel and, like *Sir Anthony Allan-a-dale*, it addresses not one but two contemporary problems: the misuse of charitable endowments and the excessive power of the press.

Placing *The Warden* side by side with novels by Disraeli, Kingsley, Dickens, and Gaskell might, however, be thought to raise an uncomfortable question. Their social-problem fiction dealt with major issues: the gap between the rich and poor (*Sybil, or, The Two Nations*); conditions in factories, mines, and workshops (*North and South, Hard Times*); conditions for workers on the land (*Yeast*); the lack of an effective divorce law, and the attitudes supposedly encouraged by Utilitarians and political economists (both in *Hard Times*). Can Trollope's book be classed as a Condition-of-England novel when, by comparison, his topics (especially the first one) seem so slight?

The answer to that question is that these issues were as substantial as any other matter dealt with in Condition-of-England fiction. Lord Brougham had criticized the management of charities in 1816 and a Charitable Trusts Commission was established to investigate it in 1818. By 1837 a series of reports had identified 28,800 institutions which together had a large and rapidly growing income, estimated in that year as £1.2 million (over £70 million in modern money) in 1837. By the 1880s, the income of London charities alone would exceed the entire public revenues of Sweden. Even more significantly, these charities were operating before the Welfare State. In the early 1850s the government provided relief for extreme poverty through the workhouses of the New Poor Law, and made a small grant to the elementary schools run by the churches. But there was no other state involvement in education, and no state-funded medicine, old-age pension, or National Insurance scheme. Responsibility for these things fell entirely on charities, and charities were, as a consequence, extremely important. If the arrangements for what we now call 'welfare' are an aspect of the 'Condition' of a nation, then charity was, at this date, just as significant as Factory Acts, wage rates, and divorce laws.

The conclusions reached by Brougham's long-running enquiry were not encouraging. Many of the country's charitable trusts were found to be of little or no practical use, partly because of fraud, but mostly because of simple mismanagement or neglect. A bill to regulate charities in 1844 had failed. But in the early 1850s this concern finally generated a major piece of legislation: the Charitable Trusts Act, which completed its passage through Parliament on 8 August 1853. As Trollope wrote the first chapter of *The Warden*, in other words, MPs were considering the bill which sought to correct the misuse of charities. It is true that cathedrals and the institutions for which they were directly responsible (such as the fictitious Hiram's Hospital) would remain 'exempt charities', not governed by the new

Charity Commission. It is true, also, that the Episcopal and Capitular Estates Bill, which sought to address the cathedral problem, was withdrawn on 3 August. But, as this indicates, ecclesiastical charities were very much in the public eye. Though eventually exempted, they had been a key target for the press campaign which created the impetus for reform.

Where did Trollope stand on this matter? He had a sympathy for ancient religious institutions, which derived from his reading of the novels of Sir Walter Scott: 'With many of us he has had an effect on our tendencies in religion, teaching us to revere establishments and perhaps endowments.'[3] But he was also a reader of the newspapers and at the beginning of the second chapter of *The Warden* specifically identifies two of the institutions recently picked out by them for criticism: 'the well-known case of the Hospital of St Cross' and 'the struggles of Mr Whiston, at Rochester' (p. 10). Both of these cases had been repeatedly featured in the press in the late 1840s and early 1850s. Yet neither of them, as Trollope seems to have noticed, was actually as straightforward as the newspapers sought to suggest.

The Hospital of St Cross in Winchester (the city where Trollope had been a schoolboy from 1827 to 1830) was a medieval almshouse rather similar to the fictitious Hiram's Hospital. Its warden, since 1808, had been the Revd Francis North, Rector of St Mary's Church in Southampton, who unexpectedly became the Earl of Guilford (not 'Guildford' as Trollope misspells it) in 1827, after the death of his bachelor cousin. The financial benefits which North derived from his wardenship had long been a matter for adverse comment: when Keats visited Winchester in 1819, he noted that St Cross was 'a charity greatly abused' by 'the appropriation of its rich rents to a relation of the Bishop'.[4] In the 1840s such private criticism turned into a public campaign.

Like Trollope's Septimus Harding, North (or Guilford) was actually a kindly warden, who dispersed the rental income of St Cross appropriately and treated the residents of his almshouse well. But he himself derived a considerable salary from the occasional 'fines', or lump sums, paid by tenants of the charity's property when they

---

[3] Anthony Trollope, 'On English Prose Fiction as a Rational Amusement' (1870), in Morris L. Parrish (ed.), *Anthony Trollope: Four Lectures* (London: Constable, 1938), 114.

[4] See Keats's letters of 28 August and 17–27 September 1819, in *The Letters of John Keats*, ed. M. Buxton Forman (London: Oxford University Press, 1952), 375, 422.

renewed their leases. By the mid-nineteenth century this traditional practice was passing into disrepute. In 1849 the MP Joseph Hume moved a parliamentary motion for 'an inquiry into the ecclesiastical and eleemosynary preferments now held by the Rev. the Earl of Guilford' and the matter was referred to the Court of Chancery. Judgment was delivered in the summer of 1853, just as Trollope was writing the first chapter of *The Warden*. Guilford's income from St Cross was reduced to £250 a year, he was forbidden to engage in further property dealings, and he was required to repay his profits from such activities since 1849. He did not, however, retire from the wardenship until 1855 and attacks on him continued, one of the most notable ('Lord Guilford seeks to evade the consequences of discovery by shift and evasion') appearing in *The Times* on 6 January 1854, as Trollope resumed work on his novel after the four-month interruption caused by his move to a new job in Belfast.[5]

The Revd Robert Whiston was headmaster of the Cathedral Grammar School at Rochester. In February 1848 he noticed that the Dean and Chapter had failed to maintain the real value of the maintenance allowances which they were required to pay to twenty scholars at the school and four former pupils at Oxford and Cambridge. Whiston's suggestion that the chapter should update these payments from the sums specified in the cathedral's statutes of 1545, as they had done with their own stipends, was brushed aside. So in 1849 he published a book entitled *Cathedral Trusts and Their Fulfilment*, and was promptly sacked. The chapter had misjudged their man. The indomitable Whiston took his case to the law courts and in October 1852 was found technically guilty of libel but not guilty of the *gravius delictum* required for dismissal. He was therefore reinstated and, a month later, the chapter belatedly increased the schoolboys' and exhibitioners' allowances.

As in Winchester, the background to this affair was the use of 'fines' to augment clerical salaries. The Rochester chapter used the rental income from the cathedral's properties to fund its running costs, including the rebuilding of the Grammar School and the provision of a free education for its scholars. For the payment of the cathedral's clergy, however, the chapter relied on fines. This was necessary because

---

[5] References to *The Times* are from *The Times Digital Archive, 1785–1985*, cited by date.

it was impossible to hire clergymen in the mid-nineteenth century on the salaries specified in the original trust deed: Archdeacon Grantly offers a version of this argument in Chapter 9 of *The Warden*, when he insists that 'the rate of pay for such services' must be 'according to their market value at the period in question' (p. 71). The 'allowances' paid to the schoolboys were a different matter. These were an archaic relic of the cathedral's transition from monastic to secular status at the time of the Reformation. Previously, the boys had been able to eat with the monks at their common table. When this was no longer possible, they were given a sum of money to compensate them for their lost meals. By the 1840s, the justification for this transitional payment had long since disappeared and the chapter let the value of the allowances wither away. Their failure to explain this properly to Whiston, and their refusal to publish the cathedral's accounts, meant that the matter remained obscure and they emerged from the legal process as the villains of the piece. In a letter to the newspapers in the autumn of 1852, Whiston declared that, 'Without the support of the Press, in forming, guiding and reflecting the irresistible supremacy of public opinion, I might have indeed appealed in vain for even that measure of justice which I have at last obtained.'[6]

Trollope mentions these two cases early in his novel, adding a third, the mismanagement of Dulwich College, in Chapter 15. In a conversation with T. H. S. Escott, he remarked that the first two Barsetshire novels 'grew out of *The Times* correspondence columns during a dull season of the fifties',[7] and Carol H. Ganzel has argued that Trollope was referring here to yet another 'scandal', suggested in a series of letters from the Revd Sidney Godolphin Osborne in the summer of 1853 about a possible case of simony at St Ervan's in Cornwall.[8] Trollope was, indeed, very likely to have noticed letters from his old adversary Godolphin Osborne. But *The Times*, like many other journals in the early 1850s, was so full of articles and letters about the abuse of charitable endowments that it is hard to say with certainty which of them might, or might not, have caught his attention. Dickens's magazine

[6] Whiston's letter, originally published in *The Times*, the *Morning Chronicle*, and a number of other newspapers, on 1 and 2 November 1852, is here quoted from Ralph Arnold, *The Whiston Matter* (London: Rupert Hart-Davis, 1961), 193.

[7] T. H. S. Escott, *Anthony Trollope: His Work, Associates and Literary Originals* (London: John Lane, 1913), 103–4.

[8] See Carol H. Ganzel, '*The Times* Correspondent and *The Warden*', *Nineteenth-Century Fiction*, 21 (1967), 325–36.

*Household Words* published a fictionalized version of the Whiston case, 'The History of a Certain Grammar School', in August 1851,[9] and denounced the caretakers of the Charterhouse, a famous London almshouse, in June 1852.[10] In April 1852 there had been a letter in *The Times* about a similar problem at Magdalen College School in Oxford, and in May of that year (the month in which Trollope first conceived *The Warden*) there was a correspondence about the 'disgraceful conduct' of the Chapter of Westminster Abbey. When, on 22 October 1852, *The Times* thundered in a leader about the end of Robert Whiston's case, it concluded that 'The abuses of cathedral trusts will henceforth become one of the great questions of the day, which can no longer be shirked or evaded.'

Rather than being seen as a piece of domestic realism which incorporates a few, incongruous episodes of social criticism, *The Warden* is best understood as a Condition-of-England novel which Trollope enriched to an exceptional degree with social and psychological interest. Most social-problem fiction suffers from a tendency to caricature and over-simplification. Trollope's novel combines a serious treatment of urgent contemporary issues with the complex realism of character and setting which would be the defining feature of the subsequent novels in the Barsetshire series. The publisher's reader to whom William Longman sent Trollope's manuscript, Joseph Cauvin, recognized, and welcomed, precisely this combination of effects:

This story takes its rise from the recent exposé of the abuses that have crept into Cathedral and Hospital Trusts. Not a very promising subject, one might infer at first sight! But such is the skill of the author that he has contrived to weave out of his materials a very interesting and amusing tale . . .[11]

By October 1854, Cauvin's professional judgement was actually more up-to-date than the advice offered to Charley Tudor a year or two before. The fashion for Condition-of-England fiction was passing

---

[9] [Theodore Buckley], 'The History of a Certain Grammar School', *Household Words*, 3 (9 August 1851), 457–61.

[10] [Henry Morley and William Thomas Moncrieff], 'The Poor Brothers of the Charterhouse', *Household Words*, 5 (12 June 1852), 285–91.

[11] Joseph Cauvin's report to William Longman, 13 October 1854, in *The Letters of Anthony Trollope*, ed. N. John Hall with the assistance of Nina Burgis, 2 vols. (Stanford, Cal.: Stanford University Press, 1983), i. 38–9.

and Trollope had joined it only just in time. *Hard Times* in 1854 and *North and South* in 1854–5 would be the last major examples of the practice in its original phase. In the later 1850s, social problems would begin to be, 'Not a very promising subject', and it was the material that Trollope added to his Condition-of-England frame-work, as much as the framework itself, which recommended the novel to his publisher. The sensitive tracing of Eleanor Harding's feelings about her disobliging lover, the delicate account of the affectionate relationship between the two elderly widowers, Septimus Harding and Bishop Grantly, the baffled aspirations of John Bold, and the triumph of the warden's conscience over the worldly-wisdom of his domineering son-in-law give this book its remarkable richness and density. Gordon N. Ray, in 1968, observed that Trollope 'left behind him more novels of lasting value than any other writer in English'.[12] This is the first of them.

Combining the two modes of social comment and psychological insight was not, of course, an easy matter, and to achieve it Trollope made liberal use of a particular literary technique: the mock heroic. With its peculiar combination of the great and the small, the sig-nificant and the trivial, the public and the private, this procedure offered a convenient way in which to link socio-political analysis with domestic comedy. Adopting a deliberately eighteenth-century manner, Trollope introduces a personified 'Scandal' in his opening pages and goes on to describe the warden's tea party (in Chapter 6) as if it were a sequel to Pope's poem *The Rape of the Lock*. There are Miltonic allusions and Homeric similes ('As the indomitable cock preparing for the combat sharpens his spurs, shakes his feathers, and erects his comb, so did the archdeacon arrange his weapons for the coming war'), and Eleanor Harding's key confrontation with the lover who is also her father's enemy is presented through an extended anal-ogy with the classical and biblical stories of Iphigenia and Jephthah's daughter. The device is amusing but also has an important formal function. The movement back and forth between the discussion of public policy and the description of private feelings might seem forced and awkward. Here those transitions are masked by the use of a consciously artificial mode which acknowledges, or foregrounds,

---

[12] Gordon N. Ray, 'Trollope at Full Length', *Huntington Library Quarterly*, 31 (August 1968), 334.

the juxtaposition of incongruous material. With the help of the mock heroic, Trollope can combine two kinds of fiction without our noticing the joins.

As well as enriching his first social problem with interests of other kinds, Trollope combined it with a second socio-political issue: the power of the press. He had clashed with opinions expressed in *The Times* by Sidney Godolphin Osborne on a previous occasion, in 1848. Then, his first-hand experience of conditions in Ireland during the potato famine led him to defend the government's management of the crisis, and to cast doubt on the accuracy of *The Times*'s denunciations. Trollope's views, published in the small-circulation *Examiner*, had had little effect when compared with Osborne's thunderings in a daily paper which sold six times as many copies as any of its rivals. But the experience did at least leave him with a healthy scepticism about crusading journalism, and the ways in which its righteous indignation can go hand in hand with moral caricature and factual over-simplification. Now, in *The Warden*, he both participates in that campaigning process (of which Condition-of-England novels were, of course, themselves a version) and questions its validity, using the sympathetic imagination of the novelist to show how the target of such a campaign can be sensitive as well as selfish, useful as well as ana-chronistic, and right as well as wrong. *The Times* itself, in its October 1852 leader about the conclusion of the Whiston case, had seen fit to remark that 'there has been excess of zeal on both sides' (the two sides here being Whiston and the Chapter of Rochester Cathedral). In *The Warden*, Trollope develops that idea into a model which includes, on one of the sides, polemical literature and the press.

As one might expect from an author who would become cele-brated for his interest in dilemmas, or problems which are not capable of simple solution, the balance is scrupulously maintained. The parodies of *Times* journalism, Dickensian social-problem fic-tion, and the cultural criticism of Thomas Carlyle, are matched by an equally set-piece caricature, in Chapter 8, of the leading bishops of the Church of England. In a more realistic register, Trollope stages a paradoxical encounter between John Bold and Dr Grantly, in which our stock expectations about aggressive reformers and meek and mild clergymen are neatly reversed. Bold, in Chapter 12, is system-atically humiliated by Grantly's superb embodiment of the Church (Establishment) Militant. This disturbing scene, which one reads with a queasy mixture of gratification and dismay, is in some ways an even more brilliant achievement than the much praised account of the long, solitary day spent in London (in Chapter 16) by the humble Christian, Septimus Harding.

In his *Autobiography*, written more than twenty years later, Trollope regretted this even-handed approach:

I had been struck by two opposite evils . . . and with an absence of all art-judgement in such matters, I thought that I might be able to expose them, or rather to describe them, both in one and the same tale . . . I had been much struck by the injustice . . . I had also often been angered by the undeserved severity of the newspapers . . . I was altogether wrong in supposing that the two things could be combined. Any writer in advocating a cause must do so after the fashion of an advocate . . . He should take up one side and cling to that, and then he may be powerful. (Chapter 5)

This is true if your purpose is to campaign, either for or against a 'reform'. But here, as so often in *An Autobiography*, Trollope is doing less than justice to his own work. *The Warden* was not a failed campaign. Rather, it was a salutary reflection on the process of campaigning—a process which had been peculiarly popular in the previous twenty years. Whether it took the form of books and pamphlets, like Newman's *Tracts for the Times*, Pugin's *Contrasts*, and Carlyle's *Latter-Day Pamphlets* (which Trollope bought, read, and profoundly disliked in 1850 or 1851),[13] or of articles in journals and newspapers, or of Condition-of-England novels, this polemical 'severity' had been one of the distinctive features of the early Victorian age. Trollope— a much more sophisticated and self-conscious artist than we have tended to assume—is implicitly debating the advantages and disadvantages of this fashionable literary manner.

The most controversial press campaign of the entire nineteenth century was *The Times*'s reporting of the Crimean War, and it began in the months in which Trollope was writing *The Warden*. It reached its climax just as the novel was published, in January 1855: Lord Aberdeen's government would fall, after fierce and persistent attacks in the press, at the end of the month. Since Trollope's novel had been completed almost four months earlier, it is not a response to that event. The most famous of *The Times*'s 'strictures upon the conduct of the war'[14] would

---

[13] See *Letters*, i. 29.
[14] *The History of 'The Times'* (London: The Times, 1935– ), ii. 191.

be printed on the day before Christmas Eve and W. H. Russell's celebrated dispatches about 'the Crimean Winter' would not appear until
January 1855.

But this is not to say that the composition of *The Warden*, in the
spring and summer of 1854, could not have been affected by the press
campaign. The build-up to the Crimean conflict was an exceptionally slow one, first prompted by the French assertion of the rights of
Roman Catholics to visit the Holy Sepulchre in 1852, and acquiring
a British dimension as early as the spring of 1853, when the British
ambassador encouraged Turkey to reject Russia's counterclaim to an
exclusive protection of Christianity in the Ottoman Empire. Russian
troops occupied Moldavia and Wallachia at the end of May 1853.
A British fleet was assembled off the Dardanelles in June, shortly
before Trollope wrote his first chapter, and would enter the Black Sea
at the beginning of January 1854, as he resumed work on the novel
after a five-month interval.

In February, a month before Britain's formal declaration of war on
31 March 1854, *The Times* was already thundering about the state of
the army's 'hospital and surgical arrangements' (17 February) and
the government's failure to appoint a minister with sole responsibility
for the imminent conflict (27 February). With British troops on their
way to the eastern Mediterranean, a dispatch from Malta on 18 March
deplored the fact that commissariat officers had not been sent out with
the troop-ships ('to speak the truth, "somebody" is to blame'), and on
10 April 1854 a leader declared that 'the existing administration of
war is indefensible'. Sidney Herbert, the Secretary at War, speaking
in the House of Commons on 28 April, suggested that newspaper
correspondents were going beyond their proper duties. A leader the
next day attacked him for 'cavilling, quibbling, and sneering' at the
truth. By the end of June, under pressure from *The Times*'s demands
for the destruction of Sebastopol, the government had switched the
army from its original mission in (modern) Bulgaria to a previously
unplanned invasion of the Crimea. Thereafter, the press campaign
steadily developed into what the paper's official history immodestly
described as 'a brilliant phase in the history of *The Times*'.[15]

Although Trollope was certainly aware of the Crimean issue in
its early stages, the question of whether it is directly reflected in

[15] *The History of 'The Times'*, ii. 179.

*The Warden* involves the problem of deciding at what date the action of the novel is set. The events take place during a single summer, 'a few years' (Chapter 1) or 'some years' (Chapter 21) prior to the book's publication in January 1855. In *Barchester Towers* we are told, more specifically, that it is 'five years' since the events of the previous novel. Since *Barchester Towers* was published in May 1857, written 1855–6, and supposedly set when 'the first threatenings of a huge war hung heavily over the nation' (Chapter 2), this points to a date between 1849 and 1852 for the summer of *The Warden*; the reference in 'The Two Heroines of Plumplington' (1882) to the controversy over Hiram's Hospital having persisted for 'forty years' would, if taken seriously, push the action back still further, into the early 1840s.[16] But, as in *The Three Clerks*, the time at which the action is set is actually ambiguous, or multiple.

Against these statements must be set the topical allusions which require the action of *The Warden* to be set in 1854. The law cases involving Rochester (1849–52) and St Cross (1849–53) are over, since Dr Grantly remembers Sir Abraham Haphazard's performance in them (Chapter 5). If, as seems likely, the fictitious 'Bishop of Beverley' in the same chapter is really the Bishop of Salisbury, then the incident involving him had taken place in the summer of 1853. The list, in Chapter 14, of topics on which the *Jupiter* (that is, *The Times*) has thundered reflects stories covered by that paper in 1853–4, and one of them is directly related to its treatment of the Crimea. The denunciation of Britain's leaders ('Look at our generals, what faults they make;—at our admirals, how inactive they are . . . how badly are our troops brought together, fed, conveyed, clothed, armed, and managed', p. 110) is a clear imitation of the stance which *The Times* had adopted in the spring of 1854. Still more specifically, in Chapter 10, there is a reference to a particular incident in the early months of that year. When John Bold's London speech about excessive clerical incomes is cut short, it is because the room has been booked for a meeting at which, 'the Quakers and Mr Cobden were to make . . . an appeal to the public in aid of the Emperor of Russia' (p. 80). The British Society of Friends sent a mission to St Petersburg in January 1854 which, on 10 February, delivered a petition to the Czar

---

[16] In practice, *Barchester Towers* seems mostly to be set in 1856, just as *The Warden* is mostly set in 1854, and the 'five-year' interval between them is a convenient fiction to allow time for events in the life of Eleanor Bold.

praying that 'the miseries and devastation of war be averted'. *The Times* deplored this amateur diplomacy on 23 February but printed the text of the petition on the 28th. The Quakers held meetings to publicize their views in March. Trollope's attempt to turn this episode into a satirical account of the anti-war views of the Manchester School Radicals, John Bright (a Quaker) and Richard Cobden, is perhaps rather heavy-handed. It does, however, help to confirm that the Crimean War is one of the significant contexts of a romantic comedy about clergymen and their families, set in an English cathedral close.

The Crimean War becomes still more significant to our reading of *The Warden* when it is considered in conjunction with the second of the novel's social problems: the long-standing concern about the power of the press. Trollope's sense of the 'undeserved severity' of the newspapers was neither new nor peculiar to him. James Mill's celebrated *Edinburgh Review* article 'The Periodical Press', arguing that bias was inherent in the nature of journalism, had appeared in January 1824. Bias would be a persistent anxiety and, in October 1855 (just ten months after the appearance of *The Warden*), the *Edinburgh Review* would publish another much discussed essay on the 'good and evil consequences' of newspapers. Henry Reeve had been a contributor to *The Times* since the early 1840s. He left the paper in 1855 and, in his new role as editor of the *Edinburgh*, wrote a long review-article known as 'The Fourth Estate'. Newspapers, he argued, had come to exercise an extraordinary power: 'Of all *puissances* in the political world,' the press was now 'the mightiest'. This was, in many ways, a good thing. The press, in Reeve's view, was, 'a necessary portion, complement, and guardian of free institutions'. But the 'tendency' of the press was 'to exaggerate', and journalists share the vices of politicians: 'They are often as scandalously unfair. They are often as unwilling to admit virtues in an opponent or errors in a partisan. They are almost as ready to bring false imputations and almost as reluctant to retract them.' This might not matter in circumstances where there were several, rival newspapers with more or less equal circulations. But, 'the case becomes widely different when . . . one single journal has so far distanced its competitors as virtually to have extinguished them . . . The "Times," it is notorious, has reached this extraordinary and dangerous eminence.'[17] These are the considered

---

[17] *Edinburgh Review*, 102 (October 1855), 482, 477, 478, 485, 492–4.

views of an experienced journalist, living at the heart of London's social, political, and intellectual life, in the autumn of 1855. Anthony Trollope, a Post Office official living in Belfast, had anticipated almost all of them in a novel written more than a year before. In Chapter 7, Archdeacon Grantly comments on what Reeve will call the '*puissance*' of *The Times*: 'In such matters it is omnipotent. What the Czar is in Russia, or the mob in America, that the *Jupiter* is in England' (p. 58). And in Chapter 14, when John Bold goes to look at the London offices of the *Jupiter*, Trollope holds forth at length about the questionable uses to which that extraordinary power is put.

Many people, of course, shared, or passively accepted, *The Times*'s judgement on the government's handling of the Crimean crisis. Many, however, did not and disliked the way in which the monopolistic power of a single newspaper swayed public opinion and dominated the conduct of political and administrative life. Trollope's novel about the *Jupiter*'s campaign against the management of an almshouse is a microcosmic version of the violent disagreement about the power of the press by which Britain was gripped in the mid-1850s. When Sebastopol fell, in September 1855, a joke went round the clubs that *The Times* was less 'the leading newspaper' than the 'misleading newspaper'.[18] In the winter of 1854–5 public opinion had been more conflicted and the poet Arthur Hugh Clough summed it up very neatly when he told his American friend Charles Eliot Norton, on 18 January 1855, that 'the Times is blamed and believed'.[19] Had Lord Raglan been an incompetent general or merely the victim of a war reporter's prejudices? Was *The Times* contributing to the strength of a democratic nation or undermining its war effort? Was the fashion for angry denunciation in novels, newspapers, and pamphlets— whether of rural clergymen or of generals and prime ministers— a good thing or a bad one? Trollope's 'delicate' and 'delightful' fiction is an enticing opening to the Chronicles of Barsetshire. It is also an unusually self-critical social-problem novel which made a subtle and timely contribution to a stormy national debate.

If Trollope found his way to a successful formula for prose fiction through an experimental use of the Condition-of-England novel,

---

[18] See Olive Anderson, *A Liberal State at War: English Politics and Economics During the Crimean War* (London: Macmillan, 1967), 76.

[19] Clough to C. E. Norton, in *The Correspondence of Arthur Hugh Clough*, ed. F. L. Mulhauser, 2 vols. (Oxford, Clarendon Press, 1957), ii. 495.

it was the social comedy and shrewd psychological observation with which he enriched it that became the basis for his subsequent work. He wrote five more Barsetshire novels and sometimes used his imagined county as background to narratives of other kinds— extensively in some of the novels in the Palliser series, more fleetingly in *The Claverings* (1866–7). At the end of *The Last Chronicle of Barset* (1866–7) he declared a 'last farewell' to the subject, and the funeral of Septimus Harding in Chapter 81 of that novel is the true conclusion to the story begun in *The Warden*. But his *Autobiography*, written in 1875–6, spoke of Barsetshire as 'the dear county', and in his introduction to the collected edition of *The Chronicles of Barsetshire*, in 1878, Trollope declared that 'to go back to it and write about it again and again have been one of the delights of my life'. Four years later, not altogether surprisingly, he broke his vow and wrote another Barsetshire fiction: the novella 'The Two Heroines of Plumplington', written as a Christmas story to appear in the magazine *Good Cheer* in December 1882.

Trollope began writing short stories in 1859 when, during a visit to New York, he offered two tales to *Harper's New Monthly Magazine*. He went on to publish more than forty stories in fifteen different journals, collecting most of them in five volumes between 1861 and 1882. Nine of them were written and published as Christmas stories, the sub-genre made prominent by Dickens in the 1840s: 'The Mistletoe Bough' (1861), 'The Two Generals' (1863), 'The Widow's Mite' (1863), 'Christmas Day at Kirkby Cottage' (1871), 'Harry Heathcote of Gangoil' (1873, subsequently republished as a novella), 'Christmas at Thompson Hall' (1876), 'Catherine Carmichael' (1878), and 'The Two Heroines of Plumplington' and 'Not if I Know It' (both published posthumously in 1882).

In England the short story remained a relatively unsophisticated form until the 1880s, and nobody would argue that Trollope's best work was done in this field. He resented the effort required to invent plots when the resulting text, because it was short, earned only a small fee, and found the Christmas format particularly burdensome: 'Nothing can be more distasteful to me than to have to give a relish of Christmas to what I write.' The festive bonhomie which Dickens could summon up with such facility came less readily to Trollope, who felt (turning one of Dickens's key words back against him) that a good deal of the obligatory seasonal sentiment was 'humbug'

(*An Autobiography*, Chapter 20). Despite these reservations, 'The Two Heroines of Plumplington' is a sharply observed, amusing, and uncloying Christmas story, though it appears here in its other status as the final episode in the annals of Barsetshire.

The narrative is an amusing anecdote about the way in which two middle-class girls outwit their fathers and contrive to marry the disapproved of, but attractive, young men they fancy. Plumplington, the 'second town' in Barsetshire (after, that is, the city of Barchester and the town of Silverbridge), is a place that we have not heard of before. But when an indignant father thinks of disinheriting his rebellious daughter, he is told that he could, instead, leave his estate to 'found a Hiram's Hospital', about which 'a discussion . . . had been going on for the last forty years'. Septimus Harding might be dead but John Bold's campaign against him is, it seems, still alive in Barsetshire. Nothing was further from the intentions of Mr Peppercorn, the manager of Du Boung's brewery (an institution previously featured in *The Prime Minister*), 'than to give his money to such an abominable institution'.

This is a charming romantic comedy, with a happy outcome entirely suitable for a Christmas story. But Trollope's sharp observation of the Church of England, and its place in English society, is as much at work here as it had been in the previous novels of the Barsetshire series. Mr Peppercorn the brewer and Mr Greenmantle the bank manager disapprove of their daughters' suitors (a travelling salesman and a bank clerk) for essentially snobbish reasons. Dr Freeborn, the Rector of Plumplington, is a benign clergyman who contrives to overcome these objections—but does so the more readily because he, as a university-educated man of old family, sees the social distinctions of the middle and lower-middle classes as vulgar and insignificant. Polly Peppercorn and Emily Greenmantle may, without objection, marry 'beneath them'. His own daughters, however, have been forced to form suitably aristocratic alliances.

Just as it had been thirty years before, Trollope's eye was on a real contemporary problem. One of the great issues confronting the Church of England in the later nineteenth century was the shift in the social status of its clergy from gentry (sons or cousins of the squire) to bourgeoisie: upwardly mobile men from much humbler backgrounds, educated in the new schools and universities. Was this a good thing or a bad one? Were vicars more effective when they had the authority of a superior gentleman or when they were socially indistinguishable from their flock? Trollope's portrait of a clergyman of the old school is in part affectionate, in part a comment on this uncomfortable dilemma. The relative quantities of social debate and romantic comedy may have shifted somewhat between *The Warden* in 1855 and 'The Two Heroines of Plumplington' in 1882. Trollope's Barsetshire fiction remains, none the less, a stimulating and distinctive blend of these two, very different modes.

# NOTE ON THE TEXT

## The Chronicles of Barsetshire

THIS edition of *The Warden* is part of the first modern edition of Trollope's Barchester novels to be based on the text of *The Chronicles of Barsetshire*, published in eight volumes by Chapman and Hall in 1878–9.

Trollope did not plan these novels as a sequence. But they share settings, themes, and characters, and Trollope wrote to George Smith, on 7 December 1867: 'I should like to see my novels touching Barchester published in a series.'[1] Smith was unwilling, in part because the copyrights of some of the novels were owned by other publishers. W. H. Smith had rights in *Doctor Thorne* (which Trollope at this stage considered 'not absolutely essential to this series'), while Longmans had a half share of *The Warden* and *Barchester Towers*.

These complicated copyright issues would not be resolved until 1878, when Trollope used Chapman and Hall to create a collected edition. On 13 February 1878 he paid Smith, Elder £50 for their copyright in *The Last Chronicle of Barset*. By 5 March, Longmans had agreed to relinquish *The Warden* and *Barchester Towers*, and W. H. Smith had released *Doctor Thorne*.[2] With these novels available, Trollope wrote to George Smith about the others. *The Small House at Allington* was not a problem because Trollope had come to feel that it, rather than *Doctor Thorne*, was now the novel which could be omitted.[3] The sticking point was *Framley Parsonage*. Trollope offered George Smith a fifth of the profits of the entire series and Smith accepted.[4]

On 11 April, Trollope wrote to Millais for advice about frontispieces—in a letter which, confusingly, both suggested that the edition would include all six titles and spoke of it as a set of only

[1] *The Letters of Anthony Trollope*, ed. N. John Hall with the assistance of Nina Burgis, 2 vols. (Stanford, Cal.: Stanford University Press, 1983), i. 405.

[2] *Letters*, ii. 760–1; Michael Sadleir, *Trollope: A Bibliography* (London: Constable, 1928; repr. with addenda and corrigenda, 1934), 245–6.

[3] Anthony Trollope, *An Autobiography* (1883; Oxford: Oxford University Press, 1961), Chapter 15.

[4] *Letters*, ii. 760, 763.

six volumes, which would be insufficient for six novels of this size.[5]
Either shortly before or shortly after this, Frederic Chapman insisted
that *The Small House at Allington* should be included.[6] The biblio-
graphical evidence shows that the books had gone into production
before the shift from six to eight volumes was made:

> the original issue contained a series-title-page . . . which . . . declared that
> 'The Chronicles of Barsetshire' were in *six* volumes. This statement pre-
> dated the decision to include *The Small House at Allington*, and, when, as
> a result of that decision, the series was destined to extend to eight volumes,
> an inset series-half-title was inserted . . . giving *eight* volumes as the limit.[7]

What seems most likely is that Chapman had initially left the preparation of the series to Trollope but intervened, in May or June, to
avoid the risk of issuing a less than complete 'collected' edition. It
is known that Trollope paid Smith, Elder 'the large sum of £500'[8]
for the copyright of *The Small House at Allington*. This seems the
most likely moment for such a transaction. The need to acquire an
additional title for a series already in production would explain the
payment of so much more than the £50 given for *The Last Chronicle*
in February. In the event, *The Chronicles of Barsetshire* would be published as six novels in eight volumes between November 1878 and
June 1879, each volume with a frontispiece by Francis Arthur Fraser.

The six novels thus collected as *The Chronicles of Barsetshire* had
previously appeared in a number of different formats. Three were first
published as books: *The Warden* (1855), *Barchester Towers* (1857), and
*Doctor Thorne* (1858). Two were originally magazine serials: *Framley
Parsonage* (*Cornhill*, January 1860–April 1861) and *The Small House at
Allington* (*Cornhill*, September 1862–April 1864). *The Last Chronicle
of Barset* first appeared in part-issue format (thirty-two weekly parts,
1 December 1866–6 July 1867). This diversity makes it difficult to
establish a consistent copy text for a modern collected edition.

Trollope wrote rapidly, relying on others to correct his mistakes,
and his own changes in proof could sometimes be new thoughts. His
manuscripts are therefore not a definitive guide. Nor are manuscripts
always available. Of the six novels in the Barsetshire series, they survive

[5] *Letters*, ii. 770.
[6] Sadleir, *Trollope: A Bibliography*, 245–6.
[7] Ibid. 246–7.
[8] Ibid. 246.

only for *The Small House at Allington* (Huntington Library), *The Last Chronicle of Barset* (Beinecke Library), and *Framley Parsonage* (Vaughan Library, Harrow School, lacking Chapters 1–18). In these circumstances, editors must turn to the 'best lifetime edition' and their decisions have been very various. Sometimes the first appearance in print has been deemed 'best': David Skilton and Peter Miles made a strong case for the serial text in their 1984 Penguin edition of *Framley Parsonage*. Julian Thompson, however, editing the other *Cornhill* novel, *The Small House at Allington*, for the same series in 1991, took a different view. He based his text not on the serial but on the first book edition, suggesting that, 'the text, apart from minor changes in punctuation, remained unaltered'. Even first book-form texts, unfortunately, do not provide a universal solution, since the first edition of *Doctor Thorne* was manifestly imperfect. Trollope was abroad and unable to read proofs. Not until the third edition, in 1859, were the numerous errors extensively corrected.

A case can, of course, be made for an eclectic edition. This was the procedure followed by David Skilton for the Trollope Society edition of the collected works. *Framley Parsonage* and *The Small House* were based on their serial versions, *Doctor Thorne* on the third book-form edition, and *The Warden*, *Barchester Towers*, and *The Last Chronicle* on their first book-form. When the Barsetshire novels are being republished as a separate series, however, there is an argument for a different policy: a return to Trollope's own revision of them, for the same purpose, in 1878–9. As the publication history shows, Trollope cared deeply about this project. Some modern editors have been scornful about the results. Robin Gilmour, editing *The Warden* in 1984, argued that, the 'alterations and additions in the 1878 text . . . leave errors uncorrected and incorporate no new material of substance', so 'cannot be considered to constitute a proper revision'. But the uncorrected errors noted by Gilmour are minor, while the new material is more substantial than he allowed. Skilton, in the Trollope Society edition of *The Warden*, sees the 1878 revisions as 'significant alterations', and retains many of the 1879 changes in his edition of *Doctor Thorne*.

Trollope's revision of his texts for *The Chronicles of Barsetshire* was not as meticulous as a modern textual editor might ideally require. But the fact remains that this was a revision, and the last revision in the author's lifetime. This was how Trollope ultimately wished readers to

see these novels. Accordingly, this edition of the *The Warden* is based
not on the first but on the last authorial version of the text, with a few
obvious errors silently corrected. In this and in the other novels in the
series, the editors draw attention in their notes to changes from previous versions that seem particularly significant. Some spellings and
punctuation have been regularized in accordance with current OUP
practice. Trollope's 'Introduction' to *The Chronicles*, which originally
appeared as a preface to the first volume of the series, is printed as an
appendix to each of the novels.

### The Warden *and* 'The Two Heroines of Plumplington'

Trollope 'conceived the story' of *The Warden* at Salisbury on 22 May
1852, started the first chapter at Tenbury in Worcestershire on 29
July 1853, and wrote the rest of the book in Belfast, between late
December 1853 and early October 1854. These facts were for many
years obscured by the misleading account of the matter in Chapter 5
of Trollope's *An Autobiography* (1883), where he gave the impression
that this process took place a year earlier. The correct dates are established by entries in Trollope's manuscript travel diary,[9] by an official
letter giving 6 September 1853 as the day on which his new job in
Belfast began,[10] and by Michael Sadleir's transcript of the records
(since destroyed) of the dates of the posting of the manuscript to his
publisher (8 October 1854), the reader's report on that manuscript,
then titled *The Precentor* (13 October 1854), and the publisher's
agreement (24 October 1854).[11] After a change of title to *The Warden*,
it was published in one volume in January 1855: reviews appeared in
*The Examiner* and *The Spectator* on 6 January 1855. Review copies
must have been issued rather earlier and Sadleir, in his *Bibliography*,
suggests publication on 20 December 1854, though in his *Commentary*
he had given the 1855 date printed on the title page.

Longmans published *The Warden* on half profits[12] and Trollope
initially made little money from the book. However, 1,000 copies were

[9]  Morris L. Parrish Collection, Princeton University Library.

[10]  Post Office Archives, 35/127, no. 6494, cited in Richard Mullen, *Anthony Trollope:
A Victorian in His World* (London: Duckworth, 1990), 694.

[11]  Michael Sadleir, *Trollope: A Commentary* (London: Constable, 1927), 165; *Letters*,
i. 38–9; Sadleir, *Trollope: A Bibliography*, 262.

[12]  Sadleir, *Trollope: A Bibliography*, 262.

printed, rather than the 500 usual in such circumstances, so the book remained available as Trollope's reputation grew in the later 1850s. Trollope sent Lord Houghton the last remaining unsold copy 'of the First Edit.' in 1866.[13] Though successive 'cheap editions' appeared in 1859, 1866, and 1870, 'in its original form *The Warden* never reached the essential honour of a second edition'.[14] There was therefore no opportunity to revise the text until the preparation of *The Chronicles of Barsetshire* in 1878, at which point more than 800 changes and corrections were made, mostly to punctuation. Trollope did not spot some of the factual errors which have since been identified in the first edition, such as his miscalculation of the total value of Harding's gift to his bedesmen in Chapter 1, or his misspelling of the name of the Earl of Guilford as 'Guildford'. Others, such as the misspelling of the name Horsman and the inconsistent identification of Mr Chadwick's London lawyers as 'Cox and Cummins', 'Cox and Cummings', and 'Cox and Cumming', were only partially corrected. He did, however, eliminate some other mistakes, and sharpened the style, throughout. Trollope, the practised professional writer and editor of the 1870s, tightened the loosely paratactic manner which he had been able to get away with in 1855, turning long sentences full of colons and semi-colons into shorter, clearer units.

He also acknowledged the passage of time since the book's first appearance by shifting one important passage from the present into the past tense. When the archdeacon is first explained to us, in the 1855 text we are told that 'Dr Grantly is by no means a bad man; he is exactly the man which such an education as his was most likely to form'. In 1878 this becomes, 'Dr Grantly was by no means a bad man; he was exactly . . .' (p. 16), and so on through the next two paragraphs. Trollope is aware that a contemporaneous reading of a topical novel is a different experience from reading that novel even twenty years later, and adjusts his language accordingly. This sense of the passing of time is also reflected in the most obvious of the 1878 changes: the four footnotes added to Chapter 16 (here to be found in the Explanatory Notes, p. 273). At the beginning of the same chapter, Trollope made his most substantial addition to the original text by providing a fuller explanation of what might be thought the one moment of misbehaviour in the otherwise admirable conduct of Septimus Harding.

[13] *Letters*, i. 363.  [14] Trollope, *An Autobiography*, Chapter 5.

Elsewhere, Trollope corrected his previously inconsistent account of the circulation of the *Jupiter* ('forty thousand copies' and 'Two hundred thousand readers' in Chapter 7; 'fifty thousand' copies in Chapter 14) by raising both to 'eighty thousand' (and 'Four hundred thousand readers'; p. 58). He also introduced a Latin quotation (from Horace's *Satires*) in Chapter 15 to make explicit what had previously been merely a subtle allusion. At a more intimate level, he changed the inscription at the end of Septimus Harding's 'private' resignation letter to Bishop Grantly from 'yours most sincerely' to 'yours most affectionately' (p. 153), and allowed Harding's daughter a grander wedding. In 1855 Eleanor is married 'at the palace' (that is, in the Bishop's private chapel). In the 1878 text, very appropriately, her marriage takes place 'in the cathedral' (p. 168).

Trollope proposed 'The Two Heroines of Plumplington' to the editor of *Good Words*, Donald Macleod, on 6 May 1882: 'I have hit upon a story, and shall be glad to know whether you will pay the £105 of 25 of your pages'; Macleod accepted the offer on 8 May.[15] *Good Words* was a monthly magazine founded in 1860 and aimed at an Evangelical readership; by 1864 it was selling more than 100,000 copies a month and had become the single most popular outlet for serialized fiction. Despite the rejection of *Rachel Ray* in 1863, because of its hostile treatment of Evangelicals, Trollope continued to publish in the magazine. He wrote to its publisher, William Isbister, on 28 June 1882 to say: 'I shall call on you tomorrow probably with my Xmas story',[16] and the story appeared in *Good Cheer* (as the Christmas issue of *Good Words* was called) in December 1882. On 3 November 1882, between the submission and publication of this story, Trollope suffered a debilitating stroke; he died on 6 December 1882. There was thus no opportunity for him to revise the story and the only authoritative text is that printed in *Good Cheer* (December 1882, 1–32). Apart from an American pirated version (Munro's Seaside Library, New York, 1883), it was not republished until 1953.[17] Since then it has been included in several collections of Trollope's short stories.

[15] *Letters*, ii. 961.    [16] Ibid. 973.
[17] *The Two Heroines of Plumplington*, with an introduction by John Hampden (London: André Deutsch, 1953; New York: Oxford University Press, 1954).

# SELECT BIBLIOGRAPHY

## Life and Letters

Trollope, Anthony, *An Autobiography* (1883; Oxford: Oxford University Press, 1961).
*The Letters of Anthony Trollope*, ed. N. John Hall with the assistance of Nina Burgis, 2 vols. (Stanford, Cal.: Stanford University Press, 1983).

Glendinning, Victoria, *Trollope* (London: Hutchinson, 1992).
Hall, N. John, *Trollope: A Biography* (Oxford: Clarendon Press, 1991).
Mullen, Richard, *Anthony Trollope: A Victorian in His World* (London: Duckworth, 1990).
Sadleir, Michael, *Trollope: A Commentary* (London: Constable, 1927).
Super, R. H., *The Chronicler of Barsetshire: A Life of Anthony Trollope* (Ann Arbor: University of Michigan Press, 1988).

## Text, Publication, and Reception History

Sadleir, Michael, *Trollope: A Bibliography* (London: Constable, 1928; repr. with addenda and corrigenda, 1934).
Smalley, Donald (ed.), *Trollope: The Critical Heritage* (London: Routledge & Kegan Paul, 1969).
Sutherland, John, *Victorian Novelists and Publishers* (London: Athlone Press, 1976).
[Tingay, Lance, David Skilton, Claire Connolly, and Christopher Edwards (eds.)], *Anthony Trollope: A Collector's Catalogue, 1847–1990* (London: The Trollope Society, 1992).

## Trollope's Work and Context

Anderson, Olive, *A Liberal State at War: English Politics and Economics During the Crimean War* (London: Macmillan, 1967).
Chadwick, Owen, *The Victorian Church*, 2 vols. (London: A. & C. Black, 1966–70).
Clark, J. W., *The Language and Style of Anthony Trollope* (London: André Deutsch, 1975).
Dewey, Clive, *The Passing of Barchester* (London: Hambledon Press, 1991).
Garrett, Peter K., *The Victorian Multiplot Novel: Studies in Dialogical Form* (New Haven, Conn.: Yale University Press, 1980).
Gatens, William J., *Victorian Cathedral Music in Theory and Practice* (Cambridge: Cambridge University Press, 1986).

Gibson, William, *Church, State and Society, 1760–1850* (Basingstoke: Macmillan, 1994).

Levine, George, *The Realistic Imagination* (Chicago: University of Chicago Press, 1981).

Machin, G. I. T., *Politics and the Churches in Great Britain, 1832 to 1868* (Oxford: Clarendon Press, 1977).

McMaster, R. D., *Trollope and the Law* (London: Macmillan, 1986).

Marsh, P. T., *The Victorian Church in Decline* (London: Routledge, 1969).

[Morrison, Stanley], *The History of 'The Times'* (London: The Times, 1935– ).

Mullen, Richard, with James Munson, *The Penguin Companion to Trollope* (London: Penguin, 1996).

Stone, Donald D., *The Romantic Impulse in Victorian Fiction* (Cambridge, Mass.: Harvard University Press, 1980).

Super, R. H., *Trollope in the Post Office* (Ann Arbor: University of Michigan Press, 1981).

Terry, R. C. (ed.), *Oxford Reader's Companion to Trollope* (Oxford: Oxford University Press, 1999).

## General Critical Studies

apRoberts, Ruth, *Trollope: Artist and Moralist* (London: Chatto & Windus / Athens: Ohio University Press, 1971) [published in the USA as *The Moral Trollope*].

Cockshut, A. O. J., *Anthony Trollope: A Critical Study* (London: Collins, 1955).

Edwards, P. D., *Anthony Trollope: His Art and Scope* (Hassocks: Harvester Press, 1978).

Flint, Kate, 'Queer Trollope', in Carolyn Dever and Lisa Niles (eds.), *The Cambridge Companion to Anthony Trollope* (Cambridge: Cambridge University Press, 2011), 99–112.

Harvey, Geoffrey, *The Art of Anthony Trollope* (London: Weidenfeld & Nicolson, 1980).

Herbert, Christopher, *Trollope and Comic Pleasure* (Chicago: University of Chicago Press, 1987).

James, Henry, 'Anthony Trollope', *Century Magazine* (New York, July 1883); repr. in *Partial Portraits* (London: Macmillan, 1888).

Kendrick, Walter M., *The Novel-Machine: The Theory and Fiction of Anthony Trollope* (Baltimore: Johns Hopkins University Press, 1980).

Kincaid, James R., *The Novels of Anthony Trollope* (Oxford: Clarendon Press, 1977).

Letwin, Shirley Robin, *The Gentleman in Trollope: Individuality and Moral Conduct* (Cambridge, Mass.: Harvard University Press, 1982).

Nardin, Jane, *Trollope and Victorian Moral Philosophy* (Athens: Ohio University Press, 1996).

Polhemus, Robert M., *The Changing World of Anthony Trollope* (Berkeley and Los Angeles: University of California Press, 1968).

Ray, Gordon N., 'Trollope at Full Length', *Huntington Library Quarterly*, 31 (1968), 313–40.

Skilton, David, *Anthony Trollope and His Contemporaries: A Study in the Theory and Conventions of Mid-Victorian Fiction* (Harlow: Longman, 1972; repr. with alterations, 1996).

Swingle, L. J., *Romanticism and Anthony Trollope: A Study in the Continuities of Nineteenth-Century Literary Thought* (Ann Arbor: University of Michigan Press, 1990).

Wall, Stephen, *Trollope and Character* (London: Faber and Faber, 1988).

Wright, Andrew, *Anthony Trollope: Dream and Art* (Chicago: Chicago University Press, 1983).

## *'The Warden'*

Best, G. F. A., 'The Road to Hiram's Hospital: A Byway of Early Victorian History', *Victorian Studies*, 5 (1961), 135–50.

Bridgham, Elizabeth, *Spaces of the Sacred and Profane: Dickens, Trollope and the Victorian Cathedral Town* (New York: Routledge, 2008).

Eade, J. C, ' "That's the way the money goes": Accounting in *The Warden*', *Notes and Queries*, 39 (1992), 182–3.

Earle, Bo, 'Policing and Performing Liberal Individuality in Anthony Trollope's *The Warden*', *Nineteenth-Century Literature*, 61 (2006), 1–31.

Ganzel, Carol H., '*The Times* Correspondent and *The Warden*', *Nineteenth-Century Fiction*, 21 (1967), 325–36.

Jenkins, Simon, 'Jupiter's Thunder', *Trollopian*, 17 (1992), 17–23.

Langford, Thomas A., 'Trollope's Satire in *The Warden*', *Studies in the Novel*, 19 (1987), 435–47.

Lyons, Paul, 'The Morality of Irony and Unreliable Narrative in Trollope's *The Warden* and *Barchester Towers*', *South Atlantic Review*, 54/1 (1989), 41–54.

Martin, Robert Bernard, 'Better than Ambition: The Master of St. Cross Hospital', in *Enter Rumour: Four Early Victorian Scandals* (New York: Norton, 1962), 137–84.

Meckier, Jerome, 'The Cant of Reform: Trollope Rewrites Dickens in *The Warden*', *Studies in the Novel*, 15 (1983), 202–23.

Newton, K. M., 'Allegory in Trollope's *The Warden*', *Essays in Criticism* 54 (2004), 128–43.

O'Gorman, Francis, 'Gaskell's *Sylvia's Lovers* and the Scandal in Trollope's *The Warden*', *Notes and Queries*, 59 (2012), 396–9.

Stevenson, Lionel, 'Dickens and the Origin of *The Warden*', *Nineteenth-Century Fiction*, 2 (1947), 83–9.

Sutherland, John, 'Trollope, the *Times*, and *The Warden*', in Barbara Garlick and Margaret Harris (eds.), *Victorian Journalism, Exotic and Domestic* (St Lucia: Queensland University Press, 1998), 62–74.

Ziegenhagen, Timothy, 'Trollope's Professional Gentlemen: Medical Training and Medical Practice in *Doctor Thorne* and *The Warden*', *Studies in the Novel*, 38 (2006), 154–71.

### *'The Two Heroines of Plumplington' and Trollope's Short Stories*

Hampden, John, 'Farewell to Barsetshire', in Anthony Trollope, *The Two Heroines of Plumplington* (London: André Deutsch, 1953), 7–13.

Niles, Lisa, 'Trollope's Short Fiction', in Carolyn Dever and Lisa Niles (eds.), *The Cambridge Companion to Anthony Trollope* (Cambridge: Cambridge University Press, 2011), 71–84.

Stone, Donald D., 'Trollope as a Short Story Writer', *Nineteenth-Century Fiction*, 31 (1976), 26–47.

Sutherland, John, Introduction to *Anthony Trollope, Late Short Stories* (Oxford: Oxford University Press, 1995).

Symons, Julian, Introduction to *'The Two Heroines of Plumplington' and Other Stories* (London: Folio Society, 1981).

Thompson, Julian, Introduction to *Anthony Trollope, The Collected Shorter Fiction* (London: Robinson Publishing, 1992).

### *Useful Websites*

<http://www.trollopesociety.org/>
<http://www.anthonytrollope.com/>
<http://www.trollope.org/>

# A CHRONOLOGY OF
# ANTHONY TROLLOPE

(Selected publications are noted here only; volume publication is given in all cases.)

| Life | Historical and Cultural Background |
|---|---|
| 1815 (24 April) AT born in London. | Battle of Waterloo and final defeat of Napoleon. |
| 1823 Enters Harrow Boys' School. | Monroe doctrine formulated to protect American interests in relation to Europe. |
| 1825 At school in Sunbury. | Stockton and Darlington Railway, first public railway, opens. |
| 1827 Admitted to Winchester College. | |
| 1830 Back at home in poverty then to Harrow School again. | Accession of William IV in Britain; in France, rioting sees overthrow of the Bourbons and accession of Louis Philippe. |
| 1832 | First Reform Act increases electorate to c.700,000 men. |
| 1834 Trollope family flee creditors to Bruges; AT takes up clerkship at London Post Office; a period of poverty and an unpromising start to work. | 'New Poor Law'; Tolpuddle martyrs (early example of, in effect, trade union membership). |
| 1839 | First commercial telegraph in UK. |
| 1841 After much misery, AT is offered the post of deputy postal surveyor's clerk at Banagher, King's county, Ireland; begins to hunt. | British occupation of Hong Kong; Robert Peel becomes Prime Minister. |
| 1843 Begins *The Macdermots of Ballycloran*. | Wordsworth becomes Poet Laureate. |
| 1844 Marries Rose Heseltine from Rotherham (d. 1917). | Factory Act shortens working day, increases minimum hours of schooling. |
| 1845 | Great Famine begins in Ireland (–1850). |
| 1846 Henry Merivale Trollope born (d. 1926). | Repeal of Corn Laws, major achievement for free trade; Lord John Russell becomes Prime Minister. |
| 1847 Frederick James Anthony Trollope born (d. 1910); *The Macdermots of Ballycloran*. | Ten Hours Factory Act (cuts working day to 10 hours for women and children). |

| *Life* | *Historical and Cultural Background* |
|---|---|
| 1848 *The Kellys and the O'Kellys.* | European revolutions; second Chartist petition. |
| 1850 *La Vendée*, a failure. | Tennyson becomes Poet Laureate; restoration of Catholic ecclesiastical hierarchy. |
| 1851 Working for the Post Office in England. | Great Exhibition, evidence of British dominance in trade. |
| 1852 Suggests the new pillar box for post on the Channel Islands. | Opening of new Palace of Westminster; Earl of Derby becomes Prime Minister followed by Earl of Aberdeen. |
| 1853 | Crimean War (–1856). |
| 1854 Post Office surveyor for the north of Ireland: family in Donnybrook. | |
| 1855 *The Warden*, first of the 'Chronicles of Barsetshire'; thereafter, he sets himself writing targets (usually 10,000 words a week). | Abolition of final newspaper tax leads to growth of new journalism and newspaper titles; Palmerston becomes Prime Minister. |
| 1857 *Barchester Towers*, a success. | Indian Mutiny; Matrimonial Causes Act extends availability of divorce. |
| 1858 *Doctor Thorne* (Barsetshire). | Jewish Disabilities Act; abolition of property qualification for MPs; Earl of Derby is Prime Minister, then Palmerston again. |
| 1860 Beginning of instalments of *Framley Parsonage*; moves to London as Post Office surveyor; meets Kate Field, an American woman, in Florence, with whom he forms a strong attachment. | Wilberforce–Huxley debate on evolution. |
| 1861 | American Civil War begins. |
| 1862 Elected to Garrick Club. | London Exposition; Lincoln's Emancipation proclamation. |
| 1864 Elected to the Athenaeum. *The Small House at Allington* (Barsetshire, but introduces Plantagenet and Glencora Palliser). | |
| 1864–5 *Can You Forgive Her?* (first of the Palliser novels; vol. 1, Sept. 1864; vol. 2, July 1865). | |

| *Life* | *Historical and Cultural Background* |
|---|---|
| 1865 | Abolition of slavery in North America; Earl Russell becomes Prime Minister. |
| 1866 | Success with commercial transatlantic cable; Earl of Derby becomes Prime Minister. |
| 1867 *The Last Chronicle of Barset*. Resigns from the Post Office to edit *Saint Pauls: A Monthly Magazine* with illustrations by Millais. | Second Reform Act (further extension of franchise to about 2 million electors). |
| 1868 Defeated as Liberal candidate for Beverley in the General Election. | Trades Union Congress formed; Disraeli becomes Prime Minister followed by Gladstone. |
| 1869 *He Knew He Was Right*; *Phineas Finn* (Palliser). | Suez Canal opened; first issue of *Nature*. |
| 1870 *The Vicar of Bullhampton*. | Forster's Education Act, widely extending provision of primary education; first Married Women's Property Act, granting married women the right to their own earnings and to inherit property in their own name. |
| 1871 Travels in Australasia. | Paris Commune; legalization of Trade Unions. |
| 1872 *The Eustace Diamonds* (Palliser). | |
| 1873 *Phineas Redux* (Palliser); *Australia and New Zealand*. | Financial crisis begins US Long Depression. |
| 1874 | First Impressionist Exhibition (Paris); Disraeli becomes Prime Minister. |
| 1875 *The Way We Live Now*. | Third Republic in France; Theosophical Society founded. |
| 1876 *The Prime Minister* (Palliser). | The telephone patented. |
| 1877 *The American Senator*. | |
| 1878 *Is He Popenjoy?*; *South Africa*. | Exposition Universelle (Paris), including arts and machinery. |
| 1879 *Thackeray* in the English Men of Letters series. | |
| 1880 Moves to South Harting, Sussex. *The Duke's Children* (Palliser); *Life of Cicero*. | First Anglo–Boer War (–1881); Gladstone becomes Prime Minister. |
| 1881 *Dr Wortle's School*. | Assassination of US President James Garfield. |

*Life*

*Historical and Cultural Background*

1882 *Lord Palmerston*; *The Fixed
     Period*, a futuristic novel.
     Suffers a stroke; (6 Dec.) dies
     in nursing home. Buried in
     Kensal Green (his grave reads:
     'He was a loving husband, a
     loving father, and a true friend');
     leaves estate worth
     £25,892 19s. 3d.

Phoenix Park Murders; Egypt now
British protectorate; second Married
Women's Property Act allowing
married women to own and control
their own property.

1883 *Mr Scarborough's Family*;
     *An Autobiography*.

Death of Richard Wagner.

1887 Publication of AT's brother,
     Thomas Adolphus Trollope's
     *What I Remember*, with
     alternative account of the family
     upbringing.

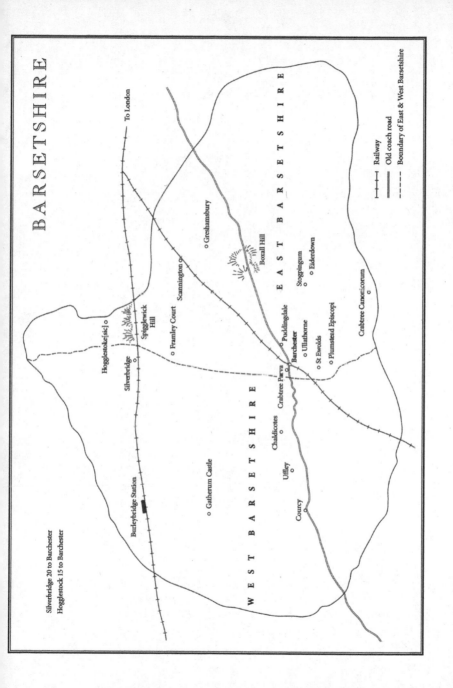

BARSETSHIRE

Silverbridge 20 to Barchester
Hogglestock 15 to Barchester

To London

WEST BARSETSHIRE

EAST BARSETSHIRE

Burleybridge Station

Gatherum Castle

Courcy

Uffley

Chaldicotes

Crabtree Parva

Silverbridge

Hogglestoke[sic]

Spigglewick Hill

Framley Court

Scannington

Greshamsbury

Boxall Hill

Stogpingum

Elderdown

Puddingdale

Barchester

Ullathorne

St Ewolds

Plumstead Episcopi

Crabtree Canonicorum

Railway
Old coach road
Boundary of East & West Barsetshire

# THE WARDEN

# CONTENTS

# CHAPTER 1

## HIRAM'S HOSPITAL

THE Rev. Septimus Harding was, a few years since, a beneficed clergyman* residing in the cathedral town of ——; let us call it Barchester.* Were we to name Wells or Salisbury, Exeter, Hereford, or Gloucester, it might be presumed that something personal was intended; and as this tale will refer mainly to the cathedral dignitaries of the town in question, we are anxious that no personality may be suspected. Let us presume that Barchester is a quiet town in the West of England, more remarkable for the beauty of its cathedral and the antiquity of its monuments, than for any commercial prosperity; that the west end of Barchester is the cathedral close,* and that the aristocracy of Barchester are the bishop, dean, and canons,* with their respective wives and daughters.

Early in life Mr Harding found himself located at Barchester. A fine voice and a taste for sacred music had decided the position in which he was to exercise his calling, and for many years he performed the easy but not highly paid duties of a minor canon. At the age of forty a small living* in the close vicinity of the town increased both his work and his income, and at the age of fifty he became precentor* of the cathedral.

Mr Harding had married early in life, and was the father of two daughters. The eldest, Susan, was born soon after his marriage; the other, Eleanor, not till ten years later. At the time at which we introduce him to our readers he was living as precentor at Barchester with his youngest daughter, then twenty-four years of age; having been many years a widower, and having married his eldest daughter to a son of the bishop, a very short time before his installation to the office of precentor.

Scandal at Barchester affirmed that had it not been for the beauty of his daughter, Mr Harding would have remained a minor canon; but here probably Scandal lied, as she so often does; for even as a minor canon no one had been more popular among his reverend brethren in the close, than Mr Harding; and Scandal, before she had reprobated Mr Harding for being made precentor by his friend the bishop, had loudly blamed the bishop for having so long omitted to do something for his friend Mr Harding. Be this as it may, Susan Harding, some twelve years since, had married the Rev. Dr Theophilus Grantly, son of the bishop, archdeacon of Barchester, and rector of Plumstead Episcopi,* and her father became, a few months later, precentor of Barchester Cathedral, that office being, as is not usual, in the bishop's gift.

Now there are peculiar circumstances connected with the precentorship which must be explained. In the year 1434 there died at Barchester one John Hiram, who had made money in the town as a woolstapler, and in his will he left the house in which he died and certain meadows and closes near the town, still called Hiram's Butts, and Hiram's Patch, for the support of twelve superannuated woolcarders,* all of whom should have been born and bred and spent their days in Barchester; he also appointed that an alms-house should be built for their abode, with a fitting residence for a warden, which warden was also to receive a certain sum annually out of the rents of the said butts and patches.* He, moreover, willed, having had a soul alive to harmony, that the precentor of the cathedral should have the option of being also warden of the alms-houses, if the bishop in each case approved.

From that day to this the charity has gone on and prospered—at least the charity had gone on, and the estates had prospered. Woolcarding in Barchester there was no longer any; so the bishop, dean, and warden, who took it in turn to put in the old men, generally appointed some hangers-on of their own; worn-out gardeners, decrepit gravediggers, or octogenarian sextons, who thankfully received a comfortable lodging and one shilling and fourpence a day, such being the stipend to which, under the will of John Hiram, they were declared to be entitled. Formerly, indeed,—that is, till within some fifty years of the present time,—they received but sixpence a day, and their breakfast and dinner was found them at a common table by the warden, such an arrangement being in stricter conformity with the absolute wording of old Hiram's will: but this was thought to be inconvenient, and to suit the tastes of neither warden nor bedesmen,* and the daily one shilling and fourpence was substituted with the common consent of all parties, including the bishop and the corporation of Barchester.

Such was the condition of Hiram's twelve old men when Mr Harding was appointed warden; but if they may be considered to have been well-to-do in the world according to their condition, the happy warden was much more so. The patches and butts which, in John Hiram's time, produced hay or fed cows, were now covered with rows of houses; the value of the property had gradually increased from year to year and century to century, and was now presumed by those who knew anything about it, to bring in a very nice income; and by some who knew nothing about it, to have increased to an almost fabulous extent.

The property was farmed* by a gentleman in Barchester, who also acted as the bishop's steward,—a man whose father and grandfather had been stewards to the bishops of Barchester, and farmers of John Hiram's estate. The Chadwicks had earned a good name in Barchester; they had lived respected by bishops, deans, canons, and precentors; they had been buried in the precincts of the cathedral; they had never been known as griping, hard men, but had always lived comfortably, maintained a good house, and held a high position in Barchester society. The present Mr Chadwick was a worthy scion of a worthy stock, and the tenants living on the butts and patches, as well as those on the wide episcopal domains of the see,* were well pleased to have to do with so worthy and liberal a steward.

For many, many years,—records hardly tell how many, probably from the time when Hiram's wishes had been first fully carried out,— the proceeds of the estate had been paid by the steward or farmer to the warden, and by him divided among the bedesmen; after which division he paid himself such sums as became his due. Times had been when the poor warden got nothing but his bare house, for the patches had been subject to floods, and the land of Barchester butts was said to be unproductive; and in these hard times the warden was hardly able to make out the daily dole* for his twelve dependents. But by degrees things mended; the patches were drained, and cottages began to rise upon the butts, and the wardens, with fairness enough, repaid themselves for the evil days gone by. In bad times the poor men had had their due, and therefore in good times they could expect no more. In this manner the income of the warden had increased; the picturesque house attached to the hospital had been enlarged and adorned, and the office had become one of the most coveted of the snug clerical sinecures* attached to our church. It was now wholly in the bishop's gift, and though the dean and chapter, in former days, made a stand on the subject, they had thought it more conducive to their honour to have a rich precentor appointed by the bishop, than a poor one appointed by themselves. The stipend of the precentor of Barchester was eighty pounds a year. The income arising from the wardenship of the hospital was eight hundred, besides the value of the house.

Murmurs, very slight murmurs, had been heard in Barchester,—few indeed, and far between,—that the proceeds of John Hiram's property had not been fairly divided: but they can hardly be said to have been of such a nature as to have caused uneasiness to any one. Still the thing had been whispered, and Mr Harding had heard it. Such was his character in Barchester, so universal was his popularity, that the very fact of his appointment would have quieted louder whispers than those which had been heard; but Mr Harding was an open-handed, just-minded man, and feeling that there might be truth in what had been said, he had, on his instalment, declared his intention of adding twopence a day to each man's pittance, making a sum of sixty-two pounds eleven shillings and fourpence,* which he was to pay out of his own pocket. In doing so, however, he distinctly and repeatedly observed to the men, that though he promised for himself, he could not promise for his successors, and that the extra twopence could only be looked on as a gift from himself, and not from the trust. The bedesmen, however, were most of them older than Mr Harding, and were quite satisfied with the security on which their extra income was based.

This munificence on the part of Mr Harding had not been unopposed. Mr Chadwick had mildly but seriously dissuaded him from it; and his strong-minded son-in-law, the archdeacon, the man of whom alone Mr Harding stood in awe, had urgently, nay, vehemently, opposed so impolitic a concession. But the warden had made known his intention to the hospital before the archdeacon had been able to interfere, and the deed was done.

Hiram's Hospital,* as the retreat is called, is a picturesque building enough, and shows the correct taste with which the ecclesiastical architects of those days* were imbued. It stands on the banks of the little river, which flows nearly round the cathedral close, being on the side furthest from the town. The London road crosses the river by a pretty one-arched bridge, and, looking from this bridge, the stranger will see the windows of the old men's rooms, each pair of windows separated by a small buttress. A broad gravel walk runs between the building and the river, which is always trim and cared for; and at the end of the walk, under the parapet of the approach to the bridge, is a large and well-worn seat, on which, in mild weather, three or four of Hiram's bedesmen are sure to be seen seated. Beyond this row of buttresses, and further from the bridge, and also further from the water which here suddenly bends, are the pretty oriel windows of Mr Harding's house, and his well-mown lawn. The entrance to the hospital is from the London road, and is made through a ponderous gateway under a heavy stone arch, unnecessary, one would suppose, at any time, for the protection of twelve old men, but greatly conducive to the good appearance of Hiram's charity. On passing through this portal, never closed to any one from six a.m. till ten p.m., and never open afterwards, except on application to a huge, intricately hung mediaeval bell, the handle of which no uninitiated intruder can possibly find, the six doors of the old men's abodes are seen, and beyond them is a slight iron screen, through which the more happy portion of the Barchester élite pass into the Elysium* of Mr Harding's dwelling.

Mr Harding is a small man, now verging on sixty years, but bearing few of the signs of age; his hair is rather grizzled than grey; his eye is very mild, but clear and bright, though the double glasses which are held swinging from his hand, unless when fixed upon his nose, show that time has told upon his sight; his hands are delicately white, and both hands and feet are small; he always wears a black frock-coat, black knee-breeches, and black gaiters,* and somewhat scandalises some of his more hyperclerical brethren by a black neck-handkerchief.*

Mr Harding's warmest admirers cannot say that he was ever an industrious man; the circumstances of his life have not called on him to be so; and yet he can hardly be called an idler. Since his appointment to his precentorship, he has published, with all possible additions of vellum, typography, and gilding, a collection of our ancient church music, with some correct dissertations on Purcell, Crotch, and Nares.* He has greatly improved the choir of Barchester, which, under his dominion, now rivals that of any cathedral in England. He has taken something more than his fair share in the cathedral services, and has played the violoncello daily to such audiences as he could collect, or, faute de mieux,* to no audience at all.

We must mention one other peculiarity of Mr Harding. As we have before stated he has an income of eight hundred a year, and has no family but his one daughter; and yet he is never quite at ease in money matters. The vellum and gilding of 'Harding's Church Music,' cost

more than any one knows, except the author, the publisher, and the
Rev. Theophilus Grantly, who allows none of his father-in-law's
extravagances to escape him. Then he is generous to his daughter,
for whose service he keeps a small carriage and pair of ponies. He is,
indeed, generous to all, but especially to the twelve old men who are
in a peculiar manner under his care. No doubt with such an income
Mr Harding should be above the world, as the saying is; but at any
rate, he is not above Archdeacon Theophilus Grantly, for he is always
more or less in debt to his son-in-law, who has, to a certain extent,
assumed the arrangement of the precentor's pecuniary affairs.

## CHAPTER 2

### THE BARCHESTER REFORMER

MR HARDING has been now precentor of Barchester for ten years;
and, alas, the murmurs respecting the proceeds of Hiram's estate
are again becoming audible. It is not that any one begrudges to Mr
Harding the income which he enjoys, and the comfortable place which
so well becomes him; but such matters have begun to be talked of in
various parts of England. Eager pushing politicians* have asserted
in the House of Commons, with very telling indignation, that the
grasping priests of the Church of England are gorged with the wealth
which the charity of former times has left for the solace of the aged,
or the education of the young. The well-known case of the Hospital of
St Cross, has even come before the law courts of the country, and the
struggles of Mr Whiston, at Rochester,* have met with sympathy and
support. Men are beginning to say that these things must be looked
into.

Mr Harding, whose conscience in the matter is clear, and who has
never felt that he had received a pound from Hiram's will to which he
was not entitled, has naturally taken the part of the church in talking
over these matters with his friend, the bishop, and his son-in-law, the
archdeacon. The archdeacon, indeed, Dr Grantly, has been somewhat loud in the matter. He is a personal friend of the dignitaries of
the Rochester Chapter, and has written letters in the public press on
the subject of that turbulent Dr Whiston, which, his admirers think,
must well-nigh set the question at rest. It is also known at Oxford,

that he is the author of the pamphlet signed 'Sacerdos'* on the subject of the Earl of Guildford and St Cross, in which it is so clearly
argued that the manners of the present times do not admit of a literal
adhesion to the very words of the founder's will, but that the interests
of the church for which the founder was so deeply concerned, are
best consulted in enabling its bishops to reward those shining lights,
whose services have been most signally serviceable to Christianity. In
answer to this, it is asserted that Henry de Blois, founder of St Cross,
was not greatly interested in the welfare of the reformed church,* and
that the masters of St Cross, for many years past, cannot be called
shining lights in the service of Christianity. It is, however, stoutly
maintained, and no doubt felt, by all the archdeacon's friends, that
his logic is conclusive, and has not, in fact, been answered.

With such a tower of strength to back both his arguments and
his conscience, it may be imagined that Mr Harding has never felt
any compunction as to receiving his quarterly sum of two hundred
pounds. Indeed, the subject has never presented itself to his mind
in that shape. He has talked not unfrequently, and heard very much
about the wills of old founders and the incomes arising from their
estates, during the last year or two; he did even, at one moment, feel
a doubt (since expelled by his son-in-law's logic) as to whether Lord
Guildford was clearly entitled to receive so enormous an income as
he does from the revenues of St Cross; but that he himself was over-
paid with his modest eight hundred pounds,—he who, out of that,
voluntarily gave up sixty-two pounds eleven shillings and fourpence
a year to his twelve old neighbours,—he who, for the money, does his
precentor's work as no precentor has done it before, since Barchester
Cathedral was built,—such an idea has never sullied his quiet, or disturbed his conscience.

Nevertheless, Mr Harding is becoming uneasy at the rumour
which he knows to prevail in Barchester on the subject. He is aware
that, at any rate, two of his old men have been heard to say, that if
every one had his own, they might each have their hundred pounds
a year, and live like gentlemen, instead of a beggarly one shilling and
sixpence a day; and that they had slender cause to be thankful for
a miserable dole of twopence, when Mr Harding and Mr Chadwick,
between them, ran away with thousands of pounds which good old
John Hiram never intended for the like of them. It is the ingratitude
of this which stings Mr Harding. One of this discontented pair, Abel

Handy, was put into the hospital by himself; he had been a stone-mason in Barchester, and had broken his thigh by a fall from a scaffolding, while employed about the cathedral; and Mr Harding had given him the first vacancy in the hospital after the occurrence, although Dr Grantly had been very anxious to put into it an insufferable clerk* of his at Plumstead Episcopi, who had lost all his teeth, and whom the archdeacon hardly knew how to get rid of by other means. Dr Grantly has not forgotten to remind Mr Harding how well satisfied with his one and sixpence a day old Joe Mutters would have been, and how injudicious it was on the part of Mr Harding to allow a radical from the town to get into the concern. Probably Dr Grantly forgot, at the moment, that the charity was intended for broken-down journeymen of Barchester.

There is living at Barchester, a young man, a surgeon, named John Bold, and both Mr Harding and Dr Grantly are well aware that to him is owing the pestilent rebellious feeling which has shown itself in the hospital; yes, and the renewal, too, of that disagreeable talk about Hiram's estates which is now again prevalent in Barchester. Nevertheless, Mr Harding and Mr Bold are acquainted with each other. We may say, are friends, considering the great disparity in their years. Dr Grantly, however, has a holy horror of the impious demagogue, as on one occasion he called Bold, when speaking of him to the precentor; and being a more prudent far-seeing man than Mr Harding, and possessed of a stronger head, he already perceives that this John Bold will work great trouble in Barchester. He considers that he is to be regarded as an enemy, and thinks that he should not be admitted into the camp on anything like friendly terms. As John Bold will occupy much of our attention, we must endeavour to explain who he is, and why he takes the part of John Hiram's bedesmen.

John Bold is a young surgeon, who passed many of his boyish years at Barchester. His father was a physician in the city of London, where he made a moderate fortune, which he invested in houses in that city. The Dragon of Wantly inn and posting-house,* belonged to him, also four shops in the High Street, and a moiety of the new row of genteel villas (so called in the advertisements), built outside the town just beyond Hiram's Hospital. To one of these Dr Bold retired to spend the evening of his life, and to die; and here his son John spent his holidays, and afterwards his Christmas vacation, when he went from school to study surgery in the London hospitals. Just as John Bold was entitled to write himself surgeon and apothecary,* old Dr Bold died, leaving his Barchester property to his son, and a certain sum in the three per cents* to his daughter Mary, who is some four or five years older than her brother.

John Bold determined to settle himself at Barchester, and look after his own property, as well as the bones and bodies of such of his neighbours as would call upon him for assistance in their troubles. He therefore put up a large brass plate, with 'John Bold, Surgeon,' on it, to the great disgust of the nine practitioners who were already trying to get a living out of the bishop, dean, and canons; and began house-keeping with the aid of his sister. At this time he was not more than twenty-four years old; and though he has now been three years in Barchester, we have not heard that he has done much harm to the nine worthy practitioners. Indeed, their dread of him has died away; for in three years he has not taken three fees.

Nevertheless, John Bold is a clever man, and would, with practice, be a clever surgeon; but he has got quite into another line of life. Having enough to live on, he has not been forced to work for bread; he has declined to subject himself to what he calls the drudgery of the profession, by which, I believe, he means the general work of a practising surgeon; and has found other employment. He frequently binds up the bruises and sets the limbs of such of the poorer classes as profess his way of thinking,—but this he does for love. Now I will not say that the archdeacon is strictly correct in stigmatising John Bold as a demagogue, for I hardly know how extreme must be a man's opinions before he can be justly so called; but Bold is a strong reformer. His passion is the reform of all abuses; state abuses, church abuses, corporation abuses (he has got himself elected a town councillor of Barchester, and has so worried three consecutive mayors, that it became somewhat difficult to find a fourth), abuses in medical practice, and general abuses in the world at large. Bold is thoroughly sincere in his patriotic endeavours to mend mankind, and there is something to be admired in the energy with which he devotes himself to remedying evil and stopping injustice; but I fear that he is too much imbued with the idea that he has a special mission for reforming. It would be well if one so young had a little more diffidence himself, and more trust in the honest purposes of others,—if he could be brought to believe that old customs need not necessarily be evil, and that changes may possibly be dangerous; but no; Bold has all the ardour, and all the self-assurance of a Danton, and hurls his anathemas against time-honoured practices with the violence of a French Jacobin.*

No wonder that Dr Grantly should regard Bold as a firebrand, falling, as he has done, almost in the centre of the quiet ancient close of Barchester Cathedral. Dr Grantly would have him avoided as the plague; but the old Doctor and Mr Harding were fast friends. Young Johnny Bold used to play as a boy on Mr Harding's lawn; he has many a time won the precentor's heart by listening with rapt attention to his sacred strains; and since those days, to tell the truth at once, he has nearly won another heart within the same walls.

Eleanor Harding has not plighted her troth to John Bold, nor has she, perhaps, owned to herself how dear to her the young reformer is; but she cannot endure that any one should speak harshly of him. She does not dare to defend him when her brother-in-law is so loud against him; for she, like her father, is somewhat afraid of Dr Grantly; but she is beginning greatly to dislike the archdeacon. She persuades her father that it would be both unjust and injudicious to banish his young friend because of his politics; she cares little to go to houses where she will not meet him, and, in fact, she is in love.

Nor is there any good reason why Eleanor Harding should not love John Bold. He has all those qualities which are likely to touch a girl's heart. He is brave, eager, and amusing; well-made and good-looking; young and enterprising; his character is in all respects good; he has sufficient income to support a wife; he is her father's friend; and, above all, he is in love with her. Then why should not Eleanor Harding be attached to John Bold?

Dr Grantly, who has as many eyes as Argus,* and has long seen how the wind blows in that direction, thinks there are various strong reasons why this should not be so. He has not thought it wise as yet to speak to his father-in-law on the subject, for he knows how foolishly indulgent is Mr Harding in everything that concerns his daughter; but he has discussed the matter with his all-trusted helpmate, within that sacred recess formed by the clerical bed-curtains at Plumstead Episcopi.

How much sweet solace, how much valued counsel has our arch-deacon received within that sainted enclosure! 'Tis there alone that he unbends, and comes down from his high church pedestal to the level of a mortal man. In the world Dr Grantly never lays aside that demeanour which so well becomes him. He has all the dignity of an ancient saint with the sleekness of a modern bishop; he is always the same; he is always the archdeacon; unlike Homer, he never nods.* Even with his father-in-law, even with the bishop and dean, he maintains that sonorous tone and lofty deportment which strikes awe into the young hearts of Barchester, and absolutely cows the whole parish of Plumstead Episcopi. 'Tis only when he has exchanged that ever-new shovel hat* for a tasselled nightcap, and those shining black habiliments for his accustomed *robe de nuit*,* that Dr Grantly talks, and looks, and thinks like an ordinary man.

Many of us have often thought how severe a trial of faith must this be to the wives of our great church dignitaries. To us these men are personifications of St Paul; their very gait is a speaking sermon; their clean and sombre apparel exacts from us faith and submission, and the cardinal virtues seem to hover round their sacred hats. A dean or archbishop, in the garb of his order, is sure of our reverence, and a well got-up bishop fills our very souls with awe. But how can this feeling be perpetuated in the bosoms of those who see the bishops without their aprons,* and the archdeacons even in a lower state of dishabille?*

Do we not all know some reverend, all but sacred, personage before whom our tongue ceases to be loud, and our step to be elastic? But were we once to see him stretch himself beneath the bed-clothes, yawn widely, and bury his face upon his pillow, we could chatter before him as glibly as before a doctor or a lawyer. From some such cause, doubtless, it arose that our archdeacon listened to the counsels of his wife, though he considered himself entitled to give counsel to every other being whom he met.

'My dear,' he said, as he adjusted the copious folds of his nightcap, 'there was that John Bold at your father's again to-day. I must say your father is very imprudent.'

'He is imprudent;—he always was,' replied. Mrs Grantly, speaking from under the comfortable bed-clothes. 'There's nothing new in that.'

'No, my dear, there's nothing new;—I know that; but, at the present juncture of affairs, such imprudence is—is—I'll tell you what, my dear, if he does not take care what he's about, John Bold will be off with Eleanor.'

'I think he will, whether papa takes care or no. And why not?'

'Why not!' almost screamed the archdeacon, giving so rough a pull at his nightcap as almost to bring it over his nose; 'why not!—that pestilent, interfering upstart, John Bold;—the most vulgar young person I ever met! Do you know that he is meddling with your father's affairs in a most uncalled for—most——' And being at a loss for an epithet sufficiently injurious, he finished his expressions of horror by muttering, 'Good heavens!' in a manner that had been found very efficacious in clerical meetings of the diocese. He must for the moment have forgotten where he was.

'As to his vulgarity, archdeacon,' (Mrs Grantly had never assumed a more familiar term than this in addressing her husband), 'I don't agree with you. Not that I like Mr Bold;—he is a great deal too conceited for me; but then Eleanor does, and it would be the best thing in the world for papa if they were to marry. Bold would never trouble himself about Hiram's Hospital if he were papa's son-in-law.' And the lady turned herself round under the bed-clothes, in a manner to which the doctor was well accustomed, and which told him, as plainly as words, that as far as she was concerned the subject was over for that night.

'Good heavens!' murmured the doctor again. He was evidently much put beside himself.

Dr Grantly was by no means a bad man; he was exactly the man which such an education as his was most likely to form; his intellect being sufficient for such a place in the world, but not sufficient to put him in advance of it. He performed with a rigid constancy such of the duties of a parish clergyman as were, to his thinking, above the sphere of his curate, but it is as an archdeacon that he shone.

We believe, as a general rule, that either a bishop or his archdeacons have sinecures. Where a bishop works, archdeacons have but little to do, and *vice versâ*. In the diocese of Barchester the Archdeacon of Barchester did the work. In that capacity he was diligent, authoritative, and, as his friends particularly boasted, judicious. His great fault was an overbearing assurance of the virtues and claims of his order, and his great foible an equally strong confidence in the dignity of his own manner and the eloquence of his own words. He was a moral man, believing the precepts which he taught, and believing also that he acted up to them; though we cannot say that he would give his coat to the man who took his cloak, or that he was prepared to forgive his brother even seven times.* He was severe enough in exacting his dues, considering that any laxity in this respect would endanger the security of the church; and, could he have had his way, he would have consigned to darkness and perdition, not only every individual reformer, but every committee and every commission that would even dare to ask a question respecting the appropriation of church revenues.

'They are church revenues: the laity admit it. Surely the church is able to administer her own revenues.' 'Twas thus he was accustomed to argue, when the sacrilegious doings of Lord John Russell* and others were discussed either at Barchester or at Oxford.

It was no wonder that Dr Grantly did not like John Bold, and that his wife's suggestion, that he should become closely connected with such a man dismayed him. To give him his dues, we must admit that the archdeacon never wanted courage; he was quite willing to meet his enemy on any field and with any weapon. He had that belief in his own arguments that he felt sure of success, could he only be sure of a fair fight on the part of his adversary. He had no idea that John Bold could really prove that the income of the hospital was malappropriated. Why, then, should peace be sought for on such bad terms? What! bribe an unbelieving enemy of the church with the sister-in-law of one dignitary, and the daughter of another,—with a young lady whose connections with the diocese and chapter of Barchester were so close as to give her an undeniable claim to a husband endowed with some of its sacred wealth! When Dr Grantly talks of unbelieving enemies, he does not mean to imply want of belief in the doctrines of the church, but an equally dangerous scepticism as to its purity in money matters.

Mrs Grantly is not usually deaf to the claims of the high order to which she belongs. She and her husband rarely disagree as to the tone with which the church should be defended. How singular, then, that in such a case as this she should be willing to succumb! The archdeacon again murmurs 'Good heavens!' as he lays himself beside her, but he does so in a voice audible only to himself, and he repeats it till sleep relieves him from deep thought.

Mr Harding himself has seen no reason why his daughter should not love John Bold. He has not been unobservant of her feelings, and perhaps his deepest regret at the part which he fears Bold is about to take regarding the hospital, arises from a dread that he may be separated from his daughter, or that she may be separated from the man she loves. He has never spoken to Eleanor about her lover; he is the last man in the world to allude to such a subject unconsulted, even with his own daughter; and had he considered that he had ground to disapprove of Bold, he would have removed her, or forbidden him his house; but he saw no such ground. He would probably have preferred a second clerical son-in-law, for Mr Harding, also, is attached to his order; and, failing in that, he would at any rate have wished that so near a connection should have thought alike with him on church matters. He would not, however, reject the man his daughter loved because he differed on such subjects with himself.

Hitherto Bold had taken no steps in the matter in any way annoying to Mr Harding personally. Some months since, after a severe battle, which cost him not a little money, he gained a victory over a certain old turnpike woman in the neighbourhood, of whose charges another old woman had complained to him. He got the act of Parliament* relating to the trust, found that his protégée had been wrongly taxed, rode through the gate himself paying the toll, then brought an action against the gate-keeper and proved that all people coming up a certain by-lane, and going down a certain other by-lane, were toll-free. The fame of his success spread widely abroad, and he began to be looked on as the upholder of the rights of the poor of Barchester. Not long after this success, he heard from different quarters that Hiram's bedesmen were treated as paupers, whereas the property to which they were, in effect, heirs, was very large; and he was instigated by the lawyer whom he had employed in the case of the turnpike to call upon Mr Chadwick for a statement as to the funds of the estate.

Bold had often expressed his indignation at the malappropriation of church funds in general, in the hearing of his friend the precentor; but the conversation had never referred to anything at Barchester; and when Finney, the attorney, induced him to interfere with the affairs of the hospital, it was against Mr Chadwick that his efforts were to be directed. Bold soon found that if he interfered with Mr Chadwick as steward, he must also interfere with Mr Harding as warden; and though he regretted the situation in which this would place him, he was not the man to flinch from his undertaking from personal motives.

As soon as he had determined to take the matter in hand, he set about his work with his usual energy. He got a copy of John Hiram's will, of the wording of which he made himself perfectly master. He ascertained the extent of the property, and as nearly as he could the value of it; and made out a schedule of what he was informed was the present distribution of its income. Armed with these particulars, he called on Mr Chadwick, having given that gentleman notice of his visit; and asked him for a statement of the income and expenditure of the hospital for the last twenty-five years.

This was of course refused, Mr Chadwick alleging that he had no authority for making public the concerns of a property in managing which he was only a paid servant.

'And who is competent to give you that authority, Mr Chadwick?' asked Bold.

'Only those who employ me, Mr Bold,' said the steward.

'And who are those, Mr Chadwick?' demanded Bold.

Mr Chadwick begged to say that if these inquiries were made merely out of curiosity, he must decline answering them: if Mr Bold had any ulterior proceeding in view, perhaps it would be desirable that any necessary information should be sought for in a professional way by a professional man. Mr Chadwick's attorneys were Messrs Cox and Cummins,* of Lincoln's Inn. Mr Bold took down the address of Cox and Cummins, remarked that the weather was cold for the time of the year, and wished Mr Chadwick good morning. Mr Chadwick said it was cold for June, and bowed him out.

He at once went to his lawyer, Finney. Now, Bold was not very fond of his attorney, but, as he said, he merely wanted a man who knew the forms of law, and who would do what he was told for his money. He had no idea of putting himself in the hands of a lawyer. He wanted law from a lawyer as he did a coat from a tailor, because he could not make it so well himself; and he thought Finney the fittest man in Barchester for his purpose. In one respect, at any rate, he was right. Finney was humility itself.

Finney advised an instant letter to Cox and Cummins, mindful of his six-and-eightpence.* 'Slap at them at once, Mr Bold. Demand categorically and explicitly a full statement of the affairs of the hospital.'

'Suppose I were to see Mr Harding first,' suggested Bold.

'Yes, yes, by all means,' said the acquiescing Finney; 'though, perhaps, as Mr Harding is no man of business, it may lead,—lead to some little difficulties; but perhaps you're right. Mr Bold, I don't think seeing Mr Harding can do any harm.' Finney saw from the expression of his client's face that he intended to have his own way.

## CHAPTER 3
### THE BISHOP OF BARCHESTER

BOLD at once repaired to the hospital. The day was now far advanced, but he knew that Mr Harding dined in the summer at four, that Eleanor was accustomed to drive in the evening, and that he might therefore probably find Mr Harding alone. It was between seven and eight when he reached the slight iron gate leading into the precentor's garden, and though, as Mr Chadwick observed, the day had been cold for June, the evening was mild, and soft, and sweet. The little gate was open. As he raised the latch he heard the notes of Mr Harding's violoncello from the far end of the garden, and, advancing before the house and across the lawn, he found him playing;—and not without an audience. The musician was seated in a garden-chair just within the summer-house, so as to allow the violoncello which he held between his knees to rest upon the dry stone flooring; before him stood a rough music desk, on which was open a page of that dear sacred book, that much-laboured and much-loved volume of church music, which had cost so many guineas; and around sat, and lay, and stood, and leaned, ten of the twelve old men who dwelt with him beneath old John Hiram's roof. The two reformers were not there. I will not say that in their hearts they were conscious of any wrong done or to be done to their mild warden, but latterly they had kept aloof from him, and his music was no longer to their taste.

It was amusing to see the positions, and eager listening faces of these well-to-do old men. I will not say that they all appreciated the music which they heard, but they were intent on appearing to do so. Pleased at being where they were, they were determined, as far as in them lay, to give pleasure in return; and they were not unsuccessful. It gladdened the precentor's heart to think that the old bedesmen whom he loved so well, admired the strains which were to him so full of almost ecstatic joy; and he used to boast that such was the air of the hospital, as to make it a precinct specially fit for the worship of St Cecilia.*

Immediately before him, on the extreme corner of the bench which ran round the summer-house, sat one old man, with his handkerchief smoothly lain upon his knees, who did enjoy the moment, or acted enjoyment well. He was one on whose large frame many years, for he was over eighty, had made small havock. He was still an upright, burly, handsome figure, with an open, ponderous brow, round which clung a few, though very few, thin grey locks. The coarse black gown of the hospital, the breeches, and buckled shoes became him well; and as he sat with his hands folded on his staff, and his chin resting on his hands, he was such a listener as most musicians would be glad to welcome.

This man was certainly the pride of the hospital. It had always been the custom that one should be selected as being to some extent in authority over the others; and though Mr Bunce, for such was his name, and so he was always designated by his inferior brethren, had no greater emoluments than they, he had assumed, and well knew how to maintain, the dignity of his elevation. The precentor delighted to call him his sub-warden, and was not ashamed, occasionally, when no other guest was there, to bid him sit down by the same parlour fire, and drink the full glass of port which was placed near him. Bunce never went without the second glass, but no entreaty ever made him take a third.

'Well, well, Mr Harding; you're too good, much too good,' he'd always say, as the second glass was filled; but when that was drunk, and the half hour over, Bunce stood erect, and with a benediction which his patron valued, retired to his own abode. He knew the world too well to risk the comfort of such halcyon* moments, by prolonging them till they were disagreeable.

Mr Bunce, as may be imagined, was most strongly opposed to innovation. Not even Dr Grantly had a more holy horror of those who would interfere in the affairs of the hospital. He was every inch a churchman; and though he was not very fond of Dr Grantly personally, that arose from there not being room in the hospital for two people so much alike as the doctor and himself, rather than from any dissimilarity in feeling. Mr Bunce was inclined to think that the warden and himself could manage the hospital without further assistance; and that, though the bishop was the constitutional visitor,* and as such entitled to special reverence from all connected with John Hiram's will, John Hiram never intended that his affairs should be interfered with by an archdeacon.

At the present moment, however, these cares were off his mind, and he was looking at his warden, as though he thought the music heavenly, and the musician hardly less so.

As Bold walked silently over the lawn, Mr Harding did not at first perceive him, and continued to draw his bow slowly across the plaintive wires; but he soon found from his audience that some stranger was there, and looking up, began to welcome his young friend with frank hospitality.

'Pray, Mr Harding——; pray don't let me disturb you,' said Bold; 'you know how fond I am of sacred music.'

'Oh! it's nothing,' said the precentor, shutting up the book and then opening it again as he saw the delightfully imploring look of his old friend Bunce. Oh, Bunce, Bunce, Bunce, I fear that after all thou art but a flatterer. 'Well, I'll just finish it then; it's a favourite little bit of Bishop's;* and then, Mr Bold, we'll have a stroll and a chat till Eleanor comes in and gives us tea.' And so Bold sat down on the soft turf to listen, or rather to think how, after such sweet harmony, he might best introduce a theme of so much discord to disturb the peace of him who was so ready to welcome him kindly.

Bold thought that the performance was soon over, for he felt that he had a somewhat difficult task, and he almost regretted the final leave-taking of the last of the old men, slow as they were in going through their adieus.

Bold's heart was in his mouth as the precentor made some ordinary but kind remark as to the friendliness of the visit.

'One evening call,' said he, 'is worth ten in the morning. It's all formality in the morning. Real social talk never begins till after dinner. That's why I dine early, so as to get as much as I can of it.'

'Quite true, Mr Harding,' said the other; 'but I fear I've reversed the order of things, and I owe you much apology for troubling you on business at such an hour; but it is on business that I have called just now.'

Mr Harding looked blank and annoyed. There was something in the tone of the young man's voice, which told him that the interview was intended to be disagreeable, and he shrank back at finding his kindly greeting so repulsed.

'I wish to speak to you about the hospital,' continued Bold.

'Well, well, anything I can tell you I shall be most happy——'

'It's about the accounts.'

'Then, my dear fellow, I can tell you nothing, for I'm as ignorant as a child. All I know is, that they pay me £800 a year. Go to Chadwick, he knows all about the accounts; and now tell me, will poor Mary Jones ever get the use of her limb again?'

'Well, I think she will, if she's careful. But, Mr Harding, I hope you won't object to discuss with me what I have to say about the hospital.'

Mr Harding gave a deep, long-drawn sigh. He did object, very strongly object, to discuss any such subject with John Bold; but he had not the business tact of Mr Chadwick, and did not know how to relieve himself from the coming evil. He sighed sadly, but made no answer.

'I have the greatest regard for you, Mr Harding,' continued Bold; 'the truest respect, the most sincere——'

'Thank ye, thank ye, Mr Bold,' interjaculated the precentor somewhat impatiently; 'I'm much obliged, but never mind that; I'm as likely to be in the wrong as another man,—quite as likely.'

'But, Mr Harding, I must express what I feel, lest you should think there is personal enmity in what I'm going to do.'

'Personal enmity! Going to do! Why you're not going to cut my throat, nor put me into the Ecclesiastical Court!'*

Bold tried to laugh, but he couldn't. He was quite in earnest, and determined in his course, and couldn't make a joke of it. He walked on awhile in silence before he recommenced his attack, during which Mr Harding, who had still the bow in his hand, played rapidly on an imaginary violoncello. 'I fear there is reason to think that John Hiram's will is not carried out to the letter, Mr Harding,' said the young man at last; 'and I have been asked to see into it.'

'Very well; I've no objection on earth; and now we need not say another word about it.'

'Only one word more, Mr Harding. Chadwick has referred me to Cox and Cummins, and I think it my duty to apply to them for some statement about the hospital. In what I do I may appear to be interfering with you, and I hope you will forgive me for doing so.'

'Mr Bold,' said the other, stopping, and speaking with some solemnity, 'if you act justly, say nothing in this matter but the truth, and use no unfair weapons in carrying out your purposes, I shall have nothing to forgive. I presume you think I am not entitled to the income I receive from the hospital, and that others are entitled to it. Whatever some may do, I shall never attribute to you base motives because you hold an opinion opposed to my own, and adverse to my interests. Pray do what you consider to be your duty. I can give you no assistance, neither will I offer you any obstacle. Let me, however, suggest to you, that you can in no wise forward your views nor I mine, by any discussion between us. Here comes Eleanor and the ponies, and we'll go in to tea.'

Bold, however, felt that he could not sit down at ease with Mr Harding and his daughter after what had passed, and therefore excused himself with much awkward apology; and merely raising his hat and bowing as he passed Eleanor and the pony chair,* left her in disappointed amazement at his departure.

Mr Harding's demeanour certainly impressed Bold with a full conviction that he as warden felt that he stood on strong grounds, and almost made him think that he was about to interfere without due warrant in the private affairs of a just and honourable man. But Mr Harding himself was anything but satisfied with his own view of the case.

In the first place, he wished for Eleanor's sake to think well of Bold and to like him, and yet he could not but feel disgusted at the arrogance of his conduct. What right had he to say that John Hiram's will was not fairly carried out? But then the question would arise within his heart,—Was that will fairly acted on? Did John Hiram mean that the warden of his hospital should receive considerably more out of the legacy than all the twelve old men together for whose behoof the hospital was built? Could it be possible that John Bold was right, and that the reverend warden of the hospital had been for the last ten years and more the unjust recipient of an income legally and equitably belonging to others? What if it should be proved before the light of day that he, whose life had been so happy, so quiet, so respected, had absorbed £8000 to which he had no title, and which he could never repay? I do not say that he feared that such was really the case; but the first shade of doubt now fell across his mind, and from this evening, for many a long, long day, our good, kind, loving warden was neither happy nor at ease.

Thoughts of this kind, these first moments of much misery, oppressed Mr Harding as he sat sipping his tea, absent and ill at ease. Poor Eleanor felt that all was not right, but her ideas as to the cause of the evening's discomfort did not go beyond her lover, and his sudden and uncivil departure. She thought there must have been some quarrel between Bold and her father, and she was half angry with both, though she did not attempt to explain to herself why she was so.

Mr Harding thought long and deeply over these things, both before he went to bed, and after it, as he lay awake, questioning within himself the validity of his claim to the income which he enjoyed. It seemed clear at any rate that, however unfortunate he might be at having been placed in such a position, no one could say that he ought either to have refused the appointment first, or to have rejected the income afterwards. All the world,—meaning the ecclesiastical world as confined to the English church,—knew that the wardenship of the Barchester Hospital was a snug sinecure, but no one had ever been blamed for accepting it. To how much blame, however, would he have been open had he rejected it! How mad would he have been thought had he declared, when the situation was vacant and offered to him, that he had scruples as to receiving £800 a year from John Hiram's property, and that he had rather some stranger should possess it! How would Dr Grantly have shaken his wise head, and have consulted with his friends in the close as to some decent retreat for the coming insanity of the poor minor canon! If he was right in accepting the place, it was clear to him also that he would be wrong in rejecting any part of the income attached to it. The patronage was a valuable appanage* of the bishopric; and surely it would not be his duty to lessen the value of that preferment which had been bestowed on himself! Surely he was bound to stand by his order!

But somehow these arguments, though they seemed logical, were not satisfactory. Was John Hiram's will fairly carried out? that was the true question: and if not, was it not his especial duty to see that this was done,—his especial duty, whatever injury it might do to his order,—however ill such duty might be received by his patron and his friends? At the idea of his friends, his mind turned unhappily to his son-in-law. He knew well how strongly he would be supported by Dr Grantly, if he could bring himself to put his case into the archdeacon's hands, and to allow him to fight the battle; but he knew also that he would find no sympathy there for his doubts, no friendly feeling, no inward comfort. Dr Grantly would be ready enough to take up his cudgel against all comers on behalf of the church militant,* but he would do so on the distasteful ground of the church's infallibility. Such a contest would give no comfort to Mr Harding's doubts. He was not so anxious to prove himself right, as to be so.

I have said before that Dr Grantly was the working man of the diocese, and that his father the bishop was somewhat inclined to an idle life. So it was; but the bishop, though he had never been an active man, was one whose qualities had rendered him dear to all who knew him. He was the very opposite to his son; he was a bland and a kind old man, opposed by every feeling to authoritative demonstrations and episcopal ostentation. It was perhaps well for him, in his situation, that his son had early in life been able to do that which he could not well do when he was younger, and which he could not have done at all now that he was over seventy. The bishop knew how to entertain the clergy of his diocese, to talk easy small talk with the rectors' wives, and put curates at their ease; but it required the strong hand of the archdeacon to deal with such as were refractory either in their doctrines or their lives.

The bishop and Mr Harding loved each other warmly. They had grown old together, and had together spent many, many years in clerical pursuits and clerical conversation. When one of them was a bishop and the other only a minor canon they were even then much together; but since their children had married, and Mr Harding had become warden and precentor, they were all in all to each other. I will not say that they managed the diocese between them; but they spent much time in discussing the man who did, and in forming little plans to mitigate his wrath against church delinquents, and soften his aspirations for church dominion.

Mr Harding determined to open his mind and confess his doubts to his old friend; and to him he went on the morning after John Bold's uncourteous visit.

Up to this period no rumour of these cruel proceedings against the hospital had reached the bishop's ears. He had doubtless heard that men existed who questioned his right to present to a sinecure of £800 a year, as he had heard from time to time of some special immorality or disgraceful disturbance in the usually decent and quiet city of Barchester; but all he did, and all he was called on to do, on such occasions, was to shake his head, and to beg his son, the great dictator, to see that no harm happened to the church.

It was a long story that Mr Harding had to tell before he made the bishop comprehend his own view of the case; but we need not follow him through the tale. At first the bishop counselled but one step, recommended but one remedy, had but one medicine in his whole pharmacopœia* strong enough to touch so grave a disorder. He prescribed the archdeacon. 'Refer him to the archdeacon,' he repeated, as Mr Harding spoke of Bold and his visit. 'The archdeacon will set you quite right about that,' he kindly said, when his friend spoke with hesitation of the justness of his cause. 'No man has got up all that so well as the archdeacon;' but the dose, though large, failed to quiet the patient. Indeed it almost produced nausea.

'But, bishop,' said he, 'did you ever read John Hiram's will?'

The bishop thought probably he had, thirty-five years ago, when first instituted to his see, but could not state positively: however, he very well knew that he had the absolute right to present to the wardenship, and that the income of the warden had been regularly settled.

'But, bishop, the question is, who has the power to settle it? If, as this young man says, the will provides that the proceeds of the property are to be divided into shares, who has the power to alter these provisions?' The bishop had an indistinct idea that they altered themselves by the lapse of years; that a kind of ecclesiastical statute of limitation* barred the rights of the twelve bedesmen to any increase of income arising from the increased value of property. He said something about tradition; more of the many learned men who by their practice had confirmed the present arrangement; then went at some length into the propriety of maintaining the due difference in rank and income between a beneficed clergyman, and certain poor old men who were dependent on charity; and concluded his argument by another reference to the archdeacon.

The precentor sat thoughtfully gazing at the fire, and listening to the good-natured reasoning of his friend. What the bishop said had a sort of comfort in it, but it was not a sustaining comfort. It made Mr Harding feel that many others,—indeed, all others of his own order,—would think him right; but it failed to prove to him that he truly was so.

'Bishop,' said he, at last, after both had sat silent for a while, 'I should deceive you and myself too, if I did not tell you that I am very unhappy about this. Suppose that I cannot bring myself to agree with Dr Grantly!—that I find, after inquiry, that the young man is right, and that I am wrong,—what then?'

The two old men were sitting near each other,—so near that the bishop was able to lay his hand upon the other's knee, and he did so with a gentle pressure. Mr Harding well knew what that pressure meant. The bishop had no further argument to adduce; he could not fight for the cause as his son would do; he could not prove all the precentor's doubts to be groundless; but he could sympathise with his friend, and he did so; and Mr Harding felt that he had received that for which he came. There was another period of silence, after which, the bishop asked with a degree of irritable energy, very unusual with him, whether this 'pestilent intruder'—meaning John Bold—had any friends in Barchester.

Mr Harding had fully made up his mind to tell the bishop everything; to speak of his daughter's love, as well as his own troubles; to talk of John Bold in his double capacity of future son-in-law and present enemy; and though he felt it to be sufficiently disagreeable, now was his time to do it.

'He is very intimate at my own house, bishop.' The bishop stared. He was not so far gone in orthodoxy and church-militancy as his son, but still he could not bring himself to understand how so declared an enemy of the establishment could be admitted on terms of intimacy into the house, not only of so firm a pillar as Mr Harding, but one so much injured as the warden of the hospital.

'Indeed, I like Mr Bold much, personally,' continued the disinterested victim; 'and to tell you the "truth," '—he hesitated as he brought out the dreadful tidings,—'I have sometimes thought it not improbable that he would be my second son-in-law.' The bishop did not whistle. We believe that they lose the power of doing so on being consecrated; and that in these days one might as easily meet a corrupt judge as a whistling bishop; but he looked as though he would have done so, but for his apron.

What a brother-in-law for the archdeacon! what an alliance for Barchester close! what a connection for even the episcopal palace! The bishop, in his simple mind, felt no doubt that John Bold, had he so much power, would shut up all cathedrals, and probably all parish churches; distribute all tithes among Methodists, Baptists, and other savage tribes;* utterly annihilate the sacred bench,* and make shovel hats and lawn sleeves as illegal as cowls, sandals, and sackcloth!* Here was a nice man to be initiated into the comfortable arcana of ecclesiastical snuggeries; one who doubted the integrity of parsons, and probably disbelieved the Trinity!*

Mr Harding saw what an effect his communication had made, and almost repented the openness of his disclosure. He, however, did what he could to moderate the grief of his friend and patron. 'I do not say that there is any engagement between them. Had there been, Eleanor would have told me. I know her well enough to be assured that she would have done so; but I see that they are fond of each other; and as a man and a father, I have had no objection to urge against their intimacy.'

'But, Mr Harding,' said the bishop, 'how are you to oppose him, if he is your son-in-law?'

'I don't mean to oppose him; it is he who opposes me; if anything is to be done in defence, I suppose Chadwick will do it. I suppose——'

'Oh, the archdeacon will see to that. Were the young man twice his brother-in-law, the archdeacon will never be deterred from doing what he feels to be right.'

Mr Harding reminded the bishop that the archdeacon and the reformer were not yet brothers, and very probably never would be; exacted from him a promise that Eleanor's name should not be mentioned in any discussion between the father bishop and son archdeacon respecting the hospital; and then took his departure, leaving his poor old friend bewildered, amazed, and confounded.

## CHAPTER 4
### HIRAM'S BEDESMEN

THE parties most interested in the movement which is about to set Barchester by the ears, were not the foremost to discuss the merit of the question, as is often the case; but when the bishop, the archdeacon, the warden, the steward, and Messrs Cox and Cummins, were all busy with the matter, each in his own way, it is not to be supposed that Hiram's bedesmen themselves were altogether passive spectators. Finney, the attorney, had been among them, asking sly questions, and raising immoderate hopes, creating a party hostile to the warden, and establishing a corps in the enemy's camp, as he figuratively calls it to himself. Poor old men! Whoever may be righted or wronged by this inquiry, they at any rate will assuredly be only injured. To them it can only be an unmixed evil. How can their lot be improved? All their wants are supplied; every comfort is administered; they have warm houses, good clothes, plentiful diet, and rest after a life of labour; and above all, that treasure so inestimable in declining years, a true and kind friend to listen to their sorrows, watch over their sickness, and administer comfort as regards this world and the world to come!

John Bold sometimes thinks of this, when he is talking loudly of the rights of the bedesmen whom he has taken under his protection; but he quiets the suggestion within his breast with the high-sounding name of justice. 'Fiat justitia ruat cœlum.'* These old men should, by rights, have one hundred pounds a year instead of one shilling and sixpence a day, and the warden should have two hundred or three hundred pounds instead of eight hundred pounds. What is unjust must be wrong; what is wrong should be righted; and if he declined the task, who else would do it?

'Each one of you is clearly entitled to one hundred pounds a year by common law!' Such had been the important whisper made by Finney into the ears of Abel Handy, and by him retailed to his eleven brethren.

Too much must not be expected from the flesh and blood even of John Hiram's bedesmen, and the positive promise of one hundred a year to each of the twelve old men, had its way with most of them. The great Bunce was not to be wiled away, and was upheld in his orthodoxy by two adherents. Abel Handy, who was the leader of the aspirants after wealth, had, alas, a stronger following. No less than five of the twelve soon believed that his views were just, making with their leader a moiety* of the hospital. The other three, volatile unstable minds, vacillated between the two chieftains, now led away by the hope of gold, now anxious to propitiate the powers that still existed.

It had been proposed to address a petition to the bishop as visitor, praying his lordship to see justice done to the legal recipients of John Hiram's Charity, and to send copies of this petition and of the reply it would elicit to all the leading London papers, and thereby to obtain notoriety for the subject. This it was thought would pave the way for ulterior legal proceedings. It would have been a great thing to have had the signatures and marks of all the twelve injured legatees; but this was impossible. Bunce would have cut his hand off sooner than have signed it. It was then suggested by Finney that if even eleven could be induced to sanction the document, the one obstinate recusant might have been represented as unfit to judge on such a question,—in fact, as being *non compos mentis*,*—and the petition would have been taken as representing the feeling of the men. But this could not be done: Bunce's friends were as firm as himself, and as yet only six crosses adorned the document. It was the more provoking, as Bunce himself could write his name legibly, and one of those three doubting souls had for years boasted of like power, and possessed, indeed, a Bible, in which he was proud to show his name written by himself some thirty years ago—'Job Skulpit.' But it was thought that Job Skulpit, having forgotten his scholarship, on that account recoiled from the petition, and that the other doubters would follow as he led them. A petition signed by half the hospital would have but a poor effect.

It was in Skulpit's room that the petition was now lying, waiting such additional signatures as Abel Handy, by his eloquence, could obtain for it. The six marks it bore were duly attested, thus:—

his                his                his
Abel + Handy,   Greg<sup>y</sup> + Moody,   Mathew + Spriggs,
mark               mark               mark

&c., and places were duly designated in pencil for those brethren who were now expected to join. For Skulpit alone was left a spot on which his genuine signature might be written in fair clerklike style. Handy had brought in the document, and spread it out on the small deal table, and was now standing by it persuasive and eager. Moody had followed with an inkhorn, carefully left behind by Finney; and Spriggs bore aloft, as though it were a sword, a well-worn ink-black pen, which from time to time he endeavoured to thrust into Skulpit's unwilling hand.

With the learned man were his two abettors in indecision, William Gazy and Jonathan Crumple. If ever the petition were to be forwarded, now was the time;—so said Mr Finney; and great was the anxiety on the part of those whose one hundred pounds a year, as they believed, mainly depended on the document in question.

'To be kept out of all that money,' as the avaricious Moody had muttered to his friend Handy, 'by an old fool saying that he can write his own name like his betters!'

'Well, Job,' said Handy, trying to impart to his own sour, ill-omened visage a smile of approbation, in which he greatly failed; 'so you're ready now, Mr Finney says; here's the place; d'ye see;'—and he put his huge brown finger down on the dirty paper;—'name or mark, it's all one. Come along, old boy; if so be we're to have the spending of this money, why the sooner the better;—that's my maxim.'

'To be sure,' said Moody. 'We a'n't none of us so young; we can't stay waiting for old Catgut* no longer.'

It was thus these miscreants named our excellent friend. The nickname he could easily have forgiven, but the allusion to the divine source of all his melodious joy would have irritated even him. Let us hope he never knew the insult.

'Only think, old Billy Gazy,' said Spriggs, who rejoiced in greater youth than his brethren, but having fallen into a fire when drunk, had had one eye burnt out, one cheek burnt through, and one arm nearly burnt off, and who, therefore, in regard to personal appearance, was not the most prepossessing of men, 'a hundred a year, and all to spend; only think, old Billy Gazy;' and he gave a hideous grin that showed off his misfortunes to their full extent.

Old Billy Gazy was not alive to much enthusiasm. Even these golden prospects did not arouse him to do more than rub his poor old bleared eyes with the cuff of his bedesman's gown, and gently mutter; 'he didn't know, not he; he didn't know.'

'But you'd know, Jonathan,' continued Spriggs, turning to the other friend of Skulpit's, who was sitting on a stool by the table, gazing vacantly at the petition. Jonathan Crumple was a meek, mild man, who had known better days; his means had been wasted by bad children, who had made his life wretched till he had been received into the hospital, of which he had not long been a member. Since that day he had known neither sorrow nor trouble, and this attempt to fill him with new hopes was, indeed, a cruelty.

'A hundred a year's a nice thing, for sartain, neighbour Spriggs,' said he. 'I once had nigh to that myself, but it didn't do me no good.' And he gave a low sigh, as he thought of the children of his own loins who had robbed him.

'And shall have again, Joe,' said Handy; 'and will have some one to keep it right and tight for you this time.'

Crumple sighed again. He had learned the impotency of worldly wealth, and would have been satisfied, if left untempted, to have remained happy with one and sixpence a day.

'Come, Skulpit,' repeated Handy, getting impatient, 'you're not going to go along with old Bunce in helping that parson to rob us all. Take the pen, man, and right yourself. Well;' he added, seeing that Skulpit still doubted, 'to see a man as is afraid to stand by hisself, is, to my thinking, the meanest thing as is.'

'Sink them all for parsons, says I,' growled Moody; 'hungry beggars, as never thinks their bellies full till they have robbed all and everything!'

'Who's to harm you, man?' argued Spriggs. 'Let them look never so black at you, they can't get you put out when you're once in;—no, not old Catgut, with Calves* to help him!' I am sorry to say the archdeacon himself was designated by this scurrilous allusion to his nether person.

'A hundred a year to win, and nothing to lose,' continued Handy, 'my eyes!—Well, how a man's to doubt about sich a bit of cheese as that passes me. But some men is timorous,—some men is born with no pluck in them,—some men is cowed at the very first sight of a gentleman's coat and waistcoat.'

Oh, Mr Harding, if you had but taken the archdeacon's advice in that disputed case, when Joe Mutters was this ungrateful demagogue's rival candidate!

'Afraid of a parson,' growled Moody, with a look of ineffable scorn. 'I tell ye what I'd be afraid of;—I'd be afraid of not getting nothing from 'em but just what I could take by might and right;—that's the most I'd be afraid on of any parson of 'em all.'

'But,' said Sculpit, apologetically, 'Mr Harding's not so bad. He did give us twopence a day, didn't he now?'

'Twopence a day!' exclaimed Spriggs with scorn, opening awfully the red cavern of his lost eye.

'Twopence a day!' muttered Moody with a curse; 'sink his twopence!'

'Twopence a day!' exclaimed Handy; 'and I'm to go, hat in hand, and thank a chap for twopence a day, when he owes me a hundred pounds a year. No, thank ye; that may do for you, but it won't for me. Come, I say Skulpit, are you a going to put your mark to this here paper, or are you not?'

Skulpit looked round in wretched indecision to his two friends. 'What d'ye think, Bill Gazy?' said he.

But Billy Gazy couldn't think. He made a noise like the bleating of an old sheep, which was intended to express the agony of his doubt, and again muttered that 'he didn't know.'

'Take hold, you old cripple,' said Handy, thrusting the pen into poor Billy's hand: 'there, so—ugh! you old fool, you've been and smeared it all,—there,—that'll do for you;—that's as good as the best name as ever was written:' and a big blotch of ink was presumed to represent Billy Gazy's acquiescence.

'Now Jonathan,' said Handy, turning to Crumple.

'A hundred a year's a nice thing, for sartain,' again argued Crumple. 'Well, neighbour Skulpit, how's it to be?'

'Oh, please yourself,' said Skulpit: 'please yourself, and you'll please me.'

The pen was thrust into Crumple's hand, and a faint, wandering, meaningless sign was made, betokening such sanction and authority as Jonathan Crumple was able to convey.

'Come Joe,' said Handy, softened by success, 'don't let 'em have to say that old Bunce has a man like you under his thumb;—a man that always holds his head in the hospital as high as Bunce himself, though you're never axed to drink wine, and sneak, and tell lies about your betters, as he does.'

Skulpit held the pen, and made little flourishes with it in the air, but still hesitated.

'And if you'll be said by me,' continued Handy, 'you'll not write your name to it at all, but just put your mark like the others;'—the cloud began to clear from Skulpit's brow;—'we all know you can do it if you like, but maybe you wouldn't like to seem uppish, you know.'

'Well, the mark would be best,' said Skulpit. 'One name and the rest marks, wouldn't look well, would it?'

'The worst in the world,' said Handy; 'there—there;' and stooping over the petition, the learned clerk made a huge cross on the place left for his signature.

'That's the game,' said Handy, triumphantly pocketing the petition; 'we're all in a boat now, that is, the nine of us; and as for old Bunce, and his cronies, they may——' But as he was hobbling off to the door, with a crutch on one side and a stick on the other, he was met by Bunce himself.

'Well, Handy, and what may old Bunce do?' said the grey-haired, upright senior.

Handy muttered something, and was departing; but he was stopped in the doorway by the huge frame of the new comer.

'You've been doing no good here, Abel Handy,' said he, ''tis plain to see that; and 'tisn't much good, I'm thinking, you ever do.'

'I mind my own business, Master Bunce,' muttered the other, 'and do you do the same; It a'n't nothing to you what I does;—and your spying and poking here won't do no good nor yet no harm.'

'I suppose then, Joe,' continued Bunce, not noticing his opponent, 'if the truth must out, you've stuck your name to that petition of theirs at last.'

Skulpit looked as though he were about to sink into the ground with shame.

'What is it to you what he signs?' said Handy. 'I suppose if we all wants to ax for our own, we needn't ax leave of you first, Mr Bunce, big a man as you are; and as to your sneaking in here, into Job's room when he's busy, and where you're not wanted——'

'I've knowed Joe Skulpit, man and boy, sixty years,' said Bunce, looking at the man of whom he spoke, 'and that's ever since the day he was born. I knowed the mother that bore him, when she and I were little wee things, picking daisies together in the close yonder; and I've lived under the same roof with him more nor ten years; and after that I may come into his room without axing leave, and yet no sneaking neither.'

'So you can, Mr Bunce,' said Skulpit; 'so you can, any hour, day or night.'

'And I'm free also to tell him my mind,' continued Bunce, looking at the one man and addressing the other; 'and I tell him now that he's done a foolish and a wrong thing. He's turned his back upon one who is his best friend; and is playing the game of others, who care nothing for him, whether he be poor or rich, well or ill, alive or dead. A hundred a year? Are the lot of you soft enough to think that if a hundred a year be to be given, it's the likes of you that will get it?'—and he pointed to Billy Gazy, Spriggs, and Crumple. 'Did any of us ever do anything worth half the money? Was it to make gentlemen of us we were brought in here, when all the world turned against us, and we couldn't longer earn our daily bread? A'n't you all as rich in your ways as he in his?'—and the orator pointed to the side on which the warden lived. 'A'n't you getting all you hoped for; ay, and more than you hoped for? Wouldn't each of you have given the dearest limb of his body to secure that which now makes you so unthankful?'

'We wants what John Hiram left us,' said Handy. 'We wants what's ourn by law. It don't matter what we expected. What's ourn by law should be ourn, and by goles* we'll have it.'

'Law!' said Bunce, with all the scorn he knew how to command,— 'law! Did ye ever know a poor man yet was the better for law, or for a lawyer? Will Mr Finney ever be as good to you, Job, as that man has been? Will he see to you when you're sick, and comfort you when you're wretched? Will he——'

'No, nor give you port wine, old boy, on cold winter nights! he won't do that, will he?' asked Handy; and laughing at the severity of his own wit, he and his colleagues retired, carrying with them, however, the now powerful petition.

There is no help for spilt milk; and Mr Bunce could only retire to his own room, disgusted at the frailty of human nature. Job Skulpit scratched his head. Jonathan Crumple again remarked, that, 'for sartain, sure a hundred a year was very nice;'—and Billy Gazy again rubbed his eyes, and lowly muttered that 'he didn't know.'

## CHAPTER 5

### DR GRANTLY VISITS THE HOSPITAL

THOUGH doubt and hesitation disturbed the rest of our poor warden, no such weakness perplexed the nobler breast of his son-in-law. As the indomitable cock preparing for the combat sharpens his spurs, shakes his feathers, and erects his comb, so did the archdeacon arrange his weapons for the coming war, without misgiving and without fear. That he was fully confident of the justice of his cause let no one doubt. Many a man can fight his battle with good courage, but with a doubting conscience. Such was not the case with Dr Grantly. He did not believe in the Gospel with more assurance than he did in the sacred justice of all ecclesiastical revenues. When he put his shoulder to the wheel to defend the income of the present and future precentors of Barchester, he was animated by as strong a sense of a holy cause, as that which gives courage to a missionary in Africa, or enables a sister of mercy to give up the pleasures of the world for the wards of a hospital. He was about to defend the holy of holies from the touch of the profane; to guard the citadel of his church from the most rampant of its enemies; to put on his good armour* in the best of fights; and secure, if possible, the comforts of his creed for coming generations of ecclesiastical dignitaries. Such a work required no ordinary vigour; and the archdeacon was, therefore, extraordinarily vigorous. It demanded a buoyant courage, and a heart happy in its toil; and the archdeacon's heart was happy, and his courage was buoyant.

He knew that he would not be able to animate his father-in-law with feelings like his own, but this did not much disturb him. He preferred to bear the brunt of the battle alone, and did not doubt that the warden would resign himself into his hands with passive submission.

'Well, Mr Chadwick,' he said, walking into the steward's office a day or two after the signing of the petition as commemorated in the last chapter: 'anything from Cox and Cummins this morning?' Mr Chadwick handed him a letter; which he read, stroking the tight-gaitered calf of his right leg as he did so. Messrs Cox and Cummins merely said that they had as yet received no notice from their adversaries; that they could recommend no preliminary steps; but that should any proceeding really be taken by the bedesmen, it would be expedient to consult that very eminent Queen's Counsel,* Sir Abraham Haphazard.

'I quite agree with them,' said Dr Grantly, refolding the letter. 'I perfectly agree with them. Haphazard is no doubt the best man; a thorough churchman, a sound Conservative, and in every respect the best man we could get. He's in the house,* too, which is a great thing.'

Mr Chadwick quite agreed.

'You remember how completely he put down that scoundrel Horseman* about the Bishop of Beverley's income;* how completely he set them all adrift in the earl's case.' Since the question of St Cross had been mooted by the public, one noble lord* had become '*the earl,*' *par excellence*, in the doctor's estimation. 'How he silenced that fellow at Rochester. Of course we must have Haphazard; and I'll tell you what, Mr Chadwick, we must take care to be in time, or the other party will forestall us.'

With all his admiration for Sir Abraham, the doctor seemed to think it not impossible that that great man might be induced to lend his gigantic powers to the side of the church's enemies.

Having settled this point to his satisfaction, the doctor stepped down to the hospital, to learn how matters were going on there; and as he walked across the hallowed close, and looked up at the ravens who cawed with a peculiar reverence as he wended his way, he thought with increased acerbity of those whose impiety would venture to disturb the goodly grace of cathedral institutions.

And who has not felt the same? We believe that Mr Horsman himself would relent, and the spirit of Sir Benjamin Hall* give way, were those great reformers to allow themselves to stroll by moonlight round the towers of some of our ancient churches. Who would not feel charity for a prebendary, when walking the quiet length of that long aisle at Winchester, looking at those decent houses, that trim grassplat, and feeling, as one must, the solemn, orderly comfort of the spot! Who could be hard upon a dean while wandering round the sweet close of Hereford, and owning that in that precinct, tone and colour, design and form, solemn tower and storied window, are all in unison, and all perfect! Who could lie basking in the cloisters of Salisbury, and gaze on Jewel's library* and that unequalled spire, without feeling that bishops should sometimes be rich!

The tone of our archdeacon's mind must not astonish us; it has been the growth of centuries of church ascendency; and though some fungi now disfigure the tree, though there be much dead wood, for how much good fruit have not we to be thankful? Who, without remorse, can batter down the dead branches of an old oak, now useless, but, ah! still so beautiful, or drag out the fragments of the ancient forest, without feeling that they sheltered the younger plants, to which they are now summoned to give way in a tone so peremptory and so harsh?

The archdeacon, with all his virtues, was not a man of delicate feeling; and after having made his morning salutations in the warden's drawing-room, he did not scruple to commence an attack on 'pestilent' John Bold in the presence of Miss Harding, though he rightly guessed that that lady was not indifferent to the name of his enemy.

'Nelly, my dear, fetch me my spectacles from the back room,' said her father, anxious to save both her blushes and her feelings.

Eleanor brought the spectacles, while her father was trying, in ambiguous phrases, to explain to her too-practical brother-in-law that it might be as well not to say anything about Bold before her, and then retreated. Nothing had been explained to her about Bold and the hospital; but, with a woman's instinct, she knew that things were going wrong.

'We must soon be doing something,' commenced the archdeacon, wiping his brows with a large, bright-coloured handkerchief, for he had felt busy, and had walked quick, and it was a broiling summer's day. 'Of course you have heard of the petition?'

Mr Harding owned, somewhat unwillingly, that he had heard of it.

'Well!' The archdeacon looked for some expression of opinion, but none coming, he continued,—'We must be doing something, you know; we mustn't allow these people to cut the ground from under us while we sit looking on.' The archdeacon, who was a practical man, allowed himself the use of every-day expressive modes of speech when among his closest intimates, though no one could soar into a more intricate labyrinth of refined phraseology when the church was the subject, and his lower brethren were his auditors.

The warden still looked mutely in his face, making the slightest possible passes with an imaginary fiddle bow, and stopping, as he did so, sundry imaginary strings with the fingers of his other hand. 'Twas his constant consolation in conversational troubles. While these vexed him sorely, the passes would be short and slow, and the upper hand would not be seen to work; nay the strings on which it operated would sometimes lie concealed in the musician's pocket, and the instrument on which he played would be beneath his chair. But as his spirit warmed to the subject,—as his trusting heart, looking to the bottom of that which vexed him, would see its clear way out,—he would rise to a higher melody, sweep the unseen strings with a bolder hand, and swiftly fingering the cords from his neck, down along his waistcoat, and up again to his very ear, create an ecstatic strain of perfect music, audible to himself and to St Cecilia, and not without effect.

'I quite agree with Cox and Cummins,' continued the archdeacon. 'They say we must secure Sir Abraham Haphazard. I shall not have the slightest fear in leaving the case in Sir Abraham's hands.' The warden played the slowest and saddest of tunes. It was but a dirge on one string. 'I think Sir Abraham will not be long in letting Master Bold know what he's about. I fancy I hear Sir Abraham cross-questioning him at the Common Pleas.'* The warden thought of his income being thus discussed, his modest life, his daily habits, and his easy work; and nothing issued from that single cord, but a low wail of sorrow. 'I suppose they've sent this petition up to my father.' The warden didn't know; he imagined they would do so this very day. 'What I can't understand is, how you let them do it, with such a command as you have in the place, or should have with such a man as Bunce. I cannot understand why you let them do it.'

'Do what?' asked the warden.

'Why, listen to this fellow Bold, and that other low pettifogger, Finney;—and get up this petition too. Why didn't you tell Bunce to destroy the petition?'

'That would have been hardly wise,' said the warden.

'Wise;—yes, it would have been very wise if they'd done it among themselves. I must go up to the palace and answer it now, I suppose. It's a very short answer they'll get, I can tell you.'

'But why shouldn't they petition, doctor?'

'Why shouldn't they!' responded the archdeacon, in a loud brazen voice, as though all the men in the hospital were expected to hear him through the walls; 'why shouldn't they? I'll let them know why they shouldn't. By-the-by, warden, I'd like to say a few words to them all together.'

The warden's mind misgave him, and even for a moment he forgot to play. He by no means wished to delegate to his son-in-law his place and authority of warden; he had expressly determined not to interfere in any step which the men might wish to take in the matter under dispute; he was most anxious neither to accuse them nor to defend himself. All these things he was aware the archdeacon would do in his behalf, and that not in the mildest manner; and yet he knew not how to refuse the permission requested. 'I'd so much sooner remain quiet in the matter,' said he, in an apologetic voice.

'Quiet!' said the archdeacon, still speaking with his brazen trumpet;* 'do you wish to be ruined in quiet?'

'Why; if I am to be ruined, certainly.'

'Nonsense, warden; I tell you something must be done. We must act; just let me ring the bell, and send the men word that I'll speak to them in the quad.'

Mr Harding knew not how to resist, and the disagreeable order was given. The quad, as it was familiarly called, was a small quadrangle, open on one side to the river, and surrounded on the others by the high wall of Mr Harding's garden, by one gable end of Mr Harding's house, and by the end of the row of buildings which formed the residences of the bedesmen. It was flagged all round, and the centre was stoned; small stone gutters ran from the four corners of the square to a grating in the centre; and attached to the end of Mr Harding's house was a conduit with four cocks covered over from the weather, at which the old men got their water, and very generally performed their morning toilet. It was a quiet, sombre place, shaded over by the trees of the warden's garden. On the side towards the river, there stood a row of stone seats, on which the old men would sit and gaze at the little fish, as they flitted by in the running stream. On the other side of the river was a rich, green meadow, running up to and joining the deanery, and as little open to the public as the garden of the dean itself. Nothing, therefore, could be more private than the quad of the hospital; and it was there that the archdeacon determined to convey to them his sense of their refractory proceedings.

The servant soon brought in word that the men were assembled in the quad, and the archdeacon, big with his purpose, rose to address them.

'Well, warden, of course you're coming,' said he, seeing that Mr Harding did not prepare to follow him.

'I wish you'd excuse me,' said Mr Harding.

'For heaven's sake, don't let us have division in the camp,' replied the archdeacon. 'Let us have a long pull and a strong pull,* but above all a pull altogether; come, warden, come; don't be afraid of your duty.'

Mr Harding was afraid; he was afraid that he was being led to do that which was not his duty. He was not, however, strong enough to resist, so he got up and followed his son-in-law.

The old men were assembled in groups in the quadrangle;—eleven of them at least, for poor old Johnny Bell was bed-ridden and couldn't come; he had, however, put his mark to the petition, as one of Handy's earliest followers. 'Tis true he could not move from the bed where he lay; 'tis true he had no friend on earth, but those whom the hospital contained; and of those the warden and his daughter were the most constant and most appreciated; 'tis true that everything was administered to him which his failing body could require, or which his faint appetite could enjoy; but still his dull eye had glistened for a moment at the idea of possessing a hundred pounds a year 'to his own cheek,' as Abel Handy had eloquently expressed it; and poor old Johnny Bell had greedily put his mark to the petition.

When the two clergymen appeared, they all uncovered their heads. Handy was slow to do it, and hesitated; but the black coat and waistcoat, of which he had spoken so irreverently in Skulpit's room, had its effect even on him, and he too doffed his hat. Bunce, advancing before the others, bowed lowly to the archdeacon, and with affectionate reverence expressed his wish, that the warden and Miss Eleanor were quite well; 'and the doctor's lady,' he added turning to the archdeacon, 'and the children at Plumstead, and my lord;' and having made his speech, he also retired among the others, and took his place with the rest upon the stone benches.

As the archdeacon stood up to make his speech, erect in the middle of that little square, he looked like an ecclesiastical statue placed there, as a fitting impersonation of the church militant here on earth; his shovel hat, large, new, and well-pronounced, a churchman's hat in every inch; declared the profession as plainly as does the Quaker's broad brim;* his heavy eyebrows, large open eyes, and full mouth and chin expressed the solidity of his order; the broad chest, amply covered with fine cloth, told how well to do was its estate; one hand ensconced within his pocket, evinced the practical hold which our mother church keeps on her temporal possessions; and the other, loose for action, was ready to fight if need be in her defence; and, below these, the decorous breeches, and neat black gaiters showing so admirably that well-turned leg, betokened the stability, the decency, the outward beauty and grace of our church establishment.

'Now, my men,' he began, when he had settled himself well in his position; 'I want to say a few words to you. Your good friend, the warden here, and myself, and my lord the bishop, on whose behalf I wish to speak to you, would all be very sorry, very sorry indeed, that you should have any just ground of complaint. Any just ground of complaint on your part would be removed at once by the warden, or by his lordship, or by me on his behalf, without the necessity of any petition on your part.' Here the orator stopped for a moment, expecting that some little murmurs of applause would show that the weakest of the men were beginning to give way; but no such murmurs came. Bunce, himself, even sat with closed lips, mute and unsatisfactory. 'Without the necessity of any petition at all,' he repeated. 'I'm told you have addressed a petition to my lord.' He paused for a reply from the men, and after a while, Handy plucked up courage, and said, 'Yes, we has.'

'You have addressed a petition to my lord, in which, as I am informed, you express an opinion that you do not receive from Hiram's estate all that is your due.' Here most of the men expressed their assent. 'Now what is it you ask for? What is it you want that you haven't got here? What is it——'

'A hundred a year,' muttered old Moody, with a voice as if it came out of the ground.

'A hundred a year!' ejaculated the archdeacon militant, defying the impudence of these claimants with one hand stretched out and closed, while with the other he tightly grasped, and secured within his breeches pocket, that symbol of the church's wealth which his own loose half-crowns* not unaptly represented. 'A hundred a year! Why, my men, you must be mad! And you talk about John Hiram's will! When John Hiram built a hospital for worn-out old men, worn-out old labouring men, infirm old men past their work, cripples, blind, bed-ridden, and such like, do you think he meant to make gentlemen of them? Do you think John Hiram intended to give a hundred a year to old single men, who earned perhaps two shillings or half-a-crown a day for themselves and families in the best of their time? No, my men! I'll tell you what John Hiram meant; he meant that twelve poor old worn-out labourers, men who could no longer support themselves, who had no friends to support them, who must starve and perish miserably if not protected by the hand of charity;—he meant that twelve such men as these should come in here in their poverty and wretchedness, and find within these walls shelter and food before their death, and a little leisure to make their peace with God. That was what John Hiram meant. You have not read John Hiram's will, and I doubt whether those wicked men who are advising you have done so. I have; I know what his will was; and I tell you that that was his will, and that that was his intention.'

Not a sound came from the eleven bedesmen, as they sat listening to what, according to the archdeacon, was their intended estate. They grimly stared upon his burly figure, but did not then express, by word or sign, the anger and disgust to which such language was sure to give rise.

'Now let me ask you,' he continued; 'do you think you are worse off than John Hiram intended to make you? Have you not shelter, and food, and leisure? Have you not much more? Have you not every indulgence which you are capable of enjoying? Have you not twice better food, twice a better bed, ten times more money in your pocket than you were ever able to earn for yourselves before you were lucky enough to get into this place? And now you sent a petition to the bishop, asking for a hundred pounds a year! I tell you what, my friends; you are deluded, and made fools of by wicked men who are acting for their own ends. You will never get a hundred pence a year more than what you have now. It is very possible that you may get less; it is very possible that my lord the bishop, and your warden, may make changes——'

'No, no, no,' interrupted Mr Harding, who had been listening with indescribable misery to the tirade of his son-in-law; 'no, my friends.

I want no changes;—at least no changes that shall make you worse off than you now are, as long as you and I live together.'

'God bless you, Mr Harding,' said Bunce; and 'God bless you, Mr Harding; God bless you, sir: we know you was always our friend,' was exclaimed by enough of the men to make it appear that the sentiment was general.

The archdeacon had been interrupted in his speech before he had quite finished it; but he felt that he could not recommence with dignity after this little ebullition,* and he led the way back into the garden, followed by his father-in-law.

'Well,' said he, as soon as he found himself within the cool retreat of the warden's garden; 'I think I spoke to them plainly.' And he wiped the perspiration from his brow; for making a speech under a broiling mid-day sun in summer, in a full suit of thick black cloth, is warm work.

'Yes, you were plain enough,' replied the warden, in a tone which did not express approbation.

'And that's everything,' said the other, who was clearly well satisfied with himself; 'that's everything. With those sort of people one must be plain, or one will not be understood. Now, I think they did understand me;—I think they knew what I meant.'

The warden agreed. He certainly thought they had understood to the full what had been said to them.

'They know pretty well what they have to expect from us; they know how we shall meet any refractory spirit on their part; they know that we are not afraid of them. And now I'll just step into Chadwick's, and tell him what I've done; and then I'll go up to the palace, and answer this petition of theirs.'

The warden's mind was very full,—full nearly to over-charging itself; and had it done so,—had he allowed himself to speak the thoughts which were working within him, he would indeed have astonished the archdeacon by the reprobation he would have expressed as to the proceeding of which he had been so unwilling a witness. But different feelings kept him silent; he was as yet afraid of differing from his son-in-law,—he was anxious beyond measure to avoid even a semblance of rupture with any of his order, and was painfully fearful of having to come to an open quarrel with any person on any subject. His life had hitherto been so quiet, so free from strife; his little early troubles had required nothing but passive fortitude; his subsequent prosperity had never forced upon him any active cares,—had never brought him into disagreeable contact with any one. He felt that he would give almost anything,—much more than he knew he ought to give,—to relieve himself from the storm which he feared was coming. It was so hard that the pleasant waters of his little stream should be disturbed and muddied by rough hands; that his quiet paths should be made a battle-field; that the unobtrusive corner of the world which had been allotted to him, as though by Providence, should be invaded and desecrated, and all within it made miserable and unsound.

Money he had none to give; the knack of putting guineas together had never belonged to him; but how willingly, with what a foolish easiness, with what happy alacrity, would he have abandoned the half of his income for all time to come, could he by so doing have quietly dispelled the clouds that were gathering over him,—could he have thus compromised the matter between the reformer and the Conservative, between his possible son-in-law, Bold, and his positive son-in-law, the archdeacon.

And this compromise would not have been made from any prudential motive of saving what would yet remain, for Mr Harding still felt little doubt but he should be left for life in quiet possession of the good things he had, if he chose to retain them. No; he would have done so from the sheer love of quiet, and from a horror of being made the subject of public talk. He had very often been moved to pity,—to that inward weeping of the heart for others' woes; but none had he ever pitied more than that old lord, whose almost fabulous wealth, drawn from his church preferments, had become the subject of so much opprobrium, of such public scorn; that wretched clerical octogenarian Croesus,* whom men would not allow to die in peace,—whom all the world united to decry and to abhor.

Was he to suffer such a fate? Was his humble name to be bandied in men's mouths, as the gormandizer* of the resources of the poor, as of one who had filched from the charity of other ages wealth which had been intended to relieve the old and the infirm? Was he to be gibbeted in the press, to become a byword for oppression, to be named as an example of the greed of the English church? Should it ever be said that he had robbed those old men, whom he so truly and so tenderly loved in his heart of hearts? As he slowly paced, hour after hour, under those noble lime-trees, turning these sad thoughts within him, he became all but fixed in his resolve that some great step must be taken to relieve him from the risk of so terrible a fate.

In the meanwhile, the archdeacon, with contented mind and unruffled spirit, went about his business. He said a word or two to Mr Chadwick, and then finding, as he expected, the petition lying in his father's library, he wrote a short answer to the men, in which he told them that they had no evils to redress, but rather great mercies for which to be thankful; and having seen the bishop sign it, he got into his brougham* and returned home to Mrs Grantly, and Plumstead Episcopi.

## CHAPTER 6

### THE WARDEN'S TEA PARTY

AFTER much painful doubting, on one thing only could Mr Harding resolve. He determined that at any rate he would take no offence, and that he would make this question no cause of quarrel either with Bold or with the bedesmen. In furtherance of this resolution, he himself wrote a note to Mr Bold, the same afternoon, inviting him to meet a few friends and hear some music on an evening named in the next week. Had not this little party been promised to Eleanor, in his present state of mind he would probably have avoided such gaiety; but the promise had been given, the invitations were to be written, and when Eleanor consulted her father on the subject, she was not ill pleased to hear him say, 'Oh, I was thinking of Bold, so I took it into my head to write to him myself; but you must write to his sister.'

Mary Bold was older than her brother, and, at the time of our story, was just over thirty. She was not an unattractive young woman, though by no means beautiful. Her great merit was the kindliness of her disposition. She was not very clever, nor very animated, nor had she apparently the energy of her brother; but she was guided by a high principle of right and wrong; her temper was sweet, and her faults were fewer in number than her virtues. Those who casually met Mary Bold thought little of her; but those who knew her well loved her well, and the longer they knew her the more they loved her. Among those who were fondest of her was Eleanor Harding; and though Eleanor had never openly talked to her of her brother, each understood the other's feelings about him. The brother and sister were sitting together when the two notes were brought in.

'How odd,' said Mary, 'that they should send two notes. Well, if Mr Harding becomes fashionable, the world is going to change.'

Her brother understood immediately the nature and intention of the peace-offering; but it was not so easy for him to behave well in the matter, as it was for Mr Harding. It is much less difficult for the sufferer to be generous than for the oppressor. John Bold felt that he could not go to the warden's party. He never loved Eleanor better than he did now; he had never so strongly felt how anxious he was to make her his wife as now, when so many obstacles to his doing so appeared in view. Yet here was her father himself, as it were, clearing away those very obstacles, and still he felt that he could not go to the house any more as an open friend.

As he sat thinking of these things with the note in his hand, his sister was waiting for his decision.

'Well,' said she, 'I suppose we must write separate answers, and both say we shall be very happy.'

'You'll go, of course, Mary,' said he; to which she readily assented. 'I cannot,' he continued, looking serious and gloomy. 'I wish I could, with all my heart.'

'And why not, John?' said she. She had as yet heard nothing of the new-found abuse which her brother was about to reform;—at least nothing which connected it with her brother's name.

He sat thinking for awhile till he determined that it would be best to tell her at once what it was that he was about. It must be done sooner or later.

'I fear I cannot go to Mr Harding's house any more as a friend, just at present.'

'Oh, John! Why not? Ah; you've quarrelled with Eleanor!'

'No, indeed,' said he; 'I've no quarrel with her as yet.'

'What is it, John?' said she, looking at him with an anxious, loving face, for she knew well how much of his heart was there in that house which he said he could no longer enter.

'Why,' said he at last, 'I've taken up the case of these twelve old men of Hiram's Hospital, and of course that brings me into contact with Mr Harding. I may have to oppose him, interfere with him,—perhaps injure him.'

Mary looked at him steadily for some time before she committed herself to reply, and then merely asked him what he meant to do for the old men.

'Why, it's a long story, and I don't know that I can make you understand it. John Hiram made a will, and left his property in charity for certain poor old men, and the proceeds, instead of going to the benefit of these men, goes chiefly into the pocket of the warden, and the bishop's steward.'

'And you mean to take away from Mr Harding his share of it?'

'I don't know what I mean yet. I mean to inquire about it. I mean to see who is entitled to this property. I mean to see, if I can, that justice be done to the poor of the city of Barchester generally, who are, in fact, the legatees under the will. I mean, in short, to put the matter right, if I can.'

'And why are you to do this, John?'

'You might ask the same question of anybody else,' said he; 'and according to that, the duty of righting these poor men would belong to nobody. If we are to act on that principle, the weak are never to be protected, injustice is never to be opposed, and no one is to struggle for the poor!' And Bold began to comfort himself in the warmth of his own virtue.

'But is there no one to do this but you, who have known Mr Harding so long? Surely, John, as a friend, as a young friend, so much younger than Mr Harding——'

'That's woman's logic, all over, Mary. What has age to do with it? Another man might plead that he was too old; and as to his friendship, if the thing itself be right, private motives should never be allowed to interfere. Because I esteem Mr Harding, is that a reason that I should neglect a duty which I owe to these old men? Or should I give up a work which my conscience tells me is a good one, because I regret the loss of his society?'

'And Eleanor, John?' said the sister, looking timidly into her brother's face.

'Eleanor, that is, Miss Harding, if she thinks fit,—that is, if her father,—or rather, if she,—or, indeed, he,—if they find it necessary——. But there is no necessity now to talk about Eleanor Harding. This I will say, that if she has the kind of spirit for which I give her credit, she will not condemn me for doing what I think to be a duty.' And Bold consoled himself with the consolation of a Roman.*

Mary sat silent for a while, till at last her brother reminded her that the notes must be answered, and she got up, and placed her desk before her, took out her pen and paper, wrote on it slowly,—

'Pakenham Villas,* Tuesday morning.

'My dear Eleanor,

'I——'

and then stopped, and looked at her brother.

'Well, Mary, why don't you write it?'

'Oh, John,' said she, 'dear John, pray think better of this.'

'Think better of what?' said he.

'Of this about the hospital,—of all this about Mr Harding,—of what you say about those old men. Nothing can call upon you,—no duty can require you to set yourself against your oldest, your best friend. Oh, John, think of Eleanor. You'll break her heart and your own.'

'Nonsense, Mary; Miss Harding's heart is as safe as yours.'

'Pray, pray, for my sake, John, give it up. You know how dearly you love her.' And she came and knelt before him on the rug. 'Pray give it up. You are going to make yourself, and her, and her father miserable. You are going to make us all miserable. And for what? For a dream of justice. You will never make those twelve men happier than they now are.'

'You don't understand it, my dear girl,' said he, smoothing her hair with his hand.

'I do understand it, John. I understand that this is a chimera,*— a dream that you have got. I know well that no duty can require you to do this mad,—this suicidal thing. I know you love Eleanor Harding with all your heart, and I tell you now that she loves you as well. If there was a plain, a positive duty before you, I would be the last to bid you neglect it for any woman's love; but this——; oh, think again, before you do anything to make it necessary that you and Mr Harding should be at variance.' He did not answer, as she knelt there, leaning on his knees, but by his face she thought that he was inclined to yield. 'At any rate let me say that you will go to this party. At any rate do not break with them while your mind is in doubt.' And she got up, hoping to conclude her note in the way she desired.

'My mind is not in doubt,' at last he said, rising. 'I could never respect myself again, were I to give way now, because Eleanor Harding is beautiful. I do love her. I would give a hand to hear her tell me what you have said, speaking on her behalf. But I cannot for her sake go back from the task which I have commenced. I hope she may hereafter acknowledge and respect my motives, but I cannot now go as a guest to her father's house.' And the Barchester Brutus* went out to fortify his own resolution by meditations on his own virtue.

Poor Mary Bold sat down, and sadly finished her note, saying that she would herself attend the party, but that her brother was unavoidably prevented from doing so. I fear that she did not admire as she should have done the self-devotion of his singular virtue.

The party went off as such parties do. There were fat old ladies, in fine silk dresses, and slim young ladies, in gauzy muslin frocks; old gentlemen stood up with their backs to the empty fire-place, looking by no means so comfortable as they would have done in their own arm-chairs at home; and young gentlemen, rather stiff about the neck, clustered near the door, not as yet sufficiently in courage to attack the muslin frocks,* who awaited the battle, drawn up in a semicircular array. The warden endeavoured to induce a charge, but failed signally, not having the tact of a general; his daughter did what she could to comfort the forces under her command, who took in refreshing rations of cake and tea, and patiently looked for the coming engagement. But she herself, Eleanor, had no spirit for the work; the only enemy whose lance she cared to encounter was not there, and she and others were somewhat dull.

Loud above all voices was heard the clear sonorous tones of the archdeacon as he dilated to brother parsons of the danger of the church, of the fearful rumours of mad reforms even at Oxford,* and of the damnable heresies of Dr Whiston.

Soon, however, sweeter sounds began timidly to make themselves audible. Little movements were made in a quarter notable for round stools and music stands. Wax candles were arranged in sconces, big books were brought from hidden recesses, and the work of the evening commenced.

How often were those pegs twisted and retwisted before our friend found that he had twisted them enough; how many discordant scrapes gave promise of the coming harmony! How much the muslin fluttered and crumpled before Eleanor and another nymph were duly seated at the piano; how closely did that tall Apollo* pack himself against the wall, with his flute, long as himself, extending high over the heads of his pretty neighbours; into how small a corner crept that round and florid little minor canon, and there with skill amazing found room to tune his accustomed fiddle!

And now the crash begins. Away they go in full flow of harmony together,—up hill and down dale,—now louder and louder, then lower and lower; now loud, as though stirring the battle; then low, as though mourning the slain. In all, through all, and above all, is heard the violoncello. Ah, not for nothing were those pegs so twisted and retwisted. Listen, listen! Now alone that saddest of instruments tells its touching tale. Silent, and in awe, stand fiddle, flute, and piano, to hear the sorrows of their wailing brother. 'Tis but for a moment. Before the melancholy of those low notes has been fully realised, again comes the full force of all the band. Down go the pedals. Away rush twenty fingers scouring over the bass notes with all the impetus of passion. Apollo blows till his stiff neckcloth is no better than a rope, and the minor canon works with both arms till he falls into a syncope* of exhaustion against the wall.

How comes it that now, when all should be silent, when courtesy, if not taste, should make men listen,—how is it at this moment the black-coated corps leave their retreat and begin skirmishing? One by one they creep forth, and fire off little guns timidly, and without precision. Ah, my men, efforts such as these will take no cities, even though the enemy should be never so open to assault. At length a more deadly artillery is brought to bear; slowly, but with effect, the advance is made; the muslin ranks are broken, and fall into confusion; the formidable array of chairs gives way; the battle is no longer between opposing regiments, but hand to hand, and foot to foot with single combatants, as in the glorious days of old, when fighting was really noble. In corners, and under the shadow of curtains, behind sofas and half hidden by doors, in retiring windows, and sheltered by hanging tapestry, are blows given and returned, fatal, incurable, dealing death.

Apart from this another combat arises, more sober and more serious. The archdeacon is engaged against two prebendaries, a pursy full-blown rector assisting him, in all the perils and all the enjoyments of short whist.* With solemn energy do they watch the shuffled pack, and, all-expectant, eye the coming trump. With what anxious nicety do they arrange their cards, jealous of each other's eyes! Why is that lean doctor so slow,—cadaverous man with hollow jaw and sunken eye, ill beseeming the richness of his mother church! Ah, why so slow, thou meagre doctor? See how the archdeacon, speechless in his agony, deposits on the board his cards, and looks to heaven or to the ceiling for support. Hark, how he sighs, as with thumbs in his waist-coat pocket he seems to signify that the end of such torment is not yet even nigh at hand! Vain is the hope, if hope there be, to disturb that meagre doctor. With care precise he places every card, weighs well the value of each mighty ace, each guarded king, and comfort-giving queen; speculates on knave and ten, counts all his suits, and sets his price upon the whole. At length a card is led, and quick three others fall upon the board. The little doctor leads again, while with lustrous eye his partner absorbs the trick. Now thrice has this been done,— thrice has constant fortune favoured the brace of prebendaries, ere the archdeacon rouses himself to the battle. But at the fourth assault he pins to the earth a prostrate king, laying low his crown and sceptre, bushy beard, and lowering brow, with a poor deuce.

'As David did Goliath,'* says the archdeacon, pushing over the four cards to his partner. And then a trump is led, then another trump; then a king,—and then an ace,—and then a long ten, which brings down from the meagre doctor his only remaining tower of strength,—his cherished queen of trumps.

'What, no second club?' says the archdeacon to his partner.

'Only one club,' mutters from his inmost stomach the pursy rector, who sits there red faced, silent, impervious, careful, a safe but not a brilliant ally.

But the archdeacon cares not for many clubs, or for none. He dashes out his remaining cards with a speed most annoying to his antagonists, pushes over to them some four cards as their allotted portion, shoves the remainder across the table to the red-faced rector; calls out 'two by cards and two by honours, and the odd trick last time,' marks a treble under the candle-stick, and has dealt round the second pack before the meagre doctor has calculated his losses.

And so went off the warden's party, and men and women arran-ging shawls and shoes declared how pleasant it had been; and Mrs Goodenough, the red-faced rector's wife, pressing the warden's hand, declared she had never enjoyed herself better;—which showed how little pleasure she allowed herself in this world, as she had sat the whole evening through in the same chair without occupation, not speaking, and unspoken to. And Matilda Johnson, when she allowed young Dickson of the bank to fasten her cloak round her neck, thought that two hundred pounds a year and a little cottage would really do for happiness;—besides, he was sure to be manager some day. And Apollo, folding his flute into his pocket, felt that he had acquitted himself with honour; and the archdeacon pleasantly jingled his gains; but the meagre doctor went off without much audible speech, muttering ever and anon as he went, 'three and thirty points!' 'three and thirty points!'

And so they all were gone, and Mr Harding was left alone with his daughter.

What had passed between Eleanor Harding and Mary Bold need not be told. It is indeed a matter of thankfulness that neither the historian nor the novelist hears all that is said by their heroes or heroines, or how would three volumes* or twenty suffice! In the present case so little of this sort have I overheard, that I live in hopes of finishing my work within 300 pages, and of completing that pleasant task— a novel in one volume; but something had passed between them, and as the warden blew out the wax candles, and put his instrument into its case, his daughter stood sad and thoughtful by the empty fireplace, determined to speak to her father, but irresolute as to what she would say.

'Well, Eleanor,' said he; 'are you for bed?'

'Yes,' said she, moving, 'I suppose so; but papa——. Mr Bold was not here to-night; do you know why not?'

'He was asked; I wrote to him myself,' said the warden.

'But do you know why he did not come, papa?'

'Well, Eleanor, I could guess; but it's no use guessing at such things, my dear. What makes you look so earnest about it?'

'Oh papa, do tell me,' she exclaimed, throwing her arms round him, and looking into his face; 'what is it he is going to do? What is it all about? Is there any—any—any—' she didn't well know what word to use—'any danger?'

'Danger, my dear, what sort of danger?'

'Danger to you, danger of trouble, and of loss, and of——. Oh papa, why haven't you told me of all this before?'

Mr Harding was not the man to judge harshly of any one, much less of the daughter whom he now loved better than any living creature; but still he did judge her wrongly at this moment. He knew that she loved John Bold; he fully sympathised in her affection; day after day he thought more of the matter, and, with the tender care of a loving father, tried to arrange in his own mind how matters might be so managed that his daughter's heart should not be made the sacrifice to the dispute which was likely to exist between him and Bold. Now, when she spoke to him for the first time on the subject, it was natural that he should think more of her than of himself, and that he should imagine that her own cares, and not his, were troubling her.

He stood silent before her awhile, as she gazed up into his face, and then kissing her forehead he placed her on the sofa.

'Tell me, Nelly,' he said (he only called her Nelly in his kindest, softest, sweetest moods; and yet all his moods were kind and sweet), 'tell me, Nelly, do you like Mr Bold—much?'

She was quite taken aback by the question. I will not say that she had forgotten herself, and her own love in thinking about John Bold, and while conversing with Mary. She certainly had not done so. She had been sick at heart to think, that a man of whom she could not but own to herself that she loved him, of whose regard she had been so proud, that such a man should turn against her father to ruin him. She had felt her vanity hurt, that his affection for her had not kept him from such a course. Had he really cared for her, he would not have risked her love by such an outrage. But her main fear had been for her father, and when she spoke of danger, it was of danger to him and not to herself.

She was taken aback by the question altogether: 'Do I like him, papa?'

'Yes, Nelly, do you like him? Why shouldn't you like him? But that's a poor word. Do you love him?' She sat still in his arms without answering him. She certainly had not prepared herself for an avowal of affection, intending, as she had done, to abuse John Bold herself, and to hear her father do so also. 'Come, my love,' said he, 'let us make a clean breast of it. Do you tell me what concerns yourself, and I will tell you what concerns me and the hospital.'

And then, without waiting for an answer, he described to her, as he best could, the accusation that was made about Hiram's will; the claims which the old men put forward; what he considered the strength and what the weakness of his own position; the course which Bold had taken, and that which he presumed he was about to take; and then by degrees, without further question, he presumed on the fact of Eleanor's love, and spoke of that love as a feeling which he could in no way disapprove. He apologised for Bold, excused what he was doing; nay, praised him for his energy and intentions; made much of his good qualities, and harped on none of his foibles; then, reminding his daughter how late it was, and comforting her with much assurance which he hardly felt himself, he sent her to her room, with flowing eyes and a full heart.

When Mr Harding met his daughter at breakfast the next morning, there was no further discussion on the matter, nor was the subject mentioned between them for some days. Soon after the party Mary Bold called at the hospital, but there were various persons in the drawing-room at the time, and she therefore said nothing about her brother. On the day following, John Bold met Miss Harding in one of the quiet sombre shaded walks of the close. He was most anxious to see her, but unwilling to call at the warden's house, and had in truth waylaid her in her private haunts.

'My sister tells me,' said he, abruptly hurrying on with his premeditated speech, 'my sister tells me that you had a delightful party the other evening. I was so sorry I could not be there.'

'We were all sorry,' said Eleanor, with dignified composure.

'I believe, Miss Harding, you understood why, at this moment——' And Bold hesitated, muttered, stopped, commenced his explanation again, and again broke down. Eleanor would not help him in the least. 'I think my sister explained to you, Miss Harding?'

'Pray don't apologise, Mr Bold; my father will, I am sure, always be glad to see you, if you like to come to the house now as formerly; nothing has occurred to alter his feelings. Of your own views you are, of course, the best judge.'

'Your father is all that is kind and generous; he always was so; but you, Miss Harding, yourself—— I hope you will not judge me harshly, because——'

'Mr Bold,' said she, 'you may be sure of one thing; I shall always judge my father to be right, and those who oppose him I shall judge to be wrong. If those who do not know him oppose him, I shall have charity enough to believe that they are wrong, through error of judgment; but should I see him attacked by those who ought to know him, and to love him, and revere him, of such I shall be constrained to form a different opinion.' And then curtseying low she sailed on, leaving her lover in anything but a happy state of mind.

## CHAPTER 7

### THE *JUPITER*

THOUGH Eleanor Harding rode off from John Bold on a high horse,* it must not be supposed that her heart was so elate as her demeanour. In the first place, she had a natural repugnance to losing her lover; and in the next, she was not quite so sure that she was so certainly in the right as she pretended to be. Her father had told her, and that now repeatedly, that Bold was doing nothing unjust or ungenerous; and why then should she rebuke him, and throw him off, when she felt herself so ill able to bear his loss? But such is human nature, and young-lady-nature especially. As she walked off from him beneath the shady elms of the close, her look, her tone, every motion and gesture of her body, belied her heart; she would have given the world to have taken him by the hand, to have reasoned with him, persuaded him, cajoled him, coaxed him out of his project; to have overcome him with all her female artillery, and to have redeemed her father at the cost of herself; but pride would not let her do this, and she left him without a look of love or a word of kindness.

Had Bold been judging of another lover and of another lady, he might have understood all this as well as we do; but in matters of love men do not see clearly in their own affairs. They say that faint heart never won fair lady. It is amazing to me how fair ladies are won, so faint are often men's hearts! Were it not for the kindness of their nature, that seeing the weakness of our courage they will occasionally descend from their impregnable fortresses, and themselves aid us in effecting their own defeat, too often would they escape unconquered if not unscathed, and free of body if not of heart.

Poor Bold crept off quite crest-fallen. He felt that as regarded Eleanor Harding his fate was sealed, unless he could consent to give up a task to which he had pledged himself, and which indeed it would not be easy for him to give up. Lawyers were engaged, and the question had to a certain extent been taken up by the public. Besides, how could a high-spirited girl like Eleanor Harding really learn to love a man for neglecting a duty which he had assumed! Could she allow her affection to be purchased at the cost of his own self-respect?

As regarded the issue of his attempt at reformation in the hospital, Bold had no reason hitherto to be discontented with his success. All

Barchester was by the ears* about it. The bishop, the archdeacon, the warden, the steward, and several other clerical allies, had daily meetings, discussing their tactics, and preparing for the great attack. Sir Abraham Haphazard had been consulted, but his opinion was not yet received. Copies of Hiram's will, copies of warden's journals, copies of leases, copies of accounts, copies of everything that could be copied, and of some that could not, had been sent to him; and the case was assuming most creditable dimensions. But above all, it had been mentioned in the daily *Jupiter*.* That all-powerful organ of the press in one of its leading thunderbolts launched at St Cross, had thus remarked: 'Another case, of smaller dimensions indeed, but of similar import, is now likely to come under public notice. We are informed that the warden or master of an old almshouse attached to Barchester Cathedral is in receipt of twenty-five times the annual income appointed for him by the will of the founder, while the sum yearly expended on the absolute purposes of the charity has always remained fixed. In other words, the legatees under the founder's will have received no advantage from the increase in the value of the property during the last four centuries, such increase having been absorbed by the so-called warden. It is impossible to conceive a case of greater injustice. It is no answer to say that some six or nine or twelve old men receive as much of the goods of this world as such old men require. On what foundation, moral or divine, traditional or legal, is grounded the warden's claim to the large income he receives for doing nothing? The contentment of these almsmen, if content they be, can give him no title to this wealth! Does he ever ask himself, when he stretches wide his clerical palm to receive the pay of some dozen of the working clergy, for what service he is so remunerated? Does his conscience ever entertain the question of his right to such subsidies? Or is it possible that the subject never so presents itself to his mind; that he has received for many years, and intends, should God spare him, to receive for years to come, these fruits of the industrious piety of past ages, indifferent as to any right on his own part, or of any injustice to others! We must express an opinion that nowhere but in the Church of England, and only there among its priests, could such a state of moral indifference be found.'

I must for the present leave my readers to imagine the state of Mr Harding's mind after reading the above article. They say that eighty thousand copies of the *Jupiter* are daily sold, and that each

copy is read by five persons at the least. Four hundred thousand readers then would hear this accusation against him; four hundred thousand hearts* would swell with indignation at the griping injustice,
the bare-faced robbery of the warden of Barchester Hospital! And
how was he to answer this? How was he to open his inmost heart to
this multitude, to these thousands, the educated, the polished, the
picked men of his own country; how show them that he was no robber,
no avaricious lazy priest scrambling for gold, but a retiring humble-
spirited man, who had innocently taken what had innocently been
offered to him?

'Write to the *Jupiter*,' suggested the bishop.

'Yes,' said the archdeacon, more worldly wise than his father; 'yes,
and be smothered with ridicule; tossed over and over again with scorn;
shaken this way and that, as a rat in the mouth of a practised terrier.
You will leave out some word or letter in your answer, and the ignorance of the cathedral clergy will be harped upon; you will make some
small mistake, which will be a falsehood, or some admission, which
will be self-condemnation; you will find yourself to have been vulgar,
ill-tempered, irreverend, and illiterate, and the chances are ten to one,
but that being a clergyman you will have been guilty of blasphemy!
A man may have the best of causes, the best of talents, and the best of
tempers; he may write as well as Addison, or as strongly as Junius;*
but even with all this he cannot successfully answer, when attacked
by the *Jupiter*. In such matters it is omnipotent. What the Czar is in
Russia, or the mob in America, that the *Jupiter* is in England. Answer
such an article! No, warden; whatever you do, don't do that. We were
to look for this sort of thing, you know; but we need not draw down
on our heads more of it than is necessary.'

The article in the *Jupiter*, while it so greatly harassed our poor warden, was an immense triumph to some of the opposite party. Sorry
as Bold was to see Mr Harding attacked so personally, it still gave
him a feeling of elation to find his cause taken up by so powerful an
advocate. And as to Finney, the attorney, he was beside himself. What!
to be engaged in the same cause and on the same side with the *Jupiter*;
to have the views he had recommended seconded, and furthered, and
battled for by the *Jupiter*! Perhaps to have his own name mentioned
as that of the learned gentleman whose efforts had been so successful
on behalf of the poor of Barchester! He might be examined before
committees of the House of Commons, with heaven knows how much

a day for his personal expenses;—he might be engaged for years on such a suit! There was no end to the glorious golden dreams which this leader in the *Jupiter* produced in the soaring mind* of Finney.

And the old bedesmen;—they also heard of this article, and had a glimmering, indistinct idea of the marvellous advocate which had now taken up their cause. Abel Handy limped hither and thither through the rooms, repeating all that he understood to have been printed, with some additions of his own which he thought should have been added. He told them how the *Jupiter* had declared that their warden was no better than a robber, and that what the *Jupiter* said was acknowledged by the world to be true. How the *Jupiter* had affirmed that each one of them—'each one of us, Jonathan Crumple, think of that!'—had a clear right to a hundred a year; and that if the *Jupiter* had said so, it was better than a decision of the Lord Chancellor. And then he carried about the paper, supplied by Mr Finney, which, though none of them could read it, still afforded in its very touch and aspect positive corroboration of what was told them; and Jonathan Crumple pondered deeply over his returning wealth; and Job Skulpit saw how right he had been in signing the petition, and said so many scores of times; and Spriggs leered fearfully with his one eye; and Moody, as he more nearly approached the coming golden age, hated more deeply than ever those who still kept possession of what he so coveted. Even Billy Gazy and poor bedridden Bell became active and uneasy. But the great Bunce stood apart with lowering brow,* with deep grief seated in his heart, for he perceived that evil days were coming.

It had been decided, the archdeacon advising, that no remonstrance, explanation, or defence should be addressed from the Barchester conclave to the Editor of the *Jupiter*; but hitherto that was the only decision to which they had come.

Sir Abraham Haphazard was deeply engaged in preparing a bill for the mortification of papists, to be called the 'Convent Custody Bill',* the purport of which was to enable any Protestant clergyman over fifty years of age to search any nun whom he suspected of being in possession of treasonable papers, or Jesuitical symbols; and as there were to be a hundred and thirty-seven clauses in the bill, each clause containing a separate thorn for the side of the papist, and as it was known the bill would be fought inch by inch, by fifty maddened Irishmen, the due construction and adequate dovetailing of it did consume much of Sir Abraham's time. The bill had all its desired effect. Of course it never passed into law; but it so completely divided the ranks of the Irish members, who had bound themselves together to force on the ministry a bill for compelling all men to drink Irish whiskey, and all women to wear Irish poplins, that for the remainder of the session the Great Poplin and Whiskey League was utterly harmless.

Thus it happened that Sir Abraham's opinion was not at once forthcoming, and the uncertainty, the expectation, and suffering of the folk of Barchester was maintained at a high pitch.

## CHAPTER 8

### PLUMSTEAD EPISCOPI

THE reader must now be requested to visit the rectory of Plumstead Episcopi; and as it is as yet still early morning, to ascend again with us into the bed-room of the archdeacon. The mistress of the mansion was at her toilet; on which we will not dwell with profane eyes, but proceed into a small inner room, where the doctor dressed and kept his boots and sermons; and here we will take our stand, premising that the door of the room was so open as to admit of a conversation between our reverend Adam and his valued Eve.

'It's all your own fault, archdeacon,' said the latter. 'I told you from the beginning how it would end, and papa has no one to thank but you.'

'Good gracious, my dear,' said the doctor, appearing at the door of his dressing-room, with his face and head enveloped in the rough towel which he was violently using; 'how can you say so? I am doing my very best.'

'I wish you had never done so much,' said the lady, interrupting him. 'If you'd just have let John Bold come and go there, as he and papa liked, he and Eleanor would have been married by this time, and we should not have heard one word about all this affair.'

'But, my dear——'

'Oh, it's all very well, archdeacon; and of course you're right; I don't for a moment think you'll ever admit that you could be wrong; but the fact is, you've brought this young man down upon papa by huffing him as you have done.'

'But, my love——'

'And all because you didn't like John Bold for a brother-in-law. How is she ever to do better? Papa hasn't got a shilling; and though Eleanor is well enough, she has not at all a taking style of beauty. I'm sure I don't know how she's to do better than marry John Bold; or as well indeed,' added the anxious sister, giving the last twist to her last shoe-string.

Dr Grantly felt keenly the injustice of this attack; but what could he say? He certainly had huffed John Bold; he certainly had objected to him as a brother-in-law, and a very few months ago the very idea had excited his wrath. But now matters were changed; John Bold had shown his power, and, though he was as odious as ever to the archdeacon, power is always respected, and the reverend dignitary began to think that such an alliance might not have been imprudent. Nevertheless, his motto was still 'no surrender;' he would still fight it out; he believed confidently in Oxford, in the bench of bishops,* in Sir Abraham Haphazard, and in himself; and it was only when alone with his wife that doubts of defeat ever beset him. He once more tried to communicate this confidence to Mrs Grantly, and for the twentieth time began to tell her of Sir Abraham.

'Oh, Sir Abraham!' said she, collecting all her house keys into her basket before she descended; 'Sir Abraham won't get Eleanor a husband; Sir Abraham won't get papa another income when he has been worreted out of the hospital. Mark what I tell you, arch-deacon. While you and Sir Abraham are fighting, papa will lose his preferment; and what will you do then with him and Eleanor on your hands? besides, who's to pay Sir Abraham? I suppose he won't take the case up for nothing?' And so the lady descended to family worship among her children and servants, the pattern of a good and prudent wife.

Dr Grantly was blessed with a happy, thriving family. There were, first, three boys, now at home from school for the holidays. They were called, respectively, Charles James, Henry, and Samuel.* The two younger,—there were five in all,—were girls; the elder, Florinda, bore the name of the Archbishop of York's wife, whose godchild she was: and the younger had been christened Grizzel,* after a sister of the Archbishop of Canterbury. The boys were all clever, and gave good promise of being well able to meet the cares and trials of the world; and yet they were not alike in their dispositions, and each had his individual character, and each his separate admirers among the doctor's friends.

Charles James was an exact and careful boy; he never committed himself; he well knew how much was expected from the eldest son of the Archdeacon of Barchester, and was therefore mindful not to mix too freely with other boys. He had not the great talents of his younger brothers, but he exceeded them in judgment and propriety of demeanour; his fault, if he had one, was an over-attention to words instead of things; there was a thought too much *finesse* about him, and, as even his father sometimes told him, he was too fond of a compromise.

The second was the archdeacon's favourite son, and Henry was indeed a brilliant boy. The versatility of his genius was surprising, and the visitors at Plumstead Episcopi were often amazed at the marvellous manner in which he would, when called on, adapt his capacity to apparently most uncongenial pursuits. He appeared once before a large circle as Luther the reformer, and delighted them with the perfect manner in which he assumed the character; and within three days he again astonished them by acting the part of a Capuchin friar* to the very life. For this last exploit his father gave him a golden guinea,* and his brothers said the reward had been promised beforehand in the event of the performance being successful. He was also sent on a tour into Devonshire; a treat which the lad was most anxious of enjoying. His father's friends there, however, did not appreciate his talents, and sad accounts were sent home of the perversity of his nature. He was a most courageous lad, game to the backbone.

It was soon known, both at home, where he lived, and within some miles of Barchester Cathedral, and also at Westminster, where he was at school, that young Henry could box well and would never own himself beat; other boys would fight while they had a leg to stand on, but he would fight with no leg at all. Those backing him would sometimes think him crushed by the weight of blows and faint with loss of blood, and his friends would endeavour to withdraw him from the contest; but no; Henry never gave in, was never weary of the battle. The ring was the only element in which he seemed to enjoy himself; and while other boys were happy in the number of their friends, he rejoiced most in the multitude of his foes.

His relations could not but admire his pluck, but they sometimes were forced to regret that he was inclined to be a bully; and those not so partial to him as his father was, observed with pain that, though he could fawn to the masters and the archdeacon's friends, he was imperious and masterful to the servants and the poor.

But perhaps Samuel was the general favourite; and dear little Soapy, as he was familiarly called, was as engaging a child as ever fond mother petted. He was soft and gentle in his manners, and attractive in his speech; the tone of his voice was melody, and every action was a grace; unlike his brothers, he was courteous to all, he was affable to the lowly, and meek even to the very scullery maid. He was a boy of great promise, minding his books and delighting the hearts of his masters. His brothers, however, were not particularly fond of him; they would complain to their mother that Soapy's civility all meant something; they thought that his voice was too often listened to at Plumstead Episcopi, and evidently feared that, as he grew up, he would have more weight in the house than either of them. There was, therefore, a sort of agreement among them to put young Soapy down. This, however, was not so easy to be done; Samuel, though young, was sharp; he could not assume the stiff decorum of Charles James, nor could he fight like Henry; but he was a perfect master of his own weapons, and contrived, in the teeth of both of them, to hold the place which he had assumed. Henry declared that he was a false, cunning creature; and Charles James, though he always spoke of him as his dear brother Samuel, was not slow to say a word against him when opportunity offered. To speak the truth, Samuel was a cunning boy, and those even who loved him best could not but own that for one so young, he was too adroit in choosing his words, and too skilled in modulating his voice.

The two little girls Florinda and Grizzel were nice little girls enough, but they did not possess the sterling qualities of their brothers; their voices were not often heard at Plumstead Episcopi; they were bashful and timid by nature, slow to speak before company even when asked to do so; and though they looked very nice in their clean white muslin frocks and pink sashes, they were but little noticed by the archdeacon's visitors.

Whatever of submissive humility may have appeared in the gait and visage of the archdeacon during his colloquy with his wife in the sanctum of their dressing-rooms, was dispelled as he entered his breakfast-parlour with erect head and powerful step. In the presence of a third person he assumed the lord and master; and that wise and talented lady too well knew the man to whom her lot for life was bound, to stretch her authority beyond the point at which it would be borne. Strangers at Plumstead Episcopi, when they saw the imperious brow with which he commanded silence from the large circle of visitors, children, and servants who came together in the morning to hear him read the word of God, and watched how meekly that wife seated herself behind her basket of keys with a little girl on each side, as she caught that commanding glance; strangers, I say, seeing this, could little guess that some fifteen minutes since she had stoutly held her ground against him, hardly allowing him to open his mouth in his own defence. But such is the tact and talent of women!

And now let us observe the well-furnished breakfast-parlour at Plumstead Episcopi, and the comfortable air of all the belongings of the rectory. Comfortable they certainly were, but neither gorgeous nor even grand; indeed, considering the money that had been spent there, the eye and taste might have been better served; there was an air of heaviness about the rooms which might have been avoided without any sacrifice to propriety; colours might have been better chosen and lights more perfectly diffused; but perhaps in doing so the thorough clerical aspect of the whole might have been somewhat marred. At any rate, it was not without ample consideration that those thick, dark, costly carpets were put down; those embossed but sombre papers hung up; those heavy curtains draped so as to half-exclude the light of the sun. Nor were these old-fashioned chairs, bought at a price far exceeding that now given for more modern goods, without a purpose. The breakfast-service on the table was equally costly and equally plain. The apparent object had been to spend money without obtaining brilliancy or splendour. The urn was of thick and solid silver, as were also the tea-pot, coffee-pot, cream-ewer, and sugar-bowl; the cups were old, dim dragon china,* worth about a pound a piece, but very despicable in the eyes of the uninitiated. The silver forks were so heavy as to be disagreeable to the hand, and the bread-basket was of a weight really formidable to any but robust persons. The tea consumed was the very best, the coffee the very blackest, the cream the very thickest; there was dry toast and buttered toast, muffins and crumpets; hot bread and cold bread, white bread and brown bread, home-made bread and bakers' bread, wheaten bread and oaten bread; and if there be other breads than these they were there; there were eggs in napkins, and crispy bits of bacon under silver covers; and there were little fishes in a little box, and devilled kidneys* frizzling on a hot-water dish;—which, by the bye, were placed closely contiguous to the plate of the worthy archdeacon himself. Over and above this, on a snow-white napkin, spread upon the sideboard, was a huge ham and a huge sirloin; the latter having laden the dinner table on the previous evening. Such was the ordinary fare at Plumstead Episcopi.

And yet I have never found the rectory a pleasant house. The fact that man shall not live by bread alone seemed to be somewhat forgotten; and noble as was the appearance of the host, and sweet and good-natured as was the face of the hostess, talented as were the children, and excellent as were the viands and the wines, in spite of these attractions, I generally found the rectory somewhat dull. After breakfast the archdeacon would retire,—of course to his clerical pursuits. Mrs Grantly, I presume, inspected her kitchen, though she had a first-rate housekeeper, with sixty pounds a year; and attended to the lessons of Florinda and Grizzel, though she had an excellent governess with thirty pounds* a year. At any rate she disappeared: and I never could make companions of the boys. Charles James, though he always looked as though there was something in him, never seemed to have much to say; and what he did say he would always unsay the next minute. He told me once, that he considered cricket, on the whole, to be a gentleman-like game for boys, provided they would play without running about; and that fives,* also, was a seemly game, so that those who played it never heated themselves. Henry once quarrelled with me for taking his sister Grizzel's part in a contest between them as to the best mode of using a watering-pot for the garden flowers; and from that day to this he has not spoken to me, though he speaks at me often enough. For half an hour or so I certainly did like Sammy's gentle speeches; but one gets tired of honey, and I found that he preferred the more admiring listeners whom he met in the kitchen-garden and back precincts of the establishment. Besides, I think I once caught Sammy fibbing.

On the whole, therefore, I found the rectory a dull house, though it must be admitted that everything there was of the very best.

After breakfast, on the morning of which we are writing, the archdeacon, as usual, retired to his study, intimating that he was going to be very busy, but that he would see Mr Chadwick if he called. On entering this sacred room he carefully opened the paper case on which he was wont to compose his favourite sermons, and spread on it a fair sheet of paper and one partly written on; he then placed his inkstand, looked at his pen, and folded his blotting paper; having done so, he got up again from his seat, stood with his back to the fire-place, and yawned comfortably, stretching out vastly his huge arms, and opening his burly chest. He then walked across the room and locked the door; and having so prepared himself, he threw himself into his easy chair, took from a secret drawer beneath his table a volume of Rabelais,* and began to amuse himself with the witty mischief of Panurge. So passed the archdeacon's morning on that day.

He was left undisturbed at his studies for an hour or two, when a knock came to the door, and Mr Chadwick was announced. Rabelais retired into the secret drawer, the easy chair seemed knowingly to betake itself off, and when the archdeacon quickly undid his bolt, he was discovered by the steward working, as usual, for that church of which he was so useful a pillar. Mr Chadwick had just come from London, and was, therefore, known to be the bearer of important news.

'We've got Sir Abraham's opinion at last,' said Mr Chadwick, as he seated himself.

'Well; well; well!' exclaimed the archdeacon impatiently.

'Oh, it's as long as my arm,' said the other; 'it can't be told in a word, but you can read it;' and he handed him a copy, in heaven knows how many spun-out folios, of the opinion which the attorney-general* had managed to cram on the back and sides, of the case as originally submitted to him.

'The upshot is,' said Chadwick, 'that there's a screw loose in their case, and we had better do nothing. They are proceeding against Mr Harding and myself, and Sir Abraham holds that, under the wording of the will, and subsequent arrangements legally sanctioned, Mr Harding and I are only paid servants. The defendants should have been either the Corporation of Barchester, or possibly the chapter, or your father.'

'W—hoo,' said the archdeacon; 'so Master Bold is on a wrong scent, is he?'

'That's Sir Abraham's opinion; but any scent almost would be a wrong scent. Sir Abraham thinks that if they'd taken the corporation, or the chapter, we could have baffled them. The bishop, he thinks, would be the surest shot; but even there we could plead that the bishop is only visitor, and that he has never made himself a consenting party to the performance of other duties.'

'That's quite clear,' said the archdeacon.

'Not quite so clear,' said the other. 'You see the will says, "My lord, the bishop, being graciously pleased to see that due justice be done." Now, it may be a question whether, in accepting and administering the patronage, your father has not accepted also the other duties assigned. It is doubtful, however; but even if they hit that nail,—and they are far off from that yet,—the point is so nice, as Sir Abraham says, that you would force them into fifteen thousand pounds' cost before they could bring it to an issue! And where's that sum of money to come from?'

The archdeacon rubbed his hands with delight. He had never doubted the justice of his case, but he had begun to have some dread of unjust success on the part of his enemies. It was delightful to him thus to hear that their cause was surrounded with such rocks and shoals;—such causes of shipwreck unseen by the landsman's eye, but visible enough to the keen eyes of practical law mariners. How wrong his wife was to wish that Bold should marry Eleanor! Bold! Why, if he should be ass enough to persevere, he would be a beggar before he knew whom he was at law with!

'That's excellent, Chadwick;—that's excellent! I told you Sir Abraham was the man for us;' and he put down on the table the copy of the opinion, and patted it fondly.

'Don't you let that be seen though, archdeacon.'

'Who?—I!—Not for worlds,' said the doctor.

'People will talk, you know, archdeacon.'

'Of course, of course,' said the doctor.

'Because, if that gets abroad, it would teach them how to fight their own battle.'

'Quite true,' said the doctor.

'No one here in Barchester ought to see that but you and I, archdeacon.'

'No, no, certainly no one else,' said the archdeacon, pleased with the closeness of the confidence; 'no one else shall.'

'Mrs Grantly is very interested in the matter, I know,' said Mr Chadwick.

Did the archdeacon wink, or did he not? I am inclined to think he did not quite wink; but that without such, perhaps, unseemly gesture he communicated to Mr Chadwick, with the corner of his eye, intimation that, deep as was Mrs Grantly's interest in the matter, it should not procure for her a perusal of that document; and at the same time he partly opened the small drawer, above spoken of, deposited the paper on the volume of Rabelais, and showed to Mr Chadwick the nature of the key which guarded these hidden treasures. The careful steward then expressed himself contented. Ah! vain man! He could fasten up his Rabelais, and other things secret, with all the skill of Bramah or of Chubb;* but where could he fasten up the key which solved these mechanical mysteries? It is probable to us that the contents of no drawer in that house were unknown to its mistress, and we think, moreover, that she was entitled to all such knowledge.

'But,' said Mr Chadwick, 'we must, of course, tell your father and Mr Harding so much of Sir Abraham's opinion as will satisfy them that the matter is doing well.'

'Oh, certainly,—yes, of course,' said the doctor.

'You had better let them know that Sir Abraham is of opinion that there is no case at any rate against Mr Harding; and that as the action is worded at present, it must fall to the ground; they must be non-suited* if they carry it on; you had better tell Mr Harding, that Sir Abraham is clearly of opinion that he is only a servant, and as such, not liable. Or if you like it, I'll see Mr Harding myself.'

'Oh, I must see him to-morrow, and my father too, and I'll explain to them exactly so much. You won't go before lunch, Mr Chadwick. Well, if you will, you must, for I know your time is precious;' and he shook hands with the diocesan steward, and bowed him out.

The archdeacon had again recourse to his drawer, and twice read through the essence of Sir Abraham Haphazard's law-enlightened and law-bewildered brains. It was very clear that to Sir Abraham, the justice of the old men's claim or the justice of Mr Harding's defence were ideas that had never presented themselves. A legal victory over an opposing party was the service for which Sir Abraham was, as he imagined, to be paid; and that he, according to his lights, had diligently laboured to achieve, and with probable hope of success. Of the intense desire which Mr Harding felt to be assured on fit authority, that he was wronging no man, that he was entitled in true equity* to his income, that he might sleep at night without pangs of conscience, that he was no robber, no spoiler of the poor; that he and all the world might be openly convinced that he was not the man which the *Jupiter* had described him to be;—of such longings on the part of

Mr Harding, Sir Abraham was entirely ignorant; nor, indeed, could it be looked on as part of his business to gratify such desires. Such was not the system on which his battles were fought, and victories gained. Success was his object, and he was generally successful. He conquered his enemies by their weakness rather than by his own strength, and it had been found almost impossible to make up a case, in which Sir Abraham, as an antagonist, would not find a flaw.

The archdeacon was delighted with the closeness of the reasoning. To do him justice, it was not a selfish triumph that he desired; he would personally lose nothing by defeat, or at least what he might lose did not actuate him. But neither was it love of justice which made him so anxious, nor even mainly solicitude for his father-in-law. He was fighting a part of a never-ending battle against a never-conquered foe,—that of the church against its enemies.

He knew Mr Harding could not pay all the expense of these doings,—for these long opinions of Sir Abraham's, these causes to be pleaded, these speeches to be made, these various courts through which the case was, he presumed, to be dragged. He knew that he and his father must at least bear the heavier portion of this tremendous cost. But to do the archdeacon justice, he did not recoil from this. He was a man fond of obtaining money, greedy of a large income, but open-handed enough in expending it, and it was a triumph to him to foresee the success of this measure, although he might be called on to pay so dearly for it himself.

## CHAPTER 9
### THE CONFERENCE

On the following morning the archdeacon was with his father betimes, and a note was sent down to the warden begging his attendance at the palace. Dr Grantly, as he cogitated on the matter, leaning back in his brougham as he journeyed into Barchester, felt that it would be difficult to communicate his own satisfaction either to his father or his father-in-law. He wanted success on his own side and discomfiture on that of his enemies. The bishop wanted peace on the subject; a settled peace if possible, but peace at any rate till the short remainder of his own days had spun itself out. Mr Harding required, not only success and peace, but demanded also that he might stand justified before the world.

The bishop, however, was comparatively easy to deal with; and before the arrival of the other, the dutiful son had persuaded his father that all was going on well, and then the warden arrived.

It was Mr Harding's wont, whenever he spent a morning at the palace, to seat himself immediately at the bishop's elbow, the bishop occupying a huge arm-chair fitted up with candlesticks, a reading table, a drawer, and other paraphernalia, the position of which chair was never moved, summer or winter; and when, as was usual, the archdeacon was there also, he confronted the two elders, who thus were enabled to fight the battle against him together;—and together submit to defeat, for such was their constant fate.

Our warden now took his accustomed place, having greeted his son-in-law as he entered, and then affectionately inquired after his friend's health. There was a gentleness about the bishop to which the soft womanly affection of Mr Harding particularly endeared itself, and it was quaint to see how the two mild old priests pressed each other's hands, and smiled and made little signs of love.

'Sir Abraham's opinion has come at last,' began the archdeacon. Mr Harding had heard so much, and was most anxious to know the result.

'It is quite favourable,' said the bishop, pressing his friend's arm. 'I am so glad.'

Mr Harding looked at the mighty bearer of the important news for confirmation of these glad tidings.

'Yes,' said the archdeacon; 'Sir Abraham has given most minute attention to the case; indeed, I knew he would;—most minute attention, and his opinion is,—and as to his opinion on such a subject being correct, no one who knows Sir Abraham's character can doubt,—his opinion is, that they haven't got a leg to stand on.'

'But as how, archdeacon?'

'Why, in the first place;———but you're no lawyer, warden, and I doubt you won't understand it; the gist of the matter is this;—under Hiram's will two paid guardians have been selected for the hospital; the law will say two paid servants, and you and I won't quarrel with the name.'

'At any rate I will not if I am one of the servants,' said Mr Harding. 'A rose, you know———.'*

'Yes, yes,' said the archdeacon, impatient of poetry at such a time. 'Well, two paid servants, we'll say; one to look after the men and the other to look after the money. You and Chadwick are these two servants, and whether either of you be paid too much, or too little, more or less in fact than the founder willed, it's as clear as daylight that no one can fall foul of either of you for receiving an allotted stipend.'

'That does seem clear,' said the bishop, who had winced visibly at the words servants and stipend, which, however, appeared to have caused no uneasiness to the archdeacon.

'Quite clear,' said he, 'and very satisfactory. In point of fact, it being necessary to select such servants for the use of the hospital, the pay to be given to them must depend on the rate of pay for such services, according to their market value at the period in question; and those who manage the hospital must be the only judges of this.'

'And who does manage the hospital?' asked the warden.

'Oh, let them find that out; that's another question; the action is brought against you and Chadwick; that's your defence, and a perfect and full defence it is. Now that I think very satisfactory.'

'Well,' said the bishop, looking inquiringly up into his friend's face, who sat silent awhile, and apparently not so well satisfied.

'And conclusive,' continued the archdeacon; 'if they press it to a jury, which they won't do, no twelve men in England will take five minutes to decide against them.'

'But according to that,' said Mr Harding, 'I might as well have sixteen hundred a year as eight, if the managers choose to allot it to me; and as I am one of the managers, if not the chief manager, myself, that can hardly be a just arrangement.'

'Oh, well; all that's nothing to the question; the question is, whether this intruding fellow, and a lot of cheating attorneys and pestilent dissenters, are to interfere with an arrangement which every one knows is essentially just and serviceable to the church. Pray don't let us be splitting hairs, and that amongst ourselves, or there'll never be an end of the cause or the cost.'

Mr Harding again sat silent for awhile, during which the bishop once and again pressed his arm, and looked in his face to see if he could catch a gleam of a contented and eased mind; but there was no such gleam, and the poor warden continued playing sad dirges on invisible stringed instruments in all manner of positions. He was ruminating in his mind on this opinion of Sir Abraham, looking to it wearily and earnestly for satisfaction, but finding none. At last he said, 'Did you see the opinion, archdeacon?'

The archdeacon said he had not,—that was to say, he had,—that was, he had not seen the opinion itself; he had seen what had been called a copy, but he could not say whether of a whole or part; nor could he say that what he had seen were the ipsissima verba* of the great man himself; but what he had seen contained exactly the decision which he had announced, and which he again declared to be to his mind extremely satisfactory.

'I should like to see the opinion,' said the warden;—'that is, a copy of it.'

'Well; I suppose you can if you make a point of it; but I don't see the use myself. Of course it is essential that the purport of it should not be known, and it is therefore unadvisable to multiply copies.'

'Why should it not be known?' asked the warden.

'What a question for a man to ask!' said the archdeacon, throwing up his hands in token of his surprise; 'but it is like you. A child is not more innocent than you are in matters of business. Can't you see that if we tell them that no action will lie against you, but that one may possibly lie against some other person or persons, that we shall be putting weapons into their hands, and be teaching them how to cut our own throats?'

The warden again sat silent, and the bishop again looked at him wistfully. 'The only thing we have now to do,' continued the archdeacon, 'is to remain quiet, hold our peace, and let them play their own game as they please.'

'We are not to make known then,' said the warden, 'that we have consulted the attorney-general, and that we are advised by him that the founder's will is fully and fairly carried out.'

'God bless my soul!' said the archdeacon, 'how odd it is that you will not see that all we are to do is to do nothing. Why should we say anything about the founder's will? We are in possession; and we know that they are not in a position to put us out; surely that is enough for the present.'

Mr Harding rose from his seat and paced thoughtfully up and down the library, the bishop the while watching him painfully at every turn, and the archdeacon continuing to pour forth his convictions that the affair was in a state to satisfy any prudent mind.

'And the *Jupiter*?' said the warden, stopping suddenly.

'Oh! the *Jupiter*,' answered the other. 'The *Jupiter* can break no bones. You must bear with that; there is much of course which it is our bounden duty to bear; it cannot be all roses* for us here,' and the archdeacon looked exceedingly moral; 'besides the matter is too trivial, of too little general interest to be mentioned again in the *Jupiter*, unless we stir up the subject.' And the archdeacon again looked exceedingly knowing and worldly wise.

The warden continued his walk; the hard and stinging words of that newspaper article, each one of which had thrust a thorn as it were into his inmost soul, were fresh in his memory; he had read it more than once, word by word, and what was worse, he fancied it was as well known to every one as to himself. Was he to be looked on as the unjust griping* priest he had been there described, was he to be pointed at as the consumer of the bread of the poor, and to be allowed no means of refuting such charges, of clearing his begrimed name, of standing innocent in the world, as hitherto he had stood? Was he to bear all this, to receive as usual his now hated income, and be known as one of those greedy priests who by their rapacity have brought disgrace on their church? And why? Why should he bear all this? Why should he die, for he felt that he could not live, under such a weight of obloquy? As he paced up and down the room he resolved in his misery and enthusiasm that he could with pleasure, if he were allowed, give up his place, abandon his pleasant home, leave the hospital, and live poorly, happily, and with an unsullied name, on the small remainder of his means.

He was a man somewhat shy of speaking of himself, even before those who knew him best, and whom he loved the most; but at last it burst forth from him, and with a somewhat jerking eloquence he declared that he could not, would not, bear this misery any longer.

'If it can be proved,' said he at last, 'that I have a just and honest right to this, as God well knows I always deemed I had;—if this salary or stipend be really my due, I am not less anxious than another to retain it. I have the well-being of my child to look to. I am too old to miss without some pain the comforts to which I have been used; and I am, as others are, anxious to prove to the world that I have been right, and to uphold the place I have held. But I cannot do it at such a cost as this. I cannot bear this. Could you tell me to do so?' And he appealed, almost in tears, to the bishop, who had left his chair, and was now leaning on the warden's arm as he stood on the further side of the table facing the archdeacon. 'Could you tell me to sit there at ease, indifferent, and satisfied, while such things as these are said loudly of me in the world?'

The bishop could feel for him and sympathise with him, but he could not advise him. He could only say, 'No, no, you shall be asked to do nothing that is painful; you shall do just what your heart tells you to be right; you shall do whatever you think best yourself. Theophilus, don't advise him, pray don't advise the warden to do anything which is painful.'

But the archdeacon, though he could not sympathise, could advise; and he saw that the time had come when it behoved him to do so in a somewhat peremptory manner.

'Why, my lord,' he said speaking to his father;—and when he called his father 'my lord,' the good old bishop shook in his shoes, for he knew that an evil time was coming. 'Why, my lord, there are two ways of giving advice; there is advice that may be good for the present day; and there is advice that may be good for days to come. Now I cannot bring myself to give the former, if it be incompatible with the other.'

'No; no; no; I suppose not,' said the bishop, reseating himself, and shading his face with his hands. Mr Harding sat down with his back to the further wall, playing to himself some air fitted for so calamitous an occasion, and the archdeacon said out his say standing, with his back to the empty fireplace.

'It is not to be supposed but that much pain will spring out of this unnecessarily raised question. We must all have foreseen that, and the matter has in no wise gone on worse than we expected. But it will be weak, yes, and wicked also, to abandon the cause and own ourselves wrong, because the inquiry is painful. It is not only ourselves we have to look to; to a certain extent the interest of the church is in our keeping. Should it be found that one after another of those who hold preferment abandoned it whenever it might be attacked, is it not plain that such attacks would be renewed till nothing was left us? and, that if so deserted, the Church of England must fall to the ground altogether? If this be true of many, it is true of one. Were you, accused as you now are, to throw up the wardenship, and to relinquish the preferment which is your property, with the vain object of proving yourself disinterested, you would fail in that object, you would inflict a desperate blow on your brother clergymen, you would encourage every cantankerous dissenter in England to make a similar charge against some source of clerical revenue, and you would do your best to dishearten those who are most anxious to defend you and uphold your position. I can fancy nothing more weak, or more wrong. It is not that you think that there is any justice in these charges, or that you doubt your own right to the wardenship. You are convinced of your own honesty, and yet would yield to them through cowardice.'

'Cowardice!' said the bishop, expostulating. Mr Harding sat unmoved, gazing on his son-in-law.

'Well; would it not be cowardice? would he not do so because he is afraid to endure the evil things which will be falsely spoken of him? Would that not be cowardice? And now let us see the extent of the evil which you dread. The *Jupiter* publishes an article which a great many, no doubt, will read; but of those who understand the subject how many will believe the *Jupiter*? Every one knows what its object is. It has taken up the case against Lord Guildford and against the Dean of Rochester, and that against half a dozen bishops; and does not every one know that it would take up any case of the kind, right or wrong, false or true, with known justice or known injustice, if by doing so it could further its own views? Does not all the world know this of the *Jupiter*? Who that really knows you will think the worse of you for what the *Jupiter* says? And why care for those who do not know you? I will say nothing of your own comfort, but I do say that you could not be justified in throwing up, in a fit of passion, for such it would be, the only maintenance that Eleanor has. And if you did so, if you really did vacate the wardenship, and submit to ruin, what would that profit you? If you have no future right to the income, you have had no past right to it; and the very fact of your abandoning your position, would create a demand for repayment of that which you have already received and spent.'

The poor warden groaned as he sat perfectly still, looking up at the hard-hearted orator who thus tormented him, and the bishop echoed the sound faintly from behind his hands. But the archdeacon cared little for such signs of weakness, and completed his exhortation.

'But let us suppose the office to be left vacant, and that your own troubles concerning it were over; would that satisfy you? Are your only aspirations in the matter confined to yourself and family? I know they are not. I know you are as anxious as any of us for the church to which we belong. And what a grievous blow would such an act of apostasy give her! You owe it to the church of which you are a member and a minister, to bear with this affliction, however severe it may be. You owe it to my father, who instituted you, to support his rights. You owe it to those who preceded you to assert the legality of their position. You owe it to those who are to come after you, to maintain uninjured for them that which you received uninjured from others. And you owe to us all the unflinching assistance of perfect brotherhood in this matter, so that upholding one another we may support our great cause without blushing and without disgrace.'

And so the archdeacon ceased, and stood self-satisfied, watching the effect of his spoken wisdom.

The warden felt himself, to a certain extent, stifled; he would have given the world to get himself out into the open air without speaking to, or noticing those who were in the room with him; but this was impossible. He could not leave without saying something, and he felt himself confounded by the archdeacon's eloquence. There was a heavy, unfeeling, unanswerable truth in what he had said; there was so much practical, but odious common sense in it, that he neither knew how to assent or to differ. If it were necessary for him to suffer, he felt that he could endure without complaint and without cowardice, providing that he was self-satisfied of the justice of his own cause. What he could not endure was, that he should be accused by others, and not acquitted by himself. Doubting, as he had begun to doubt, the justice of his own position in the hospital, he knew that his own self-confidence would not be restored because Mr Bold had been in error as to some legal form; nor could he be satisfied to escape, because, through some legal fiction, he who received the greatest benefit from the hospital might be considered only as one of its servants.

The archdeacon's speech had silenced him,—stupefied him,—annihilated him; anything but satisfied him. With the bishop it fared not much better. He did not discern clearly how things were, but he saw enough to know that a battle was to be prepared for; a battle that would destroy his few remaining comforts, and bring him with sorrow to the grave.

The warden still sat, and still looked at the archdeacon, till his thoughts fixed themselves wholly on the means of escape from his present position, and he felt like a bird fascinated by gazing on a snake.

'I hope you agree with me,' said the archdeacon at last, breaking the dread silence; 'my lord, I hope you agree with me.' Oh what a sigh

the bishop gave! 'My lord, I hope you agree with me,' again repeated
the merciless tyrant.

'Yes, I suppose so,' groaned the poor old man, slowly.

'And you, warden?'

Mr Harding was now stirred to action. He must speak and move, so
he got up and took one turn before he answered.

'Do not press me for an answer just at present; I will do nothing
lightly in the matter, and of whatever I do I will give you and the
bishop notice.' And so without another word he took his leave, escap-
ing quickly through the palace hall, and down the lofty steps; nor did
he breathe freely till he found himself alone under the huge elms of
the silent close. Here he walked long and slowly, thinking on his case
with a troubled air, and trying in vain to confute the archdeacon's
argument. He then went home, resolved to bear it all,—ignominy,
suspense, disgrace, self-doubt, and heart-burning,—and to do as
those would have him, who he still believed were most fit and most
able to counsel him aright.

## CHAPTER 10

### TRIBULATION

MR HARDING was a sadder man than he had ever yet been when he
returned to his own house. He had been wretched enough on that
well-remembered morning when he was forced to expose before his
son-in-law the publisher's account for ushering into the world his
dear book of sacred music; when after making such payments as
he could do unassisted, he found that he was a debtor of more than
three hundred pounds; but his sufferings then were as nothing to his
present misery;—then he had done wrong, and he knew it, and was
able to resolve that he would not sin in like manner again; but now
he could make no resolution, and comfort himself by no promises of
firmness. He had been forced to think that his lot had placed him in
a false position, and he was about to maintain that position against the
opinion of the world and against his own convictions.

He had read with pity, amounting almost to horror, the strictures
which had appeared from time to time against the Earl of Guildford
as master of St Cross, and the invectives that had been heaped on rich

diocesan dignitaries and overgrown sinecure pluralists.* In judging of them, he judged leniently; the old bias of his profession had taught him to think that they were more sinned against than sinning, and that the animosity with which they had been pursued was venomous and unjust; but he had not the less regarded their plight as most miserable. His hair had stood on end and his flesh had crept as he read the things which had been written; he had wondered how men could live under such a load of disgrace; how they could face their fellow-creatures while their names were bandied about so injuriously and so publicly. Now this lot was to be his. He, that shy retiring man, who had so comforted himself in the hidden obscurity of his lot, who had so enjoyed the unassuming warmth of his own little corner, he was now to be dragged forth into the glaring day, gibbeted before ferocious multitudes. He entered his own house a crest-fallen, humiliated man, without a hope of overcoming the wretchedness which affected him.

He wandered into the drawing-room where was his daughter; but he could not speak to her now, so he left it, and went into the book-room. He was not quick enough to escape Eleanor's glance, or to prevent her from seeing that he was disturbed; and in a little while she followed him. She found him seated in his accustomed chair with no book open before him, no pen ready in his hand, no ill-shapen notes of blotted music lying before him as was usual, none of those hospital accounts with which he was so precise and yet so unmethodical. He was doing nothing, thinking of nothing, looking at nothing; he was merely suffering.

'Leave me, Eleanor, my dear,' he said; 'leave me, my darling, for a few minutes, for I am busy.'

Eleanor saw well how it was, but she did leave him, and glided silently back to her drawing-room. When he had sat awhile, thus alone and unoccupied, he got up to walk again; he could make more of his thoughts walking than sitting, and was creeping out into his garden, when he met Bunce on the threshold.

'Well, Bunce,' said he, in a tone that for him was sharp, 'what is it? do you want me?'

'I was only coming to ask after your reverence,' said the old bedesman, touching his hat;—'and to inquire about the news from London,' he added after a pause.

The warden winced, and put his hand to his forehead and felt bewildered.

'Attorney Finney has been there this morning,' continued Bunce, 'and by his looks I guess he is not so well pleased as he once was, and it has got abroad somehow that the archdeacon has had down great news from London, and Handy and Moody are both as black as devils. And I hope,' said the man, trying to assume a cheery tone, 'that things are looking up, and that there'll be an end soon to all this stuff which bothers your reverence so sorely.'

'Well, I wish there may be, Bunce.'

'But about the news, your reverence?' said the old man, almost whispering. Mr Harding walked on, and shook his head impatiently. Poor Bunce little knew how he was tormenting his patron. 'If there was anything to cheer you, I should be so glad to know it,' said he, with a tone of affection which the warden in all his misery could not resist.

He stopped, and took both the old man's hands in his. 'My friend,' said he, 'my dear old friend, there is nothing; there is no news to cheer me. God's will be done.' And two small hot tears broke away from his eyes and stole down his furrowed cheeks.

'Then God's will be done,' said the other solemnly; 'but they told me that there was good news from London, and I came to wish your reverence joy; but God's will be done.' The warden again walked on, and the bedesman looking wistfully after him and receiving no encouragement to follow returned sadly to his own abode.

For a couple of hours the warden remained thus in the garden, now walking, now standing motionless on the turf, and then, as his legs got weary, sitting unconsciously on the garden seats, and then walking again. Eleanor, hidden behind the muslin curtains of the window, watched him through the trees as he came in sight, and then again was concealed by the turnings of the walk; and thus the time passed away till five, when the warden crept back to the house and prepared for dinner.

It was but a sorry meal. The demure parlour-maid, as she handed the dishes and changed the plates, saw that all was not right, and was more demure than ever. Neither father nor daughter could eat, and the hateful food was soon cleared away, and the bottle of port placed upon the table.

'Would you like Bunce to come in, papa?' said Eleanor, thinking that the company of the old man might lighten his sorrow.

'No, my dear, thank you, not to-day; but are not you going out, Eleanor, this lovely afternoon? Don't stay in for me, my dear.'

'I thought you seemed so sad, papa.'

'Sad,' said he, irritated; 'well, people must all have their share of sadness here; I am not more exempt than another. But kiss me, dearest, and go now; I will, if possible, be more sociable when you return.'

And Eleanor was again banished from her father's sorrow. Ah! her desire now was not to find him happy, but to be allowed to share his sorrows; not to force him to be sociable, but to persuade him to be trustful.

She put on her bonnet as desired, and went up to Mary Bold; this was her daily haunt, for John Bold was up in London among lawyers and church reformers, diving deep into other questions than that of the wardenship of Barchester; supplying information to one member of parliament and dining with another; subscribing to funds for the abolition of clerical incomes, and seconding at that great national meeting at the Crown and Anchor* a resolution to the effect, that no clergyman of the Church of England, be he who he might, should have more than a thousand a year, and none less than two hundred and fifty. His speech on this occasion was short, for fifteen had to speak, and the room was hired for two hours only, at the expiration of which the Quakers and Mr Cobden* were to make use of it for an appeal to the public in aid of the Emperor of Russia; but it was sharp and effective; at least he was told so by a companion with whom he now lived much, and on whom he greatly depended,—one Tom Towers,* a very leading genius, and supposed to have high employment on the staff of the *Jupiter*.

So Eleanor, as was now her wont, went up to Mary Bold, and Mary listened kindly, while the daughter spoke much of her father, and, perhaps kinder still, found a listener in Eleanor, while she spoke about her brother. In the meantime the warden sat alone, leaning on the arm of his chair; he had poured out a glass of wine, but had done so merely from habit, for he left it untouched; there he sat gazing at the open window, and thinking, if he can be said to have thought, of the happiness of his past life. All manner of past delights came before his mind, which at the time he had enjoyed without considering them; his easy days, his absence of all kind of hard work, his pleasant shady home, those twelve old neighbours whose welfare till now had been the source of so much pleasant care, the excellence of his children, the friendship of the dear old bishop, the solemn grandeur of those vaulted aisles, through which he loved to hear his own voice pealing; and then that friend of friends, that choice ally that had never deserted him, that eloquent companion that would always, when asked, discourse such pleasant music, that violoncello of his! Ah, how happy he had been! But it was over now; his easy days and absence of work had been the crime which brought on him his tribulation; his shady home* was pleasant no longer; may be it was no longer his; the old neighbours, whose welfare had been so desired by him, were his enemies; his daughter was as wretched as himself; and even the bishop was made miserable by his position. He could never again lift up his voice boldly as he had hitherto done among his brethren, for he felt that he was disgraced; and he feared even to touch his bow, for he knew how grievous a sound of wailing, how piteous a lamentation, it would produce.

He was still sitting in the same chair and the same posture, having hardly moved a limb, for two hours, when Eleanor came back to tea, and succeeded in bringing him with her into the drawing-room.

The tea seemed as comfortless as the dinner, though the warden, who had hitherto eaten nothing all day, devoured the plateful of bread and butter, unconscious of what he was doing.

Eleanor had made up her mind to force him to talk to her, but she hardly knew how to commence. She must wait till the urn was gone, till the servant would no longer be coming in and out.

At last everything was quiet, and the drawing-room door was permanently closed. Then Eleanor, getting up and going round to her father, put her arm round his neck, and said, 'Papa, won't you tell me what it is?'

'What what is, my dear?'

'This new sorrow that torments you; I know you are unhappy, papa.'

'New sorrow! it's no new sorrow, my dear; we have all our cares sometimes;' and he tried to smile, but it was a ghastly failure; 'but I shouldn't be so dull a companion; come, we'll have some music.'

'No, papa, not to-night; it would only trouble you to-night;' and she sat upon his knee, as she sometimes would in their gayest moods, and with her arm round his neck, she said, 'Papa, I will not leave you till you talk to me. Oh, if you only knew how much good it would do to you, to tell me of it all.'

The father kissed his daughter, and pressed her to his heart: but still he said nothing. It was so hard to him to speak of his own sorrows; he was so shy a man even with his own child!

'Oh, papa, do tell me what it is. I know it is about the hospital, and what they are doing up in London, and what that cruel newspaper has said; but if there be such cause for sorrow, let us be sorrowful together; we are all in all to each other now. Dear, dear papa, do speak to me.'

Mr Harding could not well speak now, for the warm tears were running down his cheeks like rain in May,* but he held his child close to his heart, and squeezed her hand as a lover might, and she kissed his forehead and his wet cheeks, and lay upon his bosom and comforted him as a woman only can do.

'My own child,' he said, as soon as his tears would let him speak, 'my own, own child, why should you too be unhappy before it is necessary? It may come to that, that we must leave this place, but till that time comes, why should your young days be clouded?'

'And is that all, papa? If that be all, let us leave it, and have light hearts elsewhere. If that be all, let us go. Oh, papa, you and I could be happy if we had only bread to eat, so long as our hearts were light.'

And Eleanor's face was lighted up with enthusiasm as she told her father how he might banish all his care; and a gleam of joy shot across his brow as this idea of escape again presented itself, and he again fancied for a moment that he could spurn away from him the income which the world envied him; that he could give the lie to that wielder of the tomahawk who had dared to write such things of him in the *Jupiter*; that he could leave Sir Abraham, and the archdeacon, and Bold, and the rest of them with their lawsuit among them, and wipe his hands altogether of so sorrow-stirring a concern. Ah, what happiness might there be in the distance, with Eleanor and him in some small cottage, and nothing left of their former grandeur but their music! Yes, they would walk forth with their music books, and their instruments, and shaking the dust from off their feet as they went, leave the ungrateful place. Never did a poor clergyman sigh for a warm benefice more anxiously than our warden did now to be rid of his.

'Give it up, papa,' she said again, jumping from his knees and standing on her feet before him, looking boldly into his face; 'give it up, papa.'

Oh, it was sad to see how that momentary gleam of joy passed away; how the look of hope was dispersed from that sorrowful face, as the remembrance of the archdeacon came back upon our poor warden, and he reflected that he could not stir from his now hated post. He was as a man bound with iron, fettered with adamant.* He was in no respect a free agent; he had no choice. 'Give it up!' oh if he only could! What an easy way that were out of all his troubles!

'Papa, don't doubt about it,' she continued, thinking that his hesitation arose from his unwillingness to abandon so comfortable a home; 'is it on my account that you would stay here? Do you think that I cannot be happy without a pony-carriage and a fine drawing-room? Papa, I never can be happy here, as long as there is a question as to your honour in staying here; but I could be gay as the day is long in the smallest tiny little cottage, if I could see you come in and go out with a light heart. Oh! papa, your face tells so much! Though you won't speak to me with your voice, I know how it is with you every time I look at you.'

How he pressed her to his heart again with almost a spasmodic pressure! How he kissed her as the tears fell like rain from his old eyes! How he blessed her, and called her by a hundred soft sweet names which now came new to his lips! How he chid himself for ever having been unhappy with such a treasure in his house, such a jewel on his bosom, with so sweet a flower in the choice garden of his heart! And then the flood-gates of his tongue were loosed, and, at length, with unsparing detail of circumstances, he told her all that he wished, and all that he could not do. He repeated those arguments of the archdea-con, not agreeing in their truth, but explaining his inability to escape from them;—how it had been declared to him that he was bound to remain where he was by the interests of his order, by gratitude to the bishop, by the wishes of his friends, by a sense of duty, which, though he could not understand it, he was fain to acknowledge. He told her how he had been accused of cowardice, and though he was not a man to make much of such a charge before the world, now in the full candour of his heart, he explained to her that such an accusation was grievous to him; that he did think it would be unmanly to desert his post, merely to escape his present sufferings, and that, there-fore, he must bear as best he might the misery which was prepared for him.

And did she find these details tedious? Oh, no; she encouraged him to dilate on every feeling he expressed, till he laid bare the inmost corners of his heart to her. They spoke together of the archdeacon, as two children might of a stern, unpopular, but still respected schoolmaster, and of the bishop as a parent kind as kind could be, but powerless against an omnipotent pedagogue.

And then, when they had discussed all this, when the father had told all to the child, she could not be less confiding than he had been; and as John Bold's name was mentioned between them, she owned how well she had learned to love him,—'had loved him once,' she said, 'but she would not, could not, do so now. No; even had her troth been plighted to him, she would have taken it back again;—had she sworn to love him as his wife, she would have discarded him, and not felt herself forsworn when he proved himself the enemy of her father.'

But the warden declared that Bold was no enemy of his, and encouraged her love; and gently rebuked, as he kissed her, the stern resolve she had made to cast him off; and then he spoke to her of happier days when their trials would all be over; and declared that her young heart should not be torn asunder to please either priest or prelate, dean or archdeacon. No, not if all Oxford were to convocate* together, and agree as to the necessity of the sacrifice!

And so they greatly comforted each other! In what sorrow will not such mutual confidence give consolation!—and with a last expression of tender love they parted, and went comparatively happy to their rooms.

## CHAPTER 11

### IPHIGENIA*

WHEN Eleanor laid her head on her pillow that night, her mind was anxiously intent on some plan by which she might extricate her father from his misery; and, in her warm-hearted enthusiasm, self-sacrifice was decided on as the means to be adopted. Was not so good an Agamemnon worthy of an Iphigenia? She would herself personally implore John Bold to desist from his undertaking; she would explain to him her father's sorrows, the cruel misery of his position; she would tell him how her father would die if he were thus dragged before the public and exposed to such unmerited ignominy; she would appeal to his old friendship, to his generosity, to his manliness, to his mercy; if need were, she would kneel to him for the favour she would ask;—but before she did this, the idea of love must be banished. There must be no bargain in the matter. To his mercy, to his generosity, she could appeal; but as a pure maiden, hitherto even unsolicited, she could not appeal to his love, nor under such circumstances could she allow him to do so. Of course when so provoked he would declare his passion; that was to be expected; there had been enough between them to make such a fact sure; but it was equally certain that he must be rejected. She could not be understood as saying, Make my father free and I am the reward. There would be no sacrifice in that;—not so had Jephthah's daughter* saved her father;—not so could she show to that kindest, dearest of parents how much she was able to bear for his good. No; to one resolve must her whole soul be bound; and so resolving, she felt that she could make her great request to Bold with as much self-assured confidence as she could have done to his grandfather.

And now I own I have fears for my heroine; not as to the upshot of her mission,—not in the least as to that; as to the full success of her generous scheme, and the ultimate result of such a project, no one conversant with human nature and novels can have a doubt; but as to the amount of sympathy she may receive from those of her own sex. Girls below twenty and old ladies above sixty will do her justice; for in the female heart the soft springs of sweet romance reopen after many years, and again gush out with waters pure as in earlier days, and greatly refresh the path that leads downwards to the grave. But I fear that the majority of those between these two eras will not approve of Eleanor's plan. I fear that unmarried ladies of thirty-five will declare that there can be no probability of so absurd a project being carried through; that young women on their knees before their lovers are sure to get kissed, and that they would not put themselves in such a position did they not expect it; that Eleanor is going to Bold, only because circumstances prevent Bold from coming to her;—that she is certainly a little fool, or a little schemer, but that in all probability she is thinking a good deal more about herself than her father.

Dear ladies, you are right as to your appreciation of the circumstances, but very wrong as to Miss Harding's character. Miss Harding was much younger than you are, and could not, therefore, know, as you may do, to what dangers such an encounter might expose her. She may get kissed; I think it very probable that she will; but I give my solemn word and positive assurance, that the remotest idea of such a catastrophe never occurred to her as she made the great resolve now alluded to.

And then she slept; and then she rose refreshed, and met her father with her kindest embrace and most loving smiles; and on the whole their breakfast was by no means so triste* as had been their dinner the day before; and then, making some excuse to her father for so soon leaving him, she started on the commencement of her operations.

She knew that John Bold was in London, and that, therefore, the scene itself could not be enacted to-day; but she also knew that he was soon to be home, probably on the next day, and it was necessary that some little plan for meeting him should be concerted with his sister Mary. When she got up to the house, she went as usual into the morning sitting-room, and was startled by perceiving, by a stick, a great coat, and sundry parcels which were lying about, that Bold must already have returned.

'John has come back so suddenly,' said Mary, coming into the room; 'he has been travelling all night.'

'Then I'll come up again some other time,' said Eleanor, about to beat a retreat in her sudden dismay.

'He's out now, and will be for the next two hours,' said the other; 'he's with that horrid Finney; he only came to see him, and he returns by the mail train to-night.'

Returns by the mail train to-night, thought Eleanor to herself, as she strove to screw up her courage;—away again to-night! Then it must be now or never; and she again sat down, having risen to go.

She wished the ordeal could have been postponed. She had fully made up her mind to do the deed, but she had not made up her mind to do it this very day; and now she felt ill at ease, astray, and in difficulty.

'Mary,' she began, 'I must see your brother before he goes back.'

'Oh yes, of course,' said the other; 'I know he'll be delighted to see you;' and she tried to treat it as a matter of course. But she was not the less surprised; for Mary and Eleanor had daily talked over John Bold and his conduct, and his love, and Mary would insist on calling Eleanor her sister, and would scold her for not calling Bold by his Christian name; and Eleanor would half confess her love, but like a modest maiden would protest against such familiarities even with the name of her lover. And so they talked hour after hour, and Mary Bold, who was much the elder, looked forward with happy confidence to the day when Eleanor would not be ashamed to call her her sister. She was, however, fully sure that just at present Eleanor would be much more likely to avoid her brother than to seek him.

'Mary, I must see your brother, now, to-day, and beg from him a great favour;' and she spoke with a solemn air, not at all usual to her; and then she went on, and opened to her friend all her plan, her well-weighed scheme for saving her father from a sorrow which would, she said, if it lasted, bring him to his grave. 'But Mary,' she continued, 'you must now, you know, cease any joking about me and Mr Bold. You must now say no more about that. I am not ashamed to beg this favour from your brother, but when I have done so, there can never be anything further between us!' And this she said with a staid and solemn air, quite worthy of Jephthah's daughter or of Iphigenia either.

It was quite clear that Mary Bold did not follow the argument. That Eleanor Harding should appeal, on behalf of her father, to Bold's better feelings, seemed to Mary quite natural; it seemed quite natural that he should relent, overcome by such filial tears, and by so much beauty; but, to her thinking, it was at any rate equally natural, that having relented, John should put his arm round his mistress's waist, and say, 'Now having settled that, let us be man and wife, and all will end happily!' Why his good nature should not be rewarded, when such reward would operate to the disadvantage of none, Mary, who had more sense than romance, could not understand; and she said as much.

Eleanor, however, was firm, and made quite an eloquent speech to support her own view of the question. She could not condescend, she said, to ask such a favour on any other terms than those proposed. Mary might, perhaps, think her high-flown, but she had her own ideas, and she could not submit to sacrifice her self-respect.

'But I am sure you love him;—don't you?' pleaded Mary; 'and I am sure he loves you better than anything in the world.'

Eleanor was going to make another speech, but a tear came to each eye, and she could not; so she pretended to blow her nose, and walked to the window, and made a little inward call on her own courage, and finding herself somewhat sustained, said sententiously,—'Mary, this is nonsense.'

'But you do love him,' said Mary, who had followed her friend to the window, and now spoke with her arms close wound round the other's waist. 'You do love him with all your heart. You know you do; I defy you to deny it.'

'I—' commenced Eleanor, turning sharply round to refute the charge; but the intended falsehood stuck in her throat, and never came to utterance. She could not deny her love, so she took plentifully to tears, and leant upon her friend's bosom and sobbed there, and protested that, love or no love, it would make no difference in her resolve, and called Mary, a thousand times, the most cruel of girls, and swore her to secrecy by a hundred oaths, and ended by declaring that the girl who could betray her friend's love, even to a brother, would be as black a traitor as a soldier in a garrison who should open the city gates to the enemy. While they were yet discussing the matter, Bold returned, and Eleanor was forced into sudden action. She had either to accomplish or abandon her plan; and having slipped into her friend's bedroom, as the gentleman closed the hall door, she washed the marks of tears from her eyes, and resolved within herself to go through with it. 'Tell him I am here,' said she, 'and coming in; and mind, whatever you do, don't leave us.' So Mary informed her brother, with a somewhat sombre air, that Miss Harding was in the next room, and was coming to speak to him.

Eleanor was certainly thinking more of her father than herself, as she arranged her hair before the glass, and removed the traces of sorrow from her face; and yet I should be untrue if I said that she was not anxious to appear well before her lover. Why else was she so sedulous with that stubborn curl that would rebel against her hand, and smooth so eagerly her ruffled ribands? Why else did she damp her eyes to dispel the redness, and bite her pretty lips to bring back the colour? Of course she was anxious to look her best, for she was but a mortal angel after all. But had she been immortal, had she flitted back to the sitting-room on a cherub's wings, she could not have had a more faithful heart, or a truer wish to save her father at any cost to herself.

John Bold had not met her since the day when she left him in dudgeon* in the cathedral close. Since that his whole time had been occupied in promoting the cause against her father,—and not unsuccessfully. He had often thought of her, and turned over in his mind a hundred schemes for showing her how disinterested was his love. He would write to her and beseech her not to allow the performance of a public duty to injure him in her estimation; he would write to

Mr Harding, explain all his views, and boldly claim the warden's daughter, urging that the untoward circumstances between them need be no bar to their ancient friendship, or to a closer tie; he would throw himself on his knees before his mistress; he would wait and marry the daughter when the father had lost his home and his income; he would give up the lawsuit and go to Australia, with her of course, leaving the *Jupiter* and Mr Finney to complete the case between them. Sometimes as he woke in the morning fevered and impatient, he would blow out his brains and have done with all his cares;—but this idea was generally consequent on an imprudent supper enjoyed in company with Tom Towers.

How beautiful Eleanor appeared to him as she slowly walked into the room! Not for nothing had all those little cares been taken. Though her sister, the archdeacon's wife, had spoken slightingly of her charms, Eleanor was very beautiful when seen aright. Hers was not one of those impassive faces, which have the beauty of a marble bust; finely chiselled features, perfect in every line, true to the rules of symmetry, as lovely to a stranger as to a friend, unvarying unless in sickness, or as age affects them. She had no startling brilliancy of beauty, no pearly whiteness, no radiant carnation. She had not the majestic contour that rivets attention, demands instant wonder, and then disappoints by the coldness of its charms. You might pass Eleanor Harding in the street without notice, but you could hardly pass an evening with her and not lose your heart.

She had never appeared more lovely to her lover than she did now. Her face was animated though it was serious, and her full dark lustrous eyes shone with anxious energy; her hand trembled as she took his, and she could hardly pronounce his name, when she addressed him. Bold wished with all his heart that the Australian scheme was in the act of realisation, and that he and Eleanor were away together, never to hear further of the lawsuit.

He began to talk, asked after her health;—said something about London being very stupid, and more about Barchester being very pleasant; declared the weather to be very hot, and then inquired after Mr Harding.

'My father is not very well,' said Eleanor.

John Bold was very sorry,—so sorry! He hoped it was nothing serious, and put on the unmeaningly solemn face, which people usually use on such occasions.

'I especially want to speak to you about my father, Mr Bold. Indeed, I am now here on purpose to do so. Papa is very unhappy, very unhappy indeed, about this affair of the hospital. You would pity him, Mr Bold, if you could see how wretched it has made him.'

'Oh Miss Harding!'

'Indeed you would;—any one would pity him; but a friend, an old friend as you are;—indeed you would. He is an altered man; his cheerfulness has all gone, and his sweet temper, and his kind happy tone of voice; you would hardly know him if you saw him, Mr Bold, he is so much altered; and—and—if this goes on, he will die.' Here Eleanor had recourse to her handkerchief, and so also had her auditors; but she plucked up her courage, and went on with her tale. 'He will break his heart, and die. I am sure, Mr Bold, it was not you who wrote those cruel things in the newspaper.'

John Bold eagerly protested that it was not, but his heart smote him as to his intimate alliance with Tom Towers.

'No, I am sure it was not; and papa has not for a moment thought so; you would not be so cruel;—but it has nearly killed him. Papa cannot bear to think that people should so speak of him, and that every body should hear him so spoken of. They have called him avaricious, and dishonest, and they say he is robbing the old men, and taking the money of the hospital for nothing.'

'I have never said so, Miss Harding. I——'

'No,' continued Eleanor, interrupting him, for she was now in the full flood tide of her eloquence; 'no, I am sure you have not; but others have said so; and if this goes on, if such things are written again, it will kill papa. Oh! Mr Bold, if you only knew the state he is in! Now papa does not care much about money.'

Both her auditors, brother and sister, assented to this, and declared on their own knowledge that no man lived less addicted to filthy lucre* than the warden.

'Oh! it's so kind of you to say so, Mary, and of you too, Mr Bold. I couldn't bear that people should think unjustly of papa. Do you know he would give up the hospital altogether;—only he cannot. The archdeacon says it would be cowardly, and that he would be deserting his order, and injuring the church. Whatever may happen, papa will not do that. He would leave the place to-morrow willingly, and give up his house, and the income and all, if the archdeacon——' Eleanor was going to say 'would let him,' but she stopped herself before she had compromised her father's dignity; and giving a long sigh, she added—'Oh, I do so wish he would!'

'No one who knows Mr Harding personally, accuses him for a moment,' said Bold.

'It is he that has to bear the punishment; it is he that suffers,' said Eleanor; 'and what for? what has he done wrong? how has he deserved this persecution? he that never had an unkind thought in his life, he that never said an unkind word!' and here she broke down, and the violence of her sobs stopped her utterance.

Bold, for the fifth or sixth time, declared that neither he nor any of his friends imputed any blame personally to Mr Harding.

'Then why should he be persecuted?' ejaculated Eleanor through her tears, forgetting in her eagerness that her intention had been to humble herself as a suppliant before John Bold;—'why should he be singled out for scorn and disgrace? why should he be made so wretched? Oh! Mr Bold,'—and she turned towards him as though the kneeling scene were about to be commenced—'oh! Mr Bold, why did you begin all this? You, whom we all so—so—valued!'

To speak the truth, the reformer's punishment was certainly come upon him; his present plight was not enviable; he had nothing for it but to excuse himself by platitudes about public duty, which it is by no means worth while to repeat, and to reiterate his eulogy on Mr Harding's character. His position was certainly a cruel one. Had any gentleman called upon him on behalf of Mr Harding he could of course have declined to enter upon the subject; but how could he do so with a beautiful girl, with the daughter of the man whom he had injured, with his own love?

In the meantime Eleanor recollected herself, and again summoned up her energies.

'Mr Bold,' said she, 'I have come here to implore you to abandon this proceeding.' He stood up from his seat, and looked beyond measure distressed. 'To implore you to abandon it, to implore you to spare my father, to spare either his life or his reason, for one or the other will pay the forfeit if this goes on. I know how much I am asking, and how little right I have to ask anything; but I think you will listen to me as it is for my father. Oh, Mr Bold, pray, pray do this for us;—pray do not drive to distraction a man who has loved you so well.'

She did not absolutely kneel to him, but she followed him as he moved from his chair, and laid her soft hands imploringly upon his arm. Ah! at any other time how exquisitely valuable would have been that touch! but now he was distraught, dumb-founded, and unmanned. What could he say to that sweet suppliant; how explain to her that the matter now was probably beyond his control; how tell her that he could not quell the storm which he had raised?

'Surely, surely, John, you cannot refuse her,' said his sister.

'I would give her my soul,' said he, 'if it would serve her.'

'Oh, Mr Bold,' said Eleanor, 'do not speak so; I ask nothing for myself; and what I ask for my father, it cannot harm you to grant.'

'I would give her my soul, if it would serve her,' said Bold, still addressing his sister; 'everything I have is hers, if she will accept it; my house, my heart, my all; every hope of my breast is centred in her; her smiles are sweeter to me than the sun, and when I see her in sorrow as she now is, every nerve in my body suffers. No man can love better than I love her.'

'No, no, no,' ejaculated Eleanor; 'there can be no talk of love between us. Will you protect my father from the evil you have brought upon him?'

'Oh, Eleanor, I will do anything; let me tell you how I love you!'

'No, no, no,' she almost screamed. 'This is unmanly of you, Mr Bold. Will you, will you, will you leave my father to die in peace in his quiet home?' And seizing him by his arm and hand, she followed him across the room towards the door. 'I will not leave you till you promise me; I'll cling to you in the street; I'll kneel to you before all the people. You shall promise me this; you shall promise me this; you shall——' And she clung to him with fixed tenacity, and reiterated her resolve with hysterical passion.

'Speak to her, John; answer her,' said Mary, bewildered by the unexpected vehemence of Eleanor's manner; 'you cannot have the cruelty to refuse her.'

'Promise me, promise me,' said Eleanor; 'say that my father is safe. One word will do. I know how true you are; say one word, and I will let you go.'

She still held him, and looked eagerly into his face, with her hair dishevelled, and her eyes all bloodshot. She had no thought now of herself, no care now for her appearance; and yet he thought he had never seen her half so lovely; he was amazed at the intensity of her beauty, and could hardly believe that it was she whom he had dared to

love. 'Promise me,' said she. 'I will not leave you till you have promised me.'

'I will,' said he at length; 'I do. All I can do, I will do.'

'Then may God Almighty bless you for ever and ever!' said
Eleanor; and falling on her knees with her face on Mary's lap, she
wept and sobbed like a child. Her strength had carried her through
her allotted task, but now it was well nigh exhausted.

In a while she was partly recovered, and got up to go, and would
have gone, had not Bold made her understand that it was necessary
for him to explain to her how far it was in his power to put an end
to the proceedings which had been taken against Mr Harding. Had
he spoken on any other subject, she would have vanished, but on
that she was bound to hear him. And now the danger of her position
commenced. While she had an active part to play, while she clung
to him as a suppliant, it was easy enough for her to reject his proffered love, and cast from her his caressing words; but now,—now
that he had yielded, and was talking to her calmly and kindly as
to her father's welfare, it was hard enough for her to do so. Then
Mary Bold assisted her; but now she was quite on her brother's side.
Mary said but little, but every word she did say gave some direct
and deadly blow. The first thing she did was to make room for her
brother between herself and Eleanor on the sofa. As the sofa was full
large for three, Eleanor could not resent this, nor could she show
suspicion by taking another seat; but she felt it to be a most unkind
proceeding. And then Mary would talk as though they three were
joined in some close peculiar bond together; as though they were in
future always to wish together, contrive together, and act together;
and Eleanor could not gainsay this; she could not make another
speech, and say, 'Mr Bold and I are strangers, Mary, and are always to
remain so!'

He explained to her that, though undoubtedly the proceeding
against the hospital had commenced solely with himself, many others
were now interested in the matter, some of whom were much more
influential than himself; that it was to him alone, however, that the
lawyers looked for instruction as to their doings, and, more important
still, for the payment of their bills. And he promised that he would at
once give them notice that it was his intention to abandon the cause.
He thought, he said, that it was not probable that any active steps
would be taken after he had seceded from the matter, though it was

possible that some passing allusion might still be made to the hospital in the daily *Jupiter*. He promised, however, that he would use his best influence to prevent any further personal allusion being made to Mr Harding. He then suggested that he would on that afternoon ride over himself to Dr Grantly, and inform him of his altered intentions on the subject, and with this view, he postponed his immediate return to London.

This was all very pleasant, and Eleanor did enjoy a sort of triumph in the feeling that she had attained the object for which she had sought this interview. But still the part of Iphigenia was to be played out. The gods had heard her prayer, granted her request, and were they not to have their promised sacrifice? Eleanor was not a girl to defraud them wilfully; so, as soon as she decently could, she got up for her bonnet.

'Are you going so soon?' said Bold, who half-an-hour since would have given a hundred pounds that he was in London, and she still at Barchester.

'Oh yes!' said she; 'I am so much obliged to you; papa will feel this to be so kind.' She did not quite appreciate all her father's feelings. 'Of course I must tell him, and I will say that you will see the archdeacon.'

'But may I not say one word for myself?' said Bold.

'I'll fetch you your bonnet, Eleanor,' said Mary, in the act of leaving the room.

'Mary, Mary,' said she, getting up and catching her by her dress; 'don't go, I'll get my bonnet myself;' but Mary, the traitress, stood fast by the door, and permitted no such retreat. Poor Iphigenia!

And with a volley of impassioned love, John Bold poured forth the feelings of his heart, swearing, as men do, some truths and many falsehoods; and Eleanor repeated with every shade of vehemence the 'No, no, no,' which had had a short time since so much effect. But now, alas! its strength was gone. Let her be never so vehement, her vehemence was not respected. All her 'No, no, no's' were met with counter asseverations, and at last were overpowered. The ground was cut from under her on every side. She was pressed to say whether her father would object; whether she herself had any aversion;— aversion! God help her, poor girl! the word nearly made her jump into his arms—; any other preference;—this she loudly disclaimed—; whether it was impossible that she should love him;—Eleanor could not say that it was impossible—; and so at last, all her defences demolished, all her maiden barriers swept away; she capitulated, or rather marched out with the honours of war, vanquished evidently, palpably vanquished, but still not reduced to the necessity of confessing it.

And so the altar on the shore of the modern Aulis* reeked with no sacrifice.

## CHAPTER 12
### MR BOLD'S VISIT TO PLUMSTEAD

WHETHER or no the ill-natured prediction made by certain ladies in the beginning of the last chapter, was or was not carried out to the letter, I am not in a position to state. Eleanor, however, certainly did feel herself to have been baffled as she returned home with all her news to her father. Certainly she had been victorious, certainly she had achieved her object, certainly she was not unhappy; and yet she did not feel herself triumphant. Everything would run smooth now. Eleanor was not at all addicted to the Lydian school of romance.* She by no means objected to her lover because he came in at the door under the name of Absolute, instead of pulling her out of a window under the name of Beverley. Yet she felt that she had been imposed upon, and could hardly think of Mary Bold with sisterly charity. 'I did believe I could have trusted Mary,' she said to herself over and over again. 'Oh that she should have dared to keep me in the room when I tried to get out!' Eleanor, however, felt that the game was up, and that she had now nothing further to do, but to add to the budget of news which was prepared for her father, that John Bold was her accepted lover.

We will, however, now leave her on her way, and go with John Bold to Plumstead Episcopi, merely premising that Eleanor on reaching home will not find things so smooth as she fondly expected. Two messengers had come, one to her father, and the other to the archdeacon, and each of them much opposed to her quiet mode of solving all their difficulties;—the one in the shape of a number of the *Jupiter*, and the other in that of a further opinion from Sir Abraham Haphazard.

John Bold got on his horse and rode off to Plumstead Episcopi; not briskly and with eager spur, as men do ride when self-satisfied with their own intentions; but slowly, modestly, thoughtfully, and somewhat in dread of the coming interview. Now and again he would, recur to the scene which was just over, support himself by the remembrance of the silence that gives consent, and exult as a happy lover. But even this feeling was not without a shade of remorse. Had he not shown himself childishly weak thus to yield up the resolve of many hours of thought to the tears of a pretty girl? How was he to meet his lawyer? How was he to back out of a matter in which his name was already so publicly concerned? What, oh what! was he to say to Tom Towers? While meditating these painful things he reached the lodge leading up to the archdeacon's glebe,* and for the first time in his life found himself within the sacred precincts.

All the doctor's children were together on the slope of the lawn, close to the road, as Bold rode up to the hall door. They were there holding high debate on matters evidently of deep interest at Plumstead Episcopi, and the voices of the boys had been heard before the lodge gate was closed.

Florinda and Grizzel, frightened at the sight of so well-known an enemy to the family, fled on the first appearance of the horseman, and ran in terror to their mother's arms. Not for them was it, tender branches, to resent injuries, or as members of a church militant to put on armour against its enemies. But the boys stood their ground like heroes, and boldly demanded the business of the intruder.

'Do you want to see anybody here, sir?' said Henry, with a defiant eye and a hostile tone, which plainly said that at any rate no one there wanted to see the person so addressed; and as he spoke he brandished aloft his garden water-pot, holding it by the spout, ready for the braining of any one.

'Henry,' said Charles James, slowly, and with a certain dignity of diction. 'Mr Bold of course would not have come without wanting to see some one. If Mr Bold has a proper ground for wanting to see some person here, of course he has a right to come.'

But Samuel stepped lightly up to the horse's head, and offered his services. 'Oh, Mr Bold,' said he, 'papa, I'm sure, will be glad to see you. I suppose you want to see papa. Shall I hold your horse for you? Oh, what a very pretty horse!' and he turned his head and winked funnily at his brothers. 'Papa has heard such good news about the old hospital to-day. We know you'll be glad to hear it, because you're such a friend of grandpapa Harding, and so much in love with aunt Nelly!'

'How d'ye do, lads?' said Bold, dismounting. 'I want to see your father if he's at home.'

'Lads!' said Henry, turning on his heel and addressing himself to his brother, but loud enough to be heard by Bold; 'lads, indeed! if we're lads, what does he call himself?'

Charles James condescended to say nothing further, but cocked his hat with much precision, and left the visitor to the care of his youngest brother.

Samuel stayed till the servant came, chatting and patting the horse; but as soon as Bold had disappeared through the front door, he stuck a switch under the animal's tail to make him kick, if possible.

The church reformer soon found himself tête à tête with the archdeacon in that same room, in that sanctum sanctorum* of the rectory, to which we have already been introduced. As he entered he heard the click of a certain patent lock, but it struck him with no surprise; the worthy clergyman was no doubt hiding from eyes profane his last much-studied sermon; for the archdeacon, though he preached but seldom, was famous for his sermons. No room, Bold thought, could have been more becoming for a dignitary of the church; each wall was loaded with theology; over each separate book-case was printed in small gold letters the names of those great divines whose works were ranged beneath; beginning from the early fathers in due chronological order, there were to be found the precious labours of the chosen servants of the church down to the last pamphlet written in opposition to the consecration of Dr Hampden;*—and raised above this were to be seen the busts of the greatest among the great; Chrysostom, St Augustine, Thomas à Becket, Cardinal Wolsey, Archbishop Laud, and Dr Phillpotts.*

Every appliance that could make study pleasant and give ease to the over-toiled brain was there; chairs made to relieve each limb and muscle; reading-desks and writing-desks to suit every attitude; lamps and candles mechanically contrived to throw their light on any favoured spot, as the student might desire; a shoal of newspapers to amuse the few leisure moments which might be stolen from the labours of the day; and then from the window a view right through a bosky vista along which ran a broad green path from the rectory to the church,—at the end of which the tawny-tinted fine old tower was seen with all its variegated pinnacles and parapets. Few parish churches in England are in better repair, or better worth keeping so, than that at Plumstead Episcopi; and yet it is built in a faulty style.* The body of the church is low;—so low, that the nearly flat leaden roof would be visible from the churchyard, were it not for the carved parapet with which it is surrounded. It is cruciform, though the transepts are irregular, one being larger than the other; and the tower is much too high in proportion to the church. But the colour of the building is perfect; it is that rich yellow grey which one finds nowhere but in the south and west of England, and which is so strong a characteristic of most of our old houses of Tudor architecture. The stone work also is beautiful; the mullions of the windows and the thick tracery of the Gothic workmanship is as rich as fancy can desire; and though in gazing on such a structure, one knows by rule that the old priests who built it, built it wrong, one cannot bring oneself to wish that they should have made it other than it is.

When Bold was ushered into the book-room, he found its owner standing with his back to the empty fire-place ready to receive him, and he could not but perceive that that expansive brow was elated with triumph, and that those full heavy lips bore more prominently than usual an appearance of arrogant success.

'Well, Mr Bold,' said he;—'well, what can I do for you? Very happy, I can assure you, to do anything for such a friend of my father-in-law.'

'I hope you'll excuse my calling, Dr Grantly.'

'Certainly, certainly,' said the archdeacon; 'I can assure you, no apology is necessary from Mr Bold;—only let me know what I can do for him.'

Dr Grantly was standing himself, and he did not ask Bold to sit, and therefore he had to tell his tale standing, leaning on the table, with his hat in his hand. He did, however, manage to tell it; and as the archdeacon never once interrupted him or even encouraged him by a single word, he was not long in coming to the end of it.

'And so, Mr Bold, I'm to understand, I believe, that you are desirous of abandoning this attack upon Mr Harding.'

'Oh, Dr Grantly, there has been no attack, I can assure you.'

'Well, well, we won't quarrel about words; I should call it an attack;—most men would so call an endeavour to take away from a man every shilling of income that he has to live upon; but it shan't be an attack, if you don't like it; you wish to abandon this,—this little game of back-gammon* you've begun to play.'

'I intend to put an end to the legal proceedings which I have commenced.'

'I understand,' said the archdeacon. 'You've already had enough of it. Well, I can't say that I am surprised. Carrying on a losing lawsuit where one has nothing to gain, but everything to pay, is not pleasant.'

Bold turned very red in the face. 'You misinterpret my motives,' said he; 'but, however, that is of little consequence. I did not come to trouble you with my motives, but to tell you a matter of fact. Good morning, Dr Grantly.'

'One moment,—one moment,' said the other. 'I don't exactly appreciate the taste which induced you to make any personal communication to me on the subject; but I dare say I'm wrong; I dare say your judgment is the better of the two; but as you have done me the honour;—as you have, as it were, forced me into a certain amount of conversation on a subject which had better, perhaps, have been left to our lawyers, you will excuse me if I ask you to hear my reply to your communication.'

'I am in a hurry, Dr Grantly.'

'Well, I am, Mr Bold; my time is not exactly leisure time, and, therefore, if you please, we'll go to the point at once. You are going to abandon this lawsuit?'—and he paused for a reply.

'Yes, Dr Grantly, I am.'

'Having exposed a gentleman who was one of your father's warmest friends, to all the ignominy and insolence which the press could heap upon his name, having somewhat ostentatiously declared that it was your duty as a man of high public virtue to protect those poor old fools whom you have humbugged there at the hospital, you now find that the game costs more than it's worth, and so you make up your mind to have done with it. A prudent resolution, Mr Bold;—but it is a pity you should have been so long coming to it. Has it struck you that we may not now choose to give over? that we may find it necessary to punish the injury you have done to us? Are you aware, sir, that we have gone to enormous expense to resist this iniquitous attempt of yours?'

Bold's face was now furiously red, and he nearly crushed his hat between his hands; but he said nothing.

'We have found it necessary to employ the best advice that money could procure. Are you aware, sir, what may be the probable cost of securing the services of the attorney-general?'

'Not in the least, Dr Grantly.'

'I dare say not, sir. When you recklessly put this affair into the hands of your friend Mr Finney, whose six and eightpences and thirteen and fourpences* may, probably, not amount to a large sum, you were indifferent as to the cost and suffering which such a proceeding might entail on others. But are you aware, sir, that these crushing costs must now come out of your own pocket?'

'Any demand of such a nature which Mr Harding's lawyer may have to make, will doubtless be made to my lawyer.'

'Mr Harding's lawyer and my lawyer! Did you come here merely to refer me to the lawyers? Upon my word I think the honour of your visit might have been spared! And now, sir, I'll tell you what my opinion is. My opinion is, that we shall not allow you to withdraw this matter from the courts.'

'You can do as you please, Dr Grantly; good morning.'

'Hear me out, sir,' said the archdeacon. 'I have here in my hands the last opinion given in this matter by Sir Abraham Haphazard. I dare say you have already heard of this. I dare say it has had something to do with your visit here to-day.'

'I know nothing whatever of Sir Abraham Haphazard or his opinion.'

'Be that as it may, here it is. He declares most explicitly that under no phasis* of the affair whatever have you a leg to stand upon; that Mr Harding is as safe in his hospital as I am here in my rectory; that a more futile attempt to destroy a man was never made, than this which you have made to ruin Mr Harding. Here,' and he slapped the paper on the table, 'I have this opinion from the very first lawyer in the land; and under these circumstances you expect me to make you a low bow for your kind offer to release Mr Harding from the toils of your net! Sir, your net is not strong enough to hold him; sir, your net has fallen to pieces, and you knew that well enough before I told you. And now, sir, I'll wish you good morning, for I am busy.'

Bold was now choking with passion. He had let the archdeacon run on, because he knew not with what words to interrupt him; but now that he had been so defied and insulted, he could not leave the room without some reply.

'Dr Grantly,' he commenced.

'I have nothing further to say or to hear,' said the archdeacon. 'I'll do myself the honour to order your horse.' And he rang the bell.

'I came here, Dr Grantly, with the warmest, kindest feelings——'

'Oh, of course you did; nobody doubts it.'

'With the kindest feelings;—and they have been most grossly outraged by your treatment.'

'Of course they have! I have not chosen to see my father-in-law ruined. What an outrage that has been to your feelings!'

'The time will come, Dr Grantly, when you will understand why I called upon you to-day.'

'No doubt; no doubt. Is Mr Bold's horse there? That's right; open the front door. Good morning, Mr Bold;' and the doctor stalked into his own drawing-room, closing the door behind him, and making it quite impossible that John Bold should speak another word to him.

As John Bold got on his horse, which he was fain to do feeling like a dog turned out of a kitchen, he was again greeted by little Sammy.

'Good-bye, Mr Bold; I hope we may have the pleasure of seeing you again before long; I am sure papa will always be glad to see you.'

That was certainly the bitterest moment in John Bold's life. Not even the remembrance of his successful love could comfort him. Nay, when he thought of Eleanor, he felt that it was that very love which had brought him to such a pass. That he should have been so insulted, and be unable to reply! That he should have given up so much to the request of a girl, and then have had his motives so misunderstood! That he should have made so gross a mistake as this visit of his to the archdeacon's! He bit the top of his whip, till he penetrated the horn of which it was made. He struck the poor animal in his anger, and then was doubly angry with himself at his futile passion. He had been so completely check-mated, so palpably overcome! And what was he to do? He could not continue his action after pledging himself to abandon it. Nor was there any revenge in that. It was the very step to which his enemy had endeavoured to goad him!

He threw the reins to the servant who came to take his horse, and rushed upstairs into his drawing-room, where his sister Mary was sitting.

'If there be a devil,' said he, 'a real devil here on earth, it is Dr Grantly.' He vouchsafed her no further intelligence, but again seizing his hat, he rushed out, and took his departure for London without another word to any one.

## CHAPTER 13

### THE WARDEN'S DECISION

THE meeting between Eleanor and her father was not so stormy as that described in the last chapter, but it was hardly more successful. On her return from Bold's house she found her father in a strange state. He was not sorrowful and silent as he had been on that memorable day when his son-in-law lectured him as to all that he owed to his order; nor was he in his usual quiet mood. When Eleanor reached the hospital, he was walking to and fro upon the lawn, and she soon saw that he was much excited.

'I am going to London, my dear,' he said as soon as he saw her.

'To London, papa!'

'Yes, my dear, to London; I will have this matter settled in some way. There are some things, Eleanor, which I cannot bear.'

'Oh, papa, what is it?' said she, leading him by the arm into the house. 'I had such good news for you, and now you make me fear I am too late.' And then, before he could let her know what had caused this sudden resolve, or could point to the fatal paper which lay on the table, she told him that the lawsuit was over, that Bold had commissioned her to assure her father in his name that it would be abandoned,— that there was no further cause for misery, and that the whole matter might be looked on as though it had never been discussed. She did not tell him with what determined vehemence she had obtained this concession in his favour, nor did she mention the price she was to pay for it. The warden did not express himself peculiarly gratified at this intelligence, and Eleanor, though she had not worked for thanks, and was by no means disposed to magnify her own good offices, felt hurt at the manner in which her news was received. 'Mr Bold can act as he thinks proper, my love,' said he; 'if Mr Bold thinks he has been wrong, of course he will discontinue what he is doing; but that cannot change my purpose.'

'Oh, papa!' she exclaimed, all but crying with vexation; 'I thought you would have been so happy;—I thought all would have been right now.'

'Mr Bold,' continued he, 'has set great people to work;—so great that I doubt they are now beyond his control. Read that, my dear.' The warden, doubling up a number of the *Jupiter*, pointed to the peculiar article which she was to read. It was to the last of the three leaders which are generally furnished daily for the support of the nation that Mr Harding directed her attention. It dealt some heavy blows on various clerical delinquents; on families who received their tens of thousands yearly for doing nothing; on men who, as the article stated, rolled in wealth which they had neither earned nor inherited, and which was in fact stolen from the poorer clergy. It named some sons of bishops, and grandsons of archbishops; men great in their way, who had redeemed their disgrace in the eyes of many by the enormity of their plunder; and then, having disposed of these leviathans,* it descended to Mr Harding.

'We alluded some weeks since to an instance of similar injustice, though in a more humble scale, in which the warden of an almshouse at Barchester has become possessed of the income of the greater part of the whole institution. Why an almshouse should have a warden we cannot pretend to explain, nor can we say what special need twelve old men can have for the services of a separate clergyman, seeing that they have twelve reserved seats for themselves in Barchester Cathedral. But be this as it may, let the gentleman call himself warden or precentor, or what he will,—let him be never so scrupulous in exacting religious duties from his twelve dependants, or never so negligent as regards the services of the cathedral,—it appears palpably clear that he can be entitled to no portion of the revenue of the hospital, excepting that which the founder set apart for him; and it is equally clear that the founder did not intend that three-fifths of his charity should be so consumed.

'The case is certainly a paltry one after the tens of thousands with which we have been dealing, for the warden's income is after all but a poor eight hundred a year. Eight hundred a year is not magnificent preferment of itself, and the warden may, for anything we know, be worth much more to the church. But if so, let the church pay him out of funds justly at its own disposal.

'We allude to the question of the Barchester almshouse at the present moment, because we understand that a plea has been set up which will be peculiarly revolting to the minds of English churchmen. An action has been taken against Mr warden Harding, on behalf of the almsmen, by a gentleman acting solely on public grounds, and it is to be argued that Mr Harding takes nothing but what he receives as a servant of the hospital, and that he is not himself responsible for the amount of stipend given to him for his work. Such a plea would doubtless be fair, if any one questioned the daily wages of a bricklayer employed on a building, or the fee of the charwoman who cleans it; but we cannot envy the feeling of a clergyman of the Church of England who could allow such an argument to be put in his mouth.

'If this plea be put forward we trust Mr Harding will be forced as a witness to state the nature of his employment; the amount of work that he does; the income which he receives; and the source from whence he obtained his appointment. We do not think he will receive much public sympathy to atone for the annoyance of such an examination.'

As Eleanor read the article her face flushed with indignation, and when she had finished it, she almost feared to look up at her father.

'Well, my dear,' said he; 'what do you think of that? Is it worth while to be a warden at that price?'

'Oh, papa;—dear papa!'

'Mr Bold can't unwrite that, my dear. Mr Bold can't say that that shan't be read by every clergyman at Oxford; nay, by every gentleman in the land.' Then he walked up and down the room, while Eleanor in mute despair followed him with her eyes. 'And I'll tell you what, my dear,' he continued, speaking now very calmly, and in a forced manner very unlike himself; 'Mr Bold can't dispute the truth of every word in that article you have just read—nor can I.' Eleanor stared at him, as though she scarcely understood the words he was speaking. 'Nor can I, Eleanor. That's the worst of all, or would be so if there were no remedy. I have thought much of all this since we were together last night;' and he came and sat beside her, and put his arm round her waist as he had done then. 'I have thought much of what the archdeacon has said, and of what this paper says; and I do believe I have no right to be here.'

'No right to be warden of the hospital, papa?'

'No right to be warden with eight hundred a year;—no right to be warden with such a house as this; no right to spend in luxury money that was intended for charity. Mr Bold may do as he pleases about his suit, but I hope he will not abandon it for my sake.'

Poor Eleanor! this was hard upon her. Was it for this she had made her great resolve! For this that she had laid aside her quiet demeanour, and taken upon her the rants of a tragedy heroine! One may work and not for thanks;—but yet feel hurt at not receiving them; and so it was with Eleanor. One may be disinterested in one's good actions, and yet feel discontented that they are not recognised. Charity may be given with the left hand so privily that the right hand does not know it, and yet the left hand may regret to feel that it has no immediate reward. Eleanor had had no wish to burden her father with a weight of obligation, and yet she had looked forward to much delight from the knowledge that she had freed him from his sorrows. Now such hopes were entirely over. All that she had done was of no avail. She had humbled herself to Bold in vain. The evil was utterly beyond her power to cure!

She had thought also how gently she would whisper to her father all that her lover had said to her about herself, and how impossible she had found it to reject him. And then she had anticipated her father's kindly kiss and close embrace as he gave his sanction to her love. Alas! she could say nothing of this now. In speaking of Mr Bold, her father put him aside as one whose thoughts and sayings and acts could be of no moment. Gentle reader, did you ever feel yourself snubbed? Did you ever, when thinking much of your own importance, find yourself suddenly reduced to a nonentity? Such was Eleanor's feeling now.

'They shall not put forward this plea on my behalf,' continued the warden. 'Whatever may be the truth of the matter, that at any rate is not true; and the man who wrote that article is right in saying that such a plea is revolting to an honest mind. I will go up to London, my dear, and see these lawyers myself, and if no better excuse can be made for me than that, I and the hospital will part.'

'But the archdeacon, papa?'

'I can't help it, my dear; there are some things which a man cannot bear. I cannot bear that;'—and he put his hand upon the newspaper.

'But will the archdeacon go with you?'

To tell the truth, Mr Harding had made up his mind to steal a march upon the archdeacon. He was aware that he could take no steps without informing his dread son-in-law; but he had resolved that he would send out a note to Plumstead Episcopi detailing his plans, but that the messenger should not leave Barchester till he himself had started for London;—so that he might be a day before the doctor, who, he had no doubt, would follow him. In that day, if he had luck, he might arrange it all. He might explain to Sir Abraham that he, as warden, would have nothing further to do with the defence about to be set up; he might send in his official resignation to his friend the bishop, and so make public the whole transaction, that even the archdeacon would not be able to undo what he had done. He knew too well the archdeacon's strength and his own weakness to suppose he could do this if they both reached London together. Indeed, he would never be able to get to London, if the archdeacon knew of his intended journey in time to prevent it.

'No, I think not,' said he. 'I think I shall start before the archdeacon could be ready. I shall go early to-morrow morning.'

'That will be best, papa,' said Eleanor, showing that her father's ruse was appreciated.

'Why, yes, my love. The fact is, I wish to do all this before the archdeacon can,—can interfere. There is a great deal of truth in all he says. He argues very well, and I can't always answer him; but there is an old saying, Nelly; "Every one knows where his own shoe pinches!" He'll say that I want moral courage, and strength of character, and power of endurance, and it's all true; but I'm sure I ought not to remain here, if I have nothing better to put forward than a quibble. So, Nelly, we shall have to leave this pretty place.'

Eleanor's face brightened up, as she assured her father how cordially she agreed with him.

'True, my love,' said he, now again quite happy and at ease in his manner. 'What good to us is this place or all the money, if we are to be ill-spoken of?'

'Oh, papa, I am so glad!'

'My darling child. It did cost me a pang at first, Nelly, to think that you should lose your pretty drawing-room, and your ponies, and your garden. The garden will be the worst of all;—but there is a garden at Crabtree, a very pretty garden.'

Crabtree Parva was the name of the small living which Mr Harding had held as a minor canon, and which still belonged to him. It was only worth some eighty pounds a year, and a small house and glebe, all of which were now handed over to Mr Harding's curate. But it was to Crabtree glebe that Mr Harding thought of retiring. This parish must not be mistaken for that other living, Crabtree Canonicorum,* as it is called. Crabtree Canonicorum is a very nice thing. There are only two hundred parishioners; there are four hundred acres of glebe; and the great and small tithes, which both go to the rector, are worth four hundred pounds a year more. Crabtree Canonicorum is in the gift of the dean and chapter, and is at this time possessed by the Honourable and Reverend Dr Vesey Stanhope, who also fills the prebendal stall of Goosegorge in Barchester Chapter, and holds the united rectory of Eiderdown and Stogpingum, or Stoke Pinquium,* as it should be written. This is the same Dr Vesey Stanhope, whose hospitable villa on the Lake of Como* is so well known to the élite of English travellers, and whose collection of Lombard butterflies* is supposed to be unique.

'Yes,' said the warden, musing, 'there is a very pretty garden at Crabtree; but I shall be sorry to disturb poor Smith.' Smith was the curate of Crabtree, a gentleman who was maintaining a wife and half a dozen children on the income arising from his profession.

Eleanor assured her father that, as far as she was concerned, she could leave her house and her ponies without a single regret. She was only so happy that he was going,—going where he would escape all this dreadful turmoil.

'But we will take the music, my dear.'

And so they went on planning their future happiness, and plotting how they would arrange it all without the interposition of the archdeacon. At last they again became confidential, and then the warden did thank her for what she had done, and Eleanor, lying on her father's shoulder, did find an opportunity to tell her secret. And the father gave his blessing to his child, and said that the man whom she loved was honest, good, and kind-hearted, and right-thinking in the main;—one who wanted only a good wife to put him quite upright;—'a man, my love,' he ended by saying, 'to whom I firmly believe that I can trust my treasure with safety.'

'But what will Dr Grantly say?'

'Well, my dear, it can't be helped. We shall be out at Crabtree then.'

And Eleanor ran upstairs to prepare her father's clothes for his journey; and the warden returned to his garden to make his last adieus to every tree, and shrub, and shady nook that he knew so well.

## CHAPTER 14

### MOUNT OLYMPUS*

WRETCHED in spirit, groaning under the feeling of the insult, self-condemning, and ill-satisfied in every way, Bold returned to his London lodgings. Ill as he had fared in his interview with the archdeacon, he was not the less under the necessity of carrying out his pledge to Eleanor; and he went about his ungracious task with a heavy heart.

The attorneys whom he had employed in London received his instructions with surprise and evident misgiving; however, they could only obey, and mutter something of their sorrow that such heavy costs should only fall upon their own employer,—especially as nothing was wanting but perseverance to throw them on the opposite party. Bold left the office which he had latterly so much frequented, shaking the dust from off his feet; and before he was down the stairs, an edict had already gone forth for the preparation of the bill.

He next thought of the newspapers. The case had been taken up by more than one; and he was well aware that the key note had been sounded by the *Jupiter*. He had been very intimate with Tom Towers, and had often discussed with him the affairs of the hospital. Bold could not say that the articles in that paper had been written at his own instigation. He did not even know as a fact that they had been written by his friend. Tom Towers had never said that such a view of the case, or such a side in the dispute, would be taken by the paper with which he was connected. Very discreet in such matters was Tom Towers, and altogether indisposed to talk loosely of the concerns of that mighty engine of which it was his high privilege to move in secret some portion. Nevertheless Bold believed that to him were owing those dreadful words which had caused such panic at Barchester,— and he conceived himself bound to prevent their repetition. With this view he betook himself from the attorneys' office to that laboratory where, with amazing chemistry, Tom Towers compounded thunderbolts for the destruction of all that is evil, and for the furtherance of all that is good, in this and other hemispheres.

Who has not heard of Mount Olympus,—that high abode of all the powers of type, that favoured seat of the great goddess Pica,* that wondrous habitation of gods and devils, from whence, with ceaseless hum of steam and never-ending flow of Castalian ink,* issue forth eighty thousand nightly edicts for the governance of a subject nation?

Velvet and gilding do not make a throne, nor gold and jewels a sceptre.* It is a throne because the most exalted one sits there;— and a sceptre because the most mighty one wields it. So it is with Mount Olympus. Should a stranger make his way thither at dull noonday, or during the sleepy hours of the silent afternoon, he would find no acknowledged temple of power and beauty, no fitting fane for the great Thunderer, no proud façades and pillared roofs to support the dignity of this greatest of earthly potentates. To the outward and uninitiated eye, Mount Olympus is a somewhat humble spot,—undistinguished, unadorned,—nay, almost mean. It stands alone,* as it were, in a mighty city, close to the densest throng of men, but partaking neither of the noise nor the crowd; a small secluded, dreary spot, tenanted, one would say, by quite unambitious people, at the easiest rents. 'Is this Mount Olympus?' asks the unbelieving stranger. 'Is it from these small, dark, dingy buildings that those infallible laws proceed which cabinets are called upon to obey; by which bishops are to be guided, lords and commons controlled,—judges instructed in law, generals in strategy, admirals in naval tactics, and orange-women in the management of their barrows?' 'Yes, my friend—from these walls. From here issue the only known infallible bulls for the guidance of British souls and bodies. This little court is the Vatican of England. Here reigns a pope, self-nominated, self-consecrated,—ay, and much stranger too,—self-believing!—a pope whom, if you cannot obey him, I would advise you to disobey as silently as possible; a pope hitherto afraid of no Luther; a pope who manages his own inquisition, who punishes unbelievers as no most skilful inquisitor* of Spain ever dreamt of doing;—one who can excommunicate thoroughly, fearfully, radically; put you beyond the pale of men's charity; make you odious to your dearest friends, and turn you into a monster to be pointed at by the finger!'

Oh heavens! and this is Mount Olympus!

It is a fact amazing to ordinary mortals that the *Jupiter* is never wrong. With what endless care, with what unsparing labour, do we not strive to get together for our great national council the men most fitting to compose it. And how we fail! Parliament is always wrong. Look at the *Jupiter*, and see how futile are their meetings, how vain their council, how needless all their trouble! With what pride do we regard our chief ministers, the great servants of state, the oligarchs of the nation on whose wisdom we lean, to whom we look for guidance in our difficulties! But what are they to the writers of the *Jupiter*? They hold council together and with anxious thought painfully elaborate their country's good; but when all is done, the *Jupiter* declares that all is nought. Why should we look to Lord John Russell;—why should we regard Palmerston and Gladstone,* when Tom Towers without a struggle can put us right? Look at our generals,* what faults they make;—at our admirals, how inactive they are. What money, honesty, and science can do, is done; and yet how badly are our troops brought together, fed, conveyed, clothed, armed, and managed. The most excellent of our good men do their best to man our ships, with the assistance of all possible external appliances; but in vain. All, all is wrong! Alas! alas! Tom Towers, and he alone, knows all about it. Why, oh why, ye earthly ministers, why have ye not followed more closely this heaven-sent messenger that is among us?

Were it not well for us in our ignorance that we confided all things to the *Jupiter*? Would it not be wise in us to abandon useless talking, idle thinking, and profitless labour? Away with majorities in the House of Commons, with verdicts from judicial bench given after much delay, with doubtful laws, and the fallible attempts of humanity! Does not the *Jupiter*, coming forth daily with eighty thousand impressions full of unerring decision on every mortal subject, set all matters sufficiently at rest? Is not Tom Towers here, able to guide us and willing?

Yes indeed,—able and willing to guide all men in all things, so long as he is obeyed as autocrat should be obeyed,—with undoubting submission! Only let not ungrateful ministers seek other colleagues than those whom Tom Towers may approve; let church and state, law and physic, commerce and agriculture,—the arts of war, and the arts of peace, all listen and obey, and all will be made perfect. Has not Tom Towers an all-seeing eye? From the diggings of Australia to those of California,* right round the habitable globe, does he not know, watch, and chronicle the doings of every one? From a bishopric in New Zealand* to an unfortunate director of a North-west passage,* is he not the only fit judge of capability? From the sewers of London to the Central Railway of India,*—from the palaces of St Petersburg to the cabins of Connaught,* nothing can escape him. Britons have but to read, obey, and be blessed. None but the fools doubt the wisdom of the *Jupiter*. None but the mad dispute its facts.

No established religion has ever been without its unbelievers, even in the country where it is the most firmly fixed; no creed has been without scoffers; no church has so prospered as to free itself entirely from dissent. There are those who doubt the *Jupiter*! They live and breathe the upper air, walking here unscathed, though scorned,—men, born of British mothers and nursed on English milk, who scruple not to say that Mount Olympus has its price, that Tom Towers can be bought for gold!

Such is Mount Olympus, the mouthpiece of all the wisdom of this great country. It may probably be said that no place in this 19th century is more worthy of notice. No treasury mandate* armed with the signatures of all the government has half the power of one of those broad sheets,* which fly forth from hence so abundantly, armed with no signature at all.

Some great man, some mighty peer,—we'll say a noble duke,— retires to rest feared and honoured by all his countrymen,—fearless himself; if not a good man, at any rate a mighty man,—too mighty to care much what men may say about his want of virtue. He rises in the morning degraded, mean, and miserable; an object of men's scorn, anxious only to retire as quickly as may be to some German obscurity, some unseen Italian privacy, or, indeed, anywhere out of sight. What has made this awful change? What has so afflicted him? An article has appeared in the *Jupiter*; some fifty lines of a narrow column have destroyed all his grace's equanimity, and banished him for ever from the world. No man knows who wrote the bitter words; the clubs talk confusedly of the matter, whispering to each other this and that name; while Tom Towers walks quietly along Pall Mall,* with his coat but-toned close against the east wind, as though he were a mortal man, and not a god dispensing thunderbolts from Mount Olympus.

It was not to Mount Olympus that our friend Bold betook himself. He had before now wandered round that lonely spot, thinking how grand a thing it was to write articles for the *Jupiter*; considering within himself whether by any stretch of the powers within him he could ever come to such distinction; wondering how Tom Towers would take any little humble offering of his talents; calculating that Tom Towers himself must have once had a beginning, have once doubted as to his own success. Towers could not have been born a writer in the *Jupiter*. With such ideas, half ambitious and half awe-struck, had Bold regarded the silent-looking workshop of the gods; but he had never yet by word or sign attempted to influence the slightest word of his unerring friend. On such a course was he now intent; and not without much inward palpitation did he betake himself to the quiet abode of wisdom,* where Tom Towers was to be found o' mornings inhaling ambrosia and sipping nectar* in the shape of toast and tea.

Not far removed from Mount Olympus, but somewhat nearer

to the blessed regions of the West, is the most favoured abode of Themis.* Washed by the rich tide which now passes from the towers of Cæsar to Barry's halls of eloquence;* and again back, with new offerings of a city's tribute, from the palaces of peers to the mart of merchants,* stand those quiet walls which Law has delighted to honour by its presence. What a world within a world is the Temple! how quiet are its 'entangled walks,' as some one lately has called them,* and yet how close to the densest concourse of humanity! how gravely respectable its sober alleys, though removed but by a single step from the profanity of the Strand and the low iniquity of Fleet Street! Old St Dunstan,* with its bell-smiting bludgeoners, has been removed; the ancient shops with their faces full of pleasant history are passing away one by one; the bar itself* is to go; its doom has been pronounced by the *Jupiter*; rumour tells us of some huge building* that is to appear in these latitudes dedicated to law, subversive of the courts of Westminster, and antagonistic to the Rolls and Lincoln's Inn. But nothing yet threatens the silent beauty of the Temple. It is the mediæval court of the metropolis.

Here, on the choicest spot of this choice ground, stands a lofty row of chambers, looking obliquely upon the sullied Thames. Before the windows, the lawn of the Temple Gardens stretches with that dim yet delicious verdure so refreshing to the eyes of Londoners. If doomed to live within the thickest of London smoke you would surely say that that would be your chosen spot. Yes, you, you whom I now address, my dear, middle-aged bachelor friend, can nowhere be so well domiciled as here. No one here will ask whether you are out or at home; alone or with friends. Here no Sabbatarian* will investigate your Sundays, no censorious landlady will scrutinise your empty bottle, no valetudinarian neighbour will complain of late hours. If you love books, to what place are books so suitable? The whole spot is redolent of typography. Would you worship the Paphian goddess,* the groves of Cyprus are not more taciturn than those of the Temple. Wit and wine are always here, and always together. The revels of the Temple are as those of polished Greece, where the wildest worshipper of Bacchus* never forgot the dignity of the god whom he adored. Where can retirement be so complete as here? Where can you be so sure of all the pleasures of society?

It was here that Tom Towers lived, and cultivated with eminent success the tenth Muse* who now governs the periodical press. But let it not be supposed that his chambers were such, or so comfortless, as are frequently the gaunt abodes of legal aspirants.* Four chairs, a half-filled deal bookcase with hangings of dingy green baize, an old office table covered with dusty papers, which are not moved once in six months, and an old Pembroke brother* with rickety legs, for all daily uses;—a despatcher* for the preparation of lobsters and coffee, and an apparatus for the cooking of toast and mutton chops; such utensils and luxuries as these did not suffice for the well-being of Tom Towers. He indulged in four rooms on the first floor, each of which was furnished, if not with the splendour, with probably more than the comfort of Stafford House.* Every addition that science and art have lately made to the luxuries of modern life was to be found there. The room in which he usually sat was surrounded by book-shelves carefully filled; nor was there a volume there which was not entitled to its place in such a collection, both by its intrinsic worth and exterior splendour. A pretty portable set of steps in one corner of the room showed that those even on the higher shelves were intended for use. The chamber contained but two works of art;—the one, an admirable bust of Sir Robert Peel, by Power,* declared the individual politics of our friend; and the other, a singularly long figure of a female devotee, by Millais,* told equally plainly the school of art to which he was addicted. This picture was not hung, as pictures usually are, against the wall. There was no inch of wall vacant for such a purpose. It had a stand or desk erected for its own accommodation; and there on her pedestal, framed and glazed, stood the devotional lady looking intently at a lily as no lady ever looked before.

Our modern artists, whom we style Præ-Raffaellites,* have delighted to go back, not only to the finish and peculiar manner, but also to the subjects of the early painters. It is impossible to give them too much praise for the elaborate perseverance with which they have equalled the minute perfections of the masters from whom they take their inspiration. Nothing probably can exceed the painting of some of these latter-day pictures. It is, however, singular into what faults they fall as regards their subjects. They are not quite content to take the old stock groups,—a Sebastian with his arrows, a Lucia with her eyes in a dish, a Lorenzo with a gridiron, or the virgin with two children.* But they are anything but happy in their change. As a rule, no figure should be drawn in a position which it is impossible to suppose any figure should maintain. The patient endurance of St Sebastian, the wild ecstasy of St John in the Wilderness, the maternal love of the virgin, are feelings naturally portrayed by a fixed posture; but the lady with the stiff back and bent neck, who looks at her flower, and is still looking from hour to hour, gives us an idea of pain without grace, and abstraction without a cause.

It was easy, from his rooms, to see that Tom Towers was a Sybarite,* though by no means an idle one. He was lingering over his last cup of tea, surrounded by an ocean of newspapers, through which he had been swimming, when John Bold's card was brought in by his tiger.* This tiger never knew that his master was at home, though he often knew that he was not, and thus Tom Towers was never invaded but by his own consent. On this occasion, after twisting the card twice in his fingers, he signified to his attendant imp that he was visible; and the inner door was unbolted, and our friend announced.

I have before said that he of the *Jupiter* and John Bold were intimate. There was no very great difference in their ages, for Towers was still considerably under forty; and when Bold had been attending the London hospitals, Towers, who was not then the great man that he had since become, had been much with him. Then they had often discussed together the objects of their ambition and future prospects. Then Tom Towers was struggling hard to maintain himself, as a briefless barrister,* by short-hand reporting for any of the papers that would engage him; then he had not dared to dream of writing leaders for the *Jupiter*, or canvassing the conduct of Cabinet ministers. Things had altered since that time. The briefless barrister was still briefless, but he now despised briefs. Could he have been sure of a judge's seat, he would hardly have left his present career. It is true he wore no ermine,* bore no outward marks of a world's respect; but with what a load of inward importance was he charged! It is true his name appeared in no large capitals; on no wall was chalked up 'Tom Towers for ever;'—'Freedom of the Press and Tom Towers;' but what member of Parliament had half his power? It is true that in far-off provinces men did not talk daily of Tom Towers, but they read the *Jupiter*, and acknowledged that without the *Jupiter* life was not worth having. This kind of hidden but still conscious glory* suited the nature of the man. He loved to sit silent in a corner of his club and listen to the loud chattering of politicians, and to think how they all were in his power;—how he could smite the loudest of them, were it worth his while to raise his pen for such a purpose. He loved to watch the great men of whom he daily wrote, and flatter himself that he was greater than any of them. Each of them was responsible to his country, each of them must answer if inquired into, each of them must endure abuse with good humour, and insolence without anger. But to whom was he, Tom Towers, responsible? No one could insult him; no one could inquire into him. He could speak out withering words, and no one could answer him. Ministers courted him, though perhaps they knew not his name; bishops feared him; judges doubted their own verdicts unless he confirmed them; and generals, in their councils of war, did not consider more deeply what the enemy would do, than what the *Jupiter* would say. Tom Towers never boasted of the *Jupiter*; he scarcely ever named the paper even to the most intimate of his friends; he did not even wish to be spoken of as connected with it; but he did not the less value his privileges, or think the less of his own importance. It is probable that Tom Towers considered himself the most powerful man in Europe; and so he walked on from day to day, studiously striving to look a man, but knowing within his breast that he was a god.

## CHAPTER 15

### TOM TOWERS, DR ANTICANT, AND MR SENTIMENT

'Ah, Bold! how are you? You haven't breakfasted?'

'Oh yes, hours ago. And how are you?'

When one Esquimaux meets another, do the two, as an invariable rule, ask after each other's health? Is it inherent in all human nature to make this obliging inquiry? Did any reader of this tale ever meet any friend or acquaintance without asking some such question, and did any one ever listen to the reply? Sometimes a studiously courteous questioner will show so much thought in the matter as to answer it himself, by declaring that had he looked at you he needn't have asked; meaning thereby to signify that you are an absolute personification of health. But such persons are only those who premeditate small effects.

'I suppose you're busy?' inquired Bold.

'Why, yes, rather;—or I should say rather not. If I have a leisure hour in the day, this is it.'

'I want to ask you if you can oblige me in a certain matter.'

Towers understood in a moment, from the tone of his friend's voice, that the certain matter referred to the newspaper. He smiled, and nodded his head, but made no promise.

'You know this lawsuit that I've been engaged in,' said Bold.

Tom Towers intimated that he was aware of the action which was pending about the hospital.

'Well, I've abandoned it.'

Tom Towers merely raised his eyebrows, thrust his hands into his trousers' pockets, and waited for his friend to proceed.

'Yes, I've given it up. I needn't trouble you with all the history; but the fact is that the conduct of Mr Harding——. Mr Harding is the——.'

'Oh yes, the master of the place; the man who takes all the money and does nothing,' said Tom Towers, interrupting him.

'Well; I don't know about that; but his conduct in the matter has been so excellent, so little selfish, so open, that I cannot proceed in the matter to his detriment.' Bold's heart misgave him as to Eleanor as he said this; and yet he felt that what he said was not untrue. 'I think nothing should now be done till the wardenship be vacant.'

'And be again filled,' said Towers, 'as it certainly would, before any one heard of the vacancy; and the same objection would again exist. It's an old story that of the vested rights of the incumbent;* but suppose the incumbent has only a vested wrong, and that the poor of the town have a vested right, if they only knew how to get at it! Is not that something the case here?'

Bold could not deny it, but thought it was one of those cases which required a good deal of management before any real good could be done. It was a pity that he had not considered this before he crept into the lion's mouth, in the shape of an attorney's office. 'It will cost you a good deal, I fear,' said Towers.

'A few hundreds,' said Bold—'perhaps three hundred. I can't help that, and am prepared for it.'

'That's philosophical. It's quite refreshing to hear a man talking of his hundreds in so purely indifferent a manner. But I'm sorry you are giving the matter up. It injures a man to commence a thing of this kind, and not carry it through. Have you seen that?' and he threw a small pamphlet across the table, which was all but damp from the press.

Bold had not seen it nor heard of it; but he was well acquainted with the author of it,—a gentleman whose pamphlets, condemnatory of all things in these modern days, had been a good deal talked about of late.

Dr Pessimist Anticant* was a Scotchman, who had passed a great portion of his early days in Germany; he had studied there with much effect, and had learnt to look with German subtilty into the root of things, and to examine for himself their intrinsic worth and worthlessness. No man ever resolved more bravely than he to accept as good nothing that was evil; to banish from him as evil nothing that was good. 'Tis a pity that he should not have recognised the fact, that in this world no good is unalloyed, and that there is but little evil that has not in it some seed of what is goodly.

Returning from Germany, he had astonished the reading public by the vigour of his thoughts, put forth in the quaintest language. He cannot write English, said the critics. No matter, said the public. We can read what he does write, and that without yawning. And so Dr Pessimist Anticant became popular. Popularity spoilt him for all further real use, as it has done many another. While, with some diffidence, he confined his objurgations to the occasional follies or short-comings of mankind; while he ridiculed the energy of the squire devoted to the slaughter of partridges, or the mistake of some noble patron who turned a poet into a gauger of beer-barrels, it was all well. We were glad to be told our faults and to look forward to the coming millennium, when all men, having sufficiently studied the works of Dr Anticant, would become truthful and energetic. But the doctor mistook the signs of the times and the minds of men, instituted himself censor of things in general, and began the great task of reprobating everything and everybody, without further promise of any millennium at all. This was not so well; and, to tell the truth, our author did not succeed in his undertaking. His theories were all beautiful, and the code of morals that he taught us was certainly an improvement on the practices of the age. We all of us could, and many of us did, learn much from the doctor while he chose to remain vague, mysterious, and cloudy. But when he became practical, the charm was gone.

His allusion to the poet and the partridges was received very well. 'Oh, my poor brother,' said he, 'slaughtered partridges a score of brace to each gun, and poets gauging ale-barrels, with sixty pounds

a year, at Dumfries,* are not the signs of a great era!—perhaps of
the smallest possible era yet written of. Whatever economies we pur-
sue, political or other, let us see at once that this is the maddest of
the uneconomic. Partridges killed by our land magnates at, shall we
say, a guinea a head, to be retailed in Leadenhall* at one shilling and
ninepence, with one poacher in limbo* for every fifty birds! our poet,
maker, creator, gauging ale, and that badly, with no leisure for making
or creating;—only a little leisure for drinking, and such like beer-
barrel avocations! Truly, a cutting of blocks with fine razors while we
scrape our chins so uncomfortably with rusty knives! Oh, my political economist, master of supply and demand, division of labour and
high pressure,—oh, my loud-speaking friend, tell me, if so much be
in you, what is the demand for poets in these kingdoms of Queen
Victoria, and what the vouchsafed supply?'

This was all very well. This gave us some hope. We might do better with our next poet, when we got one; and though the partridges
might not be abandoned, something could perhaps be done as to
the poachers. We were unwilling, however, to take lessons in politics
from so misty a professor; and when he came to tell us that the heroes
of Westminster were naught, we began to think that he had written
enough. His attack upon despatch boxes* was not thought to have
much in it; but as it is short, the doctor shall again be allowed to speak
his sentiments.

'Could utmost ingenuity in the management of red tape avail anything to men lying gasping,—we may say, all but dead; could despatch boxes with never-so-much velvet lining and Chubb's patent, be
of comfort to a people in extremis, I also, with so many others, would,
with parched tongue, call on the name of Lord John Russell; or, my
brother, at your advice, on Lord Aberdeen; or, my cousin, on Lord
Derby, at yours; being, with my parched tongue, indifferent to such
matters. 'Tis all one. Oh, Derby! Oh, Gladstone! Oh, Palmerston!
Oh, Lord John! Each comes running with serene face and despatch
box. Vain physicians! Though there were hosts of such, no despatch
box will cure this disorder! What! are there other doctors' new names,
disciples who have not yet burdened their souls with tape? Well, let us
call again. Oh Disraeli, great oppositionist, man of the bitter brow!
or, Oh, Molesworth,* great reformer, thou who promisest Utopia.
They come; each with that serene face, and each,—alas, me! alas, my
country!—each with a despatch box!

'Oh, the serenity of Downing Street!

'My brothers, when hope was over on the battle field, when no dimmest chance of victory remained, the ancient Roman could hide his face within his toga, and die gracefully. Can you and I do so now? If so, 'twere best for us. If not, oh my brothers, we must die disgracefully, for hope of life and victory I see none left to us in this world below. I for one cannot trust much to serene face and despatch box!'

There might be truth in this, there might be depth of reasoning; but Englishmen did not see enough in the argument to induce them to withdraw their confidence from the present arrangements of the government, and Dr Anticant's monthly pamphlet on the decay of the world did not receive so much attention as his earlier works. He did not confine himself to politics in these publications, but roamed at large over all matters of public interest, and found everything bad. According to him nobody was true, and not only nobody, but nothing. A man could not take off his hat to a lady without telling a lie. The lady would lie again in smiling. The ruffles of the gentleman's shirt would be fraught with deceit, and the lady's flounces full of falsehood. Was ever anything more severe than that attack of his on chip bonnets, or the anathemas with which he endeavoured to dust the powder out of the bishops' wigs?*

The pamphlet which Tom Towers now pushed across the table was entitled *Modern Charity*, and was written with the view of proving how much in the way of charity was done by our predecessors;— how little by the present age; and it ended by a comparison between ancient and modern times, very little to the credit of the latter.

'Look at this,' said Towers, getting up and turning over the pages of the pamphlet, and pointing to a passage near the end. 'Your friend the warden, who is so little selfish, won't like that, I fear.' Bold read as follows:—

'Heavens, what a sight! Let us with eyes wide open see the godly man of four centuries since, the man of the dark ages;—let us see how he does his godlike work, and, again, how the godly man of these latter days does his.

'Shall we say that the former one is walking painfully through the world, regarding, as a prudent man, his worldly work, prospering in it as a diligent man will prosper, but always with an eye to that better treasure* to which thieves do not creep in? Is there not much nobility in that old man, as, leaning on his oaken staff, he walks down the

high street of his native town, and receives from all courteous saluta-
tion and acknowledgment of his worth? A noble old man, my august
inhabitants of Belgrave Square* and such like vicinity,—a very noble
old man, though employed no better than in the wholesale carding of
wool.

'This carding of wool, however, did in those days bring with it
much profit, so that our ancient friend, when dying, was declared, in
whatever slang then prevailed, to cut up exceeding well. For sons and
daughters there was ample sustenance, with assistance of due industry; for friends and relatives some relief for grief at this great loss;—
for aged dependants comfort in declining years. This was much for
one old man to get done in that dark fifteenth century. But this was
not all. Coming generations of poor wool-carders should bless the
name of this rich one; and a hospital should be founded and endowed
with his wealth for the feeding of such of the trade as could not, by
diligent carding, any longer duly feed themselves.

' 'Twas thus that an old man in the fifteenth century did his godlike
work to the best of his power, and not ignobly, as appears to me.

'We will now take our godly man of latter days. He shall no longer
be a wool-carder, for such are not now men of mark. We will suppose him to be one of the best of the good,—one who has lacked no
opportunities. Our old friend was, after all, but illiterate. Our modern
friend shall be a man educated in all seemly knowledge; he shall, in
short, be that blessed being,—a clergyman of the Church of England!

'And now, in what perfectest manner does he in this lower world get
his godlike work done and put out of hand? Heavens! in the strangest
of manners. Oh, my brother! in a manner not at all to be believed but
by the most minute testimony of eyesight. He does it by the magni-
tude of his appetite,—by the power of his gorge! His only occupation is to swallow the bread prepared with so much anxious care for
these impoverished carders of wool,—that, and to sing indifferently
through his nose once in the week some psalm more or less long,—
the shorter the better, we should be inclined to say.

'Oh, my civilised friends!—great Britons that never will be
slaves,*—men advanced to infinite state of freedom and knowledge of
good and evil; tell me, will you, what becoming monument* you will
erect to an highly-educated clergyman of the Church of England?'

Bold certainly thought that his friend would not like that. He
could not conceive anything that he would like less than this. To what

a world of toil and trouble* had he, Bold, given rise by his indiscreet attack upon the hospital!

'You see,' said Towers, 'that this affair has been much talked of, and the public are with you. I am sorry you should give the matter up. Have you seen the first number of the *Almshouse*?'

No; Bold had not seen the *Almshouse*. He had seen advertisements of Mr Popular Sentiment's* new novel of that name, but had in no way connected it with Barchester Hospital, and had never thought a moment on the subject.

'It's a direct attack on the whole system,' said Towers. 'It'll go a long way to put down Rochester, and Barchester, and Dulwich,* and St Cross, and all such hotbeds of peculation. It's very clear that Sentiment has been down to Barchester, and got up the whole story there. Indeed, I thought he must have had it all from you. It's very well done, as you'll see. His first numbers always are.'

Bold declared that Mr Sentiment had got nothing from him, and that he was deeply grieved to find that the case had become so notorious. 'The fire has gone too far to be quenched,' said Towers; 'the building must go now; and as the timbers are all rotten, why, I should be inclined to say, the sooner the better. I expected to see you get some éclat* in the matter.'

This was all wormwood to Bold. He had done enough to make his friend the warden miserable for life, and had then backed out just when the success of his project was sufficient to make the question one of real interest. How weakly he had managed his business! He had already done the harm, and then stayed his hand when the good which he had in view was to be commenced. How delightful would it have been to have employed all his energy in such a cause,—to have been backed by the *Jupiter*, and written up to by two of the most popular authors of the day! The idea opened a vista into the very world in which he wished to live. To what might it not have given rise? what delightful intimacies,—what public praise,—to what Athenian banquets and rich flavour of Attic salt?*

This, however, was now past hope. He had pledged himself to abandon the cause; and could he have forgotten the pledge, he had gone too far to retreat. He was now, this moment, sitting in Tom Towers' room with the object of deprecating any further articles in the *Jupiter*, and, greatly as he disliked the job, his petition to that effect must be made.

'I couldn't continue it,' said he, 'because I found I was in the wrong.'

Tom Towers shrugged his shoulders. How could a successful man be in the wrong! 'In that case,' said he, 'of course you must abandon it.'

'And I called this morning to ask you also to abandon it,' said Bold.

'To ask me,' said Tom Towers with the most placid of smiles, and a consummate look of gentle surprise, as though Tom Towers was well aware that he of all men was the last to meddle in such matters.

'Yes,' said Bold, almost trembling with hesitation. 'The *Jupiter*, you know, has taken the matter up very strongly. Mr Harding has felt what it has said deeply; and I thought that if I could explain to you that he personally has not been to blame, these articles might be discontinued.'

How calmly impassive was Tom Towers' face, as this innocent little proposition was made! Had Bold addressed himself to the doorposts in Mount Olympus, they would have shown as much outward sign of assent or dissent. His quiescence was quite admirable. His discretion certainly more than human.

'My dear fellow,' said he, when Bold had quite done speaking, 'I really cannot answer for the *Jupiter*.'

'But if you saw that these articles were unjust, I think that you would endeavour to put a stop to them. Of course nobody doubts that you could, if you chose.'

'Nobody and everybody are always very kind, but unfortunately are generally very wrong.'

'Come, come, Towers,' said Bold, plucking up his courage, and remembering that for Eleanor's sake he was bound to make his best exertion; 'I have no doubt in my own mind but that you wrote the articles yourself. And very well written they were. It will be a great favour if you will in future abstain from any personal allusion to poor Harding.'

'My dear Bold,' said Tom Towers, 'I have a sincere regard for you. I have known you for many years, and value your friendship. I hope you will let me explain to you, without offence, that none who are connected with the public press can with propriety listen to interference.'

'Interference!' said Bold, 'I don't want to interfere.'

'Ah, my dear fellow, but you do. What else is it? You think that I am able to keep certain remarks out of a newspaper. Your information is probably incorrect, as most public gossip on such subjects is; but, at any rate, you think I have such power; and you ask me to use it. Now that is interference.'

'Well, if you choose to call it so.'

'And now suppose for a moment that I had this power, and used it as you wish. Isn't it clear that it would be a great abuse? Certain men are employed in writing for the public press; and if they are induced either to write or to abstain from writing by private motives, surely the public press would soon be of little value. Look at the recognised worth of different newspapers, and see if it does not mainly depend on the assurance which the public feel that such a paper is, or is not, independent. You alluded to the *Jupiter*. Surely you cannot but see that the weight of the *Jupiter* is too great to be moved by any private request, even though it should be made to a much more influential person than myself. You've only to think of this, and you'll see that I am right.'

The discretion of Tom Towers was boundless. There was no contradicting what he said, no arguing against such propositions. He took such high ground that there was no getting up on to it. 'The public is defrauded,' said he, 'whenever private considerations are allowed to have weight.' Quite true, thou greatest oracle of the middle of the nineteenth century; thou sententious proclaimer of the purity of the press. The public is defrauded when it is purposely misled. Poor public! How often is it misled! Against what a world of fraud has it to contend!

Bold took his leave, and got out of the room as quickly as he could, inwardly denouncing his friend Tom Towers as a prig and a humbug. 'I know he wrote those articles,' said Bold to himself. 'I know he got his information from me. He was ready enough to take my word for gospel when it suited his own views, and to set Mr Harding up before the public as an impostor on no other testimony than my chance conversation; but when I offer him real evidence opposed to his own views, he tells me that private motives are detrimental to public justice! Confound his arrogance! What is any public question but a conglomeration of private interests? What is any newspaper article but an expression of the views taken by one side? Truth! It takes an age to ascertain the truth of any question! The idea of Tom Towers talking of public motives and purity of purpose! Why; it wouldn't give him a moment's uneasiness to change his politics to-morrow, if the paper required it.'

Such were John Bold's inward exclamations as he made his way out of the quiet labyrinth of the Temple. And yet there was no position of worldly power so coveted in Bold's ambition as that held by the man of whom he was thinking. It was the impregnability of the place which made Bold so angry with the possessor of it, and it was the same quality which made it appear so desirable.

Passing into the Strand, he saw in a bookseller's window an announcement of the first number of the *Almshouse*; so he purchased a copy, and hurrying back to his lodgings, proceeded to ascertain what Mr Popular Sentiment had to say to the public on the subject which had lately occupied so much of his own attention.

In former times great objects were attained by great work. When evils were to be reformed, reformers set about their heavy task with grave decorum and laborious argument. An age was occupied in proving a grievance, and philosophical researches were printed in folio pages, which it took a life to write, and an eternity to read. We get on now with a lighter step, and quicker. 'Ridiculum acri Fortius et melius magnas plerumque secat res.'* Ridicule is found to be more convincing than argument, imaginary agonies touch more than true sorrows, and monthly novels convince, when learned quartos fail to do so. If the world is to be set right, the work will be done by shilling numbers.*

Of all such reformers Mr Sentiment is the most powerful. It is incredible the number of evil practices he has put down. It is to be feared he will soon lack subjects, and that when he has made the working classes comfortable, and got bitter beer put into proper-sized pint bottles, there will be nothing left for him to do. Mr Sentiment is certainly a very powerful man, and perhaps not the less so that his good poor people are so very good; his hard rich people so very hard; and the genuinely honest so very honest. Namby-pamby* in these days is not thrown away if it be introduced in the proper quarters. Divine peeresses are no longer interesting, though possessed of every virtue; but a pattern peasant or an immaculate manufacturing hero* may talk as much twaddle as one of Mrs Ratcliffe's heroines,* and still be listened to. Perhaps, however, Mr Sentiment's great attraction is in his second-rate characters. If his heroes and heroines walk upon stilts, as heroes and heroines, I fear, ever must, their attendant satellites are as natural as though one met them in the street. They walk and talk like men and women, and live among our friends a rattling, lively life; yes, live, and will live till the names of their calling shall be forgotten in their own, and Buckett and Mrs Gamp* will be the only words left to us to signify a detective police officer or a monthly nurse.

The *Almshouse* opened with a scene in a clergyman's house. Every luxury to be purchased by wealth was described as being there. All the appearances of household indulgence generally found amongst the most self-indulgent of the rich were crowded into this abode. Here the reader was introduced to the demon of the book, the Mephistopheles* of the drama. What story was ever written without a demon? What novel, what history, what work of any sort, what world, would be perfect without existing principles both of good and evil? The demon of the *Almshouse* was the clerical owner of this comfortable abode. He was a man well stricken in years, but still strong to do evil. He was one who looked cruelly out of a hot, passionate, bloodshot eye; who had a huge red nose with a carbuncle, thick lips, and a great double, flabby chin, which swelled out into solid substance, like a turkey cock's comb, when sudden anger inspired him. He had a hot, furrowed, low brow, from which a few grizzled hairs were not yet rubbed off by the friction of his handkerchief. He wore a loose unstarched white handkerchief, black, loose, ill-made clothes, and huge loose shoes, adapted to many corns and various bunions. His husky voice told tales of much daily port wine, and his language was not so decorous as became a clergyman. Such was the master of Mr Sentiment's *Almshous*e. He was a widower, but at present accompanied by two daughters, and a thin and somewhat insipid curate. One of the young ladies was devoted to her father and the fashionable world, and she of course was the favourite. The other was equally addicted to Puseyism* and the curate.

The second chapter of course introduced the reader to the more especial inmates of the hospital. Here were discovered eight old men; and it was given to be understood that four vacancies remained unfilled, through the perverse ill-nature of the clerical gentleman with the double chin. The state of these eight paupers was touchingly dreadful. Sixpence-farthing a day had been sufficient for their diet when the almshouse was founded; and on sixpence-farthing a-day were they still doomed to starve, though food was four times as dear, and money four times as plentiful. It was shocking to find how the conversation of these eight starved old men in their dormitory shamed that of the clergyman's family in his rich drawing-room. The absolute words they uttered were not perhaps spoken in the purest English, and it might be difficult to distinguish from their dialect* to what part of the country they belonged. The beauty of the sentiment,

however, amply atoned for the imperfection of the language; and it
was really a pity that these eight old men could not be sent through
the country as moral missionaries, instead of being immured and
starved in that wretched almshouse.

Bold finished the number; and as he threw it aside, he thought
that that at least had no direct appliance to Mr Harding, and that the
absurdly strong colouring of the picture would disenable the work
from doing either good or harm. He was wrong. The artist who paints
for the million must use glaring colours, as no one knew better than
Mr Sentiment when he described the inhabitants of his almshouse;
and the radical reform which has now swept over such establishments
has owed more to the twenty numbers of Mr Sentiment's novel, than
to all the true complaints which have escaped from the public for the
last half century.

## CHAPTER 16

### A LONG DAY IN LONDON

THE warden had to make use of all his very moderate powers of
intrigue to give his son-in-law the slip, and get out of Barchester
without being stopped on his road. No schoolboy ever ran away
from school with more precaution and more dread of detection; no
convict slipping down from a prison wall, ever feared to see the
gaolor more entirely than Mr Harding did to see his son-in-law, as
he drove up in the pony carriage to the railway station, on the morning of his escape to London. It was mean all this, and he knew that it
was mean; but, for the life of him, he could not help it. Had he met
the archdeacon he certainly would have lacked the courage to explain
the purpose which was carrying him up to London;—to explain it
in full.*

The evening before he went, however, he wrote a note to the archdeacon, explaining something. He said that he should start on the
morrow on his journey; that it was his intention to see the attorney-
general if possible, and to decide on his future plans in accordance
with what he heard from that gentleman; he excused himself for giving Dr Grantly no earlier notice, by stating that his resolve was very
sudden; and having entrusted this note to Eleanor, with the perfect,

though not expressed, understanding that it was to be sent over to Plumstead Episcopi without haste, he took his departure.

He also prepared and carried with him a note for Sir Abraham Haphazard, in which he stated his name, explaining that he was the defendant in the case of 'The Queen on behalf of the Wool-carders of Barchester *v.* Trustees under the will of the late John Hiram,' for so was the suit denominated, and begged the illustrious and learned gentleman to vouchsafe to him ten minutes' audience at any hour on the next day. Mr Harding calculated that for that one day he was safe; his son-in-law, he had no doubt, would arrive in town by an early train, but not early enough to reach the truant till he should have escaped from his hotel after breakfast; and, could he thus manage to see the lawyer on that very day, the deed might be done before the archdeacon could interfere.

On his arrival in town the warden drove, as was his wont, to the Chapter Hotel and Coffee House,* near St Paul's. His visits to London of late had not been frequent; but in those happy days when Harding's Church Music was going through the press, he had been often there; and as the publisher's house was in Paternoster Row,* and the printer's press in Fleet Street, the Chapter Hotel and Coffee House had been convenient. It was a quiet, sombre, clerical house, beseeming such a man as the warden, and thus he afterwards frequented it. Had he dared, he would on this occasion have gone elsewhere to throw the archdeacon further off the scent; but he did not know what violent steps his son-in-law might take for his recovery if he were not found at his usual haunt, and he deemed it not prudent to make himself the object of a hunt through London.

Arrived at his inn, he ordered dinner, and went forth to the attorney-general's chambers. There he learnt that Sir Abraham was in Court, and would not probably return that day. He would go direct from Court to the House;* all appointments were, as a rule, made at the chambers; the clerk could by no means promise an interview for the next day; was able, on the other hand, to say that such interview was, he thought, impossible; but that Sir Abraham would certainly be at the House in the course of the night, where an answer from himself might possibly be elicited.

To the House Mr Harding went, and left his note, not finding Sir Abraham there. He added a most piteous entreaty that he might be favoured with an answer that evening, for which he would return. He then journeyed back sadly to the Chapter Coffee House, digesting his great thoughts, as best he might, in a clattering omnibus, wedged in between a wet old lady and a journeyman glazier returning from his work with his tools in his lap. In melancholy solitude he discussed his mutton chop and pint of port. What is there in this world more melancholy than such a dinner? A dinner, though eaten alone, in a country hotel may be worthy of some energy; the waiter, if you are known, will make much of you; the landlord will make you a bow and perhaps put the fish on the table; if you ring you are attended to, and there is some life about it. A dinner at a London eating-house is also lively enough, if it have no other attraction. There is plenty of noise and stir about it, and the rapid whirl of voices and rattle of dishes disperses sadness. But a solitary dinner in an old, respectable, sombre, solid London inn, where nothing makes any noise but the old waiter's creaking shoes; where one plate slowly goes and another slowly comes without a sound; where the two or three guests would as soon think of knocking each other down as of talking to one another; where the servants whisper, and the whole household is disturbed if an order be given above the voice,—what can be more melancholy than a mutton chop and a pint of port in such a place?

Having gone through this Mr Harding got into another omnibus, and again returned to the House. Yes, Sir Abraham was there, and was that moment on his legs, fighting eagerly for the hundred and seventh clause of the Convent Custody Bill. Mr Harding's note had been delivered to him; and if Mr Harding would wait some two or three hours, Sir Abraham could be asked whether there was any answer. The House was not full, and perhaps Mr Harding might get admittance into the Strangers' Gallery, which admission, with the help of five shillings,* Mr Harding was able to effect.

This bill of Sir Abraham's had been read a second time and passed into committee. A hundred and six clauses had already been discussed, and had occupied only four mornings and five evening sittings. Nine of the hundred and six clauses were passed, fifty-five were withdrawn by consent, fourteen had been altered so as to mean the reverse of the original proposition, eleven had been postponed for further consideration, and seventeen had been directly negatived. The hundred and seventh ordered the bodily searching of nuns for Jesuitical symbols by aged clergymen, and was considered to be the real mainstay of the whole bill. No intention had ever existed to pass such a law as that proposed, but the Government did not intend to abandon it till their object was fully attained by the discussion of this clause. It was known that it would be insisted on with terrible vehemence by Protestant Irish members, and as vehemently denounced by the Roman Catholic; and it was justly considered that no further union between the parties would be possible after such a battle. The innocent Irish fell into the trap as they always do, and whisky and poplins became a drug in the market.*

A florid-faced gentleman with a nice head of hair, from the south of Ireland, had succeeded in catching the speaker's eye by the time that Mr Harding had got into the gallery, and was denouncing the proposed sacrilege, his whole face glowing with a fine theatrical frenzy.

'And is this a Christian country?' said he. (Loud cheers; counter cheers from the ministerial benches. 'Some doubt as to that,' from a voice below the gangway.) 'No, it can be no Christian country, in which the head of the bar, the lagal adviser (loud laughter and cheers)—yes, I say the lagal adviser of the crown (great cheers and laughter)—can stand up in his seat in this house (prolonged cheers and laughter), and attempt to lagalise indacent assaults on the bodies of religious ladies.' (Deafening cheers and laughter, which were prolonged till the honourable member resumed his seat.)

When Mr Harding had listened to this and much more of the same kind for about three hours, he returned to the door of the house, and received back from the messenger his own note, with the following words scrawled in pencil on the back of it;—'To-morrow, 10 p.m.—my chambers. A. H.'

He was so far successful. But 10 p.m.! What an hour Sir Abraham had named for a legal interview! Mr Harding felt perfectly sure that long before that Dr Grantly would be in London. Dr Grantly could not, however, know that this interview had been arranged, nor could he learn it unless he managed to get hold of Sir Abraham before that hour; and as this was very improbable, Mr Harding determined to start from his hotel early, merely leaving word that he should dine out, and unless luck were much against him, he might still escape the archdeacon till his return from the attorney-general's chambers.

He was at breakfast at nine, and for the twentieth time consulted his 'Bradshaw,'* to see at what earliest hour Dr Grantly could arrive from Barchester. As he examined the columns, he was nearly petrified by the reflection that perhaps the archdeacon might come up by

the mail-train! His heart sank within him at the horrid idea, and for
a moment he felt himself dragged back to Barchester without accomp-
lishing any portion of his object. Then he remembered that had Dr
Grantly done so, he would have been in the hotel, looking for him
long since.

'Waiter,' said he, timidly.

The waiter approached, creaking in his shoes, but voiceless.

'Did any gentleman,—a clergyman, arrive here by the night
mail-train?'

'No, sir, not one,' whispered the waiter, putting his mouth nearly
close to the warden's ear.

Mr Harding was reassured.

'Waiter,' said he again, and the waiter again creaked up. 'If any one
calls for me, I am going to dine out, and shall return about eleven
o'clock.'

The waiter nodded, but did not this time vouchsafe any reply; and
Mr Harding, taking up his hat, proceeded out to pass a long day in the
best way he could, somewhere out of sight of the archdeacon.

'Bradshaw' had told him twenty times that Dr Grantly could not
be at the Paddington station till 2 p.m., and our poor friend might
therefore have trusted to the shelter of the hotel for some hours
longer with perfect safety. But he was nervous. There was no knowing
what steps the archdeacon might take for his apprehension. A message by electric telegraph might desire the landlord of the hotel to set
a watch upon him; some letter might come which he might find himself unable to disobey; at any rate, he could not feel himself secure in
any place at which the archdeacon could expect to find him; and at 10
a.m. he started forth to spend twelve hours in London.

Mr Harding had friends in town had he chosen to seek them; but
he felt that he was in no humour for ordinary calls, and he did not
now wish to consult with any one as to the great step which he had
determined to take. As he had said to his daughter, no one knows
where the shoe pinches but the wearer. There are some points on
which no man can be contented to follow the advice of another,—
some subjects on which a man can consult his own conscience only.
Our warden had made up his mind that it was good for him at any cost
to get rid of this grievance. His daughter was the only person whose
concurrence appeared necessary to him, and she did concur with him
most heartily. Under such circumstances he would not, if he could

help it, consult any one further, till advice would be useless. Should the archdeacon catch him, indeed, there would be much advice, and much consultation of a kind not to be avoided; but he hoped better things; and as he felt that he could not now converse on indifferent subjects, he resolved to see no one till after his interview with the attorney-general.

He determined to take sanctuary in Westminster Abbey; he went, therefore, again thither in an omnibus, and finding that the doors were not open for morning service, he paid his twopence, and entered the Abbey as a sight-seer.* It occurred to him that he had no definite place of rest for the day, and that he should be absolutely worn out before his interview if he attempted to walk about from 10 a.m. to 10 p.m. So he sat himself down on a stone step, and gazed up at the figure of William Pitt,* who looks as though he had just entered the church for the first time in his life and was anything but pleased at finding himself there.

He had been sitting unmolested about twenty minutes when the verger* asked him whether he wouldn't like to walk round. Mr Harding didn't want to walk anywhere, and declined, merely observing that he was waiting for the morning service. The verger seeing that he was a clergyman, told him that the doors of the choir were now open, and showed him into a seat. This was a great point gained; the archdeacon would certainly not come to morning service at Westminster Abbey, even though he were in London; and here the warden could rest quietly, and, when the time came, duly say his prayers.

He longed to get up from his seat, and examine the music-books of the choristers, and the copy of the litany from which the service was chanted, to see how far the little details at Westminster corresponded with those at Barchester, and whether he thought his own voice would fill the church well from the Westminster precentor's seat. There would, however, be impropriety in such meddling, and he sat perfectly still, looking up at the noble roof, and guarding against the coming fatigues of the day.

By degrees two or three people entered; the very same damp old woman who had nearly obliterated him in the omnibus, or some other just like her; a couple of young ladies with their veils down, and gilt crosses conspicuous on their prayer-books; an old man on crutches; a party who were seeing the Abbey, and thought they might as well hear the service for their twopence, as opportunity served; and a young woman with her prayer-book done up in her handkerchief, who rushed in late, and, in her hurried entry, tumbled over one of the forms, and made such a noise that every one, even the officiating minor canon, was startled, and she herself was so frightened by the echo of her own catastrophe that she was nearly thrown into fits by the panic.

Mr Harding was not much edified by the manner of the service. The minor canon in question hurried in, somewhat late, in a surplice not in the neatest order, and was followed by a dozen choristers, who were also not as trim as they might have been. They all jostled into their places with a quick hurried step, and the service was soon commenced. Soon commenced and soon over,—for there was no music, and time was not unnecessarily lost in the chanting.* On the whole Mr Harding was of opinion that things were managed better at Barchester, though even there he knew that there was room for improvement.

It appears to us a question whether any clergyman can go through our church service with decorum, morning after morning, in an immense building, surrounded by not more than a dozen listeners.* The best actors cannot act well before empty benches, and though there is, of course, a higher motive in one case than the other, still even the best of clergymen cannot but be influenced by their audience. To expect that a duty should be well done under such circumstances, would be to require from human nature more than human power.

When the two ladies with the gilt crosses, the old man with his crutches, and the still palpitating housemaid were going, Mr Harding found himself obliged to go too. The verger stood in his way, and looked at him and looked at the door, and so he went. But he returned again in a few minutes, and re-entered with another twopence. There was no other sanctuary so good for him.

As he walked slowly down the nave, and then up one aisle, and then again down the nave and up the other aisle, he tried to think gravely of the step he was about to take. He was going to give up eight hundred a year voluntarily; and doom himself to live for the rest of his life on about a hundred and fifty. He knew that he had hitherto failed to realise this fact as he ought to do. Could he maintain his own independence and support his daughter on a hundred and fifty pounds a year without being a burden on any one? His son-in-law was rich, but nothing could induce him to lean on his son-in-law after acting, as he intended to do, in direct opposition to his son-in-law's counsel. The bishop was rich, but he was about to throw away the bishop's best gift, and that in a manner to injure materially the patronage of the giver. He could neither expect nor accept anything further from the bishop. There would be not only no merit, but positive disgrace, in giving up his wardenship, if he were not prepared to meet the world without it. Yes; he must from this time forward limit all his human wishes for himself and his daughter to the poor extent of so limited an income. He knew he had not thought sufficiently of this, that he had been carried away by enthusiasm, and had hitherto not brought home to himself the full reality of his position.

He thought most about his daughter, naturally. It was true that she was engaged, and he knew enough of his proposed son-in-law to be sure that his own altered circumstances would make no obstacle to such a marriage; nay, he was sure that the very fact of his poverty would induce Bold more anxiously to press the matter; but he disliked counting on Bold in this emergency, brought on, as it had been, by his doing. He did not like saying to himself,—Bold has turned me out of my house and income, and, therefore, he must relieve me of my daughter; he preferred reckoning on Eleanor as the companion of his poverty and exile,—as the sharer of his small income.

Some modest provision for his daughter had been long since made. His life was insured for three thousand pounds, and this sum was to go to Eleanor. The archdeacon, for some years past, had paid the premium, and had secured himself by the immediate possession of a small property which was to have gone to Mrs Grantly after her father's death. This matter, therefore, had been taken out of the warden's hands long since, as, indeed, had all the business transactions of his family, and his anxiety was, therefore, confined to his own life income.

Yes. A hundred and fifty per annum was very small, but still it might suffice. But how was he to chant the litany at the cathedral on Sunday mornings, and get the service done at Crabtree Parva? True, Crabtree Church was not quite a mile and a half from the cathedral; but he could not be in two places at once? Crabtree was a small village, and afternoon service might suffice, but still this went against his conscience. It was not right that his parishioners should be robbed of any of their privileges on account of his poverty. He might, to be sure, make some arrangements for doing weekday service at the cathedral;

but he had chanted the litany at Barchester so long, and had a conscious feeling that he did it so well, that he was unwilling to give up the duty.

Thinking of such things, turning over in his own mind together small desires and grave duties, but never hesitating for a moment as to the necessity of leaving the hospital, Mr Harding walked up and down the Abbey, or sat still meditating on the same stone step, hour after hour. One verger went and another came, but they did not disturb him. Every now and then they crept up and looked at him, but they did so with a reverential stare, and, on the whole, Mr Harding found his retreat well chosen. About four o'clock his comfort was disturbed by an enemy in the shape of hunger. It was necessary that he should dine, and it was clear that he could not dine in the Abbey. So he left his sanctuary not willingly, and betook himself to the neighbourhood of the Strand to look for food.

His eyes had become so accustomed to the gloom of the church, that they were dazed when he got out into the full light of day, and he felt confused and ashamed of himself, as though people were staring at him. He hurried along, still in dread of the archdeacon, till he came to Charing Cross,* and then remembered that in one of his passages through the Strand he had seen the words 'Chops and Steaks' on a placard in a shop window. He remembered the shop distinctly. It was next door to a trunk-seller's, and there was a cigar shop on the other side. He couldn't go to his hotel for dinner, which to him hitherto was the only known mode of dining in London at his own expense; and, therefore, he would get a steak at the shop in the Strand. Archdeacon Grantly would certainly not come to such a place for his dinner.

He found the house easily,—just as he had observed it, between the trunks and the cigars. He was rather daunted by the huge quantity of fish which he saw in the window. There were barrels of oysters, hecatombs of lobsters, a few tremendous-looking crabs, and a tub full of pickled salmon. Not, however, being aware of any connection between shell-fish and iniquity, he entered, and modestly asked a slatternly woman, who was picking oysters out of a great watery reservoir, whether he could have a mutton chop and a potato.

The woman looked somewhat surprised, but answered in the affirmative, and a slipshod girl ushered him into a long back room, filled with boxes for the accommodation of parties, in one of which he took his seat. In a more miserably forlorn place he could not have found himself. The room smelt of fish, and sawdust, and stale tobacco smoke, with a slight taint of escaped gas. Everything was rough, and dirty, and disreputable. The cloth which they put before him was abominable. The knives and forks were bruised, and hacked, and filthy; and everything was impregnated with fish. He had one comfort, however. He was quite alone; there was no one there to look on his dismay; nor was it probable that any one would come to do so. It was a London supper-house. About one o'clock at night the place would be lively enough, but at the present time his seclusion was as deep as it had been in the Abbey.

In about half an hour the untidy girl, not yet dressed for her evening labours, brought him his chop and potatoes, and Mr Harding begged for a pint of sherry. He was impressed with an idea, which was generally prevalent a few years since, and is not yet wholly removed from the minds of men, that to order a dinner at any kind of inn, without also ordering a pint of wine for the benefit of the landlord, was a kind of fraud;—not punishable, indeed, by law, but not the less abominable on that account. Mr Harding remembered his coming poverty, and would willingly have saved his half-crown, but he thought he had no alternative; and he was soon put in possession of some horrid mixture procured from the neighbouring public-house.

His chop and potatoes, however, were eatable, and having got over as best he might the disgust created by the knives and forks, he contrived to swallow his dinner. He was not much disturbed. One young man, with pale face and watery fish-like eyes, wearing his hat ominously on one side, did come in and stare at him, and ask the girl, audibly enough, 'Who that old cock was;' but the annoyance went no further, and the warden was left seated on his wooden bench in peace, endeavouring to distinguish the different scents arising from lobsters, oysters, and salmon.

Unknowing as Mr Harding was in the ways of London, he felt that he had somehow selected an ineligible dining-house, and that he had better leave it. It was hardly five o'clock. How was he to pass the time till ten? Five miserable hours! He was already tired, and it was impossible that he should continue walking so long. He thought of getting into an omnibus, and going out to Fulham for the sake of coming back in another. This, however, would be weary work, and as he paid his bill to the woman in the shop, he asked her if there were any place near where he could get a cup of coffee. Though she did keep a shell-fish

supper-house, she was very civil, and directed him to the cigar divan*
on the other side of the street.

Mr Harding had not a much correcter notion of a cigar divan than
he had of a London dinner-house, but he was desperately in want of
rest, and went as he was directed. He thought he must have made some
mistake when he found himself in a cigar shop, but the man behind
the counter saw immediately that he was a stranger, and understood
what he wanted. 'One shilling, sir,—thank ye, sir,—cigar, sir?—ticket
for coffee, sir;—you'll only have to call the waiter. Up those stairs, if
you please, sir. Better take the cigar, sir,—you can always give it to
a friend you know. Well, sir, thank ye, sir;—as you are so good, I'll
smoke it myself.' And so Mr Harding ascended to the divan, with his
ticket for coffee, but minus the cigar.

The place seemed much more suitable to his requirements than the
room in which he had dined. There was, to be sure, a strong smell of
tobacco, to which he was not accustomed; but after the shell-fish, the
tobacco did not seem disagreeable. There were quantities of books,
and long rows of sofas. What on earth could be more luxurious than
a sofa, a book, and a cup of coffee? An old waiter came up to him,
with a couple of magazines and an evening paper. Was ever anything
so civil? Would he have a cup of coffee, or would he prefer sherbet?*
Sherbet! Was he absolutely in an Eastern divan, with the slight addition of all the London periodicals? He had, however, an idea that
sherbet should be drank sitting cross-legged, and as he was not quite
up to this, he ordered the coffee.

The coffee came, and was unexceptionable. Why, this divan was
a paradise! The civil old waiter suggested to him a game of chess.
Though a chess player he was not equal to this, so he declined, and,
putting up his weary legs on the sofa, leisurely sipped his coffee, and
turned over the pages of his Blackwood.* He might have been so
engaged for about an hour, for the old waiter enticed him to a second
cup of coffee, when a musical clock began to play. Mr Harding then
closed his magazine, keeping his place with his finger, and lay, listening with closed eyes to the clock. Soon the clock seemed to turn into
a violoncello, with piano accompaniments, and Mr Harding began to
fancy the old waiter was the Bishop of Barchester; he was inexpress-
ibly shocked that the bishop should have brought him his coffee with
his own hands; then Dr Grantly came in, with a basket full of lobsters,
which he would not be induced to leave down stairs in the kitchen;

and then the warden couldn't quite understand why so many people would smoke in the bishop's drawing-room; and so he fell fast asleep, and his dreams wandered away to his accustomed stall in Barchester Cathedral, and the twelve old men he was so soon about to leave for ever.

He was fatigued, and slept soundly for some time. Some sudden stop in the musical clock woke him at length, and he jumped up with a start, surprised to find the room quite full. It had been nearly empty when his nap began. With nervous anxiety he pulled out his watch, and found that it was half-past nine. He seized his hat, and, hurrying down stairs, started at a rapid pace for Lincoln's Inn.

It still wanted twenty minutes to ten when the warden found himself at the bottom of Sir Abraham's stairs, so he walked leisurely up and down the quiet inn to cool himself. It was a beautiful evening at the end of August. He had recovered from his fatigue. His sleep and the coffee had refreshed him, and he was surprised to find that he was absolutely enjoying himself, when the inn clock struck ten. The sound was hardly over before he knocked at Sir Abraham's door, and was informed by the clerk who received him that the great man would be with him immediately.

## CHAPTER 17

### SIR ABRAHAM HAPHAZARD

MR HARDING was shown into a comfortable inner sitting-room, looking more like a gentleman's book-room than a lawyer's chambers, and there waited for Sir Abraham. Nor was he kept waiting long. In ten or fifteen minutes he heard a clatter of voices speaking quickly in the passage, and then the attorney-general entered.

'Very sorry to keep you waiting, Mr Warden,' said Sir Abraham, shaking hands with him; 'and sorry, too, to name so disagreeable an hour; but your notice was short, and as you said to-day, I named the very earliest hour that was not disposed of.'

Mr Harding assured him that he was aware that it was he that should apologise.

Sir Abraham was a tall thin man, with hair prematurely grey, but bearing no other sign of age. He had a slight stoop, in his neck rather than his back, acquired by his constant habit of leaning forward as he addressed his various audiences. He might be fifty years old, and would have looked young for his age, had not constant work hardened his features, and given him the appearance of a machine with a mind. His face was full of intellect, but devoid of natural expression. You would say he was a man to use, and then have done with; a man to be sought for on great emergencies, but ill-adapted for ordinary services; a man whom you would ask to defend your property, but to whom you would be sorry to confide your love. He was bright as a diamond, and as cutting, and also as unimpressionable. He knew every one whom to know was an honour, but he was without a friend; he wanted none, however, and knew not the meaning of the word in other than its parliamentary sense. A friend! Had he not always been sufficient to himself, and now, at fifty, was it likely that he should trust another? He was married, indeed, and had children; but what time had he for the soft idleness of conjugal felicity? His working days or term times were occupied from his time of rising to the late hour at which he went to rest, and even his vacations were more full of labour than the busiest days of other men. He never quarrelled with his wife, but he never talked to her. He never had time to talk, he was so taken up with speaking. She, poor lady, was not unhappy; she had all that money could give her, she would probably live to be a peeress, and she really thought Sir Abraham the best of husbands.

Sir Abraham was a man of wit, and sparkled among the brightest at the dinner-tables of political grandees. Indeed, he always sparkled; whether in society, in the House of Commons, or the courts of law, coruscations flew from him; glittering sparkles, as from hot steel; but no heat; no cold heart was ever cheered by warmth from him, no unhappy soul ever dropped a portion of its burden at his door.

With him success alone was praiseworthy, and he knew none so successful as himself. No one had thrust him forward;* no powerful friends had pushed him along on his road to power. No; he was attorney-general, and would, in all human probability, be lord chancellor by sheer dint of his own industry and his own talent. Who else in all the world rose so high with so little help? A premier, indeed! Who had ever been premier without mighty friends? An archbishop! Yes, the son or grandson of a great noble, or else, probably, his tutor. But he, Sir Abraham, had had no mighty lord at his back. His father had been a country apothecary, his mother a farmer's daughter. Why should he respect any but himself? And so he glitters along through the world, the brightest among the bright; and when his glitter is gone, and he is gathered to his fathers, no eye will be dim with a tear, no heart will mourn for its lost friend.

'And so, Mr Warden,' said Sir Abraham, 'all our trouble about this law-suit is at an end.'

Mr Harding said he hoped so, but he didn't at all understand what Sir Abraham meant. Sir Abraham, with all his sharpness, could hardly have looked into his heart and read his intentions.

'All over. You need trouble yourself no further about it. Of course they must pay the costs, and the absolute expense to you and Dr Grantly will be trifling;—that is, compared with what it might have been if it had been continued.'

'I fear I don't quite understand you, Sir Abraham.'

'Don't you know that their attorneys have noticed us that they have withdrawn the suit?'

Mr Harding explained to the lawyer that he knew nothing of this, although he had heard in a round-about way that such an intention had been talked of; and he also at length succeeded in making Sir Abraham understand that even this did not satisfy him. The attorney-general stood up, put his hands into his breeches' pockets, and raised his eyebrows, as Mr Harding proceeded to detail the grievance from which he now wished to rid himself.

'I know I have no right to trouble you personally with this matter, but as it is of most vital importance to me, as all my happiness is concerned in it, I thought I might venture to seek your advice.'

Sir Abraham bowed, and declared his clients were entitled to the best advice he could give them;—particularly a client so respectable in every way as the Warden of Barchester Hospital.

'A spoken word, Sir Abraham, is often of more value than volumes of written advice. The truth is, I am ill-satisfied with this matter as it stands at present. I do see,—I cannot help seeing, that the affairs of the hospital are not arranged according to the will of the founder.'

'None of such institutions are, Mr Harding, nor can they be. The altered circumstances in which we live do not admit of it.'

'Quite true,—that is quite true; but I can't see that those altered circumstances give me a right to eight hundred a year. I don't know whether I ever read John Hiram's will, but were I to read it now I could not understand it. What I want you, Sir Abraham, to tell me, is this;—am I, as warden, legally and distinctly entitled to the proceeds of the property, after the due maintenance of the twelve bedesmen?'

Sir Abraham declared that he couldn't exactly say in so many words that Mr Harding was legally entitled to, &c., &c., &c., and ended in expressing a strong opinion that it would be madness to raise any further question on the matter, as the suit was to be,—nay, was, abandoned.

Mr Harding, seated in his chair, began to play a slow tune on an imaginary violoncello.

'Nay, my dear sir,' continued the attorney-general, 'there is no further ground for any question. I don't see that you have the power of raising it.'

'I can resign,' said Mr Harding, slowly playing away with his right hand, as though the bow were beneath the chair in which he was sitting.

'What! throw it up altogether?' said the attorney-general, gazing with utter astonishment at his client.

'Did you see those articles in the *Jupiter*?' said Mr Harding, piteously, appealing to the sympathy of the lawyer.

Sir Abraham said he had seen them. This poor little clergyman, cowed into such an act of extreme weakness by a newspaper article, was to Sir Abraham so contemptible an object, that he hardly knew how to talk to him as to a rational being.

'Hadn't you better wait,' said he, 'till Dr Grantly is in town with you? Wouldn't it be better to postpone any serious step till you can consult with him?'

Mr Harding declared vehemently that he could not wait, and Sir Abraham began seriously to doubt his sanity.

'Of course,' said the latter, 'if you have private means sufficient for your wants, and if this——'

'I haven't a sixpence, Sir Abraham,' said the warden.

'God bless me! Why, Mr Harding, how do you mean to live?'

Mr Harding proceeded to explain to the man of law that he meant to keep his precentorship,—that was eighty pounds a year; and, also, that he meant to fall back upon his own little living of Crabtree, which was another eighty pounds. That, to be sure, the duties of the two were hardly compatible; but perhaps he might effect an exchange. And then, recollecting that the attorney-general would hardly care to hear how the service of a cathedral church is divided among the minor canons, stopped short in his explanations.

Sir Abraham listened in pitying wonder. 'I really think, Mr Harding, you had better wait for the archdeacon. This is a most serious step;—one for which, in my opinion, there is not the slightest necessity; and, as you have done me the honour of asking my advice, I must implore you to do nothing without the approval of your friends. A man is never the best judge of his own position.'

'A man is the best judge of what he feels himself. I'd sooner beg my bread till my death, than read such another article as those two that have appeared, and feel, as I do, that the writer has truth on his side.'

'Have you not a daughter, Mr Harding,—an unmarried daughter?'

'I have,' said he, now standing also, but still playing away on his fiddle with his hand behind his back. 'I have, Sir Abraham; and she and I are completely agreed on this subject.'

'Pray excuse me, Mr Harding, if what I say seems impertinent; but surely it is you that should be prudent on her behalf. She is young, and does not know the meaning of living on an income of a hundred and fifty pounds a year. On her account give up this idea. Believe me, it is sheer Quixotism.'*

The warden walked away to the window, and then back to his chair; and then, irresolute what to say, took another turn to the window. The attorney-general was really extremely patient, but he was beginning to think that the interview had been long enough.

'But if this income be not justly mine, what if she and I have both to beg?' said the warden at last, sharply, and in a voice so different from that he had hitherto used, that Sir Abraham was startled. 'If so, it would be better to beg.'

'My dear sir, nobody now questions its justness.'

'Yes, Sir Abraham, one does question it,—the most important of all witnesses against me;—I question it myself. My God knows whether or no I love my daughter; but I would sooner that she and I should both beg, than that she should live in comfort on money which is truly the property of the poor. It may seem strange to you, Sir Abraham, it is strange to myself, that I should have been ten years in that happy home, and not have thought of these things, till they were so roughly dinned into my ears. I cannot boast of my conscience, when it required the violence of a public newspaper to awaken it; but, now that it is awake, I must obey it. When I came here I did not know that the suit was withdrawn by Mr Bold, and my object was to beg you to abandon my defence. As there is no action, there can be no defence. But it is, at any rate, as well that you should know that from to-morrow I shall cease to be the warden of the hospital. My friends and I differ on this subject, Sir Abraham, and that adds much to my sorrow: but it cannot be helped.' And, as he finished what he had to say, he played up such a tune as never before had graced the chambers of any attorney-general. He was standing up, gallantly fronting Sir Abraham, and his right arm passed with bold and rapid sweeps before him, as though he were embracing some huge instrument, which allowed him to stand thus erect; and with the fingers of his left hand he stopped, with preternatural velocity, a multitude of strings, which ranged from the top of his collar to the bottom of the lappet* of his coat. Sir Abraham listened and looked in wonder. As he had never before seen Mr Harding, the meaning of these wild gesticulations was lost upon him; but he perceived that the gentleman who had a few minutes since been so subdued as to be unable to speak without hesitation, was now impassioned,—nay, almost violent.

'You'll sleep on this, Mr Harding, and to-morrow——'

'I have done more than sleep upon it,' said the warden; 'I have laid awake upon it, and that night after night. I found I could not sleep upon it. Now I hope to do so.'

The attorney-general had no answer to make to this; so he expressed a quiet hope that whatever settlement was finally made would be satisfactory; and Mr Harding withdrew, thanking the great man for his kind attention.

Mr Harding was sufficiently satisfied with the interview to feel a glow of comfort as he descended into the small old square of Lincoln's Inn.* It was a calm, bright, beautiful night, and by the light of the moon, even the chapel of Lincoln's Inn, and the sombre row of chambers, which surround the quadrangle, looked well. He stood still a moment to collect his thoughts, and reflect on what he had done, and was about to do. He knew that the attorney-general regarded him as little better than a fool, but that he did not mind; he and the attorney-general had not much in common between them; he knew also that others, whom he did care about, would think so too; but Eleanor, he was sure, would exult in what he had done, and the bishop, he trusted, would sympathise with him.

In the meantime he had to meet the archdeacon, and so he walked slowly down Chancery Lane and along Fleet Street, feeling sure that his work for the night was not yet over. When he reached the hotel he rang the bell quietly, and with a palpitating heart. He almost longed to escape round the corner, and delay the coming storm by a further walk round St Paul's Churchyard, but he heard the slow creaking shoes of the old waiter approaching, and he stood his ground manfully.

## CHAPTER 18

### THE WARDEN IS VERY OBSTINATE

'DR GRANTLY is here, sir,' greeted his ears before the door was well open, 'and Mrs Grantly. They have a sitting-room above, and are waiting up for you.'

There was something in the tone of the man's voice which seemed to indicate that even he looked upon the warden as a runaway school-boy, just recaptured by his guardian, and that he pitied the culprit, though he could not but be horrified at the crime.

The warden endeavoured to appear unconcerned, as he said, 'Oh, indeed! I'll go up-stairs at once;' but he failed signally. There was, perhaps, a ray of comfort in the presence of his married daughter; that is to say, of comparative comfort, seeing that his son-in-law was there; but how much would he have preferred that they should both have been safe at Plumstead Episcopi! However, up-stairs he went, the waiter slowly preceding him; and on the door being opened the archdeacon was discovered standing in the middle of the room, erect, indeed, as usual, but oh! how sorrowful! And on a dingy sofa behind him reclined his patient wife.

'Papa, I thought you were never coming back,' said the lady; 'it's twelve o'clock.'

'Yes, my dear,' said the warden. 'The attorney-general named ten for my meeting. To be sure ten is late, but what could I do, you know? Great men will have their own way.'

And he gave his daughter a kiss, and shook hands with the doctor, and again tried to look unconcerned.

'And you have absolutely been with the attorney-general?' asked the archdeacon.

Mr Harding signified that he had.

'Good heavens, how unfortunate!' And the archdeacon raised his huge hands in the manner in which his friends are so accustomed

to see him express disapprobation and astonishment. 'What will Sir
Abraham think of it? Did you not know that it is not customary for
clients to go direct to their counsel?'

'Isn't it?' asked the warden, innocently. 'Well, at any rate, I've done
it. Sir Abraham didn't seem to think it so very strange.'

The archdeacon gave a sigh that would have moved a man-of-war.*

'But, papa, what did you say to Sir Abraham?' asked the lady.

'I asked him, my dear, to explain John Hiram's will to me. He
couldn't explain it in the only way which would have satisfied me, and
so I resigned the wardenship.'

'Resigned it!' said the archdeacon, in a solemn voice, sad and
low, but yet sufficiently audible;—a sort of whisper that Macready*
would have envied, and the galleries have applauded with a couple of
rounds. 'Resigned it! Good heavens!' And the dignitary of the church
sank back horrified into a horse-hair arm chair.

'At least I told Sir Abraham that I would resign;—and of course
I must now do so.'

'Not at all,' said the archdeacon, catching a ray of hope. 'Nothing
that you say in such a way to your own counsel can be in any way
binding on you. Of course you were there to ask his advice. I'm sure,
Sir Abraham did not advise any such step.'

Mr Harding could not say that he had.

'I am sure he disadvised you from it,' continued the reverend
cross-examiner.

Mr Harding could not deny this.

'I'm sure Sir Abraham must have advised you to consult your
friends.'

To this proposition also Mr Harding was obliged to assent.

'Then your threat of resignation amounts to nothing, and we are
just where we were before.'

Mr Harding was now standing on the rug, moving uneasily from
one foot to the other. He made no distinct answer to the archdeacon's
last proposition, for his mind was chiefly engaged on thinking how he
could escape to bed. That his resignation was a thing finally fixed on,
a fact all but completed, was not in his mind a matter of any doubt.
He knew his own weakness; he knew how prone he was to be led; but
he was not weak enough to give way now, to go back from the position to which his conscience had driven him, after having purposely
come to London to declare his determination. He did not in the least

doubt his resolution, but he greatly doubted his power of defending it against his son-in-law.

'You must be very tired, Susan,' said he: 'wouldn't you like to go to bed?'

But Susan didn't want to go till her husband went. She had an idea that her papa might be bullied if she were away. She wasn't tired at all, or at least she said so.

The archdeacon was pacing the room, expressing, by certain noddles* of his head, his opinion of the utter fatuity of his father-in-law.

'Why,' at last he said,—and angels might have blushed at the rebuke expressed in his tone and emphasis,—'Why did you go off from Barchester so suddenly? Why did you take such a step without giving us notice, after what had passed at the palace?'

The warden hung his head, and made no reply. He could not condescend to say that he had not intended to give his son-in-law the slip; and as he had not the courage to avow it, he said nothing.

'Papa has been too much for you,' said the lady.

The archdeacon took another turn, and again ejaculated, 'Good heavens!'—this time in a very low whisper, but still audibly.

'I think I'll go to bed,' said the warden, taking up a side candle.

'At any rate, you'll promise me to take no further step without consultation,' said the archdeacon. Mr Harding made no answer, but slowly proceeded to light his candle. 'Of course,' continued the other, 'such a declaration as that you made to Sir Abraham means nothing. Come, warden, promise me this. The whole affair, you see, is already settled, and that with very little trouble or expense. Bold has been compelled to abandon his action, and all you have to do is to remain quiet at the hospital.' Mr Harding still made no reply, but looked meekly into his son-in-law's face. The archdeacon thought he knew his father-in-law, but he was mistaken; he thought that he had already talked over a vacillating man to resign his promise. 'Come,' said he, 'promise Susan to give up this idea of resigning the wardenship.'

The warden looked at his daughter, thinking probably at the moment that if Eleanor were contented with him, he need not so much regard his other child, and said, 'I am sure Susan will not ask me to break my word, or to do what I know to be wrong.'

'Papa,' said she, 'it would be madness in you to throw up your preferment. What are you to live on?'

'God, that feeds the young ravens,* will take care of me also,' said

Mr Harding, with a smile, as though afraid of giving offence by making his reference to scripture too solemn.

'Pish!' said the archdeacon, turning away rapidly. 'If the ravens persisted in refusing the food prepared for them, they wouldn't be fed.' A clergyman generally dislikes to be met in argument by any scriptural quotation; he feels as affronted as a doctor does, when recommended by an old woman to take some favourite dose, or as a lawyer when an unprofessional man attempts to put him down by a quibble.

'I shall have the living of Crabtree,' modestly suggested the warden.

'Eighty pounds a year!' sneered the archdeacon.

'And the precentorship,' said the father-in-law.

'It goes with the wardenship,' said the son-in-law. Mr Harding was prepared to argue this point, and began to do so, but Dr Grantly stopped him. 'My dear warden,' said he, 'this is all nonsense. Eighty pounds or a hundred and sixty makes very little difference. You can't live on it;—you can't ruin Eleanor's prospects for ever. In point of fact, you can't resign. The bishop wouldn't accept it. The whole thing is settled. What I now want to do is to prevent any inconvenient tittle-tattle,—any more newspaper articles.'

'That's what I want, too,' said the warden.

'And to prevent that,' continued the other, 'we mustn't let any talk of resignation get abroad.'

'But I shall resign,' said the warden, very, very, meekly.

'Good heavens! Susan, my dear, what can I say to him?'

'But, papa,' said Mrs Grantly, getting up, and putting her arm through that of her father, 'what is Eleanor to do if you throw away your income?'

A hot tear stood in each of the warden's eyes as he looked round upon his married daughter. Why should one sister who was so rich predict poverty for another? Some such idea as this was on his mind, but he gave no utterance to it. Then he thought of the pelican* feeding its young with blood from its own breast, but he gave no utterance to that either;—and then of Eleanor waiting for him at home, waiting to congratulate him on the end of all his trouble.

'Think of Eleanor, papa,' said Mrs Grantly.

'I do think of her,' said her father.

'And you will not do this rash thing?' The lady was really moved beyond her usual calm composure.

'It can never be rash to do right,' said he. 'I shall certainly resign this wardenship.'

'Then, Mr Harding, there is nothing before you but ruin,' said the archdeacon, now moved beyond all endurance. 'Ruin both for you and Eleanor. How do you mean to pay the monstrous expenses of this action?'

Mrs Grantly suggested that, as the action was abandoned, the costs would not be heavy.

'Indeed they will, my dear,' continued he. 'One cannot have the attorney-general up at twelve o'clock at night for nothing. But of course your father has not thought of this.'

'I will sell my furniture,' said the warden.

'Furniture!' ejaculated the other, with a most powerful sneer.

'Come, archdeacon,' said the lady, 'we needn't mind that at present. You know you never expected papa to pay the costs.'

'Such absurdity is enough to provoke Job,'* said the archdeacon, marching quickly up and down the room. Your father is like a child. Eight hundred pounds a-year!—Eight hundred and eighty with the house;—with nothing to do. The very place for him. And to throw that up because some scoundrel writes an article in a newspaper! Well;—I have done my duty. If he chooses to ruin his child I cannot help it. And he stood still at the fireplace, and looked at himself in a dingy mirror which stood on the chimney-piece.

There was a pause for about a minute, and then the warden, finding that nothing else was coming, lighted his candle, and quietly said, 'Good night.'

'Good night, papa,' said the lady.

And so the warden retired; but, as he closed the door behind him, he heard the well-known ejaculation,—slower, lower, more solemn, more ponderous than ever;—'Good heavens!'


## CHAPTER 19

### THE WARDEN RESIGNS

THE party met next morning at breakfast; and a very sombre affair it was;—very unlike the breakfasts at Plumstead Episcopi.

There were three thin, small, dry bits of bacon, each an inch long, served up under a huge old plated cover;* there were four three-cornered bits of dry toast, and four square bits of buttered toast; there was a loaf of bread, and some oily-looking butter; and on the sideboard there were the remains of a cold shoulder of mutton. The archdeacon, however, had not come up from his rectory to St Paul's Churchyard to enjoy himself, and therefore nothing was said of the scanty fare.

The guests were as sorry as the viands. Hardly anything was said over the breakfast-table. The archdeacon munched his toast in ominous silence, turning over bitter thoughts in his deep mind. The warden tried to talk to his daughter, and she tried to answer him; but they both failed. There were no feelings at present in common between them. The warden was thinking only of getting back to Barchester, and calculating whether the archdeacon would expect him to wait for him; and Mrs Grantly was preparing herself for a grand attack which she was to make on her father, as agreed upon between herself and her husband during their curtain confabulation* of that morning.

When the waiter had creaked out of the room with the last of the teacups, the archdeacon got up and went to the window, as though to admire the view. The room looked out on a narrow passage which runs from St Paul's Churchyard to Paternoster Row; and Dr Grantly patiently perused the names of the three shopkeepers whose doors were in view. The warden still kept his seat at the table, and examined the pattern of the table-cloth; and Mrs Grantly, seating herself on the sofa, began to knit.

After awhile the warden pulled his Bradshaw out of his pocket, and began laboriously to consult it. There was a train for Barchester at 10 a.m. That was out of the question, for it was nearly ten already. Another at 3 p.m.; another, the night-mail train, at 9 p.m. The three o'clock train would take him home to tea, and would suit very well.

'My dear,' said he, 'I think I shall go back home at three o'clock to-day. I shall get home at half-past eight. I don't think there's anything to keep me in London.'

'The archdeacon and I return by the early train to-morrow, papa. Won't you wait and go back with us?'

'Why, Eleanor will expect me to-night; and I've so much to do; and——'

'Much to do!' said the archdeacon sotto voce; but the warden heard him.

'You'd better wait for us, papa.'

'Thank ye, my dear! I think I'll go this afternoon.' The tamest animal will turn when driven too hard, and even Mr Harding was beginning to fight for his own way.

'I suppose you won't be back before three?' said the lady addressing her husband.

'I must leave this at two,' said the warden.

'Quite out of the question,' said the archdeacon, answering his wife, and still reading the shopkeepers' names; 'I don't suppose I shall be back till five.'

There was another long pause, during which Mr Harding continued to study his 'Bradshaw.'

'I must go to Cox and Cumming,' said the archdeacon at last.

'Oh, to Cox and Cumming,' said the warden. It was quite a matter of indifference to him where his son-in-law went.

The names of Cox and Cumming had now no interest in his ears. What had he to do with Cox and Cumming further, having already had his suit finally adjudicated upon in a court of conscience, a judgment without power of appeal fully registered, and the matter settled so that all the lawyers in London could not disturb it. The archdeacon could go to Cox and Cumming, could remain there all day in anxious discussion; but what might be said there was no longer matter of interest to him, who was so soon to lay aside the name of Warden of Barchester Hospital.

The archdeacon took up his shining new clerical hat, and put on his black new clerical gloves, and looked heavy, respectable, decorous, and opulent, a decided clergyman of the Church of England, every inch of him. 'I suppose I shall see you at Barchester the day after to-morrow,' said he.

The warden supposed he would.

'I must once more beseech you to take no further steps till you see my father. If you owe me nothing,' and the archdeacon looked as though he thought a great deal were due to him, 'at least you owe so much to my father.' Without waiting for a reply, Dr Grantly wended his way to Cox and Cumming.

Mrs Grantly waited till the last fall of her husband's foot was heard, as he turned out of the court into St Paul's Churchyard, and then commenced her task of talking her father over.

'Papa,' she began, 'this is a most serious business.'

'Indeed it is,' said the warden, ringing the bell.

'I greatly feel the distress of mind you must have endured.'

'I am sure you do, my dear;'—and he ordered the waiter to bring him pen, ink, and paper.

'Are you going to write, papa?'

'Yes, my dear. I am going to write my resignation to the bishop.'

'Pray, pray, papa, put it off till our return. Pray put it off till you have seen the bishop. Dear papa! for my sake, for Eleanor's!——'

'It is for your sake and Eleanor's that I do this. I hope, at least, that my children may never have to be ashamed of their father.'

'How can you talk about shame, papa?' Then she stopped while the waiter creaked in with the paper and slowly creaked out again. 'How can you talk about shame? You know what all your friends think about this question.'

The warden spread his paper on the table, placing it on the meagre blotting-book,* which the hotel afforded, and sat himself down to write.

'You won't refuse me one request, papa?' continued his daughter; 'you won't refuse to delay your letter for two short days? Two days can make no possible difference.'

'My dear,' said he naively, 'if I waited till I got to Barchester, I might, perhaps, be prevented.'

'But surely you would not wish to offend the bishop?' said she.

'God forbid! The bishop is not apt to take offence, and knows me too well to take in bad part anything that I may be called on to do.'

'But, papa——'

'Susan,' said he, 'my mind on this subject is made up. It is not without much repugnance that I act in opposition to the advice of such men as Sir Abraham Haphazard and the archdeacon; but in this matter I can take no advice; I cannot alter the resolution to which I have come.'

'But two days, papa——'

'No;—nor can I delay it. You may add to my present unhappiness by pressing me, but you cannot change my purpose; it will be a comfort to me if you will let the matter rest.' Then, dipping his pen into the inkstand, he fixed his eyes intently on the paper.

There was something in his manner which taught his daughter to perceive that he was in earnest. She had at one time ruled supreme in her father's house, but she knew that there were moments when, mild and meek as he was, he would have his way, and the present was an occasion of the sort. She returned, therefore, to her knitting, and very shortly after left the room.

The warden was now at liberty to compose his letter, and, as it was characteristic of the man, it shall be given at full length. The official letter, which, when written, seemed to him to be too formally cold to be sent alone to so dear a friend, was accompanied by a private note; and both are here inserted.

The letter of resignation ran as follows:—

'Chapter Hotel, St Paul's,
'London,—August, 18—.

'My Lord Bishop,

'It is with the greatest pain that I feel myself constrained to resign into your Lordship's hands the wardenship of the hospital at Barchester, which you so kindly conferred upon me, now nearly twelve years since.

'I need not explain the circumstances which have made this step appear necessary to me. You are aware that a question has arisen as to the right of the warden to the income which has been allotted to the wardenship. It has seemed to me that this right is not well made out, and I hesitate to incur the risk of taking an income to which my legal claim appears doubtful.

'The office of precentor of the cathedral is, as your Lordship is aware, joined to that of the warden. That is to say, the precentor has for many years been the warden of the hospital. There is, however, nothing to make the junction of the two offices necessary, and, unless you or the dean and chapter object to such an arrangement, I would wish to keep the precentorship. The income of this office will now be necessary to me. Indeed, I do not know why I should be ashamed to say that I should have difficulty in supporting myself without it.

'Your Lordship, and such others as you may please to consult on the matter, will at once see that my resignation of the wardenship need offer not the slightest bar to its occupation by another person. I am thought in the wrong by all those whom I have consulted in the matter. I have very little but an inward and an unguided conviction of my own to bring me to this step, and I shall, indeed, be hurt to find that any slur is thrown on the preferment which your kindness bestowed on me, by my resignation of it. I, at any rate for one, shall look on any successor whom you may appoint as enjoying a clerical situation of the highest respectability, and one to which your Lordship's nomination gives an indefeasible right.

'I cannot finish this official letter without again thanking your Lordship for all your great kindness, and I beg to subscribe myself

'Your Lordship's most obedient servant,

'SEPTIMUS HARDING,

'Warden of Barchester Hospital,
and Precentor of the cathedral.'

He then wrote the following private note:—

'My dear Bishop,

'I cannot send you the accompanying official letter without a warmer expression of thanks for all your kindness than would befit a document which may to a certain degree be made public. You, I know, will understand the feeling, and, perhaps, pity the weakness which makes me resign the hospital. I am not made of calibre strong enough to withstand public attack. Were I convinced that I stood on ground perfectly firm, that I was certainly justified in taking eight hundred a year under Hiram's will, I should feel bound by duty to retain the position, however unendurable might be the nature of the assault; but, as I do not feel this conviction, I cannot believe that you will think me wrong in what I am doing.

'I had at one time an idea of keeping only some moderate portion of the income; perhaps three hundred a year, and of remitting the remainder to the trustees; but it occurred to me, and I think with reason, that by so doing I should place my successors in an invidious position, and greatly damage your patronage.

'My dear friend, let me have a line from you to say that you do not blame me for what I am doing, and that the officiating vicar of Crabtree Parva will be the same to you as the warden of the hospital.

'I am very anxious about the precentorship: the archdeacon thinks it must go with the wardenship; I think not, and that, having it, I cannot be ousted. I will, however, be guided by you and the dean. No other duty will suit me so well, or come so much within my power of adequate performance.

'I thank you from my heart for the preferment which I am now giving up, and for all your kindness, and am, dear bishop, now as always,

'Yours most affectionately,*

'SEPTIMUS HARDING.

'London, —August, 18—.'

Having written these letters and made a copy of the former one for the benefit of the archdeacon, Mr Harding, whom we must now cease to call the warden,—he having designated himself so for the last time,—found that it was nearly two o'clock, and that he must prepare for his journey. Yes; from this time he never again admitted the name by which he had been so familiarly known, and in which, to tell the truth, he had rejoiced. The love of titles is common to all men, and a vicar or fellow is as pleased at becoming Mr Archdeacon or Mr Provost, as a lieutenant at getting his captaincy, or a city tallow-chandler in becoming Sir John on the occasion of a Queen's visit to a new bridge.* But warden he was no longer, and the name of precentor, though the office was to him so dear, confers in itself no sufficient distinction. Our friend, therefore, again became Mr Harding.

Mrs Grantly had gone out; he had, therefore, no one to delay him by further entreaties to postpone his journey; he had soon arranged his bag, and paid his bill, and, leaving a note for his daughter, in which he put the copy of his official letter, he got into a cab and drove away to the station with something of triumph in his heart.

Had he not cause for triumph? Had he not been supremely successful? Had he not for the first time in his life held his own purpose against that of his son-in-law, and manfully combated against great odds,—against the archdeacon's wife as well as the archdeacon? Had he not gained a great victory, and was it not fit that he should step into his cab with triumph?

He had not told Eleanor when he would return, but she was on the look out for him by every train by which he could arrive, and the pony-carriage was at the Barchester station when the train drew up at the platform.

'My dear,' said he, sitting beside her, as she steered her little vessel to one side of the road to make room for the clattering omnibuses as they passed from the station into the town; 'I hope you'll be able to feel a proper degree of respect for the vicar of Crabtree.'

'Dear papa,' said she, 'I am so glad.'

There was great comfort in returning home to that pleasant house, though he was to leave it so soon, and in discussing with his daughter all that he had done, and all that he had to do. It must take some time to get out of one house into another. The curate at Crabtree could not be abolished under six months, that is, unless other provision could be made for him; and then the furniture! The most of that must be sold to pay Sir Abraham Haphazard for sitting up till twelve at night. Mr Harding was strangely ignorant as to lawyers' bills. He had no idea, from twenty pounds to two thousand, as to the sum in which he was indebted for legal assistance. True, he had called in no lawyer himself; true, he had been no consenting party to the employment of either Cox and Cumming, or Sir Abraham; he had never been consulted on such matters;—the archdeacon had managed all this himself, never for a moment suspecting that Mr Harding would take upon him to end the matter in a way of his own. Had the lawyers' bills been ten thousand pounds, Mr Harding could not have helped it; but he was not on that account disposed to dispute his own liability. The question never occurred to him. But it did occur to him that he had very little money at his banker's, that he could receive nothing further from the hospital, and that the sale of the furniture was his only resource.

'Not all, papa,' said Eleanor, pleadingly.

'Not quite all, my dear,' said he; 'that is, if we can help it. We must have a little at Crabtree;—but it can only be a little. We must put a bold front on it, Nelly; it isn't easy to come down from affluence to poverty.'

And so they planned their future mode of life; the father taking comfort from the reflection that his daughter would soon be freed from it, and she resolving that her father would soon have in her own house a ready means of escape from the solitude of the Crabtree vicarage.

When the archdeacon left his wife and father-in-law at the Chapter Coffee House to go to Messrs Cox and Cumming, he had no very defined idea of what he had to do when he got there. Gentlemen when at law, or in any way engaged in matters requiring legal assistance, are very apt to go to their lawyers without much absolute necessity. Gentlemen when doing so, are apt to describe such attendance as quite compulsory, and very disagreeable. The lawyers, on the other hand, do not at all see the necessity, though they quite agree as to the disagreeable nature of the visit;—gentlemen when so engaged are usually somewhat gravelled* at finding nothing to say to their learned friends; they generally talk a little politics, a little weather, ask some few foolish questions about their suit, and then withdraw, having passed half an hour in a small dingy waiting-room, in company with some junior assistant-clerk, and ten minutes with the members of the firm. The business is then over for which the gentleman has come up to London, probably a distance of a hundred and fifty miles. To be sure he goes to the play, and dines at his friend's club, and has a bachelor's liberty and bachelor's recreation for three or four days; and he could not probably plead the desire of such gratifications as a reason to his wife for a trip to London.

Married ladies, when your husbands find they are positively obliged to attend their legal advisers, the nature of the duty to be performed is generally of this description.

The archdeacon would not have dreamt of leaving London without going to Cox and Cumming; and yet he had nothing to say to them. The game was up; he plainly saw that Mr Harding in this matter was not to be moved; his only remaining business on this head was to pay the bill and have done with it: and I think it may be taken for granted, that whatever the cause may be that takes a gentleman to a lawyer's chambers, he never goes there to pay his bill.

Dr Grantly, however, in the eyes of Messrs Cox and Cumming, represented the spiritualities of the diocese of Barchester, as Mr Chadwick did the temporalities, and was, therefore, too great a man to undergo the half-hour in the clerk's room. It will not be necessary that we should listen to the notes of sorrow in which the archdeacon bewailed to Mr Cox the weakness of his father-in-law, and the end of all their hopes of triumph; nor need we repeat the various exclamations of surprise with which the mournful intelligence was received. No tragedy occurred, though Mr Cox, a short and somewhat bull-necked man, was very near a fit of apoplexy when he first attempted to ejaculate that fatal word—resign!

Over and over again did Mr Cox attempt to enforce on the archdeacon the propriety of urging on Mr Warden the madness of the deed he was about to do.

'Eight hundred a year!' said Mr Cox.

'And nothing whatever to do!' said Mr Cumming, who had joined the conference.

'No private fortune, I believe,' said Mr Cox.

'Not a shilling,' said Mr Cumming, in a very low voice, shaking his head.

'I never heard of such a case in all my experience,' said Mr Cox.

'Eight hundred a year, and as nice a house as any gentleman could wish to hang up his hat in,' said Mr Cumming.

'And an unmarried daughter, I believe,' said Mr Cox, with much moral seriousness in his tone. The archdeacon only sighed as each separate wail was uttered, and shook his head, signifying that the fatuity of some people was past belief.

'I'll tell you what he might do,' said Mr Cumming, brightening up. 'I'll tell you how you might save it. Let him exchange.'

'Exchange where?' said the archdeacon.

'Exchange for a living. There's Quiverful,* of Puddingdale;—he has twelve children, and would be delighted to get the hospital. To be sure Puddingdale is only four hundred, but that would be saving something out of the fire. Mr Harding would have a curate, and still keep three hundred or three hundred and fifty.'

The archdeacon opened his eyes and listened. He really thought the scheme might do.

'The newspapers,' continued Mr Cumming, 'might hammer away at Quiverful every day for the next six months without his minding them.'

The Archdeacon took up his hat, and returned to his hotel, thinking the matter over deeply. At any rate he would sound Quiverful. A man with twelve children would do much to double his income.

## CHAPTER 20

### FAREWELL

ON the morning after Mr Harding's return home he received a note from the bishop full of affection, condolence, and praise. 'Pray come to me at once,' wrote the bishop, 'that we may see what had better be done; as to the hospital, I will not say a word to dissuade you; but I don't like your going to Crabtree. At any rate, come to me at once.'

Mr Harding did go to him at once; and long and confidential was the consultation between the two old friends. There they sat together the whole long day, plotting to get the better of the archdeacon, and to carry out little schemes of their own, which they knew would be opposed by the whole weight of his authority.

The bishop's first idea was, that Mr Harding, if left to himself, would certainly starve,—not in the figurative sense in which so many of our ladies and gentlemen do starve on incomes from one to five hundred a year; not that he would be starved as regarded dress coats, port wine, and pocket-money; but that he would positively perish of inanition for want of bread.

'How is a man to live, when he gives up all his income?' said the bishop to himself. And then the good-natured little man began to consider how his friend might be best rescued from a death so horrid and painful.

His first proposition to Mr Harding was, that they should live together at the palace. He, the bishop, positively assured Mr Harding that he wanted another resident chaplain;—not a young, working chaplain, but a steady, middle-aged chaplain; one who would dine and drink a glass of wine with him, talk about the archdeacon, and poke the fire. The bishop did not positively name all these duties, but he gave Mr Harding to understand that such would be the nature of the service required.

It was not without much difficulty that Mr Harding made his friend see that this would not suit him; that he could not throw up the bishop's preferment, and then come and hang on at the bishop's table; that he could not allow people to say of him that it was an easy matter to abandon his own income, as he was able to sponge on that of another person. He succeeded, however, in explaining that the plan would not do, and then the bishop brought forward another which he had in his sleeve. He, the bishop, had in his will left certain moneys to Mr Harding's two daughters, imagining that Mr Harding would himself want no such assistance during his own lifetime. This legacy amounted to three thousand pounds each, duty free; and he now pressed it as a gift on his friend.

'The girls, you know,' said he, 'will have it just the same when you're gone,—and they won't want it sooner,—and as for the interest during my lifetime, it isn't worth talking about. I have more than enough.'

With much difficulty and heartfelt sorrow, Mr Harding refused also this offer. No; his wish was to support himself, however poorly;—not to be supported on the charity of any one. It was hard to make the bishop understand this; it was hard to make him comprehend that the only real favour he could confer was the continuation of his independent friendship. But at last even this was done. At any rate, thought the bishop, he will come and dine with me from time to time, and if he be absolutely starving I shall see it.

Touching the precentorship, the bishop was clearly of opinion that it could be held without the other situation;—an opinion from which no one differed; and it was therefore soon settled among all the parties concerned, that Mr Harding should still be the precentor of the cathedral.

On the day following Mr Harding's return, the archdeacon reached Plumstead full of Mr Cumming's scheme regarding Puddingdale and Mr Quiverful. On the very next morning he drove over to Puddingdale, and obtained the full consent of the wretched clerical Priam,* who was endeavouring to feed his poor Hecuba and a dozen of Hectors on the small proceeds of his ecclesiastical kingdom. Mr Quiverful had no doubts as to the legal rights of the warden; his conscience would be quite clear as to accepting the income; and as to the *Jupiter*, he begged to assure the archdeacon that he was quite indifferent to any emanations from the profane portion of the periodical press.

Having so far succeeded, he next sounded the bishop; but here he was astonished by most unexpected resistance. The bishop did not think it would do. 'Not do? Why not?' and seeing that his father was not shaken, he repeated the question in a severer form; 'Why not do, my lord?'

His lordship looked very unhappy, and shuffled about in his chair, but still didn't give way. He thought Puddingdale wouldn't do for Mr Harding; it was too far from Barchester.

'Oh! of course he'll have a curate.'

The bishop also thought that Mr Quiverful wouldn't do for the hospital; such an exchange wouldn't look well at such a time; and, when pressed harder, he declared he didn't think Mr Harding would accept of Puddingdale under any circumstances.

'How is he to live?' demanded the archdeacon.

The bishop, with tears in his eyes, declared that he had not the slightest conception how life was to be sustained within him at all.

The archdeacon then left his father, and went down to the hospital; but Mr Harding wouldn't listen at all to the Puddingdale scheme. To his eyes it had no attraction. It savoured of simony,* and was likely to bring down upon him harder and more deserved strictures than any he had yet received. He positively declined to become vicar of Puddingdale under any circumstances.

The archdeacon waxed wroth, talked big, and looked bigger. He said something about dependence and beggary, spoke of the duty every man was under to earn his bread, made passing allusions to the follies of youth and waywardness of age, as though Mr Harding were afflicted by both, and ended by declaring that he had done. He felt that he had left no stone unturned to arrange matters on the best and easiest footing; that he had, in fact, so arranged them, that he had so managed that there was no further need of any anxiety in the matter. And how had he been paid? His advice had been systematically rejected; he had been not only slighted, but distrusted and avoided; he and his measures had been utterly thrown over, as had been Sir Abraham, who, he had reason to know, was much pained at what had occurred. He now found it was useless to interfere any further, and he should retire. If any further assistance were required from him, he would probably be called on, and should be again happy to come forward. And so he left the hospital, and has not since entered it from that day to this.

And here we must take leave of Archdeacon Grantly. We fear that he is represented in these pages as being worse than he is; but we have had to do with his foibles, and not with his virtues. We have seen only the weak side of the man, and have lacked the opportunity of bringing him forward on his strong ground. That he is a man somewhat too fond of his own way, and not sufficiently scrupulous in his manner of achieving it, his best friends cannot deny. That he is bigoted in favour, not so much of his doctrines as of his cloth,* is also true. And it is true that the possession of a large income is a desire that sits near his heart. Nevertheless, the archdeacon is a gentleman and a man of conscience. He spends his money liberally, and does the work he has to do with the best of his ability. He improves the tone of society of those among whom he lives. His aspirations are of a healthy, if not of the highest, kind. Though never an austere man, he upholds propriety of conduct both by example and precept. He is generous to the poor, and hospitable to the rich; in matters of religion he is sincere, and yet no Pharisee;* he is in earnest, and yet no fanatic. On the whole, the Archdeacon of Barchester is a man doing more good than harm,—a man to be furthered and supported, though perhaps also to be controlled; and it is matter of regret to us that the course of our narrative has required that we should see more of his weakness than his strength.

Mr Harding allowed himself no rest till everything was prepared for his departure from the hospital. It may be as well to mention that he was not driven to the stern necessity of selling all his furniture. He had been quite in earnest in his intention to do so, but it was soon made known to him that the claims of Messrs Cox and Cumming made no such step obligatory. The archdeacon had thought it wise to make use of the threat of the lawyer's bill, to frighten his father-in-law into compliance; but he had no intention to saddle Mr Harding with costs, which had been incurred by no means exclusively for his benefit. The amount of the bill was added to the diocesan account, and was, in fact, paid out of the bishop's pocket, without any consciousness on the part of his lordship. A great part of his furniture he did resolve to sell, having no other means to dispose of it; and the ponies and carriage were transferred, by private contract, to the use of an old maiden lady in the city.

For his present use Mr Harding took a lodging in Barchester, and thither were conveyed such articles as he wanted for daily use,—his music, books, and instruments, his own arm-chair, and Eleanor's pet sofa; her teapoy and his cellaret,* and also the slender but still sufficient contents of his wine-cellar. Mrs Grantly had much wished that her sister would reside at Plumstead, till her father's house at Crabtree should be ready for her; but Eleanor herself strongly resisted this proposal. It was in vain urged upon her, that a lady in lodgings cost more than a gentleman; and that, under her father's present circumstances, such an expense should be avoided. Eleanor had not pressed her father to give up the hospital in order that she might live at Plumstead Rectory, and he alone in his Barchester lodgings; nor did Eleanor think that she would be treating a certain gentleman very fairly, if she betook herself to the house which he would be the least desirous of entering of any in the county. So she got a little bedroom for herself behind the sitting-room, and just over the little back parlour of the chemist, with whom they were to lodge. There was somewhat of a savour of senna softened by peppermint about the place; but, on the whole, the lodgings were clean and comfortable.

The day had been fixed for the migration of the ex-warden, and all Barchester were in a state of excitement on the subject. Opinion was much divided as to the propriety of Mr Harding's conduct. The mercantile part of the community, the mayor and corporation, and council, also most of the ladies, were loud in his praise. Nothing could be more noble, nothing more generous, nothing more upright. But the gentry were of a different way of thinking,—especially the lawyers and the clergymen. They said such conduct was weak and undignified; that Mr Harding evinced a lamentable want of esprit de corps,* as well as courage; and that such an abdication must do much harm, and could do but little good.

On the evening before he left, he summoned all the bedesmen into his parlour to wish them good-bye. With Bunce he had been in frequent communication since his return from London, and had been at much pains to explain to the old man the cause of his resignation, without in any way prejudicing the position of his successor. The others, also, he had seen more or less frequently; and had heard from most of them separately some expression of regret at his departure; but he had postponed his farewell till the last evening.

He now bade the maid put wine and glasses on the table; and had the chairs arranged around the room; and sent Bunce to each of the men to request they would come and say farewell to their late warden. Soon the noise of aged scuffling feet was heard upon the gravel and in the little hall, and the eleven men who were enabled to leave their rooms were assembled.

'Come in, my friends, come in,' said the warden. He was still warden then. 'Come in, and sit down;' and he took the hand of Abel Handy, who was the nearest to him, and led the limping grumbler to a chair. The others followed slowly and bashfully; the infirm, the lame, and the blind: poor wretches! who had been so happy, had they but known it! Now their aged faces were covered with shame, and every kind word from their master was a coal of fire* burning on their heads.

When first the news had reached them that Mr Harding was going to leave the hospital, it had been received with a kind of triumph. His departure was, as it were, a prelude to success. He had admitted his want of right to the money about which they were disputing; and as it did not belong to him, of course it did to them. The one hundred a year to each of them was actually becoming a reality. Abel Handy was a hero, and Bunce a faint-hearted sycophant, worthy neither honour nor fellowship. But other tidings soon made their way into the

old men's rooms. It was first notified to them that the income abandoned by Mr Harding would not come to them; and these accounts
were confirmed by attorney Finney. They were then informed that
Mr Harding's place would be at once filled by another. That the new
warden could not be a kinder man they all knew; that he would be
a less friendly one most suspected; and then came the bitter information that, from the moment of Mr Harding's departure, the twopence
a day, his own peculiar gift, must of necessity be withdrawn.

And this was to be the end of all their mighty struggle,—of their
fight for their rights,—of their petition, and their debates and their
hopes! They were to change the best of masters for a possible bad one,
and to lose twopence a day each man! No; unfortunate as this was, it
was not the worst, or nearly the worst, as will just now be seen.

'Sit down, sit down, my friends,' said the warden; 'I want to say
a word to you, and to drink your healths, before I leave you. Come up
here, Moody, here is a chair for you; come, Jonathan Crumple.' And
by degrees he got the men to be seated. It was not surprising that
they should hang back with faint hearts, having returned so much
kindness with such deep ingratitude. Last of all of them came Bunce,
and with sorrowful mien and slow step got into his accustomed seat
near the fire-place.

When they were all in their places, Mr Harding rose to address
them; and then finding himself not quite at home on his legs, he sat
down again. 'My dear old friends,' said he, 'you all know that I am
going to leave you.'

There was a sort of murmur ran round the room, intended, perhaps, to express regret at his departure; but it was but a murmur, and
might have meant that or anything else.

'There has been lately some misunderstanding between us. You
have thought, I believe, that you did not get all that you were entitled
to, and that the funds of the hospital have not been properly disposed of. As for me, I cannot say what should be the disposition of
these moneys, or how they should be managed, and I have therefore
thought it best to go.'

'We never wanted to drive your reverence out of it,' said Handy.

'No, indeed, your reverence,' said Skulpit. 'We never thought it
would come to this. When I signed the petition,—that is, I didn't sign
it, because——'

'Let his reverence speak, can't you?' said Moody.

'No,' continued Mr Harding; 'I am sure you did not wish to turn me out; but I thought it best to leave you. I am not a very good hand at a lawsuit, as you may all guess; and when it seemed necessary that our ordinary quiet mode of living should be disturbed, I thought it better to go. I am neither angry nor offended with any man in the hospital.'

Here Bunce uttered a kind of groan, very clearly expressive of disagreement.

'I am neither angry nor displeased with any man in the hospital,' repeated Mr Harding, emphatically. 'If any man has been wrong,—and I don't say any man has,—he has erred through wrong advice. In this country all are entitled to look for their own rights, and you have done no more. As long as your interests and my interests were at variance, I could give you no counsel on this subject; but the connection between us has ceased; my income can no longer depend on your doings, and therefore, as I leave you, I venture to offer to you my advice.'

The men all declared that they would from henceforth be entirely guided by Mr Harding's opinion in their affairs.

'Some gentleman will probably take my place here very soon, and I strongly advise you to be prepared to receive him in a kindly spirit, and to raise no further question among yourselves as to the amount of his income. Were you to succeed in lessening what he has to receive, you would not increase your own allowance. The surplus would not go to you. Your wants are adequately provided for, and your position could hardly be improved.'

'God bless your reverence, we knows it,' said Spriggs.

'It's all true, your reverence,' said Skulpit. 'We sees it all now.'

'Yes, Mr Harding,' said Bunce, opening his mouth for the first time; 'I believe they do understand it now,—now that they've driven from under the same roof with them such a master as not one of them will ever know again. Now that they're like to be in sore want of a friend.'

'Come, come, Bunce,' said Mr Harding, blowing his nose, and manœuvring to wipe his eyes at the same time.

'Oh, as to that,' said Handy, 'we none of us never wanted to do Mr Harding no harm. If he's going now, it's not along of us; and I don't see for what Mr Bunce speaks up agen us that way.'

'You've ruined yourselves, and you've ruined me too, and that's why,' said Bunce.

'Nonsense, Bunce,' said Mr Harding; 'there's nobody ruined at all. I hope you'll let me leave you all friends. I hope you'll all drink a glass of wine in friendly feeling with me and with one another. You'll have a good friend, I don't doubt, in your new warden; and if ever you want any other, why after all I'm not going so far off but that I shall sometimes see you.' Then, having finished his speech, Mr Harding filled all the glasses, and himself handed each a glass to the men round him, and raising his own, said,—

'God bless you all! you have my heartfelt wishes for your welfare. I hope you may live contented, and die trusting in the Lord Jesus Christ, and thankful to Almighty God for the good things he has given you. God bless you, my friends!' And Mr Harding drank his wine.

Another murmur, somewhat more articulate than the first, passed round the circle, and this time it was intended to imply a blessing on Mr Harding. It had, however, but little cordiality in it. Poor old men! how could they be cordial with their sore consciences and shamed faces? how could they bid God bless him with hearty voices and a true benison,* knowing, as they did, that their vile cabal had driven him from his happy home, and sent him in his old age to seek shelter under a strange roof-tree? They did their best, however; they drank their wine, and withdrew.

As they left the hall-door, Mr Harding shook hands with each of the men, and spoke a kind word to them about their individual cases and ailments; and so they departed, answering his questions in the fewest words, and retreated to their dens, a sorrowful repentant crew.

All but Bunce, who still remained to make his own farewell. 'There's poor old Bell,' said Mr Harding; 'I mustn't go without saying a word to him; come through with me, Bunce, and bring the wine with you;' and so they went through to the men's cottages, and found the old man propped up as usual in his bed.

'I've come to say good-bye to you, Bell,' said Mr Harding, speaking loud, for the old man was deaf.

'And are you going away, then, really?' asked Bell.

'Indeed I am, and I've brought you a glass of wine; so that we may part friends, as we lived, you know.'

The old man took the proffered glass in his shaking hands, and drank it eagerly. 'God bless you, Bell!' said Mr Harding; 'good-bye, my old friend.'

'And so you're really going?' the man again asked.

'Indeed I am, Bell.'

The poor old bed-ridden creature still kept Mr Harding's hand in his own, and the warden thought that he had met with something like warmth of feeling in the one of all his subjects from whom it was the least likely to be expected; for poor old Bell had nearly outlived all human feelings. 'And your reverence,' said he, and then he paused, while his old palsied head shook horribly, and his shrivelled cheeks sank lower within his jaws, and his glazy eye gleamed with a momentary light; 'and your reverence, shall we get the hundred a year, then?'

How gently did Mr Harding try to extinguish the false hope of money which had been so wretchedly raised to disturb the quiet of the dying man! One other week and his mortal coil would be shuffled off.* In one short week would God resume his soul, and set it apart for its irrevocable doom. Seven more tedious days and nights of senseless inactivity, and all would be over for poor Bell in this world. And yet, with his last audible words, he was demanding his moneyed rights, and asserting himself to be the proper heir of John Hiram's Bounty? Not on him, poor sinner as he was, be the load of such sin!

Mr Harding returned to his parlour, meditating with a sick heart on what he had seen, and Bunce with him. We will not describe the parting of these two good men, for good men they were. It was in vain that the late warden endeavoured to comfort the heart of the old bedesman. Poor old Bunce felt that his days of comfort were gone. The hospital had to him been a happy home, but it could be so no longer. He had had honour there, and friendship; he had recognised his master, and been recognised; all his wants, both of soul and body, had been supplied, and he had been a happy man. He wept grievously as he parted from his friend, and the tears of an old man are bitter. 'It is all over for me in this world,' said he, as he gave the last squeeze to Mr Harding's hand; 'I have now to forgive those who have injured me;—and to die.'

And so the old man went out, and then Mr Harding gave way to his grief and wept aloud.

# CHAPTER 21

## CONCLUSION

OUR tale is now done, and it only remains to us to collect the scattered threads of our little story, and to tie them into a seemly knot. This will not be a work of labour, either to the author or to his readers. We have not to deal with many personages, or with stirring events, and were it not for the custom of the thing, we might leave it to the imagination of all concerned to conceive how affairs at Barchester arranged themselves.

On the morning after the day last alluded to, Mr Harding, at an early hour, walked out of the hospital, with his daughter under his arm, and sat down quietly to breakfast at his lodgings over the chemist's shop. There was no parade about his departure; no one, not even Bunce, was there to witness it; had he walked to the apothecary's thus early to get a piece of court plaster,* or a box of lozenges, he could not have done it with less appearance of an important movement. There was a tear in Eleanor's eye as she passed through the big gateway and over the bridge; but Mr Harding walked with an elastic step, and entered his new abode with a pleasant face.

'Now, my dear,' said he, 'you have everything ready, and you can make tea here just as nicely as in the parlour at the hospital.' So Eleanor took off her bonnet and made the tea. After this manner did the late Warden of Barchester Hospital accomplish his flitting, and change his residence.

It was not long before the archdeacon brought his father to discuss the subject of a new warden. Of course he looked upon the nomination as his own, and he had in his eye three or four fitting candidates, seeing that Mr Cumming's plan as to the living of Puddingdale could not be brought to bear. How can I describe the astonishment which confounded him, when his father declared that he would appoint no successor to Mr Harding? 'If we can get the matter set to rights, Mr Harding will return,' said the bishop; 'and if we cannot, it will be wrong to put any other gentleman into so cruel a position.'

It was in vain that the archdeacon argued and lectured, and even threatened; in vain he my-lorded his poor father in his sternest manner; in vain his 'good heavens!' were ejaculated in a tone that might have moved a whole synod, let alone one weak and aged bishop. Nothing could induce his father to fill up the vacancy caused by Mr Harding's retirement.

Even John Bold would have pitied the feelings with which the archdeacon returned to Plumstead. The church was falling, nay, already in ruins; its dignitaries were yielding without a struggle before the blows of its antagonists; and one of its most respected bishops, his own father,—the man considered by all the world as being in such matters under his, Dr Grantly's control,—had positively resolved to capitulate, and own himself vanquished!

And how fared the hospital under this resolve of its visitor? Badly indeed. It was now some years since Mr Harding left it, and the warden's house is still tenantless. Old Bell has died, and Billy Gazy; the one-eyed Spriggs has drunk himself to death, and three others of the twelve have been gathered into the churchyard mould. Six have gone, and the six vacancies remain unfilled! Yes, six have died, with no kind friend to solace their last moments, with no wealthy neighbour to administer comforts and ease the stings of death. Mr Harding, indeed, did not desert them; from him they had such consolation as a dying man may receive from his Christian pastor; but it was the occasional kindness of a stranger which ministered to them, and not the constant presence of a master, a neighbour, and a friend.

Nor were those who remained better off than those who died. Dissensions rose among them, and contests for pre-eminence; and then they began to understand that soon one among them would be the last,—some one wretched being would be alone there in that now comfortless hospital,—the miserable relic of what had once been so good and so comfortable.

The building of the hospital itself has not been allowed to go to ruins. Mr Chadwick, who still holds his stewardship, and pays the accruing rents into an account opened at a bank for the purpose, sees to that; but the whole place has become disordered and ugly. The warden's garden is a wretched wilderness, the drive and paths are covered with weeds, the flower-beds are bare, and the unshorn lawn is now a mass of long damp grass and unwholesome moss. The beauty of the place is gone; its attractions have withered. Alas! a very few years since it was the prettiest spot in Barchester, and now it is a disgrace to the city.

Mr Harding did not go out to Crabtree Parva. An arrangement was made which respected the homestead of Mr Smith and his happy family, and put Mr Harding into possession of a small living within the walls of the city. It is the smallest possible parish, containing a part of the Cathedral Close and a few old houses adjoining. The church is a singular little Gothic building, perched over a gateway, through which the Close is entered, and is approached by a flight of stone steps which leads down under the archway of the gate. It is no bigger than an ordinary room,—perhaps twenty-seven feet long by eighteen wide,—but still it is a perfect church. It contains an old carved pulpit and reading-desk, a tiny altar under a window filled with dark old-coloured glass, a font, some half-dozen pews, and perhaps a dozen seats for the poor; and also a vestry. The roof is high-pitched, and of black old oak, and the three large beams which support it run down to the side walls, and terminate in grotesquely carved faces,—two devils and an angel on one side, two angels and a devil on the other. Such is the church of St Cuthbert* at Barchester, of which Mr Harding became rector, with a clear income of seventy-five pounds* a year.

Here he performs afternoon service every Sunday, and administers the Sacrament once in every three months.* His audience is not large; and, had they been so, he could not have accommodated them. But enough come to fill his six pews, and, on the front seat of those devoted to the poor is always to be seen our old friend Mr Bunce, decently arrayed in his bedesman's gown.

Mr Harding is still precentor of Barchester; and it is very rarely the case that those who attend the Sunday morning service miss the gratification of hearing him chant the Litany, as no other man in England can do it. He is neither a discontented nor an unhappy man. He still inhabits the lodgings to which he went on leaving the hospital, but he now has them to himself. Three months after that time Eleanor became Mrs Bold, and of course removed to her husband's house.

There were some difficulties to be got over on the occasion of the marriage. The archdeacon, who could not so soon overcome his grief, would not be persuaded to grace the ceremony with his presence, but he allowed his wife and children to be there. The marriage took place in the cathedral, and the bishop himself officiated. It was the last occasion on which he ever did so; and, though he still lives, it is not probable that he will ever do so again.

Not long after the marriage, perhaps six months, when Eleanor's bridal-honours were fading, and persons were beginning to call her Mrs Bold without twittering, the archdeacon consented to meet John Bold at a dinner-party, and since that time they have become almost friends. The archdeacon firmly believes that his brother-in-law was, as a bachelor, an infidel, an unbeliever in the great truths of our religion; but that matrimony has opened his eyes, as it has those of others. And Bold is equally inclined to think that time has softened the asperities of the archdeacon's character. Friends though they are, they do not often revert to the feud of the hospital.

Mr Harding, we say, is not an unhappy man. He keeps his lodgings, but they are of little use to him, except as being the one spot on earth which he calls his own. His time is spent chiefly at his daughter's or at the palace; he is never left alone, even should he wish to be so; and within a twelvemonth of Eleanor's marriage his determination to live at his own lodging had been so far broken through and abandoned, that he consented to have his violoncello permanently removed to his daughter's house.

Every other day a message is brought to him from the bishop. 'The bishop's compliments, and his lordship is not very well to-day, and he hopes Mr Harding will dine with him.' This bulletin as to the old man's health is a myth; for though he is over eighty he is never ill, and will probably die some day, as a spark goes out, gradually and without a struggle. Mr Harding does dine with him very often, which means going to the palace at three and remaining till ten; and whenever he does not the bishop whines, and says that the port wine is corked, and complains that nobody attends to him, and frets himself off to bed an hour before his time.

It was long before the people of Barchester forgot to call Mr Harding by his long well-known name of Warden. It had become so customary to say Mr Warden, that it was not easily dropped. 'No, no;' he always says when so addressed, 'not warden now, only precentor.'

# THE TWO HEROINES OF
PLUMPLINGTON

# CHAPTER 1

### THE TWO GIRLS

IN the little town of Plumplington last year,* just about this time of the year,—it was in November,—the ladies and gentlemen forming the Plumplington Society were much exercised as to the affairs of two young ladies. They were both the only daughters of two elderly gentlemen, well known and greatly respected in Plumplington. All the world may not know that Plumplington is the second town in Barsetshire, and though it sends no member to Parliament, as does Silverbridge, it has a population of over 20,000 souls, and three separate banks. Of one of these Mr Greenmantle is the manager, and is reputed to have shares in the bank. At any rate he is known to be a warm man. His daughter Emily is supposed to be the heiress of all he possesses, and has been regarded as a fitting match by many of the sons of the country gentlemen around. It was rumoured a short time since that young Harry Gresham* was likely to ask her hand in marriage, and Mr Greenmantle was supposed at the time to have been very willing to entertain the idea. Whether Mr Gresham has ever asked or not, Emily Greenmantle did not incline her ear that way, and it came out while the affair was being discussed in Plumplington circles that the young lady much preferred one Mr Philip Hughes. Now Philip Hughes was a very promising young man, but was at the time no more than a cashier in her father's bank. It become known at once that Mr Greenmantle was very angry. Mr Greenmantle was a man who carried himself with a dignified and handsome demeanour, but he was one of whom those who knew him used to declare that it would be found very difficult to turn him from his purpose. It might not be possible that he should succeed with Harry Gresham, but it was considered out of the question that he should give his girl and his money to such a man as Philip Hughes.

The other of these elderly gentlemen is Mr Hickory Peppercorn. It cannot be said that Mr Hickory Peppercorn had ever been put on a par with Mr Greenmantle. No one could suppose that Mr Peppercorn had ever sat down to dinner in company with Mr and Miss Greenmantle. Neither did Mr or Miss Peppercorn expect to be asked on the festive occasion of one of Mr Greenmantle's dinners.

But Miss Peppercorn was not unfrequently made welcome to Miss Greenmantle's five o'clock tea-table; and in many of the affairs of the town the two young ladies were seen associated together. They were both very active in the schools, and stood nearly equal in the good graces of old Dr Freeborn.* There was, perhaps, a little jealousy on this account in the bosom of Mr Greenmantle, who was pervaded perhaps by an idea that Dr Freeborn thought too much of himself. There never was a quarrel, as Mr Greenmantle was a good church-man; but there was a jealousy. Mr Greenmantle's family sank into insignificance if you looked beyond his grandfather; but Dr Freeborn could talk glibly of his ancestors in the time of Charles I. And it cer-tainly was the fact that Dr Freeborn would speak of the two young ladies in one and the same breath.

Now Mr Hickory Peppercorn was in truth nearly as warm a man as his neighbour, and he was one who was specially proud of being warm. He was a foreman,—or rather more than foreman,—a kind of top sawyer* in the brewery establishment of Messrs Du Boung and Co.,* a firm which has an establishment also in the town of Silverbridge. His position in the world may be described by declaring that he always wears a dark coloured tweed coat and trousers, and a chimney-pot hat.* It is almost impossible to say too much that is good of Mr Peppercorn. His one great fault has been already desig-nated. He was and still is very fond of his money. He does not talk much about it; but it is to be feared that it dwells too constantly on his mind. As a servant to the firm he is honesty and constancy itself. He is a man of such a nature that by means of his very presence all the partners can be allowed to go to bed if they wish it. And there is not a man in the establishment who does not know him to be good and true. He understands all the systems of brewing, and his very existence in the brewery is a proof that Messrs Du Boung and Co. are prosperous.

He has one daughter, Polly, to whom he is so thoroughly devoted that all the other girls in Plumplington envy her. If anything is to be done Polly is asked to go to her father, and if Polly does go to her father the thing is done. As far as money is concerned it is not known that Mr Peppercorn ever refused Polly anything. It is the pride of his heart that Polly shall be, at any rate, as well dressed as Emily Greenmantle. In truth nearly double as much is spent on her clothes, all of which Polly accepts without a word to show her pride. Her father does not say much, but now and again a sigh does escape him. Then it came out, as a blow to Plumplington, that Polly too had a lover. And the last person in Plumplington who heard the news was Mr Peppercorn. It seemed from his demeanour, when he first heard the tidings, that he had not expected that any such accident would ever happen. And yet Polly Peppercorn was a very pretty, bright girl of one-and-twenty of whom the wonder was,—if it was true,—that she had never already had a lover. She looked to be the very girl for lovers, and she looked also to be one quite able to keep a lover in his place.

Emily Greenmantle's lover was a two-months'-old story when Polly's lover became known to the public. There was a young man in Barchester who came over on Thursdays dealing with Mr Peppercorn for malt.* He was a fine stalwart young fellow, six-feet-one, with bright eyes and very light hair and whiskers, with a pair of shoulders which would think nothing of a sack of wheat, a hot temper, and a thoroughly good heart. It was known to all Plumplington that he had not a shilling in the world, and that he earned forty shillings a week from Messrs Mealing's establishment at Barchester. Men said of him that he was likely to do well in the world, but nobody thought that he would have the impudence to make up to Polly Peppercorn.

But all the girls saw it and many of the old women, and some even of the men. And at last Polly told him that if he had anything to say to her he must say it to her father. 'And you mean to have him, then?' said Bessy Rolt in surprise. Her lover was by at the moment, though not exactly within hearing of Bessy's question. But Polly when she was alone with Bessy spoke up her mind freely. 'Of course I mean to have him, if he pleases. What else? You don't suppose I would go on with a young man like that and mean nothing. I hate such ways.'

'But what will your father say?'

'Why shouldn't he like it? I heard papa say that he had but 7s. 6d. a week when he first came to Du Boungs. He got poor mamma to marry him, and he never was a good-looking man.'

'But he had made some money.'

'Jack has made no money as yet, but he is a good-looking fellow. So they're quits. I believe that father would do anything for me, and when he knows that I mean it he won't let me break my heart.'

But a week after that a change had come over the scene. Jack had gone to Mr Hickory Peppercorn, and Mr Peppercorn had given him a rough word or two. Jack had not borne the rough word well, and old Hickory, as he was called, had said in his wrath, 'Impudent cub! you've got nothing. Do you know what my girl will have?'

'I've never asked.'

'You knew she was to have something.'

'I know nothing about it. I'm ready to take the rough and the smooth together. I'll marry the young lady and wait till you give her something.' Hickory couldn't turn him out on the spur of the moment because there was business to be done, but warned him not to go into his private house. 'If you speak another word to Polly, old as I am, I'll measure you across the back with my stick.' But Polly, who knew her father's temper, took care to keep out of her father's sight on that occasion.

Polly after that began the battle in a fashion that had been invented by herself. No one heard the words that were spoken between her and her father,—her father who had so idolized her; but it appeared to the people of Plumplington that Polly was holding her own. No disrespect was shown to her father, not a word was heard from her mouth that was not affectionate or at least decorous. But she took upon herself at once a certain lowering of her own social standing. She never drank tea with Emily Greenmantle, or accosted her in the street with her old friendly manner. She was terribly humble to Dr Freeborn, who however would not acknowledge her humility on any account. 'What's come over you?' said the Doctor. 'Let me have none of your stage plays or I shall take you and shake you.'

'You can shake me if you like it, Dr Freeborn,' said Polly, 'but I know who I am and what my position is.'

'You are a determined young puss,' said the Doctor, 'but I am not going to help you in opposing your own father.' Polly said not a word further, but looked very demure as the Doctor took his departure.

But Polly performed her greatest stroke in reference to a change in her dress. All her new silks, that had been the pride of her father's heart, were made to give way to old stuff gowns.* People wondered where the old gowns, which had not been seen for years, had been stowed away. It was the same on Sundays as on Mondays and Tuesdays. But the due gradation was kept between Sundays and week-days. She was quite well enough dressed for a brewer's foreman's daughter on one day as on the other, but neither on one day nor on the other was she at all the Polly Peppercorn that Plumplington had known for the last couple of years. And there was not a word said about it. But all

Plumplington knew that Polly was fitting herself, as regarded her out-side garniture,* to be the wife of Jack Hollycombe with 40s. a week. And all Plumplington said that she would carry her purpose, and that Hickory Peppercorn would break down under stress of the artillery brought to bear against him. He could not put out her clothes for her, or force her into wearing them as her mother might have done, had her mother been living. He could only tear his hair and greet,* and swear to himself that under no such artillery as this would he give way. His girl should never marry Jack Hollycombe. He thought he knew his girl well enough to be sure that she would not marry without his consent. She might make him very unhappy by wearing dowdy clothes, but she would not quite break his heart. In the meantime Polly took care that her father should have no opportunity of measuring Jack's back.

With the affairs of Miss Greenmantle much more ceremony was observed, though I doubt whether there was more earnestness felt in the matter. Mr Peppercorn was very much in earnest, as was Polly,— and Jack Hollycombe. But Peppercorn talked about it publicly, and Polly showed her purpose, and Jack exhibited the triumphant lover to all eyes. Mr Greenmantle was silent as death in respect to the great trouble that had come upon him. He had spoken to no one on the subject except to the peccant* lover, and just a word or two to old Dr Freeborn. There was no trouble in the town that did not reach Dr Freeborn's ears; and Mr Greenmantle, in spite of his little jeal-ousy, was no exception. To the Doctor he had said a word or two as to Emily's bad behaviour. But in the stiffness of his back, and the length of his face, and the continual frown which was gathered on his brows, he was eloquent to all the town. Peppercorn had no powers of looking as he looked. The gloom of the bank was awful. It was felt to be so by the two junior clerks, who hardly knew whether to hate or to pity most Mr Philip Hughes. And if Mr Greenmantle's demeanour was hard to bear down below, within the bank, what must it have been up-stairs in the family sitting-room? It was now, at this time, about the middle of November; and with Emily everything had been black and clouded for the last two months past. Polly's misfortune had only begun about the first of November. The two young ladies had had their own ideas about their own young men from nearly the same date. Philip Hughes and Jack Hollycombe had pushed themselves into prominence about the same time. But Emily's trouble had declared itself six weeks before

Polly had sent her young man to her father. The first scene which took place with Emily and Mr Greenmantle, after young Hughes had declared himself, was very impressive. 'What is this, Emily?'

'What is what, papa?' A poor girl when she is thus cross-questioned hardly knows what to say.

'One of the young men in the bank has been to me.' There was in this a great slur intended. It was acknowledged by all Plumplington that Mr Hughes was the cashier, and was hardly more fairly designated as one of the young men than would have been Mr Greenmantle himself,—unless in regard to age.

'Philip, I suppose,' said Emily. Now Mr Greenmantle had certainly led the way into this difficulty himself. He had been allured by some modesty in the young man's demeanour,—or more probably by something pleasant in his manner which had struck Emily also,—to call him Philip. He had, as it were, shown a parental regard for him, and those who had best known Mr Greenmantle had been sure that he would not forget his manifest good intentions towards the young man. As coming from Mr Greenmantle the use of the christian name had been made. But certainly he had not intended that it should be taken up in this manner. There had been an ingratitude in it, which Mr Greenmantle had felt very keenly.

'I would rather that you should call the young man Mr Hughes in anything that you may have to say about him.'

'I thought you called him Philip, papa.'

'I shall never do so again,—never. What is this that he has said to me? Can it be true?'

'I suppose it is true, papa.'

'You mean that you want to marry him?'

'Yes, papa.'

'Goodness gracious me!' After this Emily remained silent for a while. 'Can you have realised the fact that the young man has— nothing; literally nothing!' What is a young lady to say when she is thus appealed to? She knew that though the young man had nothing, she would have a considerable portion of her own. She was her father's only child. She had not 'cared for' young Gresham, whereas she had 'cared for' young Hughes. What would be all the world to her if she must marry a man she did not care for? That, she was resolved, she would not do. But what would all the world be to her if she were not allowed to marry the man she did love? And what good would it be to her to be the only daughter of a rich man if she were to be baulked in this manner? She had thought it all over, assuming to herself perhaps greater privileges than she was entitled to expect.

But Emily Greenmantle was somewhat differently circumstanced from Polly Peppercorn. Emily was afraid of her father's sternness, whereas Polly was not in the least afraid of her governor, as she was wont to call him. Old Hickory was, in a good-humoured way, afraid of Polly. Polly could order the things, in and about the house, very much after her own fashion. To tell the truth Polly had but slight fear but that she would have her own way, and when she laid by her best silks she did not do it as a person does bid farewell to those treasures which are not to be seen again. They could be made to do very well for the future Mrs Hollycombe. At any rate, like a Marlborough or a Wellington,* she went into the battle thinking of victory and not of defeat. But Wellington was a long time before he had beaten the French, and Polly thought that there might be some trouble also for her. With Emily there was no prospect of ultimate victory.

Mr Greenmantle was a very stern man, who could look at his daughter as though he never meant to give way. And, without saying a word, he could make all Plumplington understand that such was to be the case. 'Poor Emily,' said the old Doctor to his old wife; 'I'm afraid there's a bad time coming for her.' 'He's a nasty cross old man,' said the old woman. 'It always does take three generations to make a "gentleman."' For Mrs Freeborn's ancestors had come from the time of James I.*

'You and I had better understand each other,' said Mr Greenmantle, standing up with his back to the fireplace, and looking as though he were all poker from the top of his head to the heels of his boots. 'You cannot marry Mr Philip Hughes.' Emily said nothing but turned her eyes down upon the ground. 'I don't suppose he thinks of doing so without money.'

'He has never thought about money at all.'

'Then what are you to live upon? Can you tell me that? He has £220 from the bank. Can you live upon that? Can you bring up a family?' Emily blushed as she still looked upon the ground. 'I tell you fairly that he shall never have the spending of my money. If you mean to desert me in my old age,—go.'

'Papa, you shouldn't say that.'

'You shouldn't think it.' Then Mr Greenmantle looked as though he had uttered a clenching argument. 'You shouldn't think it. Now go away, Emily, and turn in your mind what I have said to you.'

## CHAPTER 2

### 'DOWN I SHALL GO'

THEN there came about a conversation between the two young ladies which was in itself very interesting. They had not met each other for about a fortnight when Emily Greenmantle came to Mr Peppercorn's house. She had been thoroughly unhappy, and among her causes for sorrow had been the severance which seemed to have taken place between her and her friend. She had discussed all her troubles with Dr Freeborn, and Dr Freeborn had advised her to see Polly. 'Here's Christmas-time coming on and you are all going to quarrel among yourselves. I won't have any such nonsense. Go and see her.'

'It's not me, Dr Freeborn,' said Emily. 'I don't want to quarrel with anybody; and there is nobody I like better than Polly.' Thereupon Emily went to Mr Peppercorn's house when Peppercorn would be certainly at the brewery, and there she found Polly at home.

Polly was dressed very plainly. It was manifest to all eyes that the Polly Peppercorn of to-day was not the same Polly Peppercorn that had been seen about Plumplington for the last twelve months. It was equally manifest that Polly intended that everybody should see the difference. She had not meekly put on her poorer dress so that people should see that she was no more than her father's child; but it was done with some ostentation. 'If father says that Jack and I are not to have his money I must begin to reduce myself by times.' That was what Polly intended to say to all Plumplington. She was sure that her father would have to give way under such shots as she could fire at him.

'Polly, I have not seen you, oh, for such a long time.'

Polly did not look like quarrelling at all. Nothing could be more pleasant than the tone of her voice. But yet there was something in her mode of address which at once excited Emily Greenmantle's attention. In bidding her visitor welcome she called her Miss Greenmantle. Now on that matter there had been some little trouble heretofore, in which the banker's daughter had succeeded in getting the better of the banker. He had suggested that Miss Peppercorn was safer than Polly; but Emily had replied that Polly was a nice dear girl, very much in Dr Freeborn's good favours, and in point of fact that Dr Freeborn wouldn't allow it. Mr Greenmantle had frowned, but had felt himself unable to stand against Dr Freeborn in such a matter. 'What's the meaning of the Miss Greenmantle?' said Emily sorrowfully.

'It's what I'm come to,' said Polly, without any show of sorrow, 'and it's what I mean to stick to as being my proper place. You have heard all about Jack Hollycombe. I suppose I ought to call him John as I'm speaking to you.'

'I don't see what difference it will make.'

'Not much in the long run; but yet it will make a difference. It isn't that I should not like to be just the same to you as I have been, but father means to put me down in the world, and I don't mean to quarrel with him about that. Down I shall go.'

'And therefore I'm to be called Miss Greenmantle.'

'Exactly. Perhaps it ought to have been always so as I'm so poorly minded as to go back to such a one as Jack Hollycombe. Of course it is going back. Of course Jack is as good as father was at his age. But father has put himself up since that and has put me up. I'm such poor stuff that I wouldn't stay up. A girl has to begin where her husband begins; and as I mean to be Jack's wife I have to fit myself for the place.'

'I suppose it's the same with me, Polly.'

'Not quite. You're a lady bred and born, and Mr Hughes is a gentleman. Father tells me that a man who goes about the country selling malt isn't a gentleman. I suppose father is right. But Jack is a good enough gentleman to my thinking. If he had a share of father's money he would break out in quite a new place.'

'Mr Peppercorn won't give it to him?'

'Well! That's what I don't know. I do think the governor loves me. He is the best fellow anywhere for downright kindness. I mean to try him. And if he won't help me I shall go down as I say. You may be sure of this,—that I shall not give up Jack.'

'You wouldn't marry him against your father's wishes?'

Here Polly wasn't quite ready with her answer. 'I don't know that father has a right to destroy all my happiness,' she said at last. 'I shall wait a long time first at any rate. Then if I find that Jack can remain constant,—I don't know what I shall do.'

'What does he say?'

'Jack? He's all sugar and promises. They always are for a time. It takes a deal of learning to know whether a young man can be true. There is not above one in twenty that do come out true when they are tried.'

'I suppose not,' said Emily sorrowfully.

'I shall tell Mr Jack that he's got to go through the ordeal. Of course he wants me to say that I'll marry him right off the reel* and that he'll earn money enough for both of us. I told him only this morning—'

'Did you see him?'

'I wrote him,—out quite plainly. And I told him that there were other people had hearts in their bodies besides him and me. I'm not going to break father's heart,—not if I can help it. It would go very hard with him if I were to walk out of this house and marry Jack Hollycombe, quite plain like.'

'I would never do it,' said Emily with energy.

'You are a little different from me, Miss Greenmantle. I suppose my mother didn't think much about such things, and as long as she got herself married decent, didn't trouble herself much what her people said.'

'Didn't she?'

'I fancy not. Those sort of cares and bothers always come with money. Look at the two girls in this house.* I take it they only act just like their mothers, and if they're good girls, which they are, they get their mothers' consent. But the marriage goes on as a matter of course. It's where money is wanted that parents become stern and their children become dutiful. I mean to be dutiful for a time. But I'd rather have Jack than father's money.'

'Dr Freeborn says that you and I are not to quarrel. I am sure I don't see why we should.'

'What Dr Freeborn says is very well.' It was thus that Polly carried on the conversation after thinking over the matter for a moment or two. 'Dr Freeborn is a great man in Plumplington, and has his own way in everything. I'm not saying a word against Dr Freeborn, and goodness knows I don't want to quarrel with you, Miss Greenmantle.'

'I hope not.'

'But I do mean to go down if father makes me, and if Jack proves himself a true man.'

'I suppose he'll do that,' said Miss Greenmantle. 'Of course you think he will.'

'Well, upon the whole I do,' said Polly. 'And though I think father will have to give up, he won't do it just at present, and I shall have to remain just as I am for a time.'

'And wear——' Miss Greenmantle had intended to inquire whether it was Polly's purpose to go about in her second-rate clothes, but had hesitated, not quite liking to ask the question.

'Just that,' said Polly. 'I mean to wear such clothes as shall be suitable for Jack's wife. And I mean to give up all my airs. I've been thinking a deal about it, and they're wrong. Your papa and my father are not the same.'

'They are not the same, of course,' said Emily.

'One is a gentleman, and the other isn't. That's the long and the short of it. I oughtn't to have gone to your house drinking tea and the rest of it; and I oughtn't to have called you Emily. That's the long and the short of that,' said she, repeating herself.

'Dr Freeborn thinks——'

'Dr Freeborn mustn't quite have it all his own way. Of course Dr Freeborn is everything in Plumplington; and when I'm Jack's wife I'll do what he tells me again.'

'I suppose you'll do what Jack tells you then.'

'Well, yes; not exactly. If Jack were to tell me not to go to church,—— which he won't,—— I shouldn't do what he told me. If he said he'd like to have a leg of mutton boiled, I should boil it. Only legs of mutton wouldn't be very common with us, unless father comes round.'

'I don't see why all that should make a difference between you and me.'

'It will have to do so,' said Polly with perfect self-assurance. 'Father has told me that he doesn't mean to find money to buy legs of mutton for Jack Hollycombe. Those were his very words. I'm determined I'll never ask him. And he said he wasn't going to find clothes for Jack Hollycombe's brats. I'll never go to him to find a pair of shoes for Jack Hollycombe or one of his brats. I've told Jack as much, and Jack says that I'm right. But there's no knowing what's inside a young man till you've tried him. Jack may fall off, and if so there's an end of him. I shall come round in time, and wear my fine clothes again when I settle down as an old maid. But father will never make me wear them, and I shall never call you anything but Miss Greenmantle, unless he consent to my marrying Jack.'

Such was the eloquence of Polly Peppercorn as spoken on that occasion. And she certainly did fill Miss Greenmantle's mind with a strong idea of her persistency. When Polly's last speech was finished the banker's daughter got up, and kissed her friend, and took her leave. 'You shouldn't do that,' said Polly with a smile. But on this one occasion she returned the caress; and then Miss Greenmantle went her way thinking over all that had been said to her.

'I'll do it too, let him persuade me ever so.' This was Polly's soliloquy to herself when she was left alone, and the 'him' spoken of on this occasion was her father. She had made up her own mind as to the line of action she would follow, and she was quite resolved never again to ask her father's permission for her marriage. Her father and Jack might fight that out among themselves, as best they could. There had already been one scene on the subject between herself and her father in which the brewer's foreman had acted the part of stern parent with considerable violence. He had not beaten his girl, nor used bad words to her, nor, to tell the truth, had he threatened her with any deprivation of those luxuries to which she had become accustomed; but he had sworn by all the oaths which he knew by heart that if she chose to marry Jack Hollycombe she should go 'bare as a tinker's brat.' 'I don't want anything better,' Polly had said. 'He'll want something else though,' Peppercorn had replied, and had bounced out of the room and banged the door.

Miss Greenmantle, in whose nature there was perhaps something of the lugubrious tendencies which her father exhibited, walked away home from Mr Peppercorn's house with a sad heart. She was very sorry for Polly Peppercorn's grief, and she was very sorry also for her own. But she had not that amount of high spirits which sustained Polly in her troubles. To tell the truth Polly had some hope that she might get the better of her father, and thereby do a good turn both to him and to herself. But Emily Greenmantle had but little hope. Her father had not sworn at her, nor had he banged the door, but he had pressed his lips together till there was no lip really visible. And he had raised his forehead on high till it looked as though one continuous poker descended from the crown of his head passing down through his entire body. 'Emily, it is out of the question. You had better leave me.' From that day to this not a word had been spoken on the 'subject.' Young Gresham had been once asked to dine at the bank, but that had been the only effort made by Mr Greenmantle in the matter.

Emily had felt as she walked home that she had not at her command weapons so powerful as those which Polly intended to use against her father. No change in her dress would be suitable to her, and were she to make any it would be altogether inefficacious. Nor would her father be tempted by his passion to throw in her teeth the lack of either boots or legs of mutton which might be the consequence of her marriage with a poor man. There was something almost vulgar in these allusions which made Emily feel that there had been some reason for her papa's exclusiveness,—but she let that go by. Polly was a dear girl, though she had found herself able to speak of the brats' feet without even a blush. 'I suppose there will be brats, and why shouldn't she,—when she's talking only to me. It must be so I suppose.' So Emily had argued to herself, making the excuse altogether on behalf of her friend. But she was sure that if her father had heard Polly he would have been offended.

But what was Emily to do on her own behalf? Harry Gresham had come to dinner, but his coming had been altogether without effect. She was quite sure that she could never care for Harry Gresham, and she did not quite believe that Harry Gresham cared very much for her. There was a rumour about in the country that Harry Gresham wanted money, and she knew well that Harry Gresham's father and her own papa had been closeted together. She did not care to be married after such a fashion as that. In truth Philip Hughes was the only young man for whom she did care.

She had always felt her father to be the most impregnable of men,—but now on this subject of her marriage he was more impregnable than ever. He had never yet entirely digested that poker which he had swallowed when he had gone so far as to tell his daughter that it was 'entirely out of the question.' From that hour her home had been terrible to her as a home, and had not been in the least enlivened by the presence of Harry Gresham. And now how was she to carry on the battle? Polly had her plans all drawn out, and was preparing herself for the combat seriously. But for Emily, there was no means left for fighting.

And she felt that though a battle with her father might be very proper for Polly, it would be highly unbecoming for herself. There was a difference in rank between herself and Polly of which Polly clearly understood the strength. Polly would put on her poor clothes, and go into the kitchen, and break her father's heart by preparing for a descent into regions which would be fitting for her were she to marry her young man without a fortune. But to Miss Greenmantle this would be impossible. Any marriage, made now or later, without her father's leave, seemed to her out of the question. She would only ruin her 'young man' were she to attempt it, and the attempt would be altogether inefficacious. She could only be unhappy, melancholy,—and perhaps morose; but she could not be so unhappy and melancholy,—or morose, as was her father. At such weapons he could certainly beat her. Since that unhappy word had been spoken, the poker within him had not been for a moment lessened in vigour. And she feared even to appeal to Dr Freeborn. Dr Freeborn could do much,—almost everything in Plumplington,—but there was a point at which her father would turn even against Dr Freeborn. She did not think that the Doctor would ever dare to take up the cudgels against her father on behalf of Philip Hughes. She felt that it would be more becoming for her to abstain and to suffer in silence than to apply to any human being for assistance. But she could be miserable;—outwardly miserable as well as inwardly;—and very miserable she was determined that she would be! Her father no doubt would be miserable too; but she was sad at heart as she bethought herself that her father would rather like it. Though he could not easily digest a poker when he had swallowed it, it never seemed to disagree with him. A state of misery in which he would speak to no one seemed to be almost to his taste. In this way poor Emily Greenmantle did not see her way to the enjoyment of a happy Christmas.

## CHAPTER 3

### MR GREENMANTLE IS MUCH PERPLEXED

THAT evening Mr Greenmantle and his daughter sat down to dinner together in a very unhappy humour. They always dined at half-past seven;* not that Mr Greenmantle liked to have his dinner at that hour better than any other, but because it was considered to be fashionable. Old Mr Gresham, Harry's father, always dined at half-past seven, and Mr Greenmantle rather followed the habits of a county gentleman's life. He used to dine at this hour when there was a dinner-party, but of late he had adopted it for the family meal. To tell the truth there had been a few words between him and Dr Freeborn while Emily had been talking over matters with Polly Peppercorn. Dr Freeborn had not ventured to say a word as to Emily's love affairs; but had so discussed those of Jack Hollycombe and Polly as to leave a strong impression on the mind of Mr Greenmantle. He had quite understood that the Doctor had been talking at himself, and that when Jack's name had been mentioned, or Polly's, the Doctor had intended that the wisdom spoken should be intended to apply to Emily and to Philip Hughes. 'It's only because he can give her a lot of money,' the Doctor had said. 'The young man is a good young man, and steady. What is Peppercorn that he should want anything better for his child? Young Hollycombe has taken her fancy, and why shouldn't she have him?'

'I suppose Mr Peppercorn may have his own views,' Mr Greenmantle had answered.

'Bother his views,' the Doctor had said. 'He has no one else to think of but the girl and his views should be confined to making her happy. Of course he'll have to give way at last, and will only make himself ridiculous. I shouldn't say a word about it only that the young man is all that he ought to be.'

Now in this there was not a word which did not apply to Mr Greenmantle himself. And the worst of it was the fact that Mr Greenmantle felt that the Doctor intended it.

But as he had taken his constitutional walk before dinner, a walk which he took every day of his life after bank hours, he had sworn to himself that he would not be guided, or in the least affected, by Dr Freeborn's opinion in the matter. There had been an underlying bitterness in the Doctor's words which had much aggravated the banker's ill-humour. The Doctor would not so have spoken of the marriage of one of his own daughters,—before they had all been married. Birth would have been considered by him almost before anything. The Peppercorns and the Greenmantles were looked down upon almost from an equal height. Now Mr Greenmantle considered himself to be infinitely superior to Mr Peppercorn, and to be almost, if not altogether, equal to Dr Freeborn. He was much the richer man of the two, and his money was quite sufficient to outweigh a century or two of blood.

Peppercorn might do as he pleased. What became of Peppercorn's money was an affair of no matter. The Doctor's argument was no doubt good as far as Peppercorn was concerned. Peppercorn was not a gentleman. It was that which Mr Greenmantle felt so acutely. The one great line of demarcation in the world was that which separated gentlemen from non-gentlemen. Mr Greenmantle assured himself that he was a gentleman, acknowledged to be so by all the county. The old Duke of Omnium had customarily asked him to dine at his annual dinner at Gatherum Castle.* He had been in the habit of staying occasionally at Greshambury,* Mr Gresham's county seat, and Mr Gresham had been quite willing to forward the match between Emily and his younger son. There could be no doubt that he was on the right side of the line of demarcation. He was therefore quite determined that his daughter should not marry the Cashier in his own bank.

As he sat down to dinner he looked sternly at his daughter, and thought with wonder at the viciousness of her taste. She looked at him almost as sternly as she thought with awe of his cruelty. In her eyes Philip Hughes was quite as good a gentleman as her father. He was the son of a clergyman who was now dead, but had been intimate with Dr Freeborn. And in the natural course of events might succeed her father as manager of the Bank. To be manager of the Bank at Plumplington was not very much in the eyes of the world; but it was the position which her father filled. Emily vowed to herself as she looked across the table into her father's face, that she would be Mrs Philip Hughes,—or remain unmarried all her life. 'Emily, shall I help you to a mutton cutlet?' said her father with solemnity.

'No thank you, papa,' she replied with equal gravity.

'On what then do you intend to dine?' There had been a sole of which she had also declined to partake. 'There is nothing else, unless you will dine off rice pudding.'

'I am not hungry, papa.' She could not decline to wear her customary clothes as did her friend Polly, but she could at any rate go without her dinner. Even a father so stern as was Mr Greenmantle could not make her eat. Then there came a vision across her eyes of a long sickness, produced chiefly by inanition, in which she might wear her father's heart out. And then she felt that she might too probably lack the courage. She did not care much for her dinner; but she feared that she could not persevere to the breaking of her father's heart. She and her father were alone together in the world, and he in other respects had always been good to her. And now a tear trickled from her eye down her nose as she gazed upon the empty plate. He ate his two cutlets one after another in solemn silence and so the dinner was ended.

He, too, had felt uneasy qualms during the meal. 'What shall I do if she takes to starving herself and going to bed, all along of that young rascal in the outer bank?' It was thus that he had thought of it, and he too for a moment had begun to tell himself that were she to be perverse she must win the battle. He knew himself to be strong in purpose, but he doubted whether he would be strong enough to stand by and see his daughter starve herself. A week's starvation or a fortnight's he might bear, and it was possible that she might give way before that time had come.

Then he retired to a little room inside the bank, a room that was half private and half official, to which he would betake himself to spend his evening whenever some especially gloomy fit would fall* upon him. Here, within his own bosom, he turned over all the circumstances of the case. No doubt he had with him all the laws of God and man. He was not bound to give his money to any such interloper as was Philip Hughes. On that point he was quite clear. But what step had he better take to prevent the evil? Should he resign his position at the bank, and take his daughter away to live in the south of France? It would be a terrible step to which to be driven by his own Cashier. He was as efficacious to do the work of the bank as ever he had been, and he would leave this enemy to occupy his place. The enemy would then be in a condition to marry a wife without a fortune; and who could tell whether he might not show his power in such a crisis by marrying Emily! How terrible in such a case would be his defeat! At any rate he might go for three months on sick leave. He had been for nearly forty years in the bank, and had never yet been absent for a day on sick leave. Thinking of all this he remained alone till it was time for him to go to bed.

On the next morning he was dumb and stiff as ever, and after breakfast sat dumb and stiff, in his official room behind the bank counter, thinking over his great trouble. He had not spoken a word to Emily since yesterday's dinner beyond asking her whether she would take a bit of fried bacon. 'No thank you, papa,' she had said; and then Mr Greenmantle had made up his mind that he must take her away somewhere at once, lest she should be starved to death. Then he went into the bank and sat there signing his name,* and meditating the terrible catastrophe which was to fall upon him. Hughes, the Cashier, had become Mr Hughes, and if any young man could be frightened out of his love by the stern look and sterner voice of a parent, Mr Hughes would have been so frightened.

Then there came a knock at the door, and Mr Peppercorn having been summoned to come in, entered the room. He had expressed a desire to see Mr Greenmantle personally, and having proved his eagerness by a double request, had been allowed to have his way. It was quite a common affair for him to visit the bank on matters referring to the brewery; but now it was evident to any one with half an eye that such at present was not Mr Peppercorn's business. He had on the clothes in which he habitually went to church instead of the light-coloured pepper and salt tweed jacket in which he was accustomed to go about among the malt and barrels. 'What can I do for you, Mr Peppercorn?' said the banker. But the aspect was the aspect of a man who had a poker still fixed within his head and gullet.

' 'Tis nothing about the brewery, sir, or I shouldn't have troubled you. Mr Hughes is very good at all that kind of thing.' A further frown came over Mr Greenmantle's face, but he said nothing. 'You know my daughter Polly, Mr Greenmantle?'

'I am aware that there is a Miss Peppercorn,' said the other. Peppercorn felt that an offence was intended. Mr Greenmantle was of course aware. 'What can I do on behalf of Miss Peppercorn?'

'She's as good a girl as ever lived.'

'I do not in the least doubt it. If it be necessary that you should speak to me respecting Miss Peppercorn, will it not be well that you should take a chair?'

Then Mr Peppercorn sat down, feeling that he had been snubbed. 'I may say that my only object in life is to do every mortal thing to make my girl happy.' Here Mr Greenmantle simply bowed. 'We sit close to you in church, where, however, she comes much more reg'lar than me, and you must have observed her scores of times.'

'I am not in the habit of looking about among young ladies at church time, but I have occasionally been aware that Miss Peppercorn has been there.'

'Of course you have. You couldn't help it. Well, now, you know the sort of appearance she has made.'

'I can assure you, Mr Peppercorn, that I have not observed Miss Peppercorn's dress in particular. I do not look much at the raiment worn by young ladies even in the outer world,—much less in church. I have a daughter of my own——'

'It's her as I'm coming to.' Then Mr Greenmantle frowned more severely than ever. But the brewer did not at the moment say a word about the banker's daughter, but reverted to his own. 'You'll see next Sunday that my girl won't look at all like herself.'

'I really cannot promise—'

'You cannot help yourself, Mr Greenmantle. I'll go bail that every one in church will see it. Polly is not to be passed over in a crowd;—at least she didn't used to be. Now it all comes of her wanting to get herself married to a young man who is altogether beneath her. Not as I mean to say anything against John Hollycombe as regards his walk of life. He is an industrious young man, as can earn forty shillings a week, and he comes over here from Barchester selling malt and such like. He may rise himself to £3 some of these days if he looks sharp about it. But I can give my girl—; well; what is quite unfit that he should think of looking for with a wife. And it's monstrous of Polly wanting to throw herself away in such a fashion. I don't believe in a young man being so covetous.'

'But what can I do, Mr Peppercorn?'

'I'm coming to that. If you'll see her next Sunday you'll think of what my feelings must be. She's a-doing of it all just because she wants to show me that she thinks herself fit for nothing better than to be John Hollycombe's wife. When I tell her that I won't have it,—this sudden changing of her toggery,* she says it's only fitting. It ain't fitting at all. I've got the money to buy things for her, and I'm willing to pay for it. Is she to go poor just to break her father's heart?'

'But what can I do, Mr Peppercorn?'

'I'm coming to that. The world does say, Mr Greenmantle, that your young lady means to serve you in the same fashion.'

Hereupon Mr Greenmantle waxed very wroth. It was terrible to his ideas that his daughter's affairs should be talked of at all by the people at Plumplington at large. It was worse again that his daughter and the brewer's girl should be lumped together in the scandal of the town. But it was worse, much worse, that this man Peppercorn should have dared to come to him, and tell him all about it. Did the man really expect that he, Mr Greenmantle, should talk unreservedly as to the love affairs of his Emily? 'The world, Mr Peppercorn, is very impertinent in its usual scandalous conversations as to its betters. You must forgive me if I do not intend on this occasion to follow the example of the world. Good morning, Mr Peppercorn.'

'It's Dr Freeborn as has coupled the two girls together.'

'I cannot believe it.'

'You ask him. It's he who has said that you and I are in a boat together.'

'I'm not in a boat with any man.'

'Well,—in a difficulty. It's the same thing. The Doctor seems to think that young ladies are to have their way in everything. I don't see it. When a man has made a tidy bit of money, as have you and I, he has a right to have a word to say as to who shall have the spending of it. A girl hasn't the right to say that she'll give it all to this man or to that. Of course, it's natural that my money should go to Polly. I'm not saying anything against it. But I don't mean that John Hollycombe shall have it. Now if you and I can put our heads together, I think we may be able to see our way out of the wood.'

'Mr Peppercorn, I cannot consent to discuss with you the affairs of Miss Greenmantle.'

'But they're both alike. You must admit that.'

'I will admit nothing, Mr Peppercorn.'

'I do think, you know, that we oughtn't to be done by our own daughters.'

'Really, Mr Peppercorn——'

'Dr Freeborn was saying that you and I would have to give way at last.'

'Dr Freeborn knows nothing about it. If Dr Freeborn coupled the two young ladies together he was I must say very impertinent; but I don't think he ever did so. Good morning, Mr Peppercorn. I am fully engaged at present and cannot spare time for a longer interview.' Then he rose up from his chair, and leant upon the table with his hands by way of giving a certain signal that he was to be left alone. Mr Peppercorn, after pausing a moment, searching for an opportunity for another word, was overcome at last by the rigid erectness of Mr Greenmantle and withdrew.

## CHAPTER 4

### JACK HOLLYCOMBE

MR PEPPERCORN'S visit to the bank had been no doubt inspired by Dr Freeborn. The Doctor had not actually sent him to the bank, but had filled his mind with the idea that such a visit might be made with good effect. 'There are you two fathers going to make two fools of yourselves,' the Doctor had said. 'You have each of you got a daughter as good as gold, and are determined to break their hearts because you won't give your money to a young man who happens to want it.'

'Now, Doctor, do you mean to tell me that you would have married your young ladies to the first young man that came and asked for them?'

'I never had much money to give my girls, and the men who came happened to have means of their own.'

'But if you'd had it, and if they hadn't, do you mean to tell me you'd never have asked a question?'

'A man should never boast that in any circumstances of his life he would have done just what he ought to do,—much less when he has never been tried. But if the lover be what he ought to be in morals and all that kind of thing, the girl's father ought not to refuse to help them. You may be sure of this,—that Polly means to have her own way. Providence has blessed you with a girl that knows her own mind.' On receipt of this compliment Mr Peppercorn scratched his head. 'I wish I could say as much for my friend Greenmantle. You two are in a boat together, and ought to make up your mind as to what you should do.' Peppercorn resolved that he would remember the phrase about the boat, and began to think that it might be good that he should see Mr Greenmantle. 'What on earth is it you two want? It is not as though you were dukes, and looking for proper alliances for two ducal spinsters.'

Now there had no doubt been a certain amount of intended venom in this. Dr Freeborn knew well the weak points in Mr Greenmantle's character; and was determined to hit him where he was weakest. He did not see the difference between the banker and the brewer nearly so clearly as did Mr Greenmantle. He would probably have said that the line of demarcation came just below himself. At any rate, he thought that he would be doing best for Emily's interest if he made her father feel that all the world was on her side. Therefore it was that he so contrived that Mr Peppercorn should pay his visit to the bank.

On his return to the brewery the first person that Peppercorn saw standing in the doorway of his own little sanctum was Jack Hollycombe. 'What is it you're wanting?' he asked gruffly.

'I was just desirous of saying a few words to yourself, Mr Peppercorn.'

'Well, here I am!' There were two or three brewers and porters about the place, and Jack did not feel that he could plead his cause well in their presence. 'What is it you've got to say,—because I'm busy? There ain't no malt wanted for the next week; but you know that, and as we stand at present you can send it in without any more words, as it's needed.'

'It ain't about malt or anything of that kind.'

'Then I don't know what you've got to say. I'm very busy just at present, as I told you.'

'You can spare me five minutes inside.'

'No I can't.' But then Peppercorn resolved that neither would it suit him to carry on the conversation respecting his daughter in the presence of the workmen, and he thought that he perceived that Jack Hollycombe would be prepared to do so if he were driven. 'Come in if you will,' he said; 'we might as well have it out.' Then he led the way into the room, and shut the door as soon as Jack had followed him. 'Now what is it you have got to say? I suppose it's about that young woman down at my house.'

'It is, Mr Peppercorn.'

'Then let me tell you that the least said will be soonest mended. She's not for you,—with my consent. And to tell you the truth I think that you have a mortal deal of brass* coming to ask for her. You've no edication suited to her edication,—and what's wus, no money.' Jack had shown symptoms of anger when his deficient education had been thrown in his teeth, but had cheered up somewhat when the lack of money had been insisted upon. 'Them two things are so against you that you haven't a leg to stand on. My word! what do you expect that I should say when such a one as you comes a-courting to a girl like that?'

'I did, perhaps, think more of what she might say.'

'I daresay;—because you knew her to be a fool like yourself. I suppose you think yourself to be a very handsome young man.'

'I think she's a very handsome young woman. As to myself I never asked the question.'

'That's all very well. A man can always say as much as that for himself. The fact is you're not going to have her.'

'That's just what I want to speak to you about, Mr Peppercorn.'

'You're not going to have her. Now I've spoken my intentions, and
you may as well take one word as a thousand. I'm not a man as was
ever known to change my mind when I'd made it up in such a matter
as this.'

'She's got a mind too, Mr Peppercorn.'

'She have, no doubt. She have a mind and so have you. But you
haven't either of you got the money. The money is here,' and Mr
Peppercorn slapped his breeches pocket. 'I've had to do with earning
it, and I mean to have to do with giving it away. To me there is no idea
of honesty at all in a chap like you coming and asking a girl to marry
you just because you know that she's to have a fortune.'

'That's not my reason.'

'It's uncommon like it. Now you see there's somebody else that's
got to be asked. You think I'm a goodnatured fellow. So I am, but I'm
not soft like that.'

'I never thought anything of the kind, Mr Peppercorn.'

'Polly told you so, I don't doubt. She's right in thinking so, because
I'd give Polly anything in reason. Or out of reason for the matter of
that, because she is the apple of my eye.' This was indiscreet on the
part of Mr Peppercorn, as it taught the young man to think that he
himself must be in reason or out of reason, and that in either case
Polly ought to be allowed to have him. 'But there's one thing I stop at;
and that is a young man who hasn't got either edication, or money,—
nor yet manners.'

'There's nothing against my manner, I hope, Mr Peppercorn.'

'Yes; there is. You come a-interfering with me in the most delicate
affair in the world. You come into my family, and want to take away my
girl. That I take it is the worst of manners.'

'How is any young lady to get married unless some young fellow
comes after her?'

'There'll be plenty to come after Polly. You leave Polly alone, and
you'll find that she'll get a young man suited to her. It's like your
impudence to suppose that there's no other young man in the world
so good as you. Why;—dash my wig; who are you? What are you?
You're merely acting for them corn-factors* over at Barsester.'

'And you're acting for them brewers here at Plumplington. What's
the difference?'

'But I've got the money in my pocket, and you've got none. That's
the difference. Put that in your pipe and smoke it. Now if you'll please

to remember that I'm very busy, you'll walk yourself off. You've had it out with me, which I didn't intend; and I've explained my mind very fully. She's not for you;—at any rate my money's not.'

'Look here, Mr Peppercorn.'

'Well?'

'I don't care a farthing for your money.'

'Don't you, now?'

'Not in the way of comparing it with Polly herself. Of course money is a very comfortable thing. If Polly's to be my wife—'

'Which she ain't.'

'I should like her to have everything that a lady can desire.'

'How kind you are.'

'But in regard to money for myself I don't value it that.' Here Jack Hollycombe snapped his fingers. 'My meaning is to get the girl I love.'

'Then you won't.'

'And if she's satisfied to come to me without a shilling, I'm satisfied to take her in the same fashion. I don't know how much you've got, Mr Peppercorn, but you can go and found a Hiram's Hospital with every penny of it.' At this moment a discussion was going on respecting a certain charitable institution in Barchester,—and had been going on for the last forty years,*—as to which Mr Hollycombe was here expressing the popular opinion of the day. 'That's the kind of thing a man should do who don't choose to leave his money to his own child.' Jack was now angry, having had his deficient education twice thrown in his teeth by one whom he conceived to be so much less educated than himself. 'What I've got to say to you, Mr Peppercorn, is that Polly means to have me, and if she's got to wait—why, I'm so minded that I'll wait for her as long as ever she'll wait for me.' So saying Jack Hollycombe left the room.

Mr Peppercorn thrust his hat back upon his head, and stood with his back to the fire, with the tails of his coat appearing over his hands in his breeches pockets, glaring out of his eyes with anger which he did not care to suppress. This man had presented to him a picture of his future life which was most unalluring. There was nothing he desired less than to give his money to such an abominable institution as Hiram's Hospital. Polly, his own dear daughter Polly, was intended to be the recipient of all his savings. As he went about among the beer barrels, he had been a happy man as he thought of Polly bright with the sheen which his money had provided for her. But it was of Polly married to some gentleman that he thought at these moments;— of Polly surrounded by a large family of little gentlemen and little ladies. They would all call him grandpapa; and in the evenings of his days he would sit by the fire in that gentleman's parlour, a welcome guest because of the means which he had provided; and the little gentlemen and the little ladies would surround him with their prattle and their noises and caresses. He was not a man whom his intimates would have supposed to be gifted with a strong imagination, but there was the picture firmly set before his mind's eye. 'Edication,' however, in the intended son-in-law was essential. And the son-in-law must be a gentleman. Now Jack Hollycombe was not a gentleman, and was not educated up to that pitch which was necessary for Polly's husband.

But Mr Peppercorn, as he thought of it all, was well aware that Polly had a decided will of her own. And he knew of himself that his own will was less strong than his daughter's. In spite of all the severe things which he had just said to Jack Hollycombe, there was present to him a dreadful weight upon his heart, as he thought that Polly would certainly get the better of him. At this moment he hated Jack Hollycombe with most un-Christian rancour. No misfortune that could happen to Jack, either sudden death, or forgery with flight to the antipodes, or loss of his good looks,—which Mr Peppercorn most unjustly thought would be equally efficacious with Polly,— would at the present moment of his wrath be received otherwise than as a special mark of good-fortune. And yet he was well aware that if Polly were to come and tell him that she had by some secret means turned herself into Mrs Jack Hollycombe, he knew very well that for Polly's sake he would have to take Jack with all his faults, and turn him into the dearest son-in-law that the world could have provided for him. This was a very trying position, and justified him in standing there for a quarter of an hour with his back to the fire, and his coat-tails over his arms, as they were thrust into his trousers pockets.

In the meantime Jack had succeeded in obtaining a few minutes' talk with Polly,—or rather the success had been on Polly's side, for she had managed the business. On coming out from the brewery Jack had met her in the street, and had been taken home by her. 'You might as well come in, Jack,' she had said, 'and have a few words with me. You have been talking to father about it, I suppose.'

'Well; I have. He says I am not sufficiently educated. I suppose he wants to get some young man from the colleges.'*

'Don't you be stupid, Jack. You want to have your own way, I suppose.'

'I don't want him to tell me I'm uneducated. Other men that I've heard of ain't any better off than I am.'

'You mean himself,—which isn't respectful.'

'I'm educated up to doing what I've got to do. If you don't want more, I don't see what he's got to do with it.'

'As the times go of course a man should learn more and more. You are not to compare him to yourself; and it isn't respectful. If you want to say sharp things against him, Jack, you had better give it all up;— for I won't bear it.'

'I don't want to say anything sharp.'

'Why can't you put up with him? He's not going to have his own way. And he is older than you. And it is he that has got the money. If you care about it——'

'You know I care.'

'Very well. Suppose I do know, and suppose I don't. I hear you say you do, and that's all I've got to act upon. Do you bide your time if you've got the patience, and all will come right. I shan't at all think so much of you if you can't bear a few sharp words from him.'

'He may say whatever he pleases.'

'You ain't educated,—not like Dr Freeborn, and men of that class.'

'What do I want with it?' said he.

'I don't know that you do want it. At any rate I don't want it; and that's what you've got to think about at present. You just go on, and let things be as they are. You don't want to be married in a week's time.'

'Why not?' he asked.

'At any rate I don't; and I don't mean to. This time five years will do very well.'

'Five years! You'll be an old woman.'

'The fitter for you, who'll still be three years older. If you've patience to wait leave it to me.'

'I haven't over much patience.'

'Then go your own way and suit yourself elsewhere.'

'Polly, you're enough to break a man's heart. You know that I can't go and suit myself elsewhere. You are all the world to me, Polly.'

'Not half so much as a quarter of malt if you could get your own price for it. A young woman is all very well just as a play-thing; but business is business;—isn't it, Jack?'

'Five years! Fancy telling a fellow that he must wait five years.'

'That'll do for the present, Jack. I'm not going to keep you here idle all the day. Father will be angry when I tell him that you've been here at all.'

'It was you that brought me.'

'Yes, I did. But you're not to take advantage of that. Now I say, Jack, hands off. I tell you I won't. I'm not going to be kissed once a week for five years. Well. Mark my words, this is the last time I ever ask you in here. No; I won't have it. Go away.' Then she succeeded in turning him out of the room and closing the house door behind his back. 'I think he's the best young man I see about anywhere. Father twits him about his education. It's my belief there's nothing he can't do that he's wanted for. That's the kind of education a man ought to have. Father says it's because he's handsome I like him. It does go a long way, and he is handsome. Father has got ideas of fashion into his head which will send him crazy before he has done with them.' Such was the soliloquy in which Miss Peppercorn indulged as soon as she had been left by her lover.

'Educated! Of course I'm not educated. I can't talk Latin and Greek as some of those fellows pretend to,—though for the matter of that I never heard it. But two and two make four, and ten and ten make twenty. And if a fellow says that it don't he is trying on some dishonest game. If a fellow understands that, and sticks to it, he has education enough for my business,—or for Peppercorn's either.' Then he walked back to the inn yard where he had left his horse and trap.

As he drove back to Barchester he made up his mind that Polly Peppercorn would be worth waiting for. There was the memory of that kiss upon his lips which had not been made less sweet by the severity of the words which had accompanied it. The words indeed had been severe; but there had been an intention and a purpose about the kiss which had altogether redeemed the words. 'She is just one in a thousand, that's about the truth. And as for waiting for her;—I'll wait like grim death, only I hope it won't be necessary!' It was thus he spoke of the lady of his love as he drove himself into the town under Barchester Towers.*

## CHAPTER 5
### DR FREEBORN AND PHILIP HUGHES

THINGS went on at Plumplington without any change for a fortnight,—that is without any change for the better. But in truth the ill-
humour both of Mr Greenmantle and of Mr Peppercorn had increased
to such a pitch as to add an additional blackness to the general haziness
and drizzle and gloom of the November weather. It was now the end of
November, and Dr Freeborn was becoming a little uneasy because the
Christmas attributes for which he was desirous were still altogether
out of sight. He was a man specially anxious for the mundane happiness of his parishioners and who would take any amount of personal
trouble to insure it; but he was in fault perhaps in this, that he considered that everybody ought to be happy just because he told them to
be so. He belonged to the Church of England certainly, but he had no
dislike to Papists or Presbyterians, or dissenters* in general, as long
as they would arrange themselves under his banner as 'Freebornites.'
And he had such force of character that in Plumplington,—beyond
which he was not ambitious that his influence should extend,—he
did in general prevail. But at the present moment he was aware that
Mr Greenmantle was in open mutiny. That Peppercorn would yield
he had strong hope. Peppercorn he knew to be a weak, good fellow,
whose affection for his daughter would keep him right at last. But
until he could extract that poker from Mr Greenmantle's throat, he
knew that nothing could be done with him.

At the end of the fortnight Mr Greenmantle called at the Rectory
about half an hour before dinner time, when he knew that the Doctor
would be found in his study before going up to dress for dinner.
'I hope I am not intruding, Dr Freeborn,' he said. But the rust of the
poker was audible in every syllable as it fell from his mouth.

'Not in the least. I've a quarter of an hour before I go and wash my
hands.'

'It will be ample. In a quarter of an hour I shall be able sufficiently to
explain my plans.' Then there was a pause, as though Mr Greenmantle
had expected that the explanation was to begin with the Doctor.
'I am thinking,' the banker continued after a while, 'of taking my
family abroad to some foreign residence.' Now it was well known to Dr
Freeborn that Mr Greenmantle's family consisted exclusively of Emily.

'Going to take Emily away?' he said.

'Such is my purpose,—and myself also.'

'What are they to do at the bank?'

'That will be the worst of it, Dr Freeborn. The bank will be the great difficulty.'

'But you don't mean that you are going for good?'

'Only for a prolonged foreign residence;—that is to say for six months. For forty years I have given but very little trouble to the Directors. For forty years I have been at my post and have never suggested any prolonged absence. If the Directors cannot bear with me after forty years I shall think them unreasonable men.' Now in truth Mr Greenmantle knew that the Directors would make no opposition to anything that he might propose; but he always thought it well to be armed with some premonitory grievance. 'In fact my pecuniary matters are so arranged that should the Directors refuse I shall go all the same.'

'You mean that you don't care a straw for the Directors.'

'I do not mean to postpone my comfort to their views,—or my daughter's.'

'But why does your daughter's comfort depend on your going away? I should have thought that she would have preferred Plumplington at present.'

That was true, no doubt. And Mr Greenmantle felt;—well; that he was not exactly telling the truth in putting the burden of his departure upon Emily's comfort. If Emily, at the present crisis of affairs, were carried away from Plumplington for six months, her comfort would certainly not be increased. She had already been told that she was to go, and she had clearly understood why. 'I mean as to her future welfare,' said Mr Greenmantle very solemnly.

Dr Freeborn did not care to hear about the future welfare of young people. What had to be said as to their eternal welfare he thought himself quite able to say. After all there was something of benevolent paganism* in his disposition. He liked better to deal with their present happiness,—so that there was nothing immoral in it. As to the world to come he thought that the fathers and mothers of his younger flock might safely leave that consideration to him. 'Emily is a remarkably good girl. That's my idea of her.'

Mr Greenmantle was offended even at this. Dr Freeborn had no right, just at present, to tell him that his daughter was a good girl. Her goodness had been greatly lessened by the fact that in regard to her marriage she was anxious to run counter to her father. 'She is a good girl. At least I hope so.'

'Do you doubt it?'

'Well, no;—or rather yes. Perhaps I ought to say no as to her life in general.'

'I should think so. I don't know what a father may want,—but I should think so. I never knew her miss church yet,—either morning or evening.'

'As far as that goes she does not neglect her duties.'

'What is the matter with her that she is to be taken off to some foreign climate for prolonged residence?' The Doctor among his other idiosyncrasies entertained an idea that England was the proper place for all Englishmen and Englishwomen who were not driven out of it by stress of pecuniary circumstances. 'Has she got a bad throat or a weak chest?'

'It is not on the score of her own health that I propose to move her,' said Mr Greenmantle.

'You did say her comfort. Of course that may mean that she likes the French way of living. I did hear that we were to lose your services for a time, because you could not trust your own health.'

'It is failing me a little, Dr Freeborn. I am already very near sixty.'

'Ten years my junior,' said the Doctor.

'We cannot all hope to have such perfect health as you possess.'

'I have never frittered it away,' said the Doctor, 'by prolonged residence in foreign parts.' This quotation of his own words was most harassing to Mr Greenmantle, and made him more than once inclined to bounce in anger out of the Doctor's study. 'I suppose the truth is that Miss Emily is disposed to run counter to your wishes in regard to her marriage, and that she is to be taken away not from consumption or a weak throat, but from a dangerous lover.' Here Mr Greenmantle's face became black as thunder. 'You see, Greenmantle, there is no good in our talking about this matter unless we understand each other.'

'I do not intend to give my girl to the young man upon whom she thinks that her affections rest.'

'I suppose she knows.'

'No, Dr Freeborn. It is often the case that a young lady does not know; she only fancies, and where that is the case absence is the best remedy. You have said that Emily is a good girl.'

'A very good girl.'

'I am delighted to hear you so express yourself. But obedience to parents is a trait in character which is generally much thought of. I have put by a little money, Dr Freeborn.'

'All Plumplington knows that.'

'And I shall choose that it shall go somewhat in accordance with my wishes. The young man of whom she is thinking—'

'Philip Hughes, an excellent fellow. I've known him all my life. He doesn't come to church quite so regularly as he ought, but that will be mended when he's married.'

'Hasn't got a shilling in the world,' continued Mr Greenmantle, finishing his sentence. 'Nor is he—just,—just—just what I should choose for the husband of my daughter. I think that when I have said so he should take my word for it.'

'That's not the way of the world, you know.'

'It's the way of my world, Dr Freeborn. It isn't often that I speak out, but when I do it's about something that I've a right to speak of. I've heard this affair of my daughter talked about all over the town. There was one Mr Peppercorn came to me——'

'One Mr Peppercorn? Why, Hickory Peppercorn is as well known in Plumplington as the church-steeple.'

'I beg your pardon, Dr Freeborn; but I don't find any reason in that for his interfering about my daughter. I must say that I took it as a great piece of impertinence. Goodness gracious me! If a man's own daughter isn't to be considered peculiar to himself I don't know what is. If he'd asked you about your daughters,—before they were married?' Dr Freeborn did not answer this, but declared to himself that neither Mr Peppercorn nor Mr Greenmantle could have taken such a liberty. Mr Greenmantle evidently was not aware of it, but in truth Dr Freeborn and his family belonged altogether to another set. So at least Dr Freeborn told himself. 'I've come to you now, Dr Freeborn, because I have not liked to leave Plumplington for a prolonged residence in foreign parts without acquainting you.'

'I should have thought that unkind.'

'You are very good. And as my daughter will of course go with me, and as this idea of a marriage on her part must be entirely given up;' the emphasis was here placed with much weight on the word entirely;—'I should take it as a great kindness if you would let my feelings on the subject be generally known. I will own that I should not have cared to have my daughter talked about, only that the mischief has been done.'

'In a little place like this,' said the Doctor, 'a young lady's marriage will always be talked about.'

'But the young lady in this case isn't going to be married.'

'What does she say about it herself?'

'I haven't asked her, Dr Freeborn. I don't mean to ask her. I shan't ask her.'

'If I understand her feelings, Greenmantle, she is very much set upon it.'

'I cannot help it.'

'You mean to say then that you intend to condemn her to unhappiness merely because this young man hasn't got as much money at the beginning of his life as you have at the end of yours?'

'He hasn't got a shilling,' said Mr Greenmantle.

'Then why can't you give him a shilling? What do you mean to do with your money?' Here Mr Greenmantle again looked offended. 'You come and ask me, and I am bound to give you my opinion for what it's worth. What do you mean to do with your money? You're not the man to found a Hiram's Hospital with it. As sure as you are sitting there your girl will have it when you're dead. Don't you know that she will have it?'

'I hope so.'

'And because she's to have it, she's to be made wretched about it all her life. She's to remain an old maid, or else to be married to some well-born pauper, in order that you may talk about your son-in-law. Don't get into a passion, Greenmantle, but only think whether I'm not telling you the truth. Hughes isn't a spendthrift.'

'I have made no accusation against him.'

'Nor a gambler, nor a drunkard, nor is he the sort of man to treat a wife badly. He's there at the bank so that you may keep him under your own eye. What more on earth can a man want in a son-in-law?'

Blood, thought Mr Greenmantle to himself; an old family name; county associations, and a certain something which he felt quite sure Philip Hughes did not possess. And he knew well enough that Dr Freeborn had married his own daughters to husbands who possessed these gifts; but he could not throw the fact back into the Rector's teeth. He was in some way conscious that the Rector had been entitled to expect so much for his girls, and that he, the banker, was not so entitled. The same idea passed through the Rector's mind. But the Rector knew how far the banker's courage would carry him. 'Good night, Dr Freeborn,' said Mr Greenmantle suddenly.

'Good night, Greenmantle. Shan't I see you again before you go?' To this the banker made no direct answer, but at once took his leave.

'That man is the greatest ass in all Plumplington,' the Doctor said to his wife within five minutes of the time of which the hall door was closed behind the banker's back. 'He's got an idea into his head about having some young county swell for his son-in-law.'

'Harry Gresham. Harry is too idle to earn money by a profession and therefore wants Greenmantle's money to live upon. There's Peppercorn wants something of the same kind for Polly. People are such fools.' But Mrs Freeborn's two daughters had been married much after the same fashion. They had taken husbands nearly as old as their father, because Dr Freeborn and his wife had thought much of 'blood.'

On the next morning Philip Hughes was summoned by the banker into the more official of the two back parlours. Since he had presumed to signify his love for Emily, he had never been asked to enjoy the familiarity of the other chamber. 'Mr Hughes, you may probably have heard it asserted that I am about to leave Plumplington for a prolonged residence in foreign parts.' Mr Hughes had heard it and so declared. 'Yes, Mr Hughes, I am about to proceed to the south of France. My daughter's health requires attention,—and indeed on my own behalf I am in need of some change as well. I have not as yet officially made known my views to the Directors.'

'There will be, I should think, no impediment with them.'

'I cannot say. But at any rate I shall go. After forty years of service in the Bank I cannot think of allowing the peculiar views of men who are all younger than myself to interfere with my comfort. I shall go.'

'I suppose so, Mr Greenmantle.'

'I shall go. I say it without the slightest disrespect for the Board. But I shall go.'

'Will it be permanent, Mr Greenmantle?'

'That is a question which I am not prepared to answer at a moment's notice. I do not propose to move my furniture for six months. It would not, I believe, be within the legal power of the Directors to take possession of the Bank house for that period.'

'I am quite sure they would not wish it.'

'Perhaps my assurance on that subject may be of more avail. At any rate they will not remove me. I should not have troubled you on this subject were it not that your position in the Bank must be affected more or less.'

'I suppose that I could do the work for six months,' said Philip Hughes.

But this was a view of the case which did not at all suit Mr Greenmantle's mind. His own duties at Plumplington had been, to his thinking, the most important ever confided to a Bank Manager. There was a peculiarity about Plumplington of which no one knew the intricate details but himself. The man did not exist who could do the work as he had done it. But still he had determined to go, and the work must be intrusted to some man of lesser competence. 'I should think it probable,' he said, 'that some confidential clerk will be sent over from Barchester. Your youth, Mr Hughes, is against you. It is not for me to say what line the Directors may determine to take.'

'I know the people better than any one can do in Barchester.'

'Just so. But you will excuse me if I say you may for that reason be the less efficient. I have thought it expedient, however, to tell you of my views. If you have any steps that you wish to take you can now take them.'

Then Mr Greenmantle paused, and had apparently brought the meeting to an end. But there was still something which he wished to say. He did think that by a word spoken in due season,—by a strong determined word, he might succeed in putting an end to this young man's vain and ambitious hopes. He did not wish to talk to the young man about his daughter; but, if the strong word might avail here was the opportunity. 'Mr Hughes,' he began.

'Yes, sir.'

'There is a subject on which perhaps it would be well that I should be silent.' Philip, who knew the manager thoroughly, was now aware of what was coming, and thought it wise that he should say nothing at the moment. 'I do not know that any good can be done by speaking of it.' Philip still held his tongue. 'It is a matter no doubt of extreme delicacy,—of the most extreme delicacy I may say. If I go abroad as I intend, I shall as a matter of course take with me—Miss Greenmantle.'

'I suppose so.'

'I shall take with me—Miss Greenmantle. It is not to be supposed that when I go abroad for a prolonged sojourn in foreign parts, that I should leave—Miss Greenmantle behind me.'

'No doubt she will accompany you.'

'Miss Greenmantle will accompany me. And it is not improbable that my prolonged residence may in her case be—still further prolonged. It may be possible that she should link her lot in life to some gentleman whom she may meet in those realms.'

'I hope not,' said Philip.

'I do not think that you are justified, Mr Hughes, in hoping anything in reference to my daughter's fate in life.'

'All the same, I do.'

'It is very,—very,—! I do not wish to use strong language, and therefore I will not say impertinent.'

'What am I to do when you tell me that she is to marry a foreigner?'

'I never said so. I never thought so. A foreigner! Good heavens! I spoke of a gentleman whom she might chance to meet in those realms. Of course I meant an English gentleman.'

'The truth is, Mr Greenmantle, I don't want your daughter to marry anyone unless she can marry me.'

'A most selfish proposition.'

'It's a sort of matter in which a man is apt to be selfish, and it's my belief that if she were asked she'd say the same thing. Of course you can take her abroad and you can keep her there as long as you please.'

'I can;—and I mean to do it.'

'I am utterly powerless to prevent you, and so is she. In this contention between us I have only one point in my favour.'

'You have no point in your favour, sir.'

'The young lady's good wishes. If she be not on my side,—why then I am nowhere. In that case you needn't trouble yourself to take her out of Plumplington. But if——'

'You may withdraw, Mr Hughes,' said the banker. 'The interview is over.' Then Philip Hughes withdrew, but as he went he shut the door after him in a very confident manner.

## CHAPTER 6

### THE YOUNG LADIES ARE TO BE TAKEN ABROAD

How should Philip Hughes see Emily before she had been carried away to 'foreign parts' by her stern father? As he regarded the matter it was absolutely imperative that he should do so. If she should be made to go, in her father's present state of mind, without having reiterated her vows, she might be persuaded by that foreign-living English gentleman whom she would find abroad, to give him her hand. Emily had no doubt confessed her love to Philip, but she had not done so in that bold unshrinking manner which had been natural to Polly Peppercorn. And her lover felt it to be incumbent upon him to receive some renewal of her assurance before she was taken away for a prolonged residence abroad. But there was a difficulty as to this. If he were to knock at the door of the private house and ask for Miss Greenmantle, the servant, though she was in truth Philip's friend in the matter, would not dare to show him up. The whole household was afraid of Mr Greenmantle, and would receive any hint that his will was to be set aside with absolute dismay. So Philip at last determined to take the bull by the horns and force his way into the drawing-room. Mr Greenmantle could not be made more hostile than he was; and then it was quite on the cards, that he might be kept in ignorance of the intrusion. When therefore the banker was sitting in his own more private room, Philip passed through from the bank into the house,* and made his way up-stairs with no one to announce him.

With no one to announce him he passed straight through into the drawing-room, and found Emily sitting very melancholy over a half-knitted stocking. It had been commenced with an idea that it might perhaps be given to Philip, but as her father's stern severity had been announced she had given up that fond idea, and had increased the size, so as to fit them for the paternal feet. 'Good gracious, Philip,' she exclaimed, 'how on earth did you get here?'

'I came up-stairs from the bank.'

'Oh, yes; of course. But did you not tell Mary that you were coming?'

'I should never have been let up had I done so. Mary has orders not to let me put my foot within the house.'

'You ought not to have come; indeed you ought not.'

'And I was to let you go abroad without seeing you! Was that what I ought to have done? It might be that I should never see you again. Only think of what my condition must be.'

'Is not mine twice worse?'

'I do not know. If it be twice worse than mine then I am the happiest man in all the world.'

'Oh, Philip, what do you mean?'

'If you will assure me of your love——'

'I have assured you.'

'Give me another assurance, Emily,' he said, sitting down beside her on the sofa. But she started up quickly to her feet. 'When you gave me the assurance before, then—then——'

'One assurance such as that ought to be quite enough.'

'But you are going abroad.'

'That can make no difference.'

'Your father says, that you will meet there some Englishman who will——'

'My father knows nothing about it. I shall meet no Englishman, and no foreigner; at least none that I shall care about. You oughtn't to get such an idea into your head.'

'That's all very well, but how am I to keep such ideas out? Of course there will be men over there; and if you come across some idle young fellow who has not his bread to earn as I do, won't it be natural that you should listen to him?'

'No, it won't be natural.'

'It seems to me to be so. What have I got that you should continue to care for me?'

'You have my word, Philip. Is that nothing?' She had now seated herself on a chair away from the sofa, and he, feeling at the time some special anxiety to get her into his arms, threw himself down on his knees before her, and seized her by both her hands. At that moment the door of the drawing-room was opened, and Mr Greenmantle appeared within the room. Philip Hughes could not get upon his feet quick enough to return the furious anger of the look which was thrown on him. There was a difficulty even in disembarrassing himself of poor Emily's hands; so that she, to her father, seemed to be almost equally a culprit with the young man. She uttered a slight scream, and then he very gradually rose to his legs.

'Emily,' said the angry father, 'retire at once to your chamber.'

'But, papa, I must explain.'

'Retire at once to your chamber, miss. As for this young man, I do not know whether the laws of his country will not punish him for this intrusion.'

Emily was terribly frightened by this allusion to her country's laws. 'He has done nothing, papa; indeed he has done nothing.'

'His very presence here, and on his knees! Is that nothing? Mr Hughes, I desire that you will retire. Your presence in the bank is required. I lay upon you my strict order never again to presume to come through that door. Where is the servant who announced you?'

'No servant announced me.'

'And did you dare to force your way into my private house, and into my daughter's presence unannounced? It is indeed time that I should take her abroad to undergo a prolonged residence in some foreign parts. But the laws of the country which you have outraged will punish you. In the meantime why do you not withdraw? Am I to be obeyed?'

'I have just one word which I wish to say to Miss Greenmantle.'

'Not a word. Withdraw! I tell you, sir, withdraw to the bank. There your presence is required. Here it will never be needed.'

'Good-bye, Emily,' he said, putting out his hand in his vain attempt to take hers.

'Withdraw, I tell you.' And Mr Greenmantle, with all the stiffness of the poker apparent about him, backed poor young Philip Hughes through the door-way on to the staircase, and then banged the door behind him. Having done this, he threw himself on to the sofa, and hid his face with his hands. He wished it to be understood that the honour of his family had been altogether disgraced by the lightness of his daughter's conduct.

But his daughter did not see the matter quite in the same light. Though she lacked something of that firmness of manner which Polly Peppercorn was prepared to exhibit, she did not intend to be altogether trodden on. 'Papa,' she said, 'Why do you do that?'

'Good heavens!'

'Why do you cover up your face?'

'That a daughter of mine should have behaved so disgracefully!'

'I haven't behaved disgracefully, papa.'

'Admitting a young man surreptitiously to my drawing-room!'

'I didn't admit him; he walked in.'

'And on his knees! I found him on his knees.'

'I didn't put him there. Of course he came,–because,–because—'

'Because what?' he demanded.

'Because he is my lover. I didn't tell him to come; but of course he wanted to see me before we went away.'

'He shall see you no more.'

'Why shouldn't he see me? He's a very good young man, and I am very fond of him. That's just the truth.'

'You shall be taken away for a prolonged residence in foreign parts before another week has passed over your head.'

'Dr Freeborn quite approves of Mr Hughes,' pleaded Emily. But the plea at the present moment was of no avail. Mr Greenmantle in his present frame of mind was almost as angry with Dr Freeborn as with Emily or Philip Hughes. Dr Freeborn was joined in this frightful conspiracy against him.

'I do not know,' said he grandiloquently, 'that Dr Freeborn has any right to interfere with the private affairs of my family. Dr Freeborn is simply the Rector* of Plumplington,—nothing more.'

'He wants to see the people around him all happy,' said Emily.

'He won't see me happy,' said Mr Greenmantle with awful pride.

'He always wishes to have family quarrels settled before Christmas.'

'He shan't settle anything for me.' Mr Greenmantle, as he so expressed himself, determined to maintain his own independence. 'Why is he to interfere with my family quarrels because he's the Rector of Plumplington? I never heard of such a thing. When I shall have taken up my residence in foreign parts he will have no right to interfere with me.'

'But, papa, he will be my clergyman all the same.'

'He won't be mine, I can tell him that. And as for settling things by Christmas, it is all nonsense. Christmas, except for going to church and taking the Sacrament, is no more than any other day.'

'Oh papa!'

'Well, my dear, I don't quite mean that. What I do mean is that Dr Freeborn has no more right to interfere with my family at this time of the year than at any other. And when you're abroad, which you will be before Christmas, you'll find that Dr Freeborn will have nothing to say to you there.' 'You had better begin to pack up at once,' he said on the following day.

'Pack up?'

'Yes, pack up. I shall take you first to London, where you will stay for a day or two. You will go by the afternoon train to-morrow.'

'To-morrow!'

'I will write and order beds to-day.'

'But where are we to go?'

'That will be made known to you in due time,' said Mr Greenmantle.

'But I've got no clothes,' said Emily.

'France is a land in which ladies delight to buy their dresses.'

'But I shall want all manner of things,—boots and underclothing,— and—and linen, papa.'

'They have all those things in France.'

'But they won't fit me. I always have my things made to fit me. And I haven't got any boxes.'

'Boxes! what boxes? work-boxes?'

'To put my things in. I can't pack up unless I've got something to pack them in. As to going to-morrow, papa, it's quite impossible. Of course there are people I must say good-bye to. The Freeborns——'

'Not the slightest necessity,' said Mr Greenmantle. 'Dr Freeborn will quite understand the reason. As to boxes, you won't want the boxes till you've bought the things to put in them.'

'But, papa, I can't go without taking a quantity of things with me. I can't get everything new; and then I must have my dresses made to fit me.' She was very lachrymose, very piteous, and full of entreaties; but still she knew what she was about. As the result of the interview, Mr Greenmantle did almost acknowledge that they could not depart for a prolonged residence abroad on the morrow.

Early on the following morning Polly Peppercorn came to call. For the last month she had stuck to her resolution,—that she and Miss Greenmantle belonged to different sets in society, and could not be brought together, as Polly had determined to wear her second-rate dresses in preparation for a second-rate marriage,—and this visit was supposed to be something altogether out of the way. It was clearly a visit with a cause, as it was made at eleven o'clock in the morning. 'Oh, Miss Greenmantle,' she said, 'I hear that you're going away to France,—you and your papa, quite at once.'

'Who has told you?'

'Well, I can't quite say; but it has come round through Dr Freeborn.' Dr Freeborn had in truth told Mr Peppercorn, with the express view of exercising what influence he possessed so as to prevent the rapid emigration of Mr Greenmantle. And Mr Peppercorn had told his daughter, threatening her that something of the same kind would have to happen in his own family if she proved obstinate about her lover. 'It's the best thing going,' said Mr Peppercorn, 'when a girl is upsetting and determined to have her own way.' To this Polly made no reply, but came away early on the following morning, so as to converse with her late friend, Miss Greenmantle.

'Papa says so; but you know it's quite impossible.'

'What is Mr Hughes to do?' asked Polly in a whisper.

'I don't know what anybody is to do. It's dreadful, the idea of going away from home in this sudden manner.'

'Indeed it is.'

'I can't do it. Only think, Polly, when I talk to him about clothes he tells me I'm to buy dresses in some foreign town. He knows nothing about a woman's clothes;—nor yet a man's for the matter of that. Fancy starting to-morrow for six months. It's the sort of thing that Ida Pfeiffer* used to do.'

'I didn't know her,' said Polly.

'She was a great traveller, and went about everywhere almost without anything. I don't know how she managed it, but I'm sure that I can't.'

'Dr Freeborn says that he thinks it's all nonsense.' As Polly said this she shook her head and looked uncommonly wise. Emily, however, made no immediate answer. Could it be true that Dr Freeborn had thus spoken of her father? Emily did think that it was all nonsense, but she had not yet brought herself to express her thoughts openly. 'To tell the truth, Miss Greenmantle,' continued Polly, 'Dr Freeborn thinks that Mr Hughes ought to be allowed to have his own way.' In answer to this Emily could bring herself to say nothing; but she declared to herself that since the beginning of things Dr Freeborn had always been as near an angel as any old gentleman could be. 'And he says that it's quite out of the question that you should be carried off in this way.'

'I suppose I must do what papa tells me.'

'Well; yes. I don't know quite about that. I'm all for doing everything that papa likes, but when he talks of taking me to France, I know I'm not going. Lord love you, he couldn't talk to anybody there.' Emily began to remember that her father's proficiency in the French language was not very great. 'Neither could I for the matter of that,' continued Polly. 'Of course, I learned it at school, but when one can only read words very slowly one can't talk them at all. I've tried it, and I know it. A precious figure father and I would make finding our way about France.'

'Does Mr Peppercorn think of going?' asked Emily.

'He says so;—if I won't drop Jack Hollycombe. Now I don't mean to drop Jack Hollycombe; not for father nor for anyone. It's only Jack himself can make me do that.'

'He won't, I suppose.'

'I don't think he will. Now it's absurd, you know, the idea of our papas both carrying us off to France because we've got lovers in Plumplington. How all the world would laugh at them! You tell your papa what my papa is saying, and Dr Freeborn thinks that that will prevent him. At any rate, if I were you, I wouldn't go and buy anything in a hurry. Of course, you've got to think of what would do for married life.'

'Oh, dear, no!' exclaimed Emily.

'At any rate I should keep my mind fixed upon it. Dr Freeborn says that there's no knowing how things may turn out.' Having finished the purport of her embassy, Polly took her leave without even having offered one kiss to her friend.

Dr Freeborn had certainly been very sly in instigating Mr Peppercorn to proclaim his intention of following the example of his neighbour the banker. 'Papa,' said Emily when her father came in to luncheon, 'Mr Peppercorn is going to take his daughter to foreign parts.'

'What for?'

'I believe he means to reside there for a time.'

'What nonsense! He reside in France! He wouldn't know what to do with himself for an hour. I never heard anything like it. Because I am going to France is all Plumplington to follow me? What is Mr Peppercorn's reason for going to France?' Emily hesitated; but Mr Greenmantle pressed the question, 'What object can such a man have?'

'I suppose it's about his daughter,' said Emily. Then the truth flashed upon Mr Greenmantle's mind, and he became aware that he must at any rate for the present abandon the idea. Then, too, there came across him some vague notion that Dr Freeborn had instigated Mr Peppercorn and an idea of the object with which he had done so.

'Papa,' said Emily that afternoon, 'am I to get the trunks I spoke about?'

'What trunks?'

'To put my things in, papa. I must have trunks if I am to go abroad for any length of time. And you will want a large portmanteau. You would get it much better in London than you would at Plumplington.' But here Mr Greenmantle told his daughter that she need not at present trouble her mind about either his travelling gear or her own.

A few days afterwards Dr Freeborn sauntered into the bank, and spoke a few words to the cashier across the counter. 'So Mr Greenmantle, I'm told, is not going abroad,' said the Rector.

'I've heard nothing more about it,' said Philip Hughes.

'I think he has abandoned the idea. There was Hickory Peppercorn thinking of going, too, but he has abandoned it. What do they want to go travelling about France for?'

'What indeed, Dr Freeborn;—unless the two young ladies have something to say to it.'

'I don't think they wish it, if you mean that.'

'I think their fathers thought of taking them out of harm's way.'

'No doubt. But when the harm's way consists of a lover it's very hard to tear a young lady away from it.' This was said so that Philip only could hear it. The two lads who attended the bank were away at their desks in distant parts of the office. 'Do you keep your eyes open, Philip,' said the Rector, 'and things will run smoother yet than you expected.'

'He is frightfully angry with me, Dr Freeborn. I made my way up into the drawing-room the other day, and he found me there.'

'What business had you to do that?'

'Well, I was wrong, I suppose. But if Emily was to be taken away suddenly I had to see her before she went. Think, Doctor, what a prolonged residence in a foreign country means. I mightn't see her again for years.'

'And so he found you up in the drawing-room. It was very improper; that's all I can say. Nevertheless, if you'll behave yourself, I shouldn't be surprised if things were to run smoother before Christmas.' Then the Doctor took his leave.

'Now, father,' said Polly, 'you're not going to carry me off to foreign parts.'

'Yes, I am. As you're so wilful it's the only thing for you.'

'What's to become of the brewery?'

'The brewery may take care of itself. As you won't want the money for your husband there'll be plenty for me. I'll give it up. I ain't going to slave and slave all my life and nothing come of it. If you won't oblige me in this the brewery may go and take care of itself.'

'If you're like that, father, I must take care of myself. Mr Greenmantle isn't going to take his daughter over.'

'Yes, he is.'

'Not a bit of it. He's as much as told Emily that she's not to get her things ready.' Then there was a pause, during which Mr Peppercorn showed that he was much disturbed. 'Now, father, why don't you give way, and show yourself what you always were,—the kindest father that ever a girl had.'

'There's no kindness in you, Polly. Kindness ought to be reciprocal.'

'Isn't it natural that a girl should like her young man?'

'He's not your young man.'

'He's going to be. What have you got to say against him? You ask Dr Freeborn.'

'Dr Freeborn, indeed! He isn't your father!'

'He's not my father, but he's my friend. And he's yours, if you only knew it. You think of it, just for another day, and then say that you'll be good to your girl.' Then she kissed him, and as she left him she felt that she was about to prevail.


# CHAPTER 7

## THE YOUNG LADIES ARE TO REMAIN AT HOME

MISS EMILY GREENMANTLE had always possessed a certain character for delicacy. We do not mean delicacy of sentiment. That of course belonged to her as a young lady,—but delicacy of health. She was not strong and robust, as her friend Polly Peppercorn. When we say that she possessed that character, we intend to imply that she perhaps made a little use of it. There had never been much the matter with her, but she had always been a little delicate. It seemed to suit her, and prevented the necessity of over-exertion. Whereas Polly, who had never been delicate, felt herself always called upon to 'run round,' as the Americans say. 'Running round' on the part of a young lady implies a readiness and a willingness to do everything that has to be done in domestic life. If a father wants his slippers or a mother her thimble, or the cook a further supply of sauces, the active young lady has to 'run round'. Polly did run round; but Emily was delicate and did not. Therefore when she did not get up one morning, and complained of a headache, the doctor was sent for. 'She's not very strong, you know,' the doctor said to her father. 'Miss Emily always was delicate.'

'I hope it isn't much,' said Mr Greenmantle.

'There is something I fear disturbing the even tenor of her thoughts,' said the doctor, who had probably heard of the hopes entertained by Mr Philip Hughes and favoured them. 'She should be kept quite quiet. I wouldn't prescribe much medicine, but I'll tell Mixet to send her in a little draught. As for diet she can have pretty nearly what she pleases. She never had a great appetite.' And so the doctor went his way. The reader is not to suppose that Emily Greenmantle intended to deceive her father, and play the old soldier.* Such an idea would have been repugnant to her nature. But when her father told her that she was to be taken abroad for a prolonged residence, and when it of course followed that her lover was to be left behind, there came upon her a natural feeling that the best thing for her would be to lie in bed, and so to avoid all the troubles of life for the present moment.

'I am very sorry to hear that Emily is so ill,' said Dr Freeborn, calling on the banker further on in the day.

'I don't think it's much, Dr Freeborn.'

'I hope not; but I just saw Miller, who shook his head. Miller never shakes his head quite for nothing.'

In the evening Mr Greenmantle got a little note from Mrs Freeborn. 'I am *so unhappy* to hear about *dear* Emily. The poor child always is *delicate. Pray* take care of her. She must see Dr Miller twice every day. Changes do take place so *frequently*. If you think she would be better here, we would be *delighted* to have her. There is so much in having the attention of a *lady*.'

'Of course I am nervous,' said Mr Philip Hughes next morning to the banker, 'I hope you will excuse me, if I venture to ask for one word as to Miss Greenmantle's health.'

'I am very sorry to hear that Miss Greenmantle has been taken so poorly,' said Mr Peppercorn, who met Mr Greenmantle in the street. 'It is not very much, I have reason to hope,' said the father, with a look of anger. Why should Mr Peppercorn be solicitous as to his daughter?

'I am told that Dr Miller is rather alarmed.' Then Polly called at the front door to make special inquiry after Miss Greenmantle's health.

Mr Greenmantle wrote to Mrs Freeborn thanking her for the offer, and expressing a hope that it might not be necessary to move Emily from her own bed. And he thanked all his other neighbours for the pertinacity of their inquiries,—feeling however all the while that there was something of a conspiracy being hatched against him. He did not quite think his daughter guilty, but in his answer made to the inquiry of Philip Hughes, he spoke as though he believed that the young man had been the instigator of it. When on the third day his daughter could not get up, and Dr Miller had ordered a more potent draught, Mr Greenmantle almost owned to himself that he had been beaten. He took a walk by himself and meditated on it. It was a cruel case. The money was his money, and the girl was his girl, and the young man was his clerk. He ought according to the rules of justice in the world to have had plenary* power over them all. But it had come to pass that his power was nothing. What is a father to do when a young lady goes to bed and remains there? And how is a soft-hearted father to make any use of his own money when all his neighbours turn against him?

'Miss Greenmantle is to have her own way, father,' Polly said to Mr Peppercorn on one of these days. It was now the second week in December, and the whole ground was hard with frost. 'Dr Freeborn will be right after all. He never is much wrong. He declared that Emily would be given to Philip Hughes as a Christmas-box.'*

'I don't believe it a bit,' said Mr Peppercorn.

'It is so all the same. I knew that when she became ill her father wouldn't be able to stand his ground. There is no knowing what these delicate young ladies can do in that way. I wish I were delicate.

'You don't wish anything of the kind. It would be very wicked to wish yourself to be sickly. What should I do if you were running up a doctor's bill?'

'Pay it,—as Mr Greenmantle does. You've never had to pay half-a-crown* for a doctor for me, I don't know when.'

'And now you want to be poorly.'

'I don't think you ought to have it both ways, you know. How am I to frighten you into letting me have my own lover? Do you think that

I am not as unhappy about him as Emily Greenmantle? There he is now going down to the brewery. You go after him and tell him that he shall have what he wants.'

Mr Peppercorn turned round and looked at her. 'Not if I know,' he said.

'Then I shall go to bed,' said Polly, 'and send for Dr Miller to-morrow. I don't see why I'm not to have the same advantage as other girls. But, father, I wouldn't make you unhappy, and I wouldn't cost you a shilling I could help, and I wouldn't not wait upon you for anything. I wouldn't pretend to be ill,—not for Jack Hollycombe.'

'I should find you out if you did.'

'I wouldn't fight my battle except on the square for any earthly consideration. But, father—'

'What do you want of me?'

'I am broken-hearted about him. Though I look red in the face, and fat, and all that, I suffer quite as much as Emily Greenmantle. When I tell him to wait perhaps for years, I know I'm unreasonable. When a young man wants a wife, he wants one. He has made up his mind to settle down, and he doesn't expect a girl to bid him remain as he is for another four or five years.'

'You've no business to tell him anything of the kind.'

'When he asks me I have a business,—if it's true. Father!'

'Well!'

'It is true. I don't know whether it ought to be so, but it is true. I'm very fond of you.'

'You don't show it.'

'Yes, I am. And I think I do show it, for I do whatever you tell me. But I like him the best.'

'What has he done for you?'

'Nothing;—not half so much as I have done for him. But I do like him the best. It's human nature. I don't take on to tell him so;—only once. Once I told him that I loved him better than all the rest,—and that if he chose to take my word for it, once spoken, he might have it. He did choose, and I'm not going to repeat it, till I tell him when I can be his own.'

'He'll have to take you just as you stand.'

'May be; but it will be worth while for him to wait just a little, till he shall see what you mean to do. What do you mean to do with it, father? We don't want it at once.'

'He's not edicated as a gentleman should be.'

'Are you?'

'No; but I didn't try to get a young woman with money. I made the money, and I've a right to choose the sort of son-in-law my daughter shall marry.'

'No; never!' she said.

'Then he must take you just as you are; and I'll make ducks and drakes* of the money after my own fashion. If you were married to-morrow what do you mean to live upon?'

'Forty shillings a week. I've got it all down in black and white.'

'And when children come;—one after another, year by year.'

'Do as others do. I'll go bail my children won't starve;—or his. I'd work for them down to my bare bones. But would you look on the while, making ducks and drakes of your money, or spending it at the pothouse, just to break the heart of your own child? It's not in you to do it. You'd have to alter your nature first. You speak of yourself as though you were strong as iron. There isn't a bit of iron about you;—but there's something a deal better. You are one of those men, father, who are troubled with a heart.'

'You're one of those women,' said he, 'who trouble the world by their tongues.' Then he bounced out of the house and banged the door.

He had seen Jack Hollycombe through the window going down to the brewery, and he now slowly followed the young man's steps. He went very slowly as he got to the entrance to the brewery yard, and there he paused for a while thinking over the condition of things. 'Hang the fellow,' he said to himself; 'what on earth has he done that he should have it all his own way. I never had it all my way. I had to work for it;—and precious hard too. My wife had to cook the dinner with only just a slip of a girl to help make the bed. If he'd been a gentleman there'd have been something in it. A gentleman expects to have things ready to his hand. But he's to walk into all my money just because he's good-looking. And then Polly tells me, that I can't help myself because I'm good-natured. I'll let her know whether I'm good-natured! If he wants a wife he must support a wife;—and he shall.' But though Mr Peppercorn stood in the doorway murmuring after this fashion he knew very well that he was about to lose the battle. He had come down the street on purpose to signify to Jack Hollycombe that he might go up and settle the day with Polly; and he himself in the midst of all his objurgations was picturing to himself the delight with which he would see Polly restored to her former mode of dressing. 'Well, Mr Hollycombe, are you here?'

'Yes, Mr Peppercorn, I am here.'

'So I perceive,—as large as life. I don't know what on earth you're doing over here so often. You're wasting your employers' time, I believe.'

'I came over to see Messrs Grist and Grindall's young man.'

'I don't believe you came to see any young man at all.'

'It wasn't any young woman, as I haven't been to your house, Mr Peppercorn.'

'What's the good of going to my house? There isn't any young woman there can do you any good.' Then Mr Peppercorn looked round and saw that there were others within hearing to whom the conversation might be attractive. 'Do you come in here. I've got something to say to you.' Then he led the way into his own little parlour, and shut the door. 'Now Mr Hollycombe, I've got something to communicate.'

'Out with it, Mr Peppercorn.'

'There's that girl of mine up there is the biggest fool that ever was since the world began.'

'It's astonishing,' said Jack, 'what different opinions different people have about the same thing.'

'I daresay. That's all very well for you; but I say she's a fool. What on earth can she see in you to make her want to give you all my money?'

'She can't do that unless you're so pleased.'

'And she won't neither. If you like to take her, there she is.'

'Mr Peppercorn, you make me the happiest man in the world.'

'I don't make you the richest;—and you're going to make yourself about the poorest. To marry a wife upon forty shillings a week! I did it myself, however,—upon thirty-five, and I hadn't any stupid old father-in-law to help me out. I'm not going to see her break her heart; and so you may go and tell her. But you needn't tell her as I'm going to make her any regular allowance. Only tell her to put on some decent kind of gown, before I come home to tea. Since all this came up the slut has worn the same dress she bought three winters ago. She thinks I didn't know it.'

And so Mr Peppercorn had given way; and Polly was to be allowed to flaunt it again this Christmas in silks and satins. 'Now you'll give me a kiss,' said Jack when he had told his tale.

'I've only got it on your bare word,' she answered, turning away from him.

'Why; he sent me here himself; and says you're to put on a proper frock to give him his tea in.'

'No.'

'But he did.'

'Then, Jack, you shall have a kiss. I am sure the message about the frock must have come from himself. Jack, are you not the happiest young man in all Plumplington?'

'How about the happiest young woman,' said Jack.

'Well, I don't mind owning up. I am. But it's for your sake. I could have waited, and not have been a bit impatient. But it's so different with a man. Did he say, Jack, what he meant to do for you?'

'He swore that he would not give us a penny.'

'But that's rubbish. I am not going to let you marry till I know what's fixed. Nor yet will I put on my silk frock.'

'You must. He'll be sure to go back if you don't do that. I should risk it all now, if I were you.'

'And so make a beggar of you. My husband shall not be dependent on any man,—not even on father. I shall keep my clothes on as I've got 'em till something is settled.'

'I wouldn't anger him if I were you,' said Jack cautiously.

'One has got to anger him sometimes, and all for his own good. There's the frock hanging up-stairs, and I'm as fond of a bit of finery as any girl. Well;—I'll put it on to-night because he has made something of a promise; but I'll not continue it till I know what he means to do for you. When I'm married my husband will have to pay for my clothes, and not father.'

'I guess you'll pay for them yourself.'

'No, I shan't. It's not the way of the world in this part of England. One of you must do it, and I won't have it done by father,—not regular. As I begin so I must go on. Let him tell me what he means to do and then we shall know how we're to live. I'm not a bit afraid of you and your forty shillings.'

'My girl!' Here was some little attempt at embracing, which, however, Polly checked.

'There's no good in all that when we're talking business. I look upon it now that we're to be married as soon as I please. Father has given way as to that, and I don't want to put you off.'

'Why no! You ought not to do that when you think what I have had to endure.'

'If you had known the picture which father drew just now of what we should have to suffer on your forty shillings a week!'

'What did he say, Polly?'

'Never mind what he said. Dry bread would be the best of it. I don't care about the dry bread;—but if there is to be anything better it must be all fixed. You must have the money for your own.'

'I don't suppose he'll do that.'

'Then you must take me without the money. I'm not going to have him giving you a five-pound note at the time and your having to ask for it. Nor yet am I going to ask for it. I don't mind it now. And to give him his due, I never asked him for a sovereign* but what he gave me two. He's very generous.'

'Is he now?'

'But he likes to have the opportunity. I won't live in the want of any man's generosity,—only my husband's. If he chooses to do anything extra that'll be as he likes it. But what we have to live upon,—to pay for meat and coals and such like,—that must be your own. I'll put on the dress to-night because I won't vex him. But before he goes to bed he must be made to understand all that. And you must understand it too, Jack. As we mean to go on so must we begin!' The interview ended, however, in an invitation given to Jack to stay in Plumplington and eat his supper. He knew the road so well that he could drive himself home in the dark.

'I suppose I'd better let them have two hundred a year to begin with,' said Peppercorn to himself, sitting alone in his little parlour. 'But I'll keep it in my own hands. I'm not going to trust that fellow further than I can see him.'

But on this point he had to change his mind before he went to bed. He was gracious enough to Jack as they were eating their supper, and insisted on having a hot glass of brandy and water afterwards,—all in honour of Polly's altered dress. But as soon as Jack was gone Polly explained her views of the case, and spoke such undoubted wisdom as she sat on her father's knee, that he was forced to yield. 'I'll speak to Mr Scribble about having it all properly settled.' Now Mr Scribble was the Plumplington attorney.

'Two hundred a year, father, which is to be Jack's own,—for ever. I won't marry him for less,—not to live as you propose.'

'When I say a thing I mean it,' said Peppercorn. Then Polly retired, having given him a final kiss.

About a fortnight after this Mr Greenmantle came to the Rectory and desired to see Dr Freeborn. Since Emily had been taken ill there had not been many signs of friendship between the Greenmantle and the Freeborn houses. But now there he was in the Rectory hall, and within five minutes had followed the Rectory footman into Dr Freeborn's study. 'Well, Greenmantle, I'm delighted to see you. How's Emily?'

Mr Greenmantle might have been delighted to see the Doctor but he didn't look it. 'I trust that she is somewhat better. She has risen from her bed to-day.'

'I'm glad to hear that,' said the Doctor.

'Yes; she got up yesterday, and to-day she seems to be restored to her usual health.'

'That's good news. You should be careful with her and not let her trust too much to her strength. Miller said that she was very weak, you know.'

'Yes; Miller has said so all through,' said the father; 'but I'm not quite sure that Miller has understood the case.'

'He hasn't known all the ins and outs you mean,—about Philip Hughes.' Here the Doctor smiled, but Mr Greenmantle moved about uneasily as though the poker were at work. 'I suppose Philip Hughes had something to do with her malady.'

'The truth is—,' began Mr Greenmantle.

'What's the truth?' asked the Doctor. But Mr Greenmantle looked as though he could not tell his tale without many efforts. 'You heard what old Peppercorn has done with his daughter?—Settled £250 a year on her for ever, and has come to me asking me whether I can't marry them on Christmas Day. Why if they were to be married by banns there would not be time.'

'I don't see why they shouldn't be married by banns,' said Mr Greenmantle, who amidst all these difficulties disliked nothing so much as that he should be put into the category with Mr Peppercorn, or Emily with Polly Peppercorn.

'I say nothing about that. I wish everybody was married by banns. Why shouldn't they? But that's not to be. Polly came to me the next day, and said that her father didn't know what he was talking about.'

'I suppose she expects a special licence* like the rest of them,' said Mr Greenmantle.

'What the girls think mostly of is their clothes. Polly wouldn't mind the banns the least in the world; but she says she can't have her things ready. When a young lady talks about her things a man has to give up. Polly says that February is a very good month to be married in.'

Mr Greenmantle was again annoyed, and showed it by the knitting of his brow, and the increased stiffness of his head and shoulders. The truth may as well be told. Emily's illness had prevailed with him and he too had yielded. When she had absolutely refused to look at her chicken-broth for three consecutive days her father's heart had been stirred. For Mr Greenmantle's character will not have been adequately described unless it be explained that the stiffness lay rather in the neck and shoulders than in the organism by which his feelings were conducted. He was in truth very like Mr Peppercorn, though he would have been infuriated had he been told so. When he found himself alone after his defeat,— which took place at once when the chicken-broth had gone down untasted for the third time,—he was ungainly and ill-natured to look at. But he went to work at once to make excuses for Philip Hughes, and ended by assuring himself that he was a manly honest sort of fellow, who was sure to do well in his profession; and ended by assuring himself that it would be very comfortable to have his married daughter and her husband living with him. He at once saw Philip, and explained to him that he had certainly done very wrong in coming up to his drawing-room without leave. 'There is an etiquette in those things which no doubt you will learn as you grow older.' Philip thought that the etiquette wouldn't much matter as soon as he had married his wife. And he was wise enough to do no more than beg Mr Greenmantle's pardon for the fault which he had committed. 'But as I am informed by my daughter,' continued Mr Greenmantle, 'that her affections are irrevocably settled upon you,'—here Philip could only bow,—'I am prepared to withdraw my opposition, which has only been entertained as long as I thought it necessary for my daughter's happiness. There need be no words now,' he continued, seeing that Philip was about to speak, 'but when I shall have made up my mind as to what it may be fitting that I shall do in regard to money, then I will see you again. In the meantime you're welcome to come into my drawing-room when it may suit you to pay your respects to Miss Greenmantle.' It was speedily settled that the marriage should take place in February, and Mr Greenmantle was now informed that Polly Peppercorn and Mr Hollycombe were to be married in the same month!

He had resolved, however, after much consideration, that he would himself inform Dr Freeborn that he had given way, and had now come for this purpose. There would be less of triumph to the enemy, and less of disgrace to himself, if he were to declare the truth. And there no longer existed any possibility of a permanent quarrel with the Doctor. The prolonged residence abroad had altogether gone to the winds. 'I think I will just step over and tell the Doctor of this alteration in our plans.' This he had said to Emily, and Emily had thanked him and kissed him, and once again had called him 'her own dear papa.' He had suffered greatly during the period of his embittered feelings, and now had his reward. For it is not to be supposed that when a man has swallowed a poker the evil results will fall only upon his companions. The process is painful also to himself. He cannot breathe in comfort so long as the poker is there.

'And so Emily too is to have her lover. I am delighted to hear it. Believe me she hasn't chosen badly. Philip Hughes is an excellent young fellow. And so we shall have the double marriage coming after all.' Here the poker was very visible. 'My wife will go and see her at once, and congratulate her; and so will I as soon as I have heard that she's got herself properly dressed for drawing-room visitors. Of course I may congratulate Philip.'

'Yes, you may do that,' said Mr Greenmantle very stiffly.

'All the town will know all about it before it goes to bed to-night. It is better so. There should never be a mystery about such matters. Good-bye, Greenmantle, I congratulate you with all my heart.'

## CHAPTER 8

### CHRISTMAS-DAY

'Now I'll tell you what we'll do,' said the Doctor to his wife a few days after the two marriages had been arranged in the manner thus described. It yet wanted ten days to Christmas, and it was known to all Plumplington that the Doctor intended to be more than ordinarily blithe during the present Christmas holidays. 'We'll have these young people to dinner on Christmas-day, and their fathers shall come with them.'

'Will that do, Doctor?' said his wife.

'Why should it not do?'

'I don't think that Mr Greenmantle will care about meeting Mr Peppercorn.'

'If Mr Peppercorn dines at my table,' said the Doctor with a certain amount of arrogance, 'any gentleman in England may meet him. What! not meet a fellow townsman on Christmas-day and on such an occasion as this!'

'I don't think he'll like it,' said Mrs Freeborn.

'Then he may lump it. You'll see he'll come. He'll not like to refuse to bring Emily here, especially as she is to meet her betrothed. And the Peppercorns and Jack Hollycombe will be sure to come. Those sort of vagaries as to meeting this man and not that, in sitting next to one woman and objecting to another, don't prevail on Christmas-day, thank God. They've met already at the Lord's Supper,* or ought to have met; and they surely can meet afterwards at the parson's table. And we'll have Harry Gresham to show that there is no ill-will. I hear that Harry is already making up to the Dean's daughter* at Barchester.'

'He won't care whom he meets,' said Mrs Freeborn. 'He has got a position of his own and can afford to meet anybody. It isn't quite so with Mr Greenmantle. But of course you can have it as you please. I shall be delighted to have Polly and her husband at dinner with us.'

So it was settled and the invitations were sent out. That to the Peppercorns was despatched first, so that Mr Greenmantle might be informed whom he would have to meet. It was conveyed in a note from Mrs Freeborn to Polly, and came in the shape of an order rather than of a request. 'Dr Freeborn hopes that your Papa and Mr Hollycombe will bring you to dine with us on Christmas-day at six o'clock.* We'll try and get Emily Greenmantle and her lover to meet you. You must come because the Doctor has set his heart upon it.'

'That's very civil,' said Mr Peppercorn. 'Shan't I get any dinner till six o'clock?'

'You can have lunch, father, of course. You must go.'

'A bit of bread and cheese when I come out of church—just when I'm most famished! Of course I'll go. I never dined with the Doctor before.'

'Nor did I; but I've drunk tea there. You'll find he'll make himself very pleasant. But what are we to do about Jack.'

'He'll come of course.'

'But what are we to do about his clothes?' said Polly. 'I don't think he's got a dress coat; and I'm sure he hasn't a white tie.* Let him come just as he pleases, they won't mind on Christmas-day as long as he's clean. He'd better come over and go to church with us; and then I'll see as to making him up tidy.' Word was sent to say that Polly and her father and her lover would come, and the necessary order was at once despatched to Barchester.

'I really do not know what to say about it,' said Mr Greenmantle when the invitation was read to him. 'You will meet Polly Peppercorn and her husband as is to be,' Mrs Freeborn had written in her note; 'for we look on you and Polly as the two heroines of Plumplington for this occasion.' Mr Greenmantle had been struck with dismay as he read the words. Could he bring himself to sit down to dinner with Hickory Peppercorn and Jack Hollycombe; and ought he to do so? Or could he refuse the Doctor's invitation on such an occasion? He suggested at first that a letter should be prepared declaring that he did not like to take his Christmas dinner away from his own house. But to this Emily would by no means consent. She had plucked up her spirits greatly since the days of the chicken-broth, and was determined at the present moment to rule both her future husband and her father. 'You must go, papa. I wouldn't not go for all the world.'

'I don't see it, my dear; indeed I don't.'

'The Doctor has been so kind. What's your objection, papa?'

'There are differences, my dear.'

'But Dr Freeborn likes to have them.'

'A clergyman is very peculiar. The rector of a parish can always meet his own flock. But rank is rank you know, and it behoves me to be careful with whom I shall associate. I shall have Mr Peppercorn slapping my back and poking me in the ribs some of these days. And moreover they have joined your name with that of the young lady in a manner that I do not quite approve. Though you each of you may be a heroine in your own way, you are not the two heroines of Plumplington. I do not choose that you shall appear together in that light.'

'That is only his joke,' said Emily.

'It is a joke to which I do not wish to be a party. The two heroines of Plumplington! It sounds like a vulgar farce.'*

Then there was a pause, during which Mr Greenmantle was thinking how to frame the letter of excuse by which he would avoid the difficulty. But at last Emily said a word which settled him. 'Oh, papa, they'll say that you were too proud, and then they'll laugh at you.' Mr Greenmantle looked very angry at this, and was preparing himself to use some severe language to his daughter. But he remembered how recently she had become engaged to be married, and he abstained. 'As you wish it, we will go,' he said. 'At the present crisis of your life I would not desire to disappoint you in anything.' So it happened that the Doctor's proposed guests all accepted; for Harry Gresham too expressed himself as quite delighted to meet Emily Greenmantle on the auspicious occasion.

'I shall be delighted also to meet Jack Hollycombe,' Harry had said. 'I have known him ever so long and have just given him an order for twenty quarters of oats.'

They were all to be seen at the Parish Church of Plumplington on that Christmas morning;—except Harry Gresham, who, if he did so at all, went to church at Greshamsbury,—and the Plumplington world all looked at them with admiring eyes. As it happened the Peppercorns sat just behind the Greenmantles, and on this occasion Jack Hollycombe and Polly were exactly in the rear of Philip Hughes and Emily. Mr Greenmantle as he took his seat observed that it was so, and his devotions were, we fear, disturbed by the fact. He walked up proudly to the altar among the earliest and most aristocratic recipients,* and as he did so could not keep himself from turning round to see whether Hickory Peppercorn was treading on his kibes. But on the present occasion Hickory Peppercorn was very modest and remained with his future son-in-law nearly to the last.

At six o'clock they all met in the Rectory drawing-room. 'Our two heroines,' said the Doctor as they walked in, one just after the other, each leaning on her lover's arm. Mr Greenmantle looked as though he did not like it. In truth he was displeased, but he could not help himself. Of the two young ladies Polly was by far the most self-possessed. As long as she had got the husband of her choice she did not care whether she were or were not called a heroine. And her father had behaved very well on that morning as to money. 'If you come out like that, father,' she had said, 'I shall have to wear a silk dress every day.' 'So you ought,' he said with true Christmas generosity. But the income then promised had been a solid assurance, and Polly was the best contented young woman in all Plumplington.

They all sat down to dinner, the Doctor with a bride on each side of him, the place of honour to his right having been of course accorded to Emily Greenmantle; and next to each young lady was her lover. Miss Greenmantle as was her nature was very quiet, but Philip Hughes made an effort and carried on, as best he could, a conversation with the Doctor. Jack Hollycombe till after pudding-time* said not a word and Polly tried to console herself through his silence by remembering that the happiness of the world did not depend upon loquacity. She herself said a little word now and again, always with a slight effort to bring Jack into notice. But the Doctor with his keen power of observation understood them all, and told himself that Jack was to be a happy man. At the other end of the table Mr Greenmantle and Mr Peppercorn sat opposite to each other, and they too, till after pudding-time, were very quiet. Mr Peppercorn felt himself to be placed a little above his proper position, and could not at once throw off the burden. And Mr Greenmantle would not make the attempt. He felt that an injury had been done him in that he had been made to sit opposite to Hickory Peppercorn. And in truth the dinner party as a dinner party would have been a failure, had it not been for Harry Gresham, who, seated in the middle between Philip and Mr Peppercorn, felt it incumbent upon him in his present position to keep up the rattle of the conversation. He said a good deal about the 'two heroines,' and the two heroes, till Polly felt herself bound to quiet him by saying that it was a pity that there was not another heroine also for him.

'I'm an unfortunate fellow,' said Harry, 'and am always left out in the cold. But perhaps I may be a hero too some of these days.'

Then when the cloth had been removed,*—for the Doctor always had the cloth taken off his table,—the jollity of the evening really began. The Doctor delighted to be on his legs on such an occasion and to make a little speech. He said that he had on his right and on his left two young ladies both of whom he had known and had loved throughout their entire lives, and now they were to be delivered over by their fathers, whom he delighted to welcome this Christmas-day at his modest board, each to the man who for the future was to be her lord and her husband. He did not know any occasion on which he, as a pastor of the church, could take greater delight, seeing that in both cases he had ample reason to be satisfied with the choice which the young ladies had made. The bridegrooms were in both instances of such a nature and had made for themselves such characters in the estimation of their friends and neighbours as to give all assurance of the happiness prepared for their wives. There was much more of it, but this was the gist of the Doctor's eloquence. And then he ended by saying that he would ask the two fathers to say a word in acknowledgment of the toast.

This he had done out of affection to Polly, whom he did not wish to distress by calling upon Jack Hollycombe to take a share in the speech-making of the evening. He felt that Jack would require a little practice before he could achieve comfort during such an operation; but the immediate effect was to plunge Mr Greenmantle into a cold bath. What was he to say on such an opportunity? But he did blunder through, and gave occasion to none of that sorrow which Polly would have felt had Jack Hollycombe got upon his legs, and then been reduced to silence. Mr Peppercorn in his turn made a better speech than could have been expected from him. He said that he was very proud of his position that day, which was due to his girl's manner and education. He was not entitled to be there by anything that he had done himself. Here the Doctor cried, 'Yes, yes, yes, certainly.' But Peppercorn shook his head. He wasn't specially proud of himself, he said, but he was awfully proud of his girl. And he thought that Jack Hollycombe was about the most fortunate young man of whom he had ever heard. Here Jack declared that he was quite aware of it.

After that the jollity of the evening commenced; and they were very jolly till the Doctor began to feel that it might be difficult to restrain the spirits which he had raised. But they were broken up before a very late hour by the necessity that Harry Gresham should return to Greshamsbury. Here we must bid farewell to the 'two heroines of Plumplington,' and to their young men, wishing them many joys in their new capacities. One little scene however must be described, which took place as the brides were putting on their hats in the Doctor's study. 'Now I can call you Emily again,' said Polly, 'and now I can kiss you, though I know I ought to do neither the one nor the other.'

'Yes, both, both, always do both,' said Emily. Then Polly walked home with her father, who, however well satisfied he might have been in his heart, had not many words to say on that evening.

# APPENDIX 1

## TROLLOPE'S INTRODUCTION TO THE CHRONICLES OF BARSETSHIRE (1878)

THESE tales were written by the Author, not one immediately after another,—not intended to be in any sequence one to another except in regard to the two first,—with an intention rather that there should be no such sequence, but that the stories should go forth to the public as being in all respects separate, the sequence being only in the Author's mind. I, the Author, had formed for myself so complete a picture of the locality, had acquired so accurate a knowledge of the cathedral town and the county in which I had placed the scene, and had become by a long-continued mental dwelling in it, so intimate with sundry of its inhabitants, that to go back to it and write about it again and again have been one of the delights of my life. But I had taught myself to believe that few novels written in continuation, one of another, had been successful. Even Scott, even Thackeray, had failed to renew a great interest. Fielding and Dickens never ventured the attempt. Therefore, when Dr Thorne, the third of the present series, was sent into the world, it was put forth almost with a hope that the locality might not be recognized. I hardly dared to do more than allude to a few of my old characters. Mrs Proudie is barely introduced, though some of the scenes are laid in the city over which she reigned.

And in Framley Parsonage, and in the Last Chronicle, though I had become bolder in going back to the society of my old friends, I had looked altogether for fresh plots and new interests in order that no intending reader might be deterred by the necessity of going back to learn what had occurred before.

But now, when these are all old stories,—not perhaps as yet quite forgotten by the readers of the day, and to my memory fresh as when they were written,—I have a not unnatural desire to see them together, so that my records of a little bit of England which I have myself created may be brought into one set, and that some possible future reader may be enabled to study in a complete form the

## CHRONICLES OF BARSETSHIRE.

# APPENDIX 2
## TROLLOPE'S BARSETSHIRE NOVELS AND THE CHURCH

ALTHOUGH it did not always seem so at the time, the Church of England which Trollope described in the Chronicles of Barsetshire (1855–67) was an institution at a peak of its authority, prosperity, and self-confidence. Anglicanism had faced a series of challenges in the second quarter of the nineteenth century. The Established Church lost its exclusive presence in Parliament with the admission of Protestant Nonconformists in 1828 and of Roman Catholics in 1829. With its behaviour attacked and its political power thus diminished, the Church felt itself to be in danger of disestablishment by the Whig government of the early 1830s, and suffered the imposition of an Ecclesiastical Commission to reform its finances and administration in 1836. Tithes were commuted in 1836 and church rates threatened. Still more worryingly, in 1833, ten Anglican bishoprics in Ireland were summarily abolished. Parliament was no longer what Richard Hooker had seen it as in the 1590s: the lay synod of the Church. Was Britain still a Christian country? A Census of Religious Worship, taken on Sunday 30 March 1851, revealed that only 29.5% of the population of England and Wales had attended an Anglican service.

None of these blows, however, was fatal and the Church of England emerged stronger and more vigorous from two decades of confrontation. Read in a less anxious way, the 1851 census showed that 60.8% of the population attended a Christian service and that 48.6% of those attending were Anglicans. No other religious group came even close to this, with the next largest, the Methodists, achieving only 25% (or 15.2% of the population). Though no longer universal, the Church of England was, it seemed, still the predominant force in the religious life of the nation.

The much feared Ecclesiastical Commission turned out, similarly, to be less threatening than it had at first appeared. Desired and implemented by the Whigs, it was actually designed by Sir Robert Peel during the brief interval of Tory government in 1834–5, and the political commissioners rarely bothered to attend the meetings. Matters were therefore left to the bishops. Spurred on by the Bishop of London, Charles Blomfield, the commission became a useful instigator of necessary reforms. Its task was to redistribute the wealth of the Church to produce a more equally rewarded and effective clergy. In 1836 the commission equalized the stipends of bishops. In 1838 a Pluralities Act limited the number of parish livings which a clergyman could hold to two, and strengthened bishops' powers to enforce residence. An Ecclesiastical Duties and Revenues Act, in 1840, suppressed the 360 non-resident **prebends** (salaried but otherwise nominal posts, attached to cathedrals), limited the number of resident canons at cathedrals, and transferred responsibility for the employment of deans and canons, together with the endowments which supported them, to the commissioners. The money thus saved was used to supplement poor livings and help new parishes. The commission's decision to link such grants to local contributions stimulated an extraordinary wave of donations: more than £25m. (£1.5 billion in modern money) would be spent on church building between 1840 and 1876.[1]

The revival of the Church was not, of course, solely the consequence of reforms introduced by the Ecclesiastical Commission. The French Revolution had had the unintended effect of making the British upper classes more religious. Without an effective Church, it seemed, relations between the rich and poor might deteriorate into violence. More profoundly, the Evangelical Revival of the eighteenth century had not just energized the dissenting sects but had deeply touched the Established Church as well. Victorian Britain had a more earnest and spiritually intense culture as a consequence.

The problems confronting the Church in the mid-century were, therefore, internal: administrative defects, or disputes with other Christian denominations, rather than threats to faith itself. As late as the 1850s, religious doubters were still a small group of untypical intellectuals. Only with the appearance of Charles Darwin's *On the Origin of Species* (1859), *Essays and Reviews* (1860), and Bishop John Colenso's *The Pentateuch and Book of Joshua Critically Examined* (1862–79) was the challenge to religion recognized as external and fundamental. Trollope was not unaware of these developments. In 1859 he interrupted the Barchester series with a novel about doubt and the difficulty of commitment: *The Bertrams*. His hero, George Bertram, thinks of becoming a clergyman. But he publishes two works of higher criticism of the Bible and settles, instead, for a career in the law (about whose claims to truth he is equally sceptical) and a love life blighted by delay and indecision. Arthur Hugh Clough's rather similar verse novel, *Amours de Voyage*, had been published in the previous year. Seven years later, in January 1866, Trollope would describe a doubting, or minimally believing, Anglican clergyman in his *Pall Mall Gazette* essay, 'The Clergyman who Subscribes for Colenso'. Things changed in the 1860s. In the decade before that, however, the Church of England had been a confident, energetic, and effective body, all the better for having passed through a process of criticism and reform.

Gladstone, writing in 1875, had no doubt that the Church had grown stronger in the course of his lifetime:

> We have received from the Almighty, within the last half-century, such gifts as perhaps were hardly ever bestowed within the same time on a religious community. We see a transformed clergy, a laity less cold and neglectful,

[1] Owen Chadwick, *The Victorian Church*, 2 vols. (London: A. & C. Black, 1966–70), ii. 240–1.

education vigorously pushed, human want and sorrow zealously cared for, sin less feebly rebuked, worship restored from frequent scandal and prevailing apathy to uniform decency and frequent reverence . . . and this by the agency . . . of men who have indeed succeeded the Apostles not less in character than in commission.[2]

The high quality of Anglican literature and art in these years confirms this impression of exceptional moral and spiritual vigour. This was the period of Tennyson's *In Memoriam* (1850), of the early poetry of Christina Rossetti, of Ruskin's *The Stones of Venice* (1851-3), of John Everett Millais's *Christ in the Carpenter's Shop* (1850), of William Holman Hunt's *The Hireling Shepherd* (1851), *The Light of the World* (1853), and *The Scapegoat* (1855), and of remarkable architecture created for Anglican congregations by Anglican architects, such as William Butterfield, G. E. Street, and Sir George Gilbert Scott. Church music revived, with the introduction of hymns to Anglican services: a new repertoire of song, first extensively collected as *Hymns, Ancient and Modern* in 1861. Intellectually, the theological forum which Parliament could no longer provide was replaced when the Anglican synod, Convocation, dormant since 1717, was restored in 1855. The Church of England with which Trollope concerned himself was not a sleepy backwater but a dynamic and influential body of belief.

Given this cultural vitality and enthusiasm for reform, why is the Anglican establishment depicted in the Barsetshire novels so full of problems? How, for example, can Barchester be burdened with a non-resident prebendary who is also an absentee pluralist, in the person of Dr Vesey Stanhope? *Barchester Towers* is set in '185-' (probably 1854). Had Trollope not heard about the Pluralities Act of 1838 and the Ecclesiastical Duties and Revenues Act of 1840? He had, and the answer is that the reforms introduced by the Ecclesiastical Commission were deliberately made in a gradual way, taking effect, 'only on the expiry of the life-interest . . . No stipend was reduced nor canonry suppressed until the death or departure of the occupant.'[3] The changes would, as a consequence, become widely effective only in the 1870s. Dr Proudie can summon Stanhope back from his villa on Lake Como because the episcopal power to require residence was an ancient one, merely strengthened by the 1838 act. The prebend itself, however, and the plurality of parishes are life-interests which pre-date that legislation, and Stanhope can retain them until his death—from apoplexy in *Doctor Thorne*. The historical circumstances here explain the tone which Trollope chose for such matters. The Church of England has already reformed itself. There is no need for denunciation: the case against such abuses has already been made and won. Instead, the

[2] W. E. Gladstone, *Gleanings of Past Years, 1851–75*, 7 vols. (London: John Murray, 1879), vii. 175; originally an article in the *Contemporary Review* (July 1875).

[3] Chadwick, *The Victorian Church*, i. 137–8.

lingering relics of an acknowledged malpractice can be treated as comic anachronisms.

This gradualism is also a reason why it was so hard for the Ecclesiastical Commission to make a significant difference to the more painful and intractable problem of unequal clerical salaries. In *Framley Parsonage*, Mark Robarts, the Vicar of Framley, has a living worth £900 a year (£55,000 in modern money). His colleague, Josiah Crawley, the Perpetual Curate of Hogglestock, is obliged to support himself on an income of just £130 (£7,800). Robarts hunts and moves in fashionable society. Crawley, not surprisingly, can hardly feed his family. Supplementing inadequate clerical stipends had been a key purpose of the 1840 Ecclesiastical Duties and Revenues Act. But the money transferred from cathedral endowments came in so slowly that the commissioners were initially obliged to borrow, would not find their accounts in surplus until 1856, and struggled even after that date to reconcile the constant need for expenditure, especially on new urban parishes, with a declining real income.

The underlying difficulty here was that the Church of England was, in a literal sense, 'reformed' rather than newly invented. The distinctively Anglican Church which emerged in the late sixteenth century inherited a medieval parochial and cathedral system, and a portfolio of ancient endowments, built up over hundreds of years and full of local anomalies. The incomes of clergymen were unequal because they were chiefly derived from tithes, commuted into a money payment in 1836 but still based on the ancient model of a tenth of the agricultural produce of the individual parish. The Ecclesiastical Commission's inability to find a quick solution to this problem meant that it was not a lingering anachronism, to be laughed at, but an enduring abuse, to be deplored. The tone in which Trollope treats it is, accordingly, very different. Chapter 14 of *Framley Parsonage* contains a polemical attack on the 'present arrangement' for paying clergymen and *The Last Chronicle of Barset* is an extended study of its ill effects.

Less controversially, the Church also retained the administrative structure and terminology of its medieval predecessor. There were two provinces, Canterbury and York, and a total of twenty-seven episcopal dioceses (twenty-eight after the addition of a Bishopric of Manchester in 1847; Barchester is an ancient but imaginary twenty-ninth). **Bishops** were spiritual leaders, not managers, and had a vote in the House of Lords. With their speeches in Parliament, and their books, sermons, and charges to the clergy, they were meant to guide the moral and religious policy of the nation. Their high incomes supported this purpose by enabling them to live on terms of equality with their fellow peers, especially during the months when the House of Lords was in session. Old Bishop Grantly of Barchester has a salary of £9,000 a year (£550,000). Since he never attends the House of Lords, he has clearly spent very little of it. Instead he has saved his income and passed his savings, as a lifetime gift, to his son, the archdeacon. His successor, Dr Proudie, has a reduced, post-1836 income of £5,000 (£300,000). He intends, none the less, to be an industrious early Victorian bishop:

> Dr Proudie was . . . quite prepared to take a conspicuous part in all theological affairs appertaining to these realms; and . . . by no means intended to bury himself in Barchester as his predecessor had done . . . London should still be his fixed residence . . . How otherwise could he . . . give to the government, in matters theological, the full benefit of his weight and talents? (*Barchester Towers*, Chapter 3)

Since Proudie's domination by his wife can sometimes make him seem more Laodicean than latitudinarian, it is worth remembering that the policy to which he intends to devote himself is the Broad Church ideal of 'Toleration'.

The management, as distinguished from leadership, of a diocese was the business of two clergymen with administrative roles: the dean and the archdeacon. **Deans** were responsible for the cathedral and its services, including the choice of preachers. After Mr Slope has given his objectionable sermon, in Chapter 6 of *Barchester Towers*, Dr Grantly points out to the dean, Dr Trefoil, that he can deny Slope any further access to the cathedral's pulpit. Except for this useful power, however, Trollope saw deans as redundant survivals of a medieval assumption that cathedrals were places of perpetual praise, 'kept up for the honour of God rather than for the welfare of the worshippers'.[4] A **precentor**, responsible for the cathedral's music, was part of this ceremonial process. Busy deans, chairing the chapter of resident canons, which governs a cathedral, and running the large staff needed for the building and its attendant schools and charities, might have resented a view of their post as a merely dignified one.

While the dean managed the cathedral, **archdeacons** managed the diocese. Bishops were required by law to 'visit the parts of their diocese' once in every three years. In the intervals between those visitations, the parishes were supervised by archdeacons who, unlike deans, had, in Trollope's view, 'a great deal to do'.[5] Some bishops, it is true, chose to play an active administrative role. But, in the mid-century, many still preferred to leave local management to their deputies. According to Trollope, in the second chapter of *The Warden*: 'We believe, as a general rule, that either a bishop or his archdeacons have sinecures: where a bishop works, archdeacons have but little to do, and vice versa. In the diocese of Barchester the Archdeacon of Barchester does the work.' Archdeacons supervised the administration of ecclesiastical property, had disciplinary powers over parish clergy, admitted churchwardens

---

[4] Anthony Trollope, 'The Normal Dean of the Present Day', *Pall Mall Gazette* (2 December 1865); collected in his *Clergymen of the Church of England* (London: Chapman & Hall, 1866), 31.

[5] Trollope, *Clergymen of the Church of England*, 42.

to office, inducted parish priests to their livings, and selected and prepared candidates for ordination. They needed to be both shrewd men of business and tactful personnel managers. There were sixty of them in early Victorian England, several of whom were, like Grantly, the sons of the bishops they worked with.

The **parish clergymen** supervised by the archdeacons were usually graduates of either Oxford or Cambridge University, or, in a few cases, of new institutions such as Durham University (1832). They were not, in other words, trained in specialized theological colleges. This meant that their education was identical with that of their non-clerical, middle-class contemporaries—or, more precisely, that their secular contemporaries took a course originally designed to train clergymen: Latin and Greek language, history, philosophy, and literature (including the Greek text of the New Testament), together with mathematics and theology. Leaders of the Church worried about the limited amount of theological knowledge which this broad syllabus provided for its ordinands. But it did mean that the clergy were at one with their educated parishioners: not a group of unfamiliar specialists but men with a common frame of intellectual reference. They were, to that extent, easier for a novelist to write about, and easier for readers to sympathize with and understand.

Once they had graduated and been ordained, such men either held college fellowships or served as temporary curates for experienced clergymen before being appointed to a parish living as rector, vicar, or perpetual curate. A **rector** received the 'great' as well as 'small' tithes of his parish. A **vicar** received only the small tithe because the great tithe (on major crops such as wheat) had once been paid to a monastery and passed to a 'lay impropriator' after the Reformation. Rectors and vicars enjoyed the same spiritual status, were canonically instituted and inducted, and received their income from funds specific to the parish. Institution protected them against the patron, often a layman, who had nominated them to the living, while the 'parson's freehold' meant that a bishop could remove them only in exceptional circumstances. **Perpetual curates**, like Josiah Crawley, were less happily situated. Before the Reformation, monasteries had sometimes provided services, on remote parts of their estate, by sending monks out from the abbey. This obligation passed, after the dissolution of the monasteries, to the new, secular owner of the land. Having no monks available, such persons were obliged to ask the bishop to license a clergyman to serve, without institution or induction, as a 'perpetual curate'. Unlike the more usual 'temporary' curates, who could be hired and fired at will, perpetual curates had tenure, since only a revocation of the bishop's licence could remove them. But they had no tithe income or glebe land and relied for their salary on a fixed payment, usually rather meagre, paid under deed by the landowner. To avoid the trouble of creating proper parishes, for which an independent Act of Parliament was required in every case, the Church Building Act of 1845 extended this ancient procedure to many of the new churches, chapels, and 'ecclesiastical districts' brought into being by industrialization and the growth of the towns.

The Church of England thus inherited some peculiar legal and material arrangements from its medieval predecessors. It also received a complicated theological structure from the 'Elizabethan compromise'. With its combination of 'Protestant Articles and a Catholic Prayer Book', Anglicanism could claim to have saved England from the wars of religion in continental Europe. But it did so by becoming a church with an exceptionally wide range of doctrinal opinion. Dr Proudie is a Broad Churchman, politically aligned with the Whig party and described as a 'latitudinarian' in Chapter 7 of *Barchester Towers*. His chaplain Obadiah Slope, however, is a Low Churchman or Evangelical whose strict Sabbatarianism and dislike of ceremonial worship suggest that he is a relatively extreme member of the Protestant wing of the Church. Dr Grantly stands on the opposite flank. Like most of the clergy of the Barchester diocese, he is a High Churchman of the traditional kind sometimes referred to as 'High and Dry', and politically a Tory, while his friend Mr Arabin is an example of the new High Church, or Anglo-Catholic, school brought into being by the Oxford Movement.

A good guide to this mixture of theological opinion is W. J. Conybeare's article on 'Church Parties' in the *Edinburgh Review* in 1853. The Church of England was divided into 'three great parties', commonly called 'the Low Church, the High Church, and the Broad Church'. Of these 'the most influential in recent times' had been the **Low Church**, with its roots in the Protestant or Puritan views of the late sixteenth century. Calvinist in its theology, and committed to the doctrines of '*justification by faith . . . conversion by grace*' and '*the sole supremacy of Scripture*',[6] it had lost adherents to the Nonconformist churches after the Savoy Conference of 1661, but revived in the eighteenth century. Under such gifted leaders as Henry Venn (1725–97), John Newton (1725–1807), and, more recently, Charles Simeon, the Vicar of Trinity Church, Cambridge (Mr Slope is a Cambridge man), and with support from members of the influential Clapham Sect, the Evangelicals could claim to have reawakened the Anglican Church in the early nineteenth century. John Sumner, Archbishop of Canterbury from 1848 to 1862, was an Evangelical, appointed by a Whig prime minister as a counter-balance to the Oxford Movement.

Despite this institutional success, the Low Church was losing its intellectual eminence: 'the Evangelical party' was, in Conybeare's words, 'too much devoted to practical work to think much of Literature'.[7] Instead, it was the members of the **Broad Church** party who were, 'to the middle of the nineteenth century, what the Low Church were to its beginning'. The clergymen

---

[6] W. J. Conybeare, 'Church Parties', *Edinburgh Review*, 98 (October 1853), 273–342, at 273 and 284 (sometimes known as 'The Divine Rule of Faith and Practice').

[7] Conybeare, 'Church Parties', 283.

who 'contributed to Classical Philology, to the Mathematical Sciences, to the Physical Sciences, to secular History', were 'all . . . Broad Churchmen'. This party was called 'Broad Church, by its friends; Latitudinarian or Indifferent by its enemies. Its distinctive character is the desire of comprehension. Its watchwords are Charity and Toleration.'[8]

Theological disputes were, in other words, unimportant, and the heterogeneous quality of the Church of England was a positive advantage. Thomas Arnold's proposal that the Church of England, as a national church, should open its doors to almost all Christians was so startling that Arnold was never made a bishop. But Whig governments were happy to appoint less intransigent Broad Churchmen to bishoprics, and two of Arnold's fellow 'Noetics' from Oriel College, Oxford, Richard Whately and R. D. Hampden, were thus promoted. As well as desiring 'comprehension', Broad Churchmen supported the uninhibited application of modern thought to religious topics. Arnold's pupil, Arthur Penrhyn Stanley, summed up the approach as 'moral thoughtfulness': morality as the common ground on which all Christians could agree, and a thoughtful, or philosophically rigorous, treatment of questions of belief.[9]

Unfortunately the Broad Church suffered from a lack of party discipline: 'this school of opinion, so rich in eminent writers, is unrepresented in the press, except by isolated publications of individuals'.[10] The **'new' High Church** or Tractarian party, which arose in the 1830s, was, by contrast, both highly organized and brilliantly publicized. Shocked by the Whig government's abolition of Anglican bishoprics in Ireland, Edward Pusey and John Newman led an 'Oxford Movement' for the independent authority of the Church, and for a reassertion of its Catholic identity. The authority of the Church of England derived, in their view, not from the Crown in Parliament but from the Apostolic Succession—the unbroken chain of ordinations and consecrations which linked contemporary Anglican bishops to Christ's disciples. Anglicanism was the *via media* or middle way: the direct descendant of the Early Church, from which both Roman Catholicism, in one direction, and Protestantism, in another, had deviated. It was thus the only true Catholic (that is, universal) Church and should assert its spiritual power against an Erastian arrangement which subordinated it to an increasingly secular State. In magazines and newspapers like the *British Critic* and *The Guardian* and, above all, in the Tracts for the Times issued between 1833 and 1841, the views of the Oxford Movement were widely and controversially disseminated.

These claims were striking but not entirely new. In a less extreme form they had been held for more than two hundred years by the **'old' High Church** party. This had its roots in the Catholic, rather than Protestant,

[8] Conybeare, 'Church Parties', 330.
[9] Arthur Penrhyn Stanley, *The Life and Correspondence of Thomas Arnold*, 6th edn. (London: B. Fellowes, 1846), 103.
[10] Conybeare, 'Church Parties', 334.

half of the 'Elizabethan compromise'. Arminian rather than Calvinist in its theology, accepting the doctrinal authority of Church as well as scripture, and ceremonial rather than spontaneous in its mode of worship, it saw itself as the successor of the institution shaped by William Laud in the early seventeenth century. As such, it valued the Apostolic Succession as something which lent weight to the Church in its relationship with the State, rather than as grounds for rejection of the establishment.

Seeking a Church more securely independent of secular government than this, Newman became a Roman Catholic in 1845. Mr Arabin, we are told in *Barchester Towers*, almost followed him. Arabin, however, is dissuaded by a curate (identified in *Framley Parsonage* as Josiah Crawley), who sets the Protestant ideal of individual judgement against the Catholic rule of Papal authority. Thereafter, Arabin remains a Tractarian Anglican or 'Puseyite'. Most of the clergymen of the diocese of Barchester are (in the terminology of *Barchester Towers*, Chapter 53) 'two degrees' lower in their 'church doctrine'. They are, that is, old High Churchmen of the kind memorably described, in 1891, as a group which inherits

> the traditions of a learned and sober Anglicanism . . . preaching, without passion or excitement, scholarlike, careful, wise . . . discourses on the capital points of faith and morals . . . There was nothing effeminate about it, as there was nothing fanatical . . . it was a manly school, distrustful of high-wrought feelings . . . cultivating self-command and shy of display, and setting up as its mark, in contrast to what seemed to it sentimental weakness, a reasonable and serious idea of duty.[11]

Puseyism would function as a stimulus to this more orthodox High Church party—sometimes an irritating one when its enthusiasm for ceremonial worship developed into what were seen as the excesses of Ritualism.

In his autobiography, Trollope claimed that, 'no one . . . could have had less reason than myself to presume himself to be able to write about clergymen'.[12] In fact, two of his uncles and both of his grandfathers were Anglican parsons, and his mother's cousin Fanny Bent, with whom he sometimes stayed, played an active part in the life of the cathedral close at Exeter. Trollope was educated at Winchester, a school with close links to a cathedral, and at Harrow, where the masters were High Anglican clergymen. During this time, he lived for more than a year alone with his father while the latter wrote his *Encyclopaedia Ecclesiastica*. Unfinished at the time of Thomas Trollope's death, this was a perceptive and wide-ranging survey of the beliefs and institutions of the Christian Church. In Ireland, Anthony Trollope got to know at least one Roman Catholic priest (possibly the Very Revd Peter

---

[11] R. W. Church, *The Oxford Movement: Twelve Years, 1833–1845*, 3rd edn. (London: Macmillan, 1909), 9–10.
[12] Anthony Trollope, *An Autobiography* (1883; Oxford: Oxford University Press, 1961), Chapter 5.

Daly)[13] sufficiently well to draw the memorable portrait of Father John McGrath in *The Macdermots of Ballycloran* (1847). Owen Dudley Edwards has argued that it was the years in Ireland which gave him 'the purchase on clerical society' needed for the Barsetshire novels; they certainly strengthened it.[14] After his death, his local vicar at South Harting in Sussex reported that he had been, 'an alert and reverent and audible worshipper, and a steady communicant'.[15]

Trollope's brother Thomas, it is true, remembered the religious practice of their childhood as 'perfunctory'.[16] But there was no lack of interest in religious ideas. Trollope's father had Broad Church sympathies. He sent his eldest son to St Alban Hall, Oxford, because Richard Whately was its principal, and argued in his *Encyclopaedia* that the word Evangelical, 'has been far too exclusively used, and may equally include all humble, devout, and pious Christians, whether Calvinists or Arminians'.[17] Trollope's mother was rather higher, and took a hostile view of Low Church clergymen, savagely caricaturing J. W. Cunningham, the Evangelical Vicar of Harrow, as the Revd W. J. Cartwright in her novel *The Vicar of Wrexhill*. Anthony Trollope's Mr Slope is a subtler and funnier version of Cartwright, and both characters are likened to Molière's hypocritical Tartuffe. Trollope, as this suggests, was no Evangelical, and he sent his sons to Bradfield College in Berkshire, a conspicuously Puseyite school. But he may have chosen it more for its generous staff–student ratio than its religious doctrine, and his own views were probably closer to those of the 'old' High Church.

More important than his private opinions is the way in which Trollope treats religion in his novels. In Chapter 6 of *Barchester Towers*, he acknowledges that, because he is 'to a certain extent forced to speak of sacred things', he might 'be thought to scoff at the pulpit'. This, he insists, does not imply any 'doubt as to the thing to be taught'. In Chapter 42 of *Framley Parsonage*, and again in Chapter 84 of *The Last Chronicle of Barset*, he responds to the opposite criticism: that, far from trespassing on the sacred, he has negligently omitted the spiritual dimension of his subject:

> I have described many clergymen, they say, but have spoken of them all as though their professional duties, their high calling, their daily workings for the good of those around them, were matters of no moment, either to

[13] See Richard Mullen, *Anthony Trollope: A Victorian in His World* (London: Duckworth, 1990), 680.

[14] Owen Dudley Edwards, Introduction to *The Macdermots of Ballycloran* (London: Trollope Society, 1991), p. xlv.

[15] *The Guardian* (13 December 1882).

[16] Thomas Adolphus Trollope, *What I Remember*, ed. Herbert Van Thal (London: William Kimber, 1973), 7.

[17] Thomas Anthony Trollope, *An Encyclopaedia Ecclesiastica* (London: John Murray, 1834), 526.

me, or in my opinion, to themselves. I would plead, in answer to this, that my object has been to paint the social and not the professional lives of clergymen. (*The Last Chronicle of Barset*, Chapter 84)

The truth lies somewhere between the two claims. He actually gives us rather more of the moral and spiritual experiences of his clerical characters than his disclaimer might suggest. But it is also the case that he takes an unusually close interest in their social lives, and in the mundane aspects of their professional routine: their practical duties, their rivalries, their rewards, and their morale.

Just as Trollope could be said to look at politicians, in his political novels, through the eyes of a civil servant, so he takes an administrator's view of clergymen. This, it could be argued, is his more original achievement, and it is one that is made all the more interesting by the curious combination of strength and contentiousness in the institution which he was describing. In Chapter 20 of *Barchester Towers*, Trollope argued that 'We are much too apt to look at schism in our church as an unmitigated evil. Moderate schism, if there may be such a thing, at any rate calls attention to the subject, draws in supporters who would otherwise have been inattentive to the matter, and teaches men to think upon religion.' The mid-nineteenth century Church of England had energy, reforming zeal, and intellectual self-confidence— but also, in the disputes between its 'parties', the stimulating quality which Trollope here calls 'moderate schism'. It made, as he realized, a remarkable subject for the novelist.

*Nicholas Shrimpton*

# EXPLANATORY NOTES

THESE notes are built on foundations laid by previous annotators, especially David Skilton (World's Classics, Oxford University Press, 1980) and Robin Gilmour (Penguin, 1984). The present editor gratefully acknowledges his debt to their work and to W. G. and J. T. Gerould for their *A Guide to Trollope* (1948), to Richard Mullen, with James Munson, for their *Penguin Companion to Trollope* (1996), and to R. C. Terry for his *Oxford Reader's Companion to Trollope* (1999). References to the Bible are to the King James version; definitions are derived from the *Oxford English Dictionary* (*OED*); references to Shakespeare are to the text of *The Complete Works*, ed. Stanley Wells and Gary Taylor (Oxford: Clarendon Press, 1988); references to Trollope's letters are to *The Letters of Anthony Trollope*, ed. N. John Hall with the assistance of Nina Burgis, 2 vols. (1983); references to *The Times* newspaper are to *The Times Digital Archive, 1785–1985*. Conversions of Victorian money to modern values are necessarily approximate but an online currency converter is provided by the National Register of Archives (<http://www.national archives.gov.uk/currency>) which updates values to 2005; 1850 should be used as the base date for *The Warden* and 1880 for *The Two Heroines of Plumplington*. There has been further inflation since then and figures for incomes should be seen as net, since income tax was levied only on the very rich, and at very low rates, before 1914; as a rough guide, values from the 1850s should be multiplied by 70, and values from the 1880s by 60.

## THE WARDEN

5  *beneficed clergyman*: a member of the clergy holding a church appointment with an endowed income.

*Barchester*: in October 1882 Trollope told the historian E. A. Freeman that the city and cathedral of Barchester were based on Winchester (Hampshire) 'where he was at school', while his model for the county of Barsetshire was Somerset (*Macmillan's Magazine*, 47 (June 1883), 239). Trollope had the idea for this novel, however, at Salisbury (Wiltshire), was familiar with Hereford, and had stayed with his mother's cousin Fanny Bent in the close at Exeter (Devon), where the cathedral, unusually, has not one but two 'Towers'. Barchester is an imaginary cathedral city in the south-west of England, suggested by some or all of these places.

*close*: the precinct of a cathedral enclosed by buildings, usually the homes of clergymen and their families, and sometimes protected by a gate closed at night.

*bishop, dean, and canons*: see Appendix 2.

*living*: a benefice or endowed post for a clergyman.

5 *precentor*: the cathedral cleric responsible for choral services; Trollope's original title for this novel was *The Precentor* (see Note on the Text, p. xxxii).

6 *Plumstead Episcopi*: the name suggests that it is a rich living in the gift of the bishop (*episcopi*: Latin, 'of the bishop'). 'Plum' is both a fruit and an adjective meaning 'fat' or 'soft'; in nineteenth-century financial slang 'plum' meant £100,000 (£5.9 million at modern values). Contrast Crabtree Parva, where the fruit imagery has different implications (see note to p. 106).

*woolstapler . . . wool-carders*: a woolstapler is a merchant who buys wool from farmers and sells it on to spinners and weavers; wool-carders were workmen who combed out raw wool so that it could be spun into thread.

*butts and patches*: butts were fields that had been used, in the Middle Ages, for archery practice; patches were areas of agricultural land (as in 'potato patch').

*bedesmen*: inmates of an almshouse, who, before the Reformation, would have been expected to pray for the soul of their benefactor (*bead*: Old English, 'prayer').

7 *farmed*: managed in respect of the drawing up of leases and collection of rents.

*see*: the office of being bishop in a particular diocese, originally his 'seat' or throne.

*dole*: a charitable gift or payment.

*sinecures*: nominal, paid, employments with no duties (Latin, 'without cares'); originally a benefice without cure of souls.

8 *twopence . . . sixty-two pounds eleven shillings and fourpence*: an error, uncorrected in the 1878 revision: the annual cost to Mr Harding of paying twopence a day to twelve bedesmen would actually be £36 10s. J. C. Eade (*Notes and Queries*, 39/2, 1992) suggests that Trollope might have arrived at his erroneous total by assuming that the supplement would not be paid on Sundays and either misremembering it as 4*d*., rather than 2*d*., or thinking that there were twenty-four bedesmen, rather than twelve. But he also notes the error in Chapter 4 whereby the reformers assume that there is £1,500 to redistribute rather than the £1,100 (£300 to the bedesmen, £800 to the warden) actually available. Trollope's financial mistakes cast doubt on his claim to have mastered the accounts of rural post offices (*An Autobiography*, Chapter 4).

*Hospital*: almshouse or old-people's home (not here used in the more modern sense of a place for medical treatment).

*the ecclesiastical architects of those days*: church architecture was a topic of intense interest in the 1850s because of the controversial publications of A. W. N. Pugin (*The True Principles of Pointed or Christian Architecture*, 1841) and John Ruskin (*The Seven Lamps of Architecture*, 1849) and the activity of the Ecclesiological Society (founded in 1839 as the Cambridge

Camden Society but renamed and based in London from 1845). The Ecclesiologists functioned as the architectural arm of the Oxford Movement (see Appendix 2) and campaigned for a return to Gothic, or 'Catholick', building, by which they meant, specifically, churches with chancels, designed in the 'Middle Pointed' or Decorated style of the thirteenth century. Other styles were not, in Trollope's word, 'correct', and the newsletter of the society fiercely criticized new churches which failed to adhere to it.

9 *Elysium*: Elysium, or the Elysian Fields, was the paradise of ancient Greek religion, where the souls of the virtuous enjoyed a life like that of the gods.

*gaiters*: a covering of leather or cloth for the lower leg and ankle. In black cotton or silk, with buttons up the side, they were part of the dress of Anglican bishops and archdeacons until the mid-twentieth century. Originally practical (because such clergy were meant to be out and about, on horseback, visiting the diocese), they became a symbol of office (see note to p. 33, 'Calves').

*hyperclerical . . . a black neck-handkerchief*: 'hyperclerical' means extremely clergyman-like (perhaps a coinage by Trollope; not in *OED*). Anglican clergymen began to adopt a distinct style of neckwear in the mid-nineteenth century, encouraged by the Tractarian stress on the special status of the priesthood. The white cravat customary in the eighteenth century had been worn by other men as well as clergymen; it gradually evolved into the distinctively clerical, stiff, white 'dog collar'. Mr Harding continues to wear a cravat, and shocks younger clergy by not always even wearing a white one.

*Purcell, Crotch, and Nares*: Henry Purcell (1659–95), John Nares (1715–83), and William Crotch (1775–1847) had been the leading composers of English church music in the previous two hundred years. All of them were also cathedral organists (Purcell at Westminster Abbey, Nares at York Minster, Crotch at Christ Church, Oxford); Crotch's edition of Thomas Tallis's *Litany* (1803) was a precedent for Harding's 'collection of our ancient church music'.

*faute de mieux*: (French) 'for want of a better'.

10 *Eager pushing politicians*: see notes to p. 37 ('Horseman' and 'Sir Benjamin Hall').

*Hospital of St Cross . . . Mr. Whiston at Rochester*: see Introduction (pp. xv–xvi).

11 *'Sacerdos'*: (Latin) 'priest'.

*the welfare of the reformed church*: like the fictitious John Hiram (who died in 1434), Henry de Blois (1096–1171), Bishop of Winchester and Abbot of Glastonbury, would have entrusted his bequest to the pre-Reformation Roman Catholic Church, not to the Anglican Church of the later sixteenth century, by which the endowment has since been held and administered.

12 *clerk*: a parish clerk is the church official, usually a layman, who assists

the priest by leading the congregation's responses and reading the epistle (the first of the two passages of New Testament scripture read out during a service). Until 1921 the office was a freehold (owned by its holder, rather than a conventional employment), which is why Dr Grantly found it so hard to get rid of the inaudible Joe Mutters.

12 *The Dragon of Wantly inn and posting-house*: this pub, at which 'posting horses' for mail-coaches were kept (in the pre-railway age), will become a familiar part of the urban landscape of Barchester. Here, in its first appearance, it provides an ironic anticipation of the plot of *The Warden* by alluding to the seventeenth-century satirical poem 'The Dragon of Wantley', collected in Thomas Percy's *Reliques of Ancient English Poetry* (1765). This ballad describes a dragon which preys on Wantley (or Wharncliffe), near Rotherham in Yorkshire, but is killed by a knight called More. Percy interprets the ballad as an attack on Sir Francis Wortley, owner of the ecclesiastical tithes of the parish, who tried to increase them at the expense of the parishioners and 'an hospital . . . built at Sheffield, for women'. More was the local lawyer who sued Wortley to prevent this. John Bold, who owns the Dragon of Wantly inn, is similarly involved in an attack on what he sees as the improper exploitation of ecclesiastical property. Trollope's wife, Rose Heseltine, came from Rotherham.

13 *physician . . . surgeon and apothecary*: both 'physician' and 'surgeon-apothecary' at this date meant what would now be called a general practitioner; 'physician' had originally meant a junior doctor, not yet qualified as a surgeon. In the late nineteenth century the terms would change their meanings again to produce the modern distinction between apothecary (pharmaceutical chemist), physician (general practitioner), and surgeon.

*the three per cents*: government stocks paying an interest rate of 3 per cent a year, widely used in the nineteenth century as a secure and convenient source of investment income.

14 *Danton . . . French Jacobin*: Georges Jacques Danton (1759–94) was a leader of 'the Mountain', the extreme wing of the French Revolutionary regime (by which he was himself executed in April 1794), and a remarkable orator. The Jacobins (who met in a Dominican house in the Rue St Jacques) were a French political society which became increasingly extreme after 1791 and organized the Reign of Terror of 1793–4. Trollope's previous novel *La Vendée* (1850) had been set during the French Revolution and referred to the way in which, in 1792, Danton 'ceased . . . to curb the licence of his tongue' (Chapter 1).

*Argus*: in Greek mythology, a herdsman with eyes all over his body, whom Hera set to watch Io when Zeus was seeking to seduce her.

15 *Homer . . . nods*: 'Quandoque bonus dormitat Homerus' (Horace, *Ars poetica*, 359), 'Even good Homer sometimes slumbers'—that is, makes a mistake. Homer was the Greek epic poet (or poets) to whom the *Iliad* and *Odyssey*, both probably written in the 8th century BC, are attributed.

*shovel hat*: the shovel hat was a stiff, broad-brimmed black hat, worn by many nineteenth-century clergymen; the brim was turned up at the sides and had a projecting, shovel-like curve in front and behind.

*robe de nuit*: (French) 'nightshirt'.

*aprons*: the 'apron', which formed part of the distinctive dress of Anglican bishops, was a shortened, knee-length version of the cassock, the ankle-length garment (derived from the *vestis talaris* of ancient Rome) worn by other clergy. The Anglican Canons of 1604 forbade clergymen to appear in public 'in their doublet and hose, without coats or cassocks'.

*dishabille*: (from French, *déshabillé*) a state of undress.

16  *give his coat . . . even seven times*: see Luke 6:29: 'And . . . him that taketh away thy cloak forbid not to take thy coat also,' and Matthew 18:21–2: 'Then came Peter to him, and said, Lord, how oft shall my brother sin against me, and I forgive him? till seven times? Jesus saith unto him, I say not unto thee, Until seven times: but, Until seventy times seven.'

17  *the sacrilegious doings of Lord John Russell*: the Whig government (1846–52) of Lord John Russell established, in 1850, the Church Estates Commission, a lay subcommittee of the Ecclesiastical Commission (see Appendix 2), to oversee the management of the property of the Church of England. The three salaried commissioners were not clergymen and two of them were appointed by the Crown (that is, the government).

18  *turnpike woman . . . act of Parliament*: turnpike trusts, each requiring a separate Act of Parliament, collected tolls for road maintenance. By 1838 there were more than 1,000 trusts, administering 30,000 miles of road, and collecting fees at 8,000 turnpikes (toll-gates named after the barriers of pikes used against cavalry in warfare). They were often unpopular with local people, and the Rebecca Rioters in south Wales (1839–43) attacked toll-gates (together with the houses of Anglican clergymen, similarly disliked for their collection of tithes from a largely Nonconformist population). The railways undermined the finances of turnpike trusts and the Local Government Act of 1888 transferred their responsibilities to county councils.

19  *Messrs Cox and Cummins*: a fictitious firm of London solicitors who became 'Cox and Cummings' in the latter part of Chapter 5 (corrected by Trollope in his 1878 revision) and 'Cox and Cumming' in Chapter 19 (uncorrected). Lord Ballindine's attorney in *The Kellys and the O'Kellys* (1848) had been 'Mr Cummings' (Chapter 39), though he may be a Dublin, rather than a London, lawyer.

*six-and-eightpence*: 6s. 8d., or a third of a pound (£20 at modern values), was the fee for a basic legal service (usually a short consultation and the writing of a letter) in the fixed tariff that preceded the modern practice of 'hourly billing', or charging clients for time spent on the work.

20  *St Cecilia*: Roman martyr of the second–third century AD; the patron saint of music and musicians.

21 *halcyon*: calm, as in 'halcyon days': fourteen days of calm weather, supposed to occur at the winter solstice when the halcyon, or kingfisher, was hatching its young.

*constitutional visitor*: an inspector who has legal authority to 'visit', or supervise, an institution to ensure that it is properly run.

22 *a favourite little bit of Bishop's*: Henry Rowley Bishop (1786–1855) was conductor at Covent Garden and Drury Lane and a prolific composer of operas. In 1848 he succeeded William Crotch (see note to p. 9) as Professor of Music at Oxford. The 'favourite little bit' of his music is almost certainly his most famous tune, 'Home, Sweet Home', written for the opera *Clari, or The Maid of Milan* (1823) with words by the American writer John Howard Payne. The song was reissued as a parlour ballad in 1852. Payne's words provide an ironic comment on Hiram's Hospital as a 'home' for the pensioners: 'Mid pleasures and palaces though we may roam, | Be it ever so humble, there's no place like home.' How a secular song by a modern composer has found its way into 'that dear sacred book', Harding's *Church Music* ('a collection of our ancient church music'), remains a mystery.

23 *Ecclesiastical Court!*: in the Church of England the bishops' Consistory Courts can try clergy for 'uncleanliness and wickedness of life'; appeals from the Consistory Courts can be made to the Court of Arches, and from there to the Judicial Committee of the Privy Council. Mr Harding may be thinking of the Gorham Case (1847–50), in which a dispute between a clergyman and his bishop (Henry Phillpotts of Exeter, see note to p. 97), on a doctrinal rather than a moral issue (so heard, in the first instance, by the Court of Arches), had been controversially decided, on appeal, by the Judicial Committee of the Privy Council.

24 *pony chair*: a pony-chaise or light carriage, drawn by two ponies or a small horse.

25 *appanage*: a perquisite or gift, either of money or of a job (originally the provision made for the maintenance of the younger children of monarchs).

*church militant*: the Church on earth in its role of fighting against evil (from medieval Latin, *ecclesia militans*).

26 *pharmacopœia*: (Latin, from Greek) a book containing formulas for preparing drugs and medicines.

27 *statute of limitation*: in law, statutory rules limit the time within which civil actions can be brought: six years from the cause of action in cases of contract and tort, twelve years in cases involving land or deeds.

28 *tithes among Methodists . . . and other savage tribes*: tithes, a 10 per cent annual charge on the produce of a parish, were the chief source of income for Anglican clergymen. They were levied on all eligible residents including non-Anglicans, such as Methodists and Baptists, who resented paying

to support a Church which was not their own and wanted them to be either shared or abolished.

*sacred bench*: twenty-six bishops of the Church of England sit in the House of Lords as 'Lords Spiritual', thus forming part of the nation's legislature (as did, from 1801 to 1871, four bishops of the Church of Ireland). The bench on which they sit (actually three benches) is on the right-hand, or government, side of the throne on which the monarch sits when present in the house, to indicate their importance, though they do not have a party allegiance.

*shovel hats and lawn sleeves . . . cowls, sandals, and sackcloth!*: shovel hats (see note to p. 15) and lawn sleeves were worn (on different occasions) by Anglican bishops. Lawn sleeves, made of a light linen cloth (from Laon in France), are part of the white rochet, or surplice, which is worn under the chimere (an academic gown without sleeves) as the liturgical dress of bishops. Cowls, sandals, and sackcloth are the characteristic dress of monks. When the bishop thinks of them as 'illegal', he is right about the letter of the law but wrong about its effects. Henry VIII had suppressed all English monasteries in 1536–41 and the Roman Catholic Relief Acts of 1778 and 1829 restated that prohibition. In practice, however, the law was held 'in abeyance' and Catholic religious communities were gradually re-established; Mount St Bernard's Abbey, a Cistercian house in Leicestershire, was founded in 1835. Female communities for Anglican women began to appear in the 1840s; the first male Anglican monastic community would be founded in 1866.

*disbelieved the Trinity!*: the doctrine of the Trinity, the belief that the One God exists in Three Persons and One Substance, is a central dogma of Christian theology but was challenged from the seventeenth century onwards by Unitarianism, the view that God is a single Person. Although the Unitarian view was widely accepted by English Presbyterians, and championed by the scientist Joseph Priestley, the Penal Laws against Unitarianism did not lapse until 1813. In 1881 the Anglican Broad Churchman A. P. Stanley, Dean of Westminster, would be criticized for allowing a Unitarian, who had been one of the team of scholars working on the Revised Version of the Bible, to take communion in Westminster Abbey.

30 *'Fiat justitia ruat cœlum'*: (Latin) 'Let justice be done even though the heavens fall.' In a slightly different form ('Fiat justitia et pereat mundus'), this had been the motto of Ferdinand I (1503–64), Holy Roman Emperor.

*moiety*: half.

*non compos mentis*: (Latin) 'not of sound mind'.

31 *old Catgut*: Harding's nickname is derived from his passion for music: the strings of violins, violas, harps, and cellos are made from 'catgut' (actually a cord made from the intestines of sheep or goats, not cats; originally 'kitgut' from the word 'kit', meaning a small violin or fiddle).

33 *Calves*: Grantly wears gaiters (see note to p. 9) as a symbol of his office as archdeacon. It is popularly assumed that he is proud of the way in which these black silk garments show off his 'nether person': his calves or shapely lower legs.

35 *by goles*: euphemism for the oath 'By God'.

36 *to put on his good armour*: 'Put on the whole armour of God, that ye may be able to stand against the wiles of the devil' (Ephesians 6:11).

37 *Queen's Counsel*: a Queen's Counsel (King's Counsel when there is a male monarch) is a senior barrister, chosen by the Crown and recognized by the courts. The role was first invented as a personal appointment for Sir Francis Bacon in 1596, but Queen's Counsels began to be created in significant numbers in the 1830s and gradually superseded the Serjeants-at-Law (previously the most senior category of advocate), entirely replacing them after 1873.

*a sound Conservative . . . in the house*: Haphazard sits in the House of Commons as a Tory MP (and, as we shall be told in Chapter 8, is the Attorney-General; see note to p. 66). He is an invented figure whose closest parallel is with Sir Fitzroy Kelly (1796–1880), a formidable advocate, Queen's Counsel, Tory MP, and Solicitor-General (not Attorney-General) in the Derby government of February to December 1852. Kelly acted for the Dean and Chapter of Rochester against Robert Whiston in the Queen's Bench hearing which 'silenced that fellow', though, in reality, no one lawyer handled all the cases which Grantly lists here. More fully described in Chapter 17 below, he will be mentioned again in *Doctor Thorne*.

*Horseman*: Edward Horsman (1807–76) was a Whig MP and a leading parliamentary critic of the Church of England. He persistently attacked the ecclesiastical policies of the Russell (1846–52), Derby (1852), and Aberdeen (1852–5) governments as too favourable to the bishops. In his 1878 revision Trollope would correct the spelling of the name to 'Horsman' on its second, though not first, occurrence.

*Bishop of Beverley's income*: the Bishop of Beverley is a fiction: there was no Anglican see at Beverley, which lies in the diocese of York, though its parish church, Beverley Minster, is larger than many cathedrals. A Roman Catholic see had been created at Beverley in 1850 by the restoration of the English hierarchy, but Grantly is certainly not thinking of that. Rather, the name functions as a substitute for Salisbury, whose bishop spoke in the Lords on 24 June and 28 July 1853, after attacks in *The Times*, to reject 'the charge of having received more than the legitimate Income of his See'. Since this statement was made in the Lords, the government lawyer who supported him was not the Attorney-General but the Lord Chancellor, Lord Cranworth (a Whig).

*one noble lord*: the Revd Francis North, 6th Earl of Guilford (1772–1861). North was a clergyman and warden of the Hospital of St Cross in Winchester (see Introduction, p. xv), who unexpectedly inherited the Earldom of Guilford from his cousin in 1827.

*Sir Benjamin Hall*: Benjamin Hall (1802–67), a baronet from 1838, Baron Llanover from 1859, was a Welsh Liberal MP, who campaigned for the abolition of church rates and for ecclesiastical reform. He published his speech on the Ecclesiastical Commission Bill (see note to p. 17) in July 1850 as a pamphlet; his books *A Letter to His Grace the Archbishop of Canterbury on the State of the Church* (1850) and *A Letter to the Rev. C. Phillips* (1852) also argued for a radical redistribution of church property. 'Big Ben', the bell in the clock tower (1858) of the Palace of Westminster, is named after him.

38 *Jewel's library*: Trollope seems to be in error here. The library of Salisbury Cathedral is within the cloisters but dates from 1445. The famous 'library' (in another sense) assembled by John Jewel (1522–71), Bishop of Salisbury from 1560 and author of the first systematic defence of the authority of the Church of England, was purchased after Jewel's death by Magdalen College, Oxford.

39 *Common Pleas*: a common-law court, dating from the late twelfth century, which heard cases between subject and subject, as distinct from those involving the Crown (which were heard in the Court of the King's or Queen's Bench). It sat in Westminster Hall and had exclusive jurisdiction over matters of real property. In 1873 a single High Court of Justice was created; Common Pleas would be fully absorbed into the Queen's Bench Division of that court in 1880.

40 *brazen trumpet*: literally a brass trumpet but figuratively a loud noise, thus in Act 4 of Purcell's opera *Dioclesian* (1690; words by Thomas Betterton): 'Sound, Fame, thy brazen trumpet sound!'

41 *a long pull and a strong pull*: a traditional saying, originally associated with sailors hauling the ropes of sailing ships, to denote concerted effort.

42 *Quaker's broad brim*: Quakers (see note to p. 80) wore distinctive dress, including (for men) a hat with a broad, flat brim. Although some (known as 'gay Friends' rather than 'plain Friends') had long disregarded this dress code, it would not be formally abolished until 1860.

43 *half-crowns*: a half-crown was a coin worth 2s. 6d., or one eighth of a pound.

44 *ebullition*: agitation (literally 'boiling').

45 *octogenarian Croesus*: an octogenarian is between 80 and 89 years old; Croesus, King of Lydia in the sixth century BC, was proverbial for his wealth. The reference is to the Revd Francis North, 6th Earl of Guilford (1772–1861), who turned eighty in 1852 (see Introduction, p. xv).

*gormandizer*: glutton, greedy consumer.

46 *brougham*: a one-horse closed carriage.

48 *consolation of a Roman*: in ancient Roman culture the *consolatio* was a familiar literary and philosophical topos. Reason was the supreme consoler:
one should remember that fortune is all powerful, that men are mortal,
and that death is the end of all ills; Seneca's *Ad Marciam* and *Ad Hel-
viam* are famous examples. Trollope describes Cicero's struggle to console
himself for the death of his daughter Tullia in his *Life of Cicero* (1880, ii.
Chapter 7). A Roman in public life could also console himself with the
thought that his private suffering had contributed to the general good.

49 *Pakenham Villas*: Bold's house, one of the 'genteel villas' developed by
his father, takes its address from the family name of the Irish Earls of
Longford, probably in honour of Major-General Sir Edward Pakenham
(1778–1815). Pakenham was killed while commanding the British forces
at the Battle of New Orleans in January 1815. This battle was unnecessary because a ceasefire between Britain and America had been agreed by
the Treaty of Ghent on 24 December 1814, news of which did not reach
Louisiana in time to prevent the fighting and a British defeat. As with the
Dragon of Wantly (see note to p. 12), a place name is being used to comment on Bold's campaign.

*chimera*: (Greek) a grotesque monster made up of parts of different ani-
mals, hence an impossible fantasy.

50 *Brutus*: a reference either to the semi-legendary Lucius Junius Brutus,
who condemned his own sons to death for treason in the sixth century BC,
or to Marcus Junius Brutus (78–42 BC), the Roman statesman who joined
the conspiracy against Julius Caesar in 44 BC and killed himself after
defeat at the Battle of Philippi: the internal narrator of Trollope's *The
Fixed Period* (1881–2) speaks of the 'grandeur' of his suicide (Chapter 3).
In his *Life of Cicero* (1880) Trollope accepts the claim, in Shakespeare's
play *Julius Caesar*, that 'Brutus was an honourable man' but comments
that, 'as far as the public service was concerned', he was 'unpractical' and
'useless' (ii. Chapter 8).

*to attack the muslin frocks*: muslin is a light cotton fabric, originally from
Mosul in Iraq; by the mid-nineteenth century the word 'frock' (previously a term for children's clothes) was used of women's dresses. Trollope's description of the party as a battle is a use of the mock-heroic
mode, found in Pope's poem *The Rape of the Lock* (1714), in which modern social events are treated as if they were episodes in the epic poems
of Homer or Virgil, though in a novel written and published during the
Crimean War (1854–6) it may also ironically reflect the military atmos-
phere of its era.

*mad reforms even at Oxford*: the Whig government of 1846–52 set up
a Royal Commission to inquire into the condition of Oxford University in
1850; after much debate, an Act for the Reform of Oxford University was
passed in July 1854. This freed matriculation and degrees (except in Theology) from religious tests and was the first step in the process by which
Oxford ceased to be an exclusively Anglican institution.

*Apollo*: the Greek sun god, also the god of music, but here probably an ironic reference to the ideal of male beauty provided by the Apollo Belvedere, a Roman copy in marble, now in the Vatican Museum, of a Greek bronze statue of Apollo from the fourth century BC.

51 *a syncope*: a failure of the action of the heart, resulting in a loss of consciousness.

*short whist*: whist is a card game in which a full pack of fifty-two cards is dealt face down to four players, playing in pairs. The player to the dealer's left leads to the first trick, and the remaining players must follow suit if they can, or trump, or discard. The winner of a trick leads to the next until the thirteen tricks have been played. Every trick won in excess of six scores 1 point. In 'short whist' a game is won by the first side to score 5 points, and a score of two games out of three wins the 'rubber'. The high trumps (ace, king, queen, jack) are 'honours': if, after the tricks have been taken, one side holds all four honours, they score 4 additional points, if three honours, 2 additional points; 3 further points can be won by achieving a 'treble', or outscoring your opponents by 5 or more points to 0. Here, the archdeacon and the rector win the first hand by seven tricks to six (1 point to 0), the second by eight to five (2 points to 0), and score 2 points for honours (since they hold ace, king, and jack). At 5 points to 0, they also take a 'treble', thus winning 8 points in the first game. The eventual margin of 'three and thirty points' appears to be their score after two rubbers. Betting would involve an agreed price per point, usually a shilling. Trollope loved playing whist and published an article about it, 'Whist at Our Club', *Blackwood's Edinburgh Magazine*, 121 (1877), 597–604.

52 *'As David did Goliath'*: Goliath, a Philistine giant, challenged any individual Israelite to fight him. David, later King of Judah but at this date a young shepherd from Bethlehem, responded by using a sling to hurl a stone at the giant's forehead, knocking him unconscious, and then beheading him with his own sword (1 Samuel 17:4–51). The archdeacon has trumped a king with a mere two.

53 *three volumes*: the dominant format for the publication of new novels from the 1820s to 1894 was the 'three-decker', in which a novel was split into three bound volumes. This suited circulating libraries because they could issue a single title to three readers at the same time. Although novels sometimes appeared in one volume (*The Warden*, as Trollope notes here, is an example of this), they rarely extended to more than three: George Eliot's *Middlemarch* (1872) and Trollope's *The Prime Minister* (1876), both four volumes, are notable exceptions. Trollope did not quite manage to make *The Warden* as short as he here hopes: the first edition has 336 pages.

56 *on a high horse*: (traditional) in a proud and domineering way.

57 *by the ears*: in an agitated and quarrelsome state, as in the opening lines of Samuel Butler's poem *Hudibras* (1662–80), describing the outbreak of the English Civil War: 'When hard words, jealousies, and fears, | Set folks together by the ears'.

57 *the daily Jupiter*: Trollope's fictional equivalent of *The Times* news-paper, which was founded in 1785 and known as 'The Thunderer'. This nickname was acquired when it was 'thundering for reform' in the early 1830s, though the immediate cause was a demand for more sensational details after the inquest into the suicide of Lord Graves in January 1829. Attacked by rival papers, *The Times* acknowledged that it had 'thundered out' its views (11 February 1829); a writer in the *Morning Herald*, prob-ably William Maginn, mocked it as '*The Thunderer*' on 15 February 1830. Carlyle identified the leader-writer Edward Sterling (1773–1847) as the chief 'Thunderer' of *The Times* in his *Life of John Sterling* (1851); George Meredith's novel *Diana of the Crossways* (1885, but set in the 1840s) calls the editor of *The Times* 'Mr Tonans' (from Latin, 'thundering'). Trollope goes behind the phrase to Jupiter Tonans, the thunderbolt-hurling (or 'fulminating') god of ancient Roman religion, who lived (like his Greek counterpart, Zeus) on Mount Olympus (see note to p. 107).

58 *eighty thousand copies . . . Four hundred thousand readers . . . four hundred thousand hearts*: in the first edition (1855), 'forty thousand copies . . . Two hundred thousand readers . . . two hundred thousand hearts'. The correct figure for *The Times* in 1855 was actually about 58,000 copies a day, with its nearest rival, the *Morning Advertiser*, selling between 7,000 and 8,000.

*Addison . . . Junius*: Joseph Addison (1672–1719), poet, dramatist, polit-ician, and prose writer: the essays which he published in the *Tatler* and *The Spectator* (1709–12) had a formative influence on modern English prose style; Dr Johnson, in 1781, described him as 'the model of the middle style'. Junius was the pseudonym of the author (possibly Sir Philip Fran-cis) of a series of powerful letters which appeared in the *Public Advertiser* (1769–72), attacking King George III and his ministers.

59 *soaring mind*: an ironic allusion to Milton, who was identified with the con-cept of the mind that soars above the material and literal. See the open-ing of *Paradise Lost*, where the poet 'intends to soar | Above th' *Aonian* Mount' (Book I, ll. 14–15), and 'At a Vacation Exercise': 'where the deep transported mind may soare | Above the wheeling poles' (ll. 33–4).

*the great Bunce stood apart with lowering brow*: a mock-heroic echo of Rich-ard Glover's blank-verse tragedy *Boadicea* (1753), where Venusia pleads with the enraged Queen of the Iceni: 'Stand apart, | At my request, Iceni-ans. [To Boadicea] O unbend | That lowering brow, and hear a suppliant sister!' (Act 2, Scene 1).

*'Convent Custody Bill'*: an exaggerated version of the Recovery of Personal Liberty Bill, proposed by Thomas Chambers, MP for Hertford, in May 1853: the measure was seen by Chambers as a way of ensuring that women were not held in convents against their will, but by the MP for Drogheda, James McCann (a Catholic), as the 'desecration of nunneries'. It was a pri-vate member's bill and the real Attorney-General, Sir Alexander Cock-burn, not only did not design it but voted against it; Lord John Russell made the government's opposition clear on 10 May 1853. David Skilton

notes that on 23 June 1853 the House of Commons considered both the Excise Duties on Spirits Bill and the Recovery of Personal Liberty Bill. But the latter debate was merely a brief reconsideration of an amendment which had reduced the Personal Liberty Bill to a proposal for an inquiry (the substantive discussions had been on 10 May and 22 June), and even this was adjourned until after the end of the session, so that the bill lapsed. There is no evidence to support Trollope's suggestion that the Personal Liberty Bill was a cunning device to divide Irish votes on the Excise Bill: Protestant, as well as Catholic, Irish MPs spoke against the 'Convent Custody Bill', seeing it as an inflammatory measure which would cause civil unrest.

61  *the bench of bishops*: see note to p. 28.

*Charles James, Henry, and Samuel*: Grantly's sons are caricatures of three contemporary Anglican bishops. Charles is Charles James Blomfield (1787–1857), Bishop of London. An energetic reformer and key member of the Ecclesiastical Commission (see Appendix 2), he was an inconsistent Churchman: Low in his support of the Jerusalem bishopric in 1841 but High in his dissent from the judgment in the Gorham Case, 1850 (see note to p. 23). Henry is Henry Phillpotts (1778–1869), Bishop of Exeter from 1830 and a notoriously combative High Churchman (see notes to p. 23 and p. 97); his appointment to the see of Exeter ('sent on a tour into Devonshire') was indeed unpopular: on Guy Fawkes night 1831 he summoned the 7th Yeomanry to defend the Bishop's Palace while a crowd outside burned him in effigy. Samuel is Samuel Wilberforce (1805–73), Bishop of Oxford, a High Churchman whose charming manner made him popular at Court (where he was the Prince Consort's chaplain) but earned him the nickname 'Soapy Sam'. Henry James, in 1883, would call this passage 'ponderous allegory'; in later Barchester novels all three sons will reappear as realistic characters, but only Henry, as Major Grantly, will play a prominent role (in *The Last Chronicle of Barset*).

*Florinda . . . Grizzel*: although Dr Grantly shares the conservative views of the actual archbishops, these names are invented. The wives of the current and immediately preceding Archbishops of York were Catherine and Anne respectively; there is no evidence that William Howley had a sister called Grizzel. (Howley was Archbishop of Canterbury, 1828–48, and thus at the time of the christening; Grantly would not have liked Howley's Evangelical successor John Sumner.) Trollope may have chosen the unusual names to make it clear that no literal reference was intended.

62  *Luther . . . Capuchin friar*: Martin Luther (1483–1546), Protestant theologian, whose Ninety-Five Theses of 1517 launched the Reformation. The Capuchin Friars, founded in the 1520s, are a branch of the Franciscan Order and played an important role in the Catholic Counter-Reformation.

*guinea*: a guinea was a coin worth 21*s*., or £1 1*s*. (£62 at modern values).

64  *dim dragon china*: antique Chinese porcelain.

65 *devilled kidneys*: lambs' kidneys fried in a piquant and spicy sauce, using cayenne pepper; an English breakfast dish dating from the eighteenth century.

*sixty pounds . . . thirty pounds*: £60 (£3,520) . . . £30 (£1,760).

*fives*: a game played by throwing a ball against the walls of a three-sided court. Originally played between the buttresses of churches and chapels, it developed as a school sport, especially at Eton, Rugby, and Trollope's second school, Winchester.

66 *Rabelais*: François Rabelais (1494–1553), author of *Gargantua and Pantagruel* (1533–64). A rambling satirical fantasy, often comically obscene, it was translated into English in the late seventeenth century but continued to be thought of as indecent: the English adjective 'Rabelaisian' means 'exuberantly and coarsely humorous' (*OED*). In the first book (*Pantagruel*, 1533), Panurge, a cunning rogue, becomes Pantagruel's constant companion. By the third book (1546), Panurge has evolved into a loquacious buffoon and the irresponsible ruler of Salmigondin; there is a long (and misogynistic) discussion of whether or not he should marry.

*attorney-general*: although Sir Abraham Haphazard has been described in Chapter 5, this is the first time we are told that he is the Attorney-General: the Crown's representative in the law courts and the government's senior legal adviser. In the twentieth century the role became increasingly a political one and the Attorney-General now usually appoints 'Treasury Counsel' to appear in court for him on government business. Until 1890, however, the Attorney-General was allowed to continue his own practice at the bar, in combination with his appearances in court for the government and his duties in Parliament.

68 *Bramah . . . Chubb*: Joseph Bramah (1748–1814) was an inventor who opened the Bramah Locks Company in Piccadilly in 1784. From 1790 the company exhibited a 'Challenge Lock', offering 200 guineas (£12,300) to anybody who could pick it; the picking of the Challenge Lock by the American locksmith Alfred Hobbs was a celebrated event (taking sixteen days) at the Great Exhibition of 1851. Charles Chubb (1779–1845), originally an ironmonger in Winchester, improved the lock patented by his brother Jeremiah in 1818 and built a large business in Wolverhampton and London. The Chubb company was the sole supplier of locks to the General Post Office, and made the secure case for the display of the Koh-i-Noor diamond at the 1851 Great Exhibition.

*nonsuited*: a nonsuit is the stoppage of a suit by the judge when the plaintiff fails to make out a legal case or to produce sufficient evidence. In the English High Court, nonsuit was abolished and replaced by discontinuance in 1881.

*equity*: fairness, natural justice. In law, equity is a system of doctrines and procedures evolved in the Court of Chancery to stand beside and correct the common law when it seems to have produced an unfair outcome.

John Bold's case, as Sir Abraham Haphazard has pointed out, will fail in law. Mr Harding feels that in equity the matter might look very different. Trollope's father practised as a Chancery barrister from 1806 until the late 1820s.

70 *'A rose, you know——.'* : 'What's in a name? That which we call a rose | By any other word would smell as sweet', Shakespeare, *Romeo and Juliet*, Act 2, Scene 1, ll. 85–6.

72 *ipsissima verba*: (Latin) 'the very words'.

73 *it cannot be all roses*: (proverbial) life is not a bed of roses, or unvaryingly pleasant.

*griping*: grasping, avaricious.

78 *sinecure pluralists*: holders of more than one church office, with incomes but no duties (see note to p. 7).

80 *Crown and Anchor*: a pub on the corner of the Strand and Arundel Street remembered for its association with Radical politics. It served a controversial dinner in July 1791 to celebrate the second anniversary of the Fall of the Bastille. Both the London Corrresponding Society and the Society for Constitutional Information held meetings there. Although it was sometimes used by groups with other views, and for other purposes, Bold's speech at this address confirms his status as a Radical. The pub would be destroyed by a fire in 1857.

*Quakers and Mr Cobden*: the Quakers, or Society of Friends, are a religious group formed by George Fox in the 1650s. They are pacifists and campaigned in 1854 against British entry into the Crimean War. Richard Cobden (1804–65) was a Radical MP, famous for his leadership of the Anti-Corn Law League in the 1840s. Unlike his parliamentary ally John Bright, he was not himself a Quaker, but his free-trade views meant that he opposed war as an impediment to commerce. A leading member of the Peace Society from 1849, Cobden spoke frequently in Parliament in the winter of 1853–4 to oppose conflict with Russia; once war had been declared (31 March 1854), he largely dropped the topic. This reference places the action of Chapter 10 in the spring of 1854 (see Introduction, p. xxiii).

*Tom Towers*: Trollope rejected a suggestion, made in a *Times* review, that Towers was based on an actual 'editor or manager' of that newspaper; *The Warden* was written before he began to be friendly with London journalists (*An Autobiography*, Chapter 5). Although Towers is actually a leader-writer, not an editor or manager, it is also the case that he does not directly resemble the writers of *The Times*' leading articles in this period: Thomas Mozley (Wiltshire clergyman), Henry Woodham (Cambridge don), Henry Reeve (civil servant and foreign policy specialist), and Robert Lowe (Oxford don, successful lawyer, and MP). Towers's career as a briefless barrister who has drifted into journalism was, however, not uncommon, and his lifestyle reflects the high salaries paid to *Times* leader-writers: £1,200 to £1,800 a year (£70,250 to £105,360). Towers reappears in

*Barchester Towers* and *Framley Parsonage*. His name alludes to Tom Tower, the belfry over the gate of Christ Church, Oxford.

81 *shady home*: an echo of Goldsmith's poem *The Deserted Village* (1770): 'How blest is he who crowns, in shades like these, | A youth of labour with an age of ease'; Goldsmith's portrait of 'the village preacher', an ideal clergyman noted for his kindness to the elderly poor, may have helped to suggest the character of Mr Harding (see note to p. 112).

82 *like rain in May*: an indirect echo of Tennyson's line 'Like Summer tempest came her tears' in the lyric 'Home they brought her warrior dead', added to *The Princess* in its third edition (1850).

83 *fettered with adamant*: adamant is an exceptionally hard substance, such as diamond; Satan, in Milton's *Paradise Lost*, is to be bound 'In Adamantin Chains' (Book I, 1. 48).

84 *convocate*: to sit in Convocation, the parliament of Oxford University, consisting of all doctors and masters (that is, graduates with the degree of MA). The powers of Convocation are now limited to the election of the Chancellor and the Professor of Poetry, with Congregation (current members of the faculties) assuming the general power over the governance of the university which Convocation held in the nineteenth century.

*Iphigenia*: daughter of Agamemnon and Clytemnestra. The goddess Artemis required her death in return for the wind needed to propel the becalmed Greek fleet from Aulis to Troy, and Agamemnon agreed to sacrifice her. In Euripides' tragedy *Iphigenia in Aulis*, she initially pleads for her life but eventually goes nobly to the sacrifice.

85 *Jephthah's daughter*: Jephthah was persuaded by the Israelites to lead a military expedition against the Ammonites, and vowed to God that, if successful, he would sacrifice whatever first emerged from his house on his return. To his dismay, this proved to be his daughter (his only child); she piously accepted her fate and became 'a burnt offering' two months later (Judges 11:30–40).

86 *triste*: (French) 'sad'.

88 *in dudgeon*: ill-humoured, resentful, offended.

90 *filthy lucre*: wealth (in a disapproving sense). 'A bishop then must be blameless . . . Not given to wine, no striker, not greedy of filthy lucre . . . not covetous' (1 Timothy 3:2–3; see also Titus 1:7). The phrase is first found in William Tyndale's translation of the New Testament (1526).

95 *Aulis*: the Greek port near Tanagra in northern Boetia where Iphigenia was sacrificed before the Trojan expedition (see note to p. 84).

*Lydian school of romance*: not the ancient Greek kingdom of Lydia (see note to p. 45, Croesus) but a reference to Lydia Languish, heroine of Sheridan's play *The Rivals* (1775), who is so addicted to novels, or 'romances', that she insists on marrying a poor man who will elope with her against her family's wishes. Captain Absolute, the wealthy suitor approved of by her aunt, must therefore pretend to be his own 'rival', Ensign Beverley, and to plan an elopement.

96 *glebe*: land belonging to a benefice and either farmed or rented out by the parish priest to provide part of his income; glebe ceased to belong to individual incumbents in 1976, when it was transferred to the diocese. The glebe at Plumstead Episcopi is so extensive that it has its own entrance 'lodge' (see note to p. 6).

97 *sanctum sanctorum*: (Latin) 'holy of holies'.

*Dr Hampden*: Renn Dickson Hampden (1793–1868) was a Broad Churchman (see Appendix 2) and a Fellow of Oriel College, Oxford. High Churchmen attacked his appointment to the Chair of Divinity in 1836, and suspended him from the board appointing Select Preachers in 1837. In 1847 they fiercely attacked his appointment as Bishop of Hereford, the topic of this 'last pamphlet'.

*Chrysostom . . . Dr Phillpotts*: the busts in Dr Grantly's library form a phalanx of High Church heroes, notable for their defence of Church against State, with a mild bathos at the end of the list. St John Chrysostom (*c.*347–407) was a gifted preacher and Bishop of Constantinople, whose denunciation of Byzantine morality offended the Empress Eudoxia and led to his banishment and death. St Augustine is either Augustine of Hippo (354–430), author of the *Confessions* and the *City of God*, or, more probably, Augustine of Canterbury (d. 604), the first missionary to pagan Anglo-Saxon Kent and first Archbishop of Canterbury. St Thomas Becket (1118–70), Archdeacon of Canterbury from 1154, Archbishop from 1162, resisted King Henry II's attempt to establish civil jurisdiction over clergy accused of criminal offences; he was assassinated in his cathedral in December 1170. Thomas Wolsey (1474–1530), Archbishop of York from 1514, a cardinal from 1515, offended King Henry VIII by failing to obtain the Pope's agreement to the King's divorce; accused of high treason, he died on his way to London for trial. William Laud (1573–1645), Archbishop of Canterbury from 1633, opposed the Calvinist wing of the reformed Church of England, sought to restore pre-Reformation liturgical practice, and in 1640 introduced new canons requiring an oath never to 'consent to alter the government of this Church by archbishops, deans, and archdeacons'; impeached and imprisoned in the Tower of London in 1641, he was executed in 1645. Henry Phillpotts (1778–1869) was the combative Bishop of Exeter who had attempted to deprive a clergyman of his living in the controversial Gorham Case (1850) and threatened to excommunicate the Archbishop of Canterbury when judgment was given against him by the Judicial Committee of the Privy Council (see notes to p. 23 and p. 61).

98 *a faulty style*: see note to p. 8. Sadleir suggests a resemblance between the church at Plumstead Episcopi and that at Huish Episcopi in Somerset (*Things Past*, 1944, 23–4), which does, indeed, have an exceptionally high west tower; Pevsner (*South and West Somerset*, 1958, 201–2) notes that the

nave and transepts are fourteenth century and later, rather than in the thirteenth-century style deemed 'correct' by the Ecclesiologists. Huish Episcopi also has high walls and a low roof: qualities which the Ecclesiologists objected to in the 'Commissioners' Churches' built by the Church Building Commission between 1815 and 1856.

98 *back-gammon*: a game, using dice, for two players who compete to move their pieces in opposite directions around a board; Grantly is punning on the word 'gammon' which can mean 'nonsense' or 'rubbish', as in the dismissive phrase 'It's all gammon and spinach'.

100 *thirteen and fourpences*: 13s. 4d. (£40), or two-thirds of a pound, was the second point on the fixed scale of lawyers' charges, for work more complicated than that done for the basic 'six and eightpence' (see note to p. 19).

*phasis*: (Greek) 'aspect'.

103 *leviathans*: (Hebrew) 'whales' or enormous sea serpents.

106 *Crabtree Parva . . . Crabtree Canonicorum*: a crabtree is a wild apple tree; unlike cultivated apple trees, it produces only very small fruit, not fit to be eaten unless roasted or made into jelly. Crabtree Parva (Latin, 'small') is therefore a very meagre living for a clergyman: contrast Plumstead Episcopi (see note to p. 6). Crabtree Canonicorum (Latin, 'of the canons') is a richer benefice, its status as a desirable perquisite of the canons outweighing the exiguous implications of the first part of its name.

107 *prebendal stall of Goosegorge . . . Stoke Pinquium*: a prebend is the income from one of the manors owned by a cathedral, used to support a canon (a member of the cathedral clergy and of the 'Chapter', or governing body, of the cathedral, to whom a 'stall', or fixed seat in the choir, was assigned for services). Goosegorge is a lucrative manor; its name alludes to the practice of force-feeding geese to produce *foie gras*, an expensive pâté made from goose liver. The parish livings which Dr Vesey Stanhope holds (in addition to Crabtree Canonicorum) are also very comfortable ones, as 'Eiderdown' implies; Stoke Pinquium is a 'rich place' (*pinguis*: Latin, 'fat, plump, rich').

*Lake of Como*: a large and beautiful lake in Lombardy, northern Italy, with views of the Alps but a sub-tropical climate. Nineteenth-century residents of the elegant villas on its shores included Byron, Mary Shelley, Caroline of Brunswick (estranged wife of George IV), Rossini, Stendhal, Liszt, and Verdi, who was writing *La traviata* there in 1853. Trollope's short story 'The Man Who Kept His Money in a Box' (1861) would be set there.

*collection of Lombard butterflies*: although Dr Stanhope's hobby might suggest a frivolous distraction from his duties as a clergyman, there were some distinguished clerical entomologists at this time, including the Revd Henry Harpur-Crewe (1828–83) and Frederick William Hope (1797–1862), who resigned his curacy to devote himself to the study of insects: the gift of his collection to Oxford in 1849 led to the foundation of the Hope Department of Entomology. The greatest collector of northern Italian butterflies, however, was a secular absentee: the Irish entomologist Alexander Henry Haliday (1806–70). A friend of Darwin, he was appointed High Sheriff of Antrim in 1842 but lived mostly at Lucca, in Tuscany, where he collected both flies (Diptera) and butterflies (Lepidoptera).

*Mount Olympus*: a mountain on the border of Greece and Thessaly, held in ancient Greek and Roman religion to be the home of the king of the gods, Zeus or Jupiter. Here, mock-heroically, the premises of the *Jupiter* (or *Times*) newspaper.

108 *Pica*: a size of type, now standardized as 12 point (4.2 mm), here turned into a quasi-classical goddess of newsprint.

*Castalian ink*: the Castalian spring on Mount Parnassus was sacred to the Muses; its water inspired those who drank it with the gift of poetry. The ink used to print newspapers is here ironically substituted.

*Velvet and gilding . . . a sceptre*: adapted from Richard Lovelace's poem, 'To Althea, from Prison' (1642): 'Stone walls do not a prison make | Nor iron bars a cage; | Minds innocent and quiet take | That for a hermitage'.

109 *It stands alone*: *The Times* newspaper was published, between 1785 and 1874, from Printing House Square, Blackfriars, in the City of London. This was a secluded courtyard off St Andrew's Hill, close to St Paul's Cathedral, which until 1770 had been the premises of the King's Printing House. The modest, two-storey brick building, dating from 1740, would be used until 1868, when it was demolished and replaced with a much larger building on the same site, with a frontage to the new Queen Victoria Street, cut through the lanes of the old City in 1867–71 to link Blackfriars Bridge to the Mansion House.

*bulls . . . Vatican . . . inquisitor*: Trollope is equating the influence of *The Times* with that of the Roman Catholic Church. 'Bulls' (from *bulla*: Latin, 'seal') are mandates sealed with the Pope's signet ring; the Vatican, in Rome, is the home of the Pope and the headquarters of the Church; the Inquisition is the ecclesiastical court responsible for the persecution of heresy, most famously active from the late fifteenth century in Spain, where it was concerned with the detection of Jews and Muslims remaining in the country after the reconquest.

*Lord John Russell . . . Palmerston and Gladstone*: cabinet ministers in the coalition government of 1852–5, which took Britain into the Crimean War. Russell, previously Prime Minister from 1846 to 1852, was Minister without Portfolio from February 1853 to June 1854, then Lord President of the Council; Palmerston was Home Secretary; Gladstone was Chancellor of the Exchequer. Both Palmerston (1784–1865) and Gladstone (1809–98) would later serve as Prime Minister. Trollope would publish an admiring memoir, *Lord Palmerston*, in 1882, and call the capital of Britannula 'Gladstonopolis' in *The Fixed Period* (1881–2).

110 *Look at our generals*: a reference to criticism of the conduct of the Crimean War conducted by *The Times* in 1854–5 (see Introduction, p. xxi).

110 *the diggings of Australia . . . California*: the Australian gold rush began in
1851, generating wealth but also a population explosion and social ten-
sions which would lead, in November 1854, to the rebellion at the Eureka
Stockade. The California gold rush began in 1848. A *Times* leader on 16
January 1854 considered both of them.

*bishopric in New Zealand*: the first Bishop of New Zealand, from 1841
to 1858, was George Selwyn (1809–78), who visited England in 1854 to
campaign for the subdivision of the diocese into several sees. *The Times*
reported the parliamentary discussion, in June and July 1854, of whether
the bishop's salary should continue to be paid from public funds.

*North-west passage*: the north-west passage is the ice-bound sea route
through the Arctic Ocean along the northern shore of North America. Sir
John Franklin's expedition to traverse it in 1845 had been lost. Searching for survivors (there were none), Robert McClure in HMS *Investiga-
tor* made the first complete crossing in 1851–3, partly by ship but in the
later stages by sled. McClure's commanding officer, Captain Sir Edward
Belcher, would be court-martialled (but honourably acquitted) in October
1854 for the loss of the ships left in the ice. The 'unfortunate director',
however, is Franklin: *The Times* on 14 December 1853 referred to 'poor
Sir John Franklin' and stated that 'of Arctic expeditions we have had more
than enough'.

*sewers of London . . . Central Railway of India*: the Metropolitan Commission of Sewers, formed in 1847, ordered the 200,000 cesspits beneath
houses in London to be closed, with the unfortunate result that sewage
was, instead, discharged directly into the Thames. After outbreaks of
cholera in 1848–9 and 1853, the General Board of Health recommended
the construction of a comprehensive system of sewers, though the problem would not be solved until after the 'Great Stink' of 1858, when Joseph
Bazalgette was given the funds to build, between 1858 and 1875, 1,182
miles of drains to carry sewage away from the city. *The Times* published
a leader on the Metropolitan Commissioners on 15 March 1853 ('we may
now be really on the eve of getting our city made sweet and habitable') and
frequent reports on their activities. The first railway in India was built
in 1853, from Bombay (Mumbai) to Thane in Maharashtra; it would be
gradually expanded through central India. A *Times* leader on 18 August
1853 noted that 'The Presidency of Bombay enjoys the honour of possessing the first and only railway opened in Asia', and reported with pleasure
that the Governor-General had just sent home 'a large and comprehensive
plan of railways'.

*palaces of St Petersburg . . . cabins of Connaught*: *The Times* commented
constantly in 1853 and 1854 on the behaviour of the Czar's government
in St Petersburg during the tension between Russia and Turkey that
would lead to the Crimean War. Connaught (Connacht) is a province
in the west of Ireland, which includes the counties of Galway, Leitrim,
Mayo, Roscommon, and Sligo. It had been the region worst affected by the

Famine of the 1840s and many of the people who lived in the 'cabins', or rudimentary cottages, of the area had died or emigrated. Trollope's novel *The Kellys and the O'Kellys* (1848) had been set there and *Times* leaders in the autumn of 1853 discussed the effects, for Connaught and the rest of Ireland, of the Encumbered Estates Acts of 1848 and 1849, which had sought to bring new capital into Irish agriculture by facilitating the sale of estates whose owners were unable to redeem their mortgages.

111 *treasury mandate*: instruction or official order from the government, endorsed by its most senior ministers. In 1660 the role of the King's Lord Treasurer was assigned to a group of commissioners known as the Lords of the Treasury; since the 1720s the First Lord of the Treasury has become known, alternatively, as the Prime Minister, and the Second Lord of the Treasury as the Chancellor of the Exchequer.

*broad sheets*: broadsheet is the largest newspaper format, usually with a page size 29.5 × 23.5 inches (749 × 597mm); it was developed after the introduction, in 1712, of a tax on newspapers based on the number of their pages. *The Times* moved from broadsheet to tabloid format in November 2004.

*Pall Mall*: on his way back from his club, Towers walks east (into the wind) along Pall Mall, where many gentlemen's clubs were located; his rooms in the Temple are conveniently half way between his club and the offices of *The Times* in Printing House Square.

*quiet abode of wisdom*: the Inner and Middle Temple, London base of the Knights Templars until their suppression in 1312, and thereafter two Inns of Court or centres for lawyers. Set just inside the old city walls, with halls and a chapel, and gardens sloping down to the river, the Inns resemble an Oxford or Cambridge college. Most of the rooms are legal 'chambers', or offices, but it is also possible to live in the Temple: nineteenth-century residents included William Makepeace Thackeray and Charles Lamb. J. T. Delane, editor of *The Times*, 1841–77, lived in bachelor chambers at 16 Serjeants' Inn, at the north-east corner of the Temple, from 1847, after his wife's decline into mental illness. This encouraged suggestions, denied by Trollope, that Towers was based on Delane (see note to p. 80).

*ambrosia . . . nectar*: (Greek) the food and drink of the gods on Olympus.

112 *blessed regions of the West . . . abode of Themis*: in ancient Greek legend, the Islands of the Blest (*Fortunatae insulae*) were set, like the paradisical Garden of the Hesperides, at the western end of the Mediterranean. Here, punningly, the reference is also to the West End, or the domestic and social districts of middle- and upper-class London, as distinct from the workaday City (where the *Jupiter* has its offices) and the proletarian East End. Themis, originally a Titan, became a wife of Zeus and the goddess of justice, often depicted with a sword in one hand and a pair of scales in the other. The Temple is her abode because it is occupied by lawyers.

*tide . . . from the towers of Cæsar to Barry's halls of eloquence*: the Thames in London is a tidal river; a rising tide flows upstream from the Tower of

London (actually Norman, though supposedly built by Julius Caesar during his invasion of Britain in 54 BC, as in Shakespeare's *Richard II*, Act 5, Scene 1), past the Inner and Middle Temple, to the Houses of Parliament, redesigned, after a fire in 1834, by the architects Sir Charles Barry and Augustus Pugin. The new 'halls of eloquence', or debating chambers, were completed in 1847 (Lords) and 1852 (Commons). The tide is 'rich . . . with new offerings of a city's tribute' because London's raw sewage was, at this date, discharged directly into the Thames (see note to p. 110).

112 *palaces of peers . . . mart of merchants*: the palatial town houses of aristocratic families (such as Devonshire House, Stafford House, and Lansdowne House) stood in the West End of London, from which a falling tide carries the waters of the Thames eastwards to the 'mart', or market, of businessmen in the City of London.

*'entangled walks,' as some one lately has called them*: Trollope appears to have misread Thackeray's account of Goldsmith's former chambers in the Temple in his *The English Humourists of the Eighteenth Century* (as lectures 1851, published 1853), which quotes Goldsmith's description of 'tangling walks' from his poem *The Deserted Village* (1770). Although the poem was written in the Temple, Goldsmith was not here describing its gardens but 'Auburn', the deserted village of his title. Wordsworth, in the 'Residence in London' book of his poem *The Prelude* (first published 1850), speaks of the things which 'entangle our impatient steps' when walking to the Temple. These, however, are the 'courts', 'lanes', and 'labyrinths' through which he has to pass, not the 'gardens green' which he finds when he gets there (Book 7, ll. 180–8).

*Old St Dunstan*: St Dunstan-in-the-West, Fleet Street: an old church, first mentioned in 1237, but entirely rebuilt in the early 1830s, on a slightly different site, to permit road-widening. The prominent clock (1671), with its giant figures striking bells on the hours and quarters, was removed in 1828 and not restored to the church until 1935: Trollope must be drawing on a childhood memory.

*the bar itself*: Temple Bar is a neo-classical arched gateway of 1670–2 which stood in Fleet Street on the site of one of the ancient gates of the walled, medieval city. Long seen as an inconvenient obstacle to traffic, it would be removed in 1880 and re-erected at Theobalds Park in Hertfordshire. It has now been returned to the City as one of the entrances to the new Paternoster Square (see note to p. 127).

*some huge building*: though long 'rumoured', the new Royal Courts of Justice, on a site between the Strand and Lincoln's Inn, would not be built until 1874–82. The 'huge building', designed by G. E. Street, gathered in one place all the higher courts concerned with civil (non-criminal) law. These had previously met in Westminster Hall and elsewhere. The eighteenth-century Rolls House (where legal records or 'rolls' were stored) and medieval Rolls Chapel (where the Rolls' Court met when Westminster Hall was not available) were on the other side of Chancery Lane from the Law Courts site but were replaced by the new Public Record Office (1851–96). Rolls House was demolished in the 1850s, the chapel in 1895. Lincoln's Inn was, in the event, untouched by the spate of building which accompanied the great mid-Victorian reform of the English legal system.

*Sabbatarian*: a believer that the Lord's Day should be kept holy, and recreation prohibited on Sundays.

*Paphian goddess*: Aphrodite, or Venus, the goddess of love, who emerged from the sea at Paphos in Cyprus. Bachelor chambers in the Temple (at that date an almost entirely male community) are, Trollope suggests, as convenient a place as the groves of Cyprus for illicit sex, perhaps with prostitutes picked up in the theatres of the West End.

*worshipper of Bacchus*: Bacchus, or Dionysus, was the Greek and Roman god of wine.

*tenth Muse*: in ancient Greek myth there were nine Muses, the goddesses of literature and the arts (epic poetry, history, tragedy, comedy, sacred song, dance, flute playing, the lyre, and astronomy). A tenth is now (ironically) needed for journalism.

113 *legal aspirants*: trainee or under-employed barristers without an established practice.

*Pembroke brother*: a Pembroke table is a small table with a drop-leaf extension on each side, possibly named after Henry Herbert, Earl of Pembroke (1693–1751), amateur architect and designer.

*despatcher*: a device for cutting, cracking (lobster shells), and grinding (coffee).

*Stafford House*: a London mansion (now known as Lancaster House), originally built for the Duke of York but enlarged in the 1830s for the wealthy Duke of Sutherland, first by Benjamin Wyatt and Robert Smirke and then, from 1838, by Charles Barry. The decoration is in the Baroque manner, especially in the gallery and its anteroom, which have ceiling paintings by Guercino and Veronese. Queen Victoria is supposed to have remarked to the Duchess of Sutherland, on arriving for a reception, 'I have come from my house to your palace.'

*Power*: Hiram Powers (1805–73), American sculptor, whose statue *The Greek Slave* (1843) was much admired at the Great Exhibition of 1851. Trollope's mother and brother Tom had known Powers in Cincinnati in 1827 and became friends with him again when Tom moved to Florence in 1846. The portrait bust is of Sir Robert Peel (1788–1850), Conservative Prime Minister, 1834–5 and 1841–6, so Towers is a Peelite, or liberal Conservative.

*Millais*: John Everett Millais (1829–96; knighted 1885), painter and a founder of the Pre-Raphaelite Brotherhood (see note on next page). The painting described here is not actually by Millais (though it was painted with his advice), since it appears to be *Convent Thoughts* by Charles Alston

Collins (1828–73), exhibited at the Royal Academy in 1851 and, in reality, bought by Thomas Combe, Superintendent of Oxford University Press. Towers shares Combe's taste for avant-garde art, if not his Tractarian piety (reflected in this painting's subject). Highly controversial in 1850 and 1851, Millais's work soon became more popular; he was elected an Associate Member of the Royal Academy in 1853. Trollope met him in 1860 and they became close friends. Millais would provide illustrations for *Framley Parsonage*, *Orley Farm*, *The Small House at Allington*, *Phineas Finn*, and *Kept in the Dark*; Trollope would seek his advice in 1878 on the choice of a suitable illustrator for *The Chronicles of Barsetshire* (see Note on the Text, p. xxix).

113 *Præ-Raffaellites*: the Pre-Raphaelite Brotherhood was founded in London in 1848 by a group of art students dissatisfied with the old-fashioned training provided in the Royal Academy Schools: a view of art derived from the High Renaissance and the example of Raphael (Rafaello Sanzio da Urbino, 1483–1520). Instead, they wished to base modern art on the new values of the Romantic Movement: truth to Nature and a return to the religious sincerity of medieval culture. This medievalist enthusiasm for 'the early painters' was expressed in a deliberately awkward and angular style of drawing, which seemed, at the time, shockingly different from the elegant modelling of Raphael and his followers. Trollope's friendship with Millais (see previous note) may have influenced his later view that 'Raphael's grace' was 'the grace of fiction, and not the grace of nature', and 'prepared absolute ruin for all who were to come after him' ('The National Gallery', *St James's Magazine*, September 1861).

*Sebastian . . . Lucia . . . Lorenzo . . . the virgin with two children*: the martyrdoms of St Sebastian, St Lucy (who plucked out her eyes to destroy her beauty and thus repulse a pagan who wished to marry her), and St Lawrence, and the Virgin Mary with Jesus and John the Baptist as children were stock subjects for seventeenth-century Bolognese and Roman Baroque painters, such as Domenichino, Guido Reni, and Guercino. These artists were widely admired until John Ruskin (1819–1900) condemned them in his book *Modern Painters* (1843–60). Ruskin was both an inspiration for the Pre-Raphaelites (see note above) and their chief defender in the early 1850s.

114 *Sybarite*: a person devoted to luxury or pleasure (from the ancient Greek city of Sybaris in southern Italy, notorious for its luxury).

*tiger*: a smartly liveried boy-servant.

*a briefless barrister*: a would-be advocate with no 'briefs' or instructions, so no work or fees; Gilbert à Beckett's 'Mr Briefless', a struggling barrister, was a recurring comic character in *Punch* in the 1840s and '50s.

*ermine*: the fur used to trim the robes of judges.

*hidden . . . glory*: writing in *The Times*, as in most journals at this date, was published anonymously. When Trollope helped to found the *Fortnightly Review* in 1865 he insisted that its articles should be signed.

116 *the vested rights of the incumbent*: the reform of the finances of the Church of England in the 1830s and '40s was done in a way which respected the interests of the current holders of ecclesiastical posts, and took effect only after their death or retirement (see Appendix 2).

117 *Dr Pessimist Anticant*: a satirical version of the writer Thomas Carlyle (1795–1881), charting the change between his much admired early work and what was widely seen as the bitter and reactionary temper of his *Latter-Day Pamphlets* (1850). Carlyle did not, in fact, pass 'a great portion of his early days in Germany'; he learned his German in Edinburgh and first visited the country in 1852. But he established his reputation in the 1820s as a critic and translator of German literature, and published *Sartor Resartus*, a witty philosophical novel about post-Kantian German thought, in 1833–4; its hero is a professor 'of things in general' ('Professor der Allerley-Wissenschaft', Book First, Chapter 3). 'Signs of the Times' (1829), an essay arguing that the modern era was both literally and intellectually 'mechanical', launched his career as a social commentator, which continued in works such as *Past and Present* (1843), parodied here by Trollope as *Modern Charity*. The image of the poet Robert Burns (1759–1796), obliged to earn his living as an Excise officer ('a gauger of beer-barrels') while a philistine aristocracy is preoccupied with field sports ('shooting the partridges of England', *Past and Present*, Book 3, Chapter 8), is a recurrent motif, while the book's structure, as a contrast between a degenerate 'Present' and a 'Past' represented by an idealized medieval abbey, anticipates the debate about the past and present condition of Hiram's Hospital in Trollope's novel. Carlyle's hatred of 'cant' took a more pessimistic turn in *Latter-Day Pamphlets*, where his criticism of a 'do-nothing' government turned into a denunciation of democracy and an assertion of inarticulate wisdom against public discussion and empirical enquiry. The third section, 'Downing Street' (parodied here as the first 'small pamphlet' which Towers throws across the table), condemned contemporary British politicians and civil servants. Trollope (a civil servant at the time) bought a copy of the book and wrote to his mother that 'the grain of sense is . . . smothered up in a sack of the sheerest trash' (*Letters*, i. 29); he would interrupt the composition of *Barchester Towers* in February 1855 to spend fifteen months writing his own, counter-Carlylean version of Carlyle's text: *The New Zealander* (first published in 1972).

118 *Dumfries*: Burns moved to Dumfries in 1791 to work as an Excise officer.

*Leadenhall*: Leadenhall Market, in the City of London, was founded in the fourteenth century for the sale of poultry and game. Rebuilt 1794–1812, it would be demolished and rebuilt again in 1880–1. Partridges sold here for 'one shilling and ninepence' would, it is suggested, have cost 'a guinea' to rear for sport on country estates. Carlyle had frequently attacked political economists of the Classical school (such as Adam Smith, who identified 'division of labour' as a key factor in economic growth) and questioned their claim that prices were scientifically determined by the interaction of 'supply and demand'.

118 *poacher in limbo*: the notoriously harsh and elaborate Game Laws of the eighteenth century, by which landowners protected their exclusive right to hunt, shoot, and fish on their estates, were simplified by the Night Poaching Act (1829) and the Game Act (1831). The laws remained harsh (a third conviction for poaching could be punished with seven years' imprisonment) and there were frequent prosecutions.

*despatch boxes*: two wooden despatch boxes (originally used for carrying documents) are used as the lecterns from which ministers and shadow ministers deliver speeches in Parliament.

*Lord Aberdeen . . . Lord Derby . . . Disraeli . . . Molesworth*: George Hamilton-Gordon, 4th Earl of Aberdeen (1784–1860) was a Peelite Conservative and Prime Minister of the coalition government of 1852–5. Edward Stanley, 14th Earl of Derby (1799–1869), originally a Whig, was Tory Prime Minister in 1852, 1858–9, and 1866–8. Benjamin Disraeli (1805–81; created Earl of Beaconsfield in 1876), was leader of the Tory party in the Commons in the 1850s (but an 'oppositionist' because the party was at this date almost always in opposition), and Prime Minister in 1868 and 1874–80. Sir William Molesworth (1810–55), was a Radical MP with Benthamite views and an interest in model colonial settlements. In 1853 Molesworth unexpectedly agreed to serve in Lord Aberdeen's cabinet, in which capacity he would defend the war in the Crimea and argue that *The Times* should censor William Howard Russell's reports on it.

119 *chip bonnets . . . anathemas . . . bishops' wigs*: a chip bonnet was a straw hat for women, made from woven palm fibre; an anathema (Greek) is a denunciation or condemnation; bishops, in the first half of the nineteenth century, continued to wear the formal, powdered wigs which had been conventional male dress in the eighteenth century (and are still worn, in the twenty-first century, by lawyers in courtrooms). Trollope is mimicking the 'clothes philosophy' of Carlyle's *Sartor Resartus* ('The Tailor Retailored') of 1833–4.

*that better treasure*: for the idea of a spiritual or moral treasure which is better than material wealth see Job 28 (where the treasure is wisdom) and Matthew 6:19–21.

120 *Belgrave Square*: a fashionable district of large and elegant houses, between Buckingham Palace and Sloane Street, developed 1820–50.

*Britons . . . never will be slaves*: 'Rule Britannia! Britannia rules the waves. | Britons never, never, never shall be slaves', the chorus (as conventionally sung, rather than as originally written) of the patriotic song 'Rule, Britannia!' (1740) by James Thomson and Thomas Arne.

*monument*: in his seventh of his *Latter-Day Pamphlets*, 'Hudson's Statue', Carlyle makes satirical use of the idea of a monument to the railway developer and speculator George Hudson (1800–71), whose financial malpractice had been exposed in 1848. The back-handed compliments paid in the same pamphlet to 'the Bishop of our Diocese' may have suggested the account of the 'clergyman of the Church of "England"' here.

121 *toil and trouble*: Shakespeare, *Macbeth* Act 4, Scene 1, ll. 10, 20, and 35.

*the Almshouse . . . Mr. Popular Sentiment*: a satirical portrait of the novelist and journalist Charles Dickens (1812–70), for which Trollope invents an imaginary novel, *The Almshouse*. This attacks abuses in charitable foundations, rather as *Oliver Twist* (1837–9) had attacked workhouses and *Bleak House* (1852–3) had recently denounced the Court of Chancery. Dickens's magazine *Household Words* had printed a fictionalized version of the Whiston case, 'The History of a Certain Grammar School' (published anonymously, but actually by Theodore Buckley) on 9 August 1851, and a denunciation of the management of a famous London almshouse, 'The Poor Brothers of the Charterhouse', on 12 June 1852 (again anonymous; actually by Henry Morley and William Thomas Moncrieff). Trollope turns these vicarious attacks into the first part issue of a novel by Dickens himself, parodically suggesting the tendency to exaggeration and caricature in Dickens's writing, while acknowledging the powerful effect of his polemical manner. Dickens had 'been down to' Preston, to research his novel *Hard Times* (1854), just as Sentiment is supposed to have 'been down to Barchester' here.

*Dulwich*: in 1619 the Elizabethan actor Edward Alleyn established a charitable foundation at Dulwich in Surrey, which combined an almshouse for twelve elderly men and women with a school for 'twelve poor scholars'. The peculiar terms of the foundation (such as the requirement that the warden should always have Alleyn's surname and be unmarried) meant that it struggled to fulfil its purposes and was much criticized, especially after 1808, when developments on its land made it very wealthy. In 1841 an attempt was made to amend the statutes and a small grammar school was created. This was still thought to be an inadequate use of the funds and in 1854 a commission was set up, under the terms of the 1853 Charitable Trusts Act, to investigate the matter. As a result, in 1857, the Dulwich College Act would be passed, dissolving the original charity, pensioning off the warden, and creating a large public school.

*éclat*: (French) 'brilliance, striking success'.

*Athenian banquets . . . Attic salt*: by an 'Athenian banquet' Bold means a symposium, or intellectual drinking party, of the kind described in Plato's Socratic dialogue *Symposium*; 'Attic salt' (Latin, *sal Atticum*) is the refined and delicate wit found in the culture of ancient Athens.

124 *'Ridiculum acri Fortius et melius magnas plerumque secat res.'*: (Latin) 'Humour often cuts the knot of serious questions more forcefully and effectively than severity' (Horace, *Satires*, 1.10.14–15). Added to the text in Trollope's 1878 revision.

*learned quartos . . . shilling numbers*: learned quartos are academic texts (literally, books with a page size determined by folding a sheet of paper twice, to make four leaves); Dickens's novels were usually first published not as books but as monthly 'parts' or 'numbers', each costing a shilling (£3) and gradually building up, over a period of nineteen months, to the complete novel.

124 *Namby-pamby*: sentimental, insipid, affectedly simple; a term coined by Henry Carey and Alexander Pope to mock the poetry of Ambrose Philips (1695–1749).

*immaculate manufacturing hero*: such as Mr Rouncewell in Dickens's *Bleak House* (1852–3).

*Mrs Ratcliffe's heroines*: Ann Radcliffe (1764–1823), author of five popular Gothic novels, published between 1789 and 1797, whose heroines respond decorously to terrifying threats: Emily St Aubert, in *The Mysteries of Udolpho* (1794), is carried off to a castle in the Apennines where she is surrounded with (apparently) supernatural dangers. Jane Austen mocked them in *Northanger Abbey* (1818) and Trollope, in his essay 'Novel-Reading' (*Nineteenth Century*, January 1879), would observe that these 'awe-striking mysterious romances . . . left little behind beyond a slightly morbid tone of the imagination'.

*Buckett and Mrs Gamp*: Inspector Bucket is the detective in Dickens's *Bleak House* (1852–3); Mrs Gamp is the nurse in his *Martin Chuzzlewit* (1843–4).

125 *Mephistopheles*: the evil spirit of the Faust legend who persuades Faust to sell his soul; sometimes seen as the Devil's agent, sometimes as the Devil himself.

*Puseyism*: a popular term for the Tractarian or Oxford Movement (see Appendix 2), derived from the name of Edward Bouverie Pusey (1800–82), Professor of Hebrew at Oxford, and leader of the Oxford Movement after Newman's withdrawal in 1841.

*their dialect*: Dickens's brilliant transcriptions of London speech in his earlier novels had not been matched by the awkward attempt to reproduce Lancashire dialect in *Hard Times* (1854).

126 *It was mean all this . . . to explain it in full*: added in Trollope's 1878 revision.

127 *Chapter Hotel and Coffee House*: the Chapter Coffee House in Paternoster Row was opened in 1715 and was frequented by booksellers, publishers, and writers, later also by clergymen and their families: Charlotte and Emily Brontë stayed there with their father on their way to Brussels in 1842, and Charlotte and Ann Brontë in 1848.

*Paternoster Row*: a street north of St Paul's Churchyard, originally built against the wall which surrounded the precinct of the medieval cathedral. It became the centre of the English book trade until destroyed by bombing on 29 December 1940. The street has now vanished beneath Paternoster Square, created by post-war rebuilding.

*the House*: the House of Commons.

128 *Strangers' Gallery . . . five shillings*: a gallery within the chamber of the House of Commons from which members of the public can watch debates. In the early 1850s admission could be achieved by tipping an attendant 5*s.* (£15). Since then the process has become more formal: a (free) ticket may be obtained by applying to one's MP, or one can enter without booking after a long wait in a queue. Trollope's footnote (1878): 'How these pleasant things have been altered since this was written a quarter of a century ago!'

129 *a drug in the market*: 'drug' in the sense (now rare) of a commodity which is no longer in demand. Trollope's note (1878): 'Again what a change!' is probably a reference to the greater effectiveness of Irish MPs in the 1870s rather than to any change in the demand for Irish whiskey and poplin (an upholstery fabric made, chiefly in Dublin, from silk and wool). After the 1874 election, Irish MPs supporting Home Rule began to 'obstruct' parliamentary business to draw attention to their cause.

*'Bradshaw'*: railway timetable. George Bradshaw (1801–53) was a Manchester publisher, who began to produce his *Railway Time Tables* in 1839. It became an indispensable handbook in the railway age, with monthly updates coordinating the schedules of the numerous train companies.

131 *twopence . . . entered the Abbey as a sight-seer*: Trollope's note (1878): 'Again what a change!' The charge to visit Westminster Abbey as a sightseer has increased steadily since the 1850s, the fee is now (2013) £18. The 2*d.* charge for entering St Paul's Cathedral and Westminster Abbey, other than for services, had been much criticized in the 1840s and was suspended during the Great Exhibition of 1851. Imposed as much to keep out 'undesirables' as to generate revenue, it was reintroduced thereafter and frequently increased.

*William Pitt*: there are monuments to two William Pitts in Westminster Abbey. One is a statue of William Pitt the Younger (1759–1806; Prime Minister, 1783–1800 and 1804–6) by Richard Westmacott above the west door. The other, in the north transept, is of Pitt the Elder (William Pitt, 1st Earl of Chatham, 1708–78; Prime Minister, 1766–8) by John Bacon. The latter more closely resembles Trollope's description and the north transept would be a more conveniently inconspicuous place for Mr Harding to sit than immediately inside the main entrance.

*verger*: attendant responsible for the care and supervision of the interior of a church.

132 *lost in the chanting*: 'Again the changes which years have made should be noted' (Trollope's footnote, added 1878).

*It appears to us a question . . . listeners*: Trollope was to develop this 'question' in his essay 'The Normal Dean of the Present Day' (*Pall Mall Gazette*, 2 December 1865; repr. as Chapter 3 of *Clergymen of the Church of England*, 1866) by suggesting that 'cathedral services' in the absence of a congregation are an anachronistic survival of a medieval assumption that worship must be 'kept up for the honour of God rather than for the welfare of the worshippers'.

134  *the Strand . . . Charing Cross*: Mr Harding walks east along Whitehall to Charing Cross, where the Strand begins, though in 1854 neither Charing Cross station (opened 1864) nor the medieval cross (destroyed 1647; reconstructed in replica 1865) were to be seen there. Instead, the site was occupied by the old Hungerford Market. The Strand was known for its restaurants, pubs, smoking-rooms, and places of entertainment, but there were still some houses: George Eliot was living at Frederic Chapman's house, No. 142, from 1851 to 1855.

136  *cigar divan*: a smoking-room furnished with sofas, attached to a cigar shop and usually decorated in an Oriental style.

*sherbet*: originally a Persian drink made from snow and fruit juice; the Western imitation was made with lemons, water, and sugar or, by the mid-nineteenth century, with lemonade powder (bicarbonate of soda, tartaric acid, and sugar).

*Blackwood*: *Blackwood's Edinburgh Magazine*, a popular monthly magazine, with Tory views, published from 1817 to 1980 and notable for its serial fiction. Five of Trollope's own novels would be serialized in *Blackwood's*: *Nina Balakta* (1866–7), *Linda Tressel* (1867–8), *John Caldigate* (1878–9), *Doctor Wortle's School* (1880), and *The Fixed Period* (1881–2). In the spring of 1854, when Mr Harding makes his trip to London, the novel being serialized in *Blackwood's* was Margaret Oliphant's *The Quiet Heart*, in which the heroine, Menie Laurie, moves from Dumfriesshire to London ('London—Babylon—great battle-ground of vexed humanity—the crisis scene of Menie Laurie's fate', *Blackwood's Edinburgh Magazine*, 75 (January 1854), 33) and recovers her 'quiet heart' only after returning to genteel poverty in rural Scotland.

138  *No one had thrust him forward*: Haphazard may in part be based on Sir Fitzroy Kelly (see note to p. 37); the *Times* obituary for Kelly, on 20 September 1880, noted that he had achieved his success without introductions or influence, and solely 'by his own fearless energy, sound learning, and unwearied combativeness'.

141  *Quixotism*: the holding of foolishly impractical ideals or schemes for the general good, as in the case of the hero of Cervantes' satirical novel *Don Quixote de la Mancha* (1605).

142  *lappet*: lapel.

*old square of Lincoln's Inn*: a small courtyard of sixteenth- and seventeenth-century buildings, with the Inn's chapel on one side of it. Trollope's father had chambers at 23 Old Square, Lincoln's Inn, when he was practising as a Chancery barrister. Trollope spent a summer holiday there, while his mother was in America, probably in 1828, and amused himself by reading

Shakespeare and 'wandering about among those old deserted buildings' (deserted because it was the legal, as well as the school, vacation; *An Autobiography*, Chapter 1).

144 *a sigh that would have moved a man-of-war*: warships still had sails in the 1850s; this sigh is (figuratively) powerful enough to propel a large ship.

*Macready*: William Charles Macready (1793–1873), a distinguished actor, notable for his Richard III and King Lear, who became the leading London actor–manager in the 1830s and '40s; he retired from the stage in 1851. Not physically impressive, he was admired for his intelligence and his remarkable voice.

145 *noddles*: a noddle is actually a popular term for a head; here nods or movements of the head.

*God, that feeds the young ravens*: Psalm 147: 'Praise ye the LORD . . . He giveth to the beast his food, and to the young ravens which cry.'

146 *pelican*: in the Middle Ages pelicans were believed to feed their young with their own blood; as a consequence the pelican became a familiar emblem of Christ and of the sacrament of the Eucharist.

147 *Job*: Job, in the Old Testament Book of Job, is an upright man afflicted with suffering as a test of his faith. Although Job is not always meekly accepting (in Chapter 3 he curses 'the day . . . wherein I was born'), the patience with which he endures both his own sorrows and the interference of his four 'comforters' became proverbial.

148 *plated cover*: silver-plating was a process, invented in Sheffield in 1743, for making items out of copper with a thin surface layer of silver. It was much cheaper than the 'thick and solid silver' found on the archdeacon's own breakfast table in Chapter 8.

*curtain confabulation*: a conversation between husband and wife within the drawn curtains of their four-poster bed; Douglas Jerrold's *Mrs Caudle's Curtain Lectures* (originally a serial in *Punch*, January–November 1845; as a book 1846), a series of comic sketches of a domineering wife, was very popular in the mid-nineteenth century.

150 *blotting-book*: a book consisting of leaves of blotting paper for drying wet ink on writing paper.

153 *Yours most affectionately*: 'Yours most sincerely' in the first edition (1855).

*Mr Provost . . . visit to a new bridge*: 'Provost' is the title of the head of three Oxford colleges (Oriel, Queen's, and Worcester); 'captain' is the army rank next above lieutenant; a City alderman (such as a member of the Tallow Chandler's Company, the medieval guild originally involved in the sale of candles made from animal fat, rather than wax, and later in the trade in edible oils) might hope to be knighted on the occasion of a royal visit to open a new bridge. In London, Chelsea Bridge was built 1851–8 and Westminster Bridge rebuilt 1854–62.

155 *gravelled*: perplexed, puzzled.

156 *Quiverful*: the name is ironically derived from Psalm 127: 3–5: 'Lo, children are an heritage of the LORD: and the fruit of the womb is his reward. As arrows are in the hand of a mighty man; so are children of the youth. Happy is the man that hath his quiver full of them.' Henry James, objecting to the use of comic names in realistic fiction, observed in 1883 that 'We can believe in the name and we can believe in the children; but we cannot manage the combination.' Mr Quiverful will reappear in *Barchester Towers* (by which time there are fourteen children) and *The Last Chronicle of Barset*, his wife Letitia also in *Framley Parsonage*.

158 *Priam*: King of Troy at the time of the Trojan War and father (by his wife Hecuba and numerous concubines) of Hector and more than fifty other sons and daughters.

159 *simony*: the selling of ecclesiastical preferment. Forbidden by the Council of Chalcedon in 451 and by the Anglican canonical legislation of 1604, this was the topic of Sidney Godolphin Osborne's letters to *The Times* in the summer of 1853 (see Introduction, p. xvii). A Simony Law Amendment Bill was debated in July 1853, but not enacted; the problem would be addressed by the Benefices Act of 1898.

*his cloth*: clerical dress seen as the emblem of the clergy as a professional body or order.

*Pharisee*: a self-righteous formalist, originally a member of a Jewish sect in the New Testament era, known for its strict adherence to the traditional and written law (see Luke 11:37–44).

160 *teapoy . . . cellaret*: a teapoy is a small pedestal table (the name, originally Hindi, means 'three footed'), which by the nineteenth century usually had a built-in caddy for holding tea; a cellaret is a small wooden cabinet for bottles of wine.

161 *esprit de corps*: (French) loyalty to the members and values of a group.

*a coal of fire*: Proverbs 25:21–2 and Romans 12:19–20, both suggesting that forgiveness and kind treatment from someone who has been wronged cause the offender to feel shame.

164 *benison*: blessing.

165 *mortal coil . . . shuffled off*: Shakespeare, *Hamlet*, Act 3, Scene 1, ll. 68–70: 'For in that sleep of death what dreams may come | When we have shuffled off this mortal coil | Must give us pause.'

166 *court plaster*: sticking plaster, so called because they were originally the black 'beauty spots' worn on the face by ladies at Court.

168 *the church of St Cuthbert*: this church somewhat resembles St Swithun in Winchester, similarly 'little' and 'perched' above the fourteenth-century Kingsgate, though the stained glass in the east window above the altar was brought here (from another medieval church) only in 1961. The 'grotesquely carved faces' with their counterpoised devils and angels are also

Trollope's invention. Trollope would have walked under it as a Winchester schoolboy but seems not to have gone inside.

*seventy-five pounds*: Mr Harding also receives a stipend as precentor of £80 a year.

*Sacrament once in every three months*: the celebration of Holy Communion, or the Eucharistic Sacrament, became very infrequent in parish churches in the later Middle Ages. The Lateran Council of 1215 had merely required Christians to communicate 'at least once a year', and the Anglican Church inherited that assumption. One of the consequences of the Oxford Movement of the 1830s (see Appendix 2) was a return to weekly communion; Mr Harding's pattern of communion three or four times a year marks him out as a clergyman of an older generation.

## THE TWO HEROINES OF PLUMPLINGTON

173 *Plumplington last year*: Plumplington is the second town in Barsetshire (after Silverbridge, the railway town, and the city, Barchester), not previously mentioned in Trollope's account of the territory but possibly close to Plumstead Episcopi; the rich and comfortable implications of that name (see note to p. 6) would also apply to this flourishing town with its prosperous banker and brewer. 'Last year' refers to 1881, since the story was written and published in 1882. In Chapter 4 we shall be told that 'forty years' have passed since the events described in *The Warden* (1855). In fact both novels are immediately contemporary in setting, so the true interval is thirty years (see Introduction, pp. xxiii and xxvii).

*Harry Gresham*: a son of Frank Gresham and Mary Thorne, whose courtship was described in *Doctor Thorne* (1858). Frank Gresham had reappeared in *The Prime Minister* (1876), by which time he was 'not as yet quite forty . . . with a large family' (Chapter 34). Harry is the 'younger son' (see Chapter 3, below) of that family; his brother, the elder son and heir to Greshambury Park (who, following family tradition, would probably be called Francis), would be too grand to be a suitor for a bank manager's daughter. Trollope had himself married a bank manager's daughter, Rose Heseltine, in 1844.

174 *Dr Freeborn*: the rector's name suggests his status as a man of ancient family: though not aristocratic, he can trace his ancestors back to 'the time of Charles I' (r. 1625–49). The idea of the Freeborn Englishman emerged from Magna Carta (1215) but was established in the early seventeenth century in the legal action known as Calvin's Case (1608). There is also a religious association with St Paul: 'And Paul said, But I was free born' (Acts 22:28).

*top sawyer*: superior worker. When timber was sawn into planks by hand, it was laid over a pit with one man pulling the saw from below and the other pushing it from above; the 'top sawyer' was more expert and more highly paid.

174 *Du Boung and Co.*: the Du Boung family are prosperous brewers in both Silverbridge and Plumplington who have changed their name from the more plebian 'Bung' (used to keep beer in barrels). Mr Du Boung appears in *The Prime Minister* (1875–6), Chapter 34, as the third candidate in the Silverbridge election. In *The Duke's Children* (1879–80), Chapter 14, he withdraws from a subsequent contest in favour of Plantagenet Palliser's heir, Lord Silverbridge, wrongly assuming him to be a fellow Liberal.

*chimney-pot hat*: a tall 'top hat', cylindrical, with slightly convex sides (as distinguished from the straight-sided stovepipe hat), a flat crown and a curling brim, finished in black silk 'hatter's plush'. Top hats were at their tallest in the 1840s and '50s; Prince Albert started to wear one in 1850.

175 *malt*: a product used in brewing beer, made by soaking and partially germinating barley, which is then dried and crushed before being mixed with water and fermented with yeast by the brewer.

176 *stuff gowns*: stuff was a thick woven cloth made of wool.

177 *garniture*: decoration, appurtenances.

*greet*: weep.

*peccant*: offending.

179 *a Marlborough or a Wellington*: John Churchill, 1st Duke of Marlborough (1650–1722), led armies which won victories at Blenheim (1704), Ramillies (1706), Oudenarde (1708), and Malplaquet (1709); Arthur Wellesley, 1st Duke of Wellington (1769–1852), was the victorious commander of British forces in India (1803) and the Iberian Peninsula (1809–15), and at Waterloo (1815). The six-year campaign of the Peninsular War is what prompts the reference to the 'long time' required for beating the French.

*James I*: Mrs Freeborn can trace her ancestors back even further than her husband can: to the reign of King James I (1603–25) (see note to p. 174).

182 *right off the reel*: immediately, without pause or hesitation.

*two girls in this house*: female servants.

186 *dined at half-past seven*: in the second half of the nineteenth century the time at which dinner was eaten was closely linked to social class. The working classes ate immediately after the end of the working day, at four or five, the aristocracy rather later, between six and half-past seven, with the middle classes gravitating anxiously between the two extremes. In Chapter 8 Mr Peppercorn, who is used to eating earlier, worries that an invitation to Christmas dinner at Dr Freeborn's house means that he will not 'get any dinner till six o'clock'. In *The Warden* Mr Harding 'dined in the summer at four' (Chapter 3): though middle-class, he is a man of the old school and retains old-fashioned habits.

188 *The old Duke of Omnium . . . Gatherum Castle*: 'the old Duke' is usually Plantagenet Palliser's uncle and predecessor, who held the title *c.*1833–70. If the reference is still to him, then Mr Greenmantle has not been

entertained at Gatherum Castle for more than a decade. The 'new' duke, as a widower with grown-up children, seems very mature in *The Duke's Children* (1880) but is actually only in his fifties and unlikely to be thought of as 'old' in 1881. Gatherum Castle is an enormous country house in west Barsetshire, built in the 1830s or '40s by the old Duke of Omnium (*Can You Forgive Her?*, Chapter 18) and used for entertaining rather than domestic life; Lord Silverbridge calls it 'the great barrack' (*The Duke's Children*, Chapter 14). Constructed of 'white stone' and 'Italian in its style' (*Doctor Thorne*, Chapter 19), it resembles the Italianate mansions designed by Sir Charles Barry, such as Trentham Hall (1834–40) and Cliveden House (1850–1). 'Omnium Gatherum' is a mock-Latin phrase for a miscellaneous assembly.

*Greshambury*: Greshambury House, in east Barsetshire, is a mansion 'in the purest style of Tudor architecture', which resembles Longleat and Hatfield (*Doctor Thorne*, Chapter 1). The Greshams are an old-established family of squires, or country gentlemen, without an aristocratic title but with a grand house and park, and with a fortune re-established (in *Doctor Thorne*) by a fortunate marriage.

189 *gloomy fit would fall*: 'But when the melancholy fit shall fall | Sudden from heaven like a weeping cloud' (Keats, 'Ode on Melancholy', ll. 11–12).

*signing his name*: to orders transferring money or to business letters written for him by his clerks.

191 *toggery*: dress (togs or toggery, jokingly derived from Latin, *toga*).

194 *brass*: impudence.

195 *corn-factors*: dealers in grain, including the barley used to make malt for beer.

196 *Hiram's Hospital . . . forty years*: Hiram's Hospital is an almshouse, or old-people's home, in Barchester for twelve elderly men, endowed by John Hiram in 1434. Readers of *The Warden* will remember that Septimus Harding resigned as the hospital's warden, despite John Bold's abandoning his legal campaign against the misuse (as he saw it) of the endowment. The press campaign, however, continued and in Chapter 2 of *Barchester Towers* a parliamentary bill 'for regulating the affairs of Barchester' was passed, whereby the warden's salary was reduced from £800 to £450, a steward appointed at £150 a year, and an additional hospital established for twelve elderly women, supervised by a matron. Notice is given 'some months after the death of the old bishop' (in July) that the reform is 'about to be carried out'; in October a self-congratulatory leader in the *Jupiter* announces that 'Hiram's hospital will be immediately re-opened under new auspices' (Chapter 43). But in the same chapter it is said that the new warden, Mr Quiverful, will 'get [his] income doubled' from his previous clerical stipend of £400, suggesting that the old £800 salary has not in fact been altered, and nothing is heard of the new arrangements in subsequent novels: Trollope may simply have forgotten them. Here, in 'The

Two Heroines of Plumplington', the issue seems still unresolved in the early 1880s. However, 'forty years' is an overstatement. Since *The Warden* was set in the early 1850s (see Introduction, p. xxiii), the interval is actually thirty years. Trollope is either miscalculating, or trying to suggest a longer chronological span for the action of the Barsetshire series than he had, in practice, allowed.

198  *the colleges*: of Oxford and Cambridge Universities.

199  *Barchester Towers*: the towers of Barchester Cathedral, possibly based on the remarkable twelfth-century north and south towers of Exeter Cathedral; the phrase was used as the title of the second novel in the Barsetshire series, *Barchester Towers* (1857).

200  *Papists . . . Presbyterians . . . dissenters*: respectively Roman Catholics, Protestants who believe that the Church should be governed not by bishops but by presbyters representing their congregations, and Protestant Nonconformists.

201  *benevolent paganism*: 'virtuous pagans' are people in the pre-Christian era who upheld ethical standards equivalent to those of Christianity, but are excluded from the full bliss of the beatific vision, so that their souls remain in Limbo rather than in Heaven or Hell. Their customary representative is the Stoic philosopher Seneca (4 BC–AD 65) who was (mistakenly) believed to have corresponded with St Paul.

208  *into the house*: as would have been usual at this time in a provincial bank, Mr Greenmantle lives 'above the shop', with his office and counting-room on the ground floor and his family residence on the upper storeys of the same building.

211  *Rector*: a parish priest, technically one who retains the full tithe (see Appendix 2).

213  *Ida Pfeiffer*: like Trollope's mother, Ida Pfeiffer (1797–1858) was a traveller and travel writer, though her journeys were more extensive and exotic than Frances Trollope's. She published *A Vienna Woman's Trip to the Holy Land* (1843), *A Journey to Iceland, Sweden, and Norway* (1846, trans. 1852), *A Woman's Journey Round the World* (1850, trans. 1854), *A Second Journey Round the World* (1856, trans. 1857), and *A Trip to Madagascar* (1861, with a biography by her son), and was a member of the German and French Geographical Societies.

217  *play the old soldier*: make cunning use of long experience to avoid duties or obtain privileges.

218  *plenary*: complete, not subject to exceptions or limitations.

*Christmas-box*: a present or gratuity given to servants and tradesmen on Boxing Day (26 December).

*half-a-crown*: a coin worth 2s. 6d., or one eighth of a pound.

220  *make ducks and drakes*: to throw something away, as in the game of Ducks and Drakes, played by skimming stones across the surface of a sheet of water.

223 *a sovereign*: a £1 coin.

225 *special licence*: a licence gives permission for a marriage to take place without the calling of banns (a public announcement in the couple's parish church for three Sundays before the wedding); a special licence was granted by the Archbishop of Canterbury or his officials and allowed a marriage to take place without banns and in any Anglican church.

227 *the Lord's Supper*: the service of Holy Communion.

*the Dean's daughter*: Susan (Posy) Arabin, daughter of the Revd Francis Arabin who became Dean of Barchester and married Eleanor Bold in *Barchester Towers* (1857). Posy appears in *The Last Chronicle of Barset* (1867) as a 5-year-old, where she is the favourite companion of her grandfather, Mr Harding. She would now be in her late teens or early twenties; a courtship between Harry Gresham and Posy Arabin hints at the possibility of yet more Barsetshire fiction.

*at six o'clock*: see note to p. 186.

228 *dress coat . . . white tie*: dressing for dinner at this date involved, for men, wearing what we would now call white tie and tails: a black tail-coat and trousers, with a white shirt, white waistcoat, and white tie or cravat.

229 *vulgar farce*: farces at this date were still short, one-act pieces, used as comic intermissions between the longer plays which made up an evening's entertainment in the theatre. The more substantial modern three-act farce began to appear later in the 1880s.

*recipients*: those taking, or receiving, the bread and wine at the Communion service.

230 *pudding-time*: the sweet course—puddings, pies, or tarts—would be served before the dessert (fruit and nuts); on this occasion it would be a Christmas pudding.

*the cloth had been removed*: there would be a tablecloth covering the table for the first three courses (fish or soup, meat, and pudding) of a Victorian dinner of this formal kind; it would then be removed and the dessert (fruit, nuts, and wine) would be served on the polished surface of the table, so that the decanters of wine could circulate smoothly.

*The Oxford World's Classics Website*

**www.worldsclassics.co.uk**

- Browse the full range of Oxford World's Classics online

- Sign up for our monthly e-alert to receive information on new titles

- Read extracts from the Introductions

- Listen to our editors and translators talk about the world's greatest literature with our Oxford World's Classics audio guides

- Join the conversation, follow us on Twitter at OWC_Oxford

- Teachers and lecturers can order inspection copies quickly and simply via our website

**www.worldsclassics.co.uk**

American Literature

British and Irish Literature

Children's Literature

Classics and Ancient Literature

Colonial Literature

Eastern Literature

European Literature

Gothic Literature

History

Medieval Literature

Oxford English Drama

Philosophy

Poetry

Politics

Religion

The Oxford Shakespeare

A complete list of Oxford World's Classics, including Authors in Context, Oxford English Drama, and the Oxford Shakespeare, is available in the UK from the Marketing Services Department, Oxford University Press, Great Clarendon Street, Oxford OX2 6DP, or visit the website at www.oup.com/uk/worldsclassics.

In the USA, visit www.oup.com/us/owc for a complete title list.

Oxford World's Classics are available from all good bookshops. In case of difficulty, customers in the UK should contact Oxford University Press Bookshop, 116 High Street, Oxford OX1 4BR.

| | |
|---|---|
| | **Late Victorian Gothic Tales** |
| JANE AUSTEN | **Emma** |
| | **Mansfield Park** |
| | **Persuasion** |
| | **Pride and Prejudice** |
| | **Selected Letters** |
| | **Sense and Sensibility** |
| MRS BEETON | **Book of Household Management** |
| MARY ELIZABETH BRADDON | **Lady Audley's Secret** |
| ANNE BRONTË | **The Tenant of Wildfell Hall** |
| CHARLOTTE BRONTË | **Jane Eyre** |
| | **Shirley** |
| | **Villette** |
| EMILY BRONTË | **Wuthering Heights** |
| ROBERT BROWNING | **The Major Works** |
| JOHN CLARE | **The Major Works** |
| SAMUEL TAYLOR COLERIDGE | **The Major Works** |
| WILKIE COLLINS | **The Moonstone** |
| | **No Name** |
| | **The Woman in White** |
| CHARLES DARWIN | **The Origin of Species** |
| THOMAS DE QUINCEY | **The Confessions of an English Opium-Eater** |
| | **On Murder** |
| CHARLES DICKENS | **The Adventures of Oliver Twist** |
| | **Barnaby Rudge** |
| | **Bleak House** |
| | **David Copperfield** |
| | **Great Expectations** |
| | **Nicholas Nickleby** |
| | **The Old Curiosity Shop** |
| | **Our Mutual Friend** |
| | **The Pickwick Papers** |

ÉMILE ZOLA

**L'Assommoir**
**The Attack on the Mill**
**La Bête humaine**
**La Débâcle**
**Germinal**
**The Kill**
**The Ladies' Paradise**
**The Masterpiece**
**Nana**
**Pot Luck**
**Thérèse Raquin**